THE
TORCH
BETRAYAL

A CONOR THORN NOVEL

THE
TORCH
BETRAYAL

A CONOR THORN NOVEL

GLENN DYER

TMR PRESS, LLC

TMR PRESS, LLC
2057 MAHRE DRIVE
PARK CITY, UTAH 84098

The Torch Betrayal. A Conor Thorn Novel (Book 1)

www.glenndyer.net

First Edition

ISBN 978-0-9991173-0-9
Library of Congress Control Number: 2017916639

Printed in the United States of America

Cover and Interior Design: JD Smith Design

To my wife Chris

Who stood by me quietly and patiently nurturing my dream

The best way to use the gold of the Redeemer is
for the redemption of those in peril.

- Saint Ambrose

There is a unanimity of opinion of Army officers here that the
proposed operation [Torch] appears hazardous to the extent of
less than a 50 percent chance of success.

- Cable regarding the invasion of North Africa from General
George Marshall, Army Chief of Staff, to General Dwight
Eisenhower, August 15, 1942

As desperate a venture as has ever been undertaken
by any force in the world's history.

- General George S. Patton

PROLOGUE

0130 Hours, Friday, October 2, 1942
US Army Air Forces Film Lab, Camp Griffiss, London

The cognac-induced buzzing in his head ramped up. The warm air passing over the frosted ground created a moist fog that, coupled with the diversion he'd put in motion earlier, guaranteed that the odds of being undetected were in his favor. Nonetheless, he silently rehearsed his story if he was found on the base so late at night.

His breathing was still a bit labored from his sprint from the maintenance shed, where he'd set kerosene-soaked cloth fuses into the near-empty fifty-gallon drums of aviation fuel. He estimated he had six or seven minutes until the heavy material of the rags burned their way into the drums. He lit a cigarette to calm himself, and when that failed, he flicked it into the fog and pulled a flask from his inside breast pocket and took a long pull, draining it. The cognac's warm trail was less intense than it had been the first time. He returned the flask to his breast pocket and pulled his pack of Player's Navy Cut cigarettes back out. As he shook the pack, he heard the first explosion; then, three seconds later, the second. He dropped his cigarettes.

"Shit," he hissed. He crouched and lost his balance slightly. Both booms were unexpected. He had only been counting on a fire. When he'd tipped each drum, it had seemed there was only an inch or two of fuel—a careless miscalculation, but one that overdelivered on his need for a diversion. He heard shouts in the fog followed by two rifle shots. He checked his jacket pockets for his tools. Feeling the hard shapes of both the wire cutters and the ball-peen hammer, he began to slink across the frost-covered grass, toward the rear of the film lab. At the top of the stairwell that descended to the rear door, he stopped and turned to survey the grounds behind the building. Nothing was visible but fog and the top portion of the stand of trees he'd just exited. He headed down the stairwell. At the bottom, the drain was clogged with leaves and twigs, creating a small puddle. The fetid water threw off a sharp stench, and his leather shoes wicked up the foul water.

The shouts of security personnel sounded farther away from down in the stairwell, and its thick concrete walls easily absorbed the sound of the hammer as he smashed through the dense pane of opaque security glass. Most of the shards landed inside, but a few pieces clung to the wire mesh embedded in the glass. He made quick work of the wire with the cutters, but when he started to push his hand through, it was too small. He reached again for his wire cutters, the handle catching on the lining of his pocket and tumbling out of his hand, into the putrid water at his feet.

The shouts were getting louder, so he forgot the cutters and shoved his hand back through the hole, the wire leaving several rows of scratches on the back of his hand and wrist, and up his arm, like a neatly plowed, bloody field.

The deadbolt slipped in his fingers at first, but he managed to get it unlocked, glass crunching under his feet once he finally stepped inside. The hallway was narrow, and with his right hand out, groping into the darkness so he didn't run into anything, he took small, quick steps deeper into the building. The chemical smell that wafted from the film processors he crept past made his eyes water and the buzzing in his head got higher pitched. The fumes weakened his focus, but the sound of a pump in one of the processors engaging snapped him back to the present. He pressed on, the dim light from low-watt, naked bulbs hanging above each processor aiding his way.

He was looking for one document. Only one. He headed for a metal locker marked "Lt. Johannson," located near the front counter of the lab. Once he found the locker, he looked in the deeply stained coffee mug; the key to the file cage was there. The locker reeked of perspiration. A jar of hair pomade along with a comb wedged into a hairbrush's bristles sat in the bottom of the locker.

Inside the chain-link file cage, where there were rows of file cabinets, he hunted for the one marked "G.D.D.E." Inside, among dozens of manila files, was the familiar leather satchel, a set of handcuffs attached to its brown Bakelite handle, and a small key to the lock on the satchel's clasp. He opened the satchel and put its contents on a small wooden table in the center of the room and pulled his lighter out. He used the index finger on his uninjured hand to sift through the myriad documents. He was halfway through the pile when he found it, and adrenaline shot through his veins. He raised his eyes to the ceiling, and his breathing quickened. It was a piece of letter-sized onionskin. Typed instructions with dates and times filled the page. The number *117* was in the upper-right corner. The paper crinkled sharply when he folded it and slid it into his inside breast pocket.

After returning the satchel to the file drawer, he locked the enclosure gate and raced back to Johannson's locker. He dumped the key back into the mug and shut the locker. As he approached the rear door of the lab, he skidded to a stop, realizing he didn't have a handkerchief or rag to clean up his blood, nor did he have the time to search for one. He pulled down the right sleeve of his jacket and swiped at the mess, but the drying blood was stubborn. As he pressed harder, he heard shouts from outside, closer this time. Plenty of people had his blood type—it was time to go. He stepped into the stairwell, his right foot landing unevenly in the puddle. *The wire cutters.* As he bent over to retrieve them, the buzzing in his head intensified.

Outside, the air was choked with the smell of burning aviation fuel. The fire seemed to be sapping the fog of its moisture. As he raced away from the shouting, he was pleased with his performance—but he would be happier once he put his hands on more cognac.

CHAPTER ONE

1000 Hours, Saturday, October 3, 1942
Headquarters of the European Theater of Operations, United States
Army (ETOUSA), London

The humiliation that Lieutenant Commander Harry Butcher, USNR, suffered over losing his lunch was slightly lessened by his having Miss Weddington leave his office beforehand.

He couldn't believe it had taken him only nine weeks to screw up his plum assignment as General Eisenhower's aide. Visions of boarding a slow boat back to the States by order of the general and being reassigned to a desk deep in the bowels of the navy's communications department filled his head. That selfish thought was soon overpowered by the magnitude of what Weddington had just told him: a document—one containing the directives of the Allies' first joint offensive action against the Nazis—was missing.

"Miss Weddington, you can come back in now," Butcher shouted as he shoved the fouled wastebasket behind the blackout curtains. He looked out his window. Heavy, gray card stock checker-boarded the large window where panes of glass existed before the Blitz. Through the window's few remaining glass panes, he watched an invasion of low, black clouds marching swiftly northward from the English Channel.

As Elizabeth Nassar Weddington, Butcher's secretary, entered the office and approached his desk, Butcher noticed her eyes were red and swollen. The slender-built woman was the only daughter of a long-tenured British Foreign Service diplomat and a mother who came from a prosperous Egyptian family. As Weddington stood before him in a faded blue dress, she tugged nervously at a handkerchief, contrasting with her normal poise.

Weddington's nose wrinkled—no doubt she had caught the stench that drifted from the wastebasket in the cramped office he shared with the general's stenographer. Butcher dropped his gaze and cleared his throat. "Tell me again—slowly. And don't leave anything out."

"I am at a complete loss to explain it. I cannot begin to tell you how sorry I am. I simply do not understand how I . . . misplaced . . . it," she said.

"Miss Weddington," he tried again, stifling his mounting frustration. "Start again from the beginning. And speak slowly." Weddington fired off a string of words in her Egyptian Arabic –tinged British accent, mumbling half of them as she tried to explain, but he caught a phrase here, another there. She paused and inhaled noisily through an open mouth, then began speaking more slowly.

"I started merging the official documents with the personal ones, renumbered them, as I always do, into one set of pages. Then I placed all the pages in the satchel. Staff Sergeant Billings handcuffed the satchel to my wrist, per required protocol. Then, the sergeant and I left for the film lab."

"Where did you gather the pages?"

"Outside your office, at my desk. And I had the outer office door locked."

Satisfied that Weddington had followed protocols, Butcher nodded. "Go on."

"We took a staff car to the film lab, and from the time we entered the lab to the time we left, nothing out of the norm happened." Weddington again tugged at her belt.

"Whom did you pass the diary pages to?"

"The same lab technician I always do—Lieutenant Johannson. I work only with the lieutenant because of his security clearance. I picked up the prior batch of microfilm and left the lab. I told Lieutenant Johannson I would be back on Saturday to collect what I had just dropped off."

Butcher rested his chin on his clasped hands and lowered his gaze to his desk blotter. Tucked into a corner of the blotter was a picture of him shaking Eisenhower's hand on his first day as the general's naval aide.

"You're absolutely sure about the specific page that's missing?" Butcher asked.

"Yes, sir, I'm afraid I'm sure," she said.

Butcher slumped back in his chair.

"Today's batch included pages 103 to 150. Every typewritten page with any pasted or stapled notes still attached came back except page 117."

Butcher began to sweat. "Thanks, Miss Weddington."

Weddington, with her handkerchief pressed tightly against her lips and her eyes welling up, turned to escape the office.

"Call over to the lab," he called after her, causing her to briefly slow her exit. "Tell whoever is in charge that no personnel are to leave until we get there."

Weddington scurried out of the office without responding and closed the door behind her. A brown-framed wall clock, its face pale yellow, ticked off the seconds noisily.

It was time to deliver his news.

#

Butcher's head began to throb, which made it difficult to focus on what he was going to say to Eisenhower. He took a deep breath and exhaled fully as he rapped on the man's office door. For a moment, there was nothing but silence on either side. Then a muffled voice said, "Enter."

Butcher pushed aside the heavy oak door to General Dwight David "Ike" Eisenhower's office. The sturdy and graying Colonel William "Wild Bill" Donovan settled back in his chair as Butcher entered. Donovan was the director of the Office of Strategic Services (OSS), the fledgling secret intelligence organization that had been formed a mere four months prior. Eisenhower loomed over maps of the North African coastline, their corners pinned down by ashtrays that overflowed with cigarette butts and

Hershey's candy bar wrappers. He held a foot-long rubber-tipped pointer in his hand.

"What can I do for you?" he asked, his face leaden with fatigue.

"General, excuse the interruption, but I need a minute."

"My guess, given your face, is that it can't wait."

"You would be right, General. It concerns Torch."

Eisenhower cocked his head, the tiredness on his face giving way to confusion. "What about Torch?"

A bead of perspiration trickled down Butcher's spine. "Simply put, General, a page that was sent over to the army film lab on Thursday to be microfilmed along with a large batch of documents has been reported . . . um . . ." Butcher stopped. He realized that he didn't know if it had been misplaced, accidently destroyed, or . . . stolen.

"Butch, I am sure this is important enough for you to interrupt Colonel Donovan and me, so get to the point," Eisenhower said, tossing the pointer onto the desk.

"Yes, sir. A page sent to be microfilmed has been reported . . . missing. Specifically, it was page 117. That was the page from the combined chiefs of staff that detailed the objectives of Operation Torch."

"My God," blurted Donovan.

Eisenhower glowered at Butcher. Their time spent together in Washington—while Eisenhower had been assigned as assistant to the chief of staff for the assistant secretary of war and Butcher was vice president and general manager of the CBS radio station WJSV—had allowed them and their spouses to establish a strong friendship. But Butcher couldn't help but think that Eisenhower was now questioning his decision to have Butcher assigned as his aide. Eisenhower didn't ask much of Butcher, just had him run interference with the press, hold the blue-haired British socialites at bay, be the one person he could talk to without having to worry about being told what people believed he wanted to hear, and keep his personal diary.

Eisenhower came around his desk to face Butcher. "Butch, you and Miss Weddington have been doing this for months. What the hell happened?" Eisenhower's neck above his starched collar was turning pink.

"We sent forty-eight pages to be microfilmed. All the original documents were returned except for one—the directives from the combined chiefs for Torch. I don't have an explanation beyond that."

Eisenhower turned away from Butcher, walked to the window behind his desk, and stood motionless for a several moments. "The prime minister, as you both know well, has been relentless in his pursuit of a firm date for Operation Torch. Up to this point, my reluctance was based on concerns over logistics, controllable military matters," he stated, his voice calm and clear. Then he turned toward his desk and grabbed the back of his chair. "What we now have, among other things, is another example for the British of our inability to manage confidential matters. Amateurs, they say. Well, that characterizes it kindly, I'd say."

"General, maybe we're overreacting," Donovan said, rising from his chair.

"I don't believe overreaction is possible, given what's at stake. If the invasion of North Africa is successful in drawing off men and materiel from the eastern front, and we think it will be, it will be critical for the survival of the Soviet Union. And Torch's success is not possible if the element of surprise isn't maintained." Eisenhower stabbed the pointer at the south coast of England. "Not to mention we have ships from both the eastern and western task forces taking on the last of their cargoes with tentative embarkation dates of October 22 and 23." Eisenhower shook his head slowly and dropped the pointer on the desk. "Setting a firm date for the invasion is something I must do within days; otherwise, it will throw our whole plan into utter confusion," he finished, his eyes locked on Butcher.

"General, we have time to get to the bottom of this," Butcher offered.

Eisenhower pulled out his chair and slumped into its leather cushion. "Butch, get back to the lab and trace where that document went. Find it before those task forces set sail."

"Yes, sir. On my way," Butcher said, relieved at having received an order instead of being sacked, and made a quick move for the door.

"I'll take my leave, General." Donovan grabbed his trench coat and hat.

"Wait a minute," Eisenhower said. Both Butcher and Donovan stopped in their tracks. "Here's a heads up, Bill. We have an invasion to finish planning. That is my top priority. If Butch doesn't turn up something within the next few hours, I'm turning this over to the OSS."

"Forewarned is forearmed, General," Donovan said, quickly making for the office door. Butcher held the door open and lowered his head as Donovan passed.

Before Butcher exited, he saw Eisenhower reach for a cigarette and his Zippo. As he quietly closed the door, the ticking desk clock underscored Eisenhower as he shook his head and muttered, "Son of a bitch."

CHAPTER TWO

1200 Hours, Saturday, October 3, 1942
District de Police Le Port, Tangier, Spanish Morocco

Thorn hated sitting on his ass, waiting for something to happen. It made him uneasy. And he didn't like being uneasy one bit. The cooling temperatures and slight breeze from the Port of Tangier brought the scent of spices—pepper, ginger, and turmeric—mixed with the stench of oil and rotting fish. One moment, the air was blissfully fragrant; the next, nauseating.

Thorn, a twenty-six-year-old former lieutenant in the US Navy newly assigned to the OSS station in Tangier, had been waiting behind the wheel of the dark-green 1939 Chevrolet Deluxe four-door sedan for twenty long minutes. He sat, eyes locked on the rearview mirror, as he incessantly rotated a gold wedding band around his finger. The car was parked on the Rue Skiredj, a constricted street no more than one hundred yards long that was barely wide enough for two-way traffic. The Rue Skiredj was more like an alley that ran along the backside of the two-story buildings that housed residents of the Arab quarter. There were no vendor stands on the street, which was one reason it was chosen for the pickup.

The quiet that enveloped the area was occasionally shattered by the high-pitched voice of a woman screaming the names of her children. The setting sun was pushing the shadows of the buildings across the narrow street, and Thorn observed his partner,

Chester Booth, an anthropologist and field archaeologist for Yale University who had spent time digging up Morocco in 1939, lounging in the backseat, loading his ever-present pipe with cheap Moroccan tobacco.

It was a quiet night in Tangier. *Too damn quiet. Something's not right.*

With his ass starting to numb, Thorn got out from behind the wheel and took a screwdriver and a soiled rag from the glove box. Booth stayed in the backseat, feeding a flame from his lighter into the bowl of his pipe. Thorn, feigning engine trouble, opened the long hood of the sedan and stuck his head under it without compromising his line of sight in either direction. Darkness was fast approaching, as was the time for Tassels to make his appearance.

Colonel Eddy, who headed up the OSS Tangier station, believed it was a notable achievement to have recruited Tassels. *Tassels* was the code name for a notorious tribal leader from the mountainous Riff region of Morocco and who was also an important part of the OSS's underground organization of informants among Arabs and the Berber tribes. The information that Tassels provided was critical in helping plan the invasion of North Africa. Thorn was well aware that if the authorities saw Tassels with the Americans, he would be shot—which was a good reason to disguise him as an Arab woman for transport to his meetings with Colonel Eddy.

After resetting the engine's six sparkplug wires for the second time, Thorn spotted Tassels turning the corner onto Rue Skiredj, then stopping to look over his shoulder. Apparently seeing nothing of worry, he continued toward the sedan. Thorn wiped his hands on the rag and slammed shut the engine hood. Once Tassels recognized Thorn, he picked up his pace and Thorn opened one of the back doors for him. Booth slid over and Tassels, who was sweating freely, jumped in.

"Ahh, Mr. Lincoln, Mr. Jefferson. A pleasure to see you both again," said Tassels as he wiped perspiration from his forehead. Every time someone used the cover name bestowed on him by Colonel Eddy, Thorn imagined Honest Abe shaking his head in disgust. Thorn slid behind the wheel, started the car, grabbed the gearshift, and forced the car into first. As he popped the clutch, he saw the dim headlights of a dark-colored Mercedes behind them in his rearview mirror, no more than fifty yards away and moving slowly. He slammed on the brakes and turned to look out the back. The Mercedes had stopped, choosing not to close the distance between them. Despite the waning light as the sun set, Thorn was able to identify the car from the damage to its left front fender. While on a survey of the harbor the day before, he'd witnessed the Mercedes plow into the rear of a delivery truck. The driver had emerged from the car shaking his left fist as he screamed at the truck driver. He'd recognized the driver of the Mercedes from the headshots of local Gestapo agents he'd studied upon his arrival in Tangier. Thorn felt for his KA-BAR knife in its sheath, strapped upside down against the inside his left forearm.

"Well, that's not good," Thorn muttered.

"What is it?" asked Booth, who was busy tending to Tassels's disguise.

"That Mercedes, the car of choice of the Gestapo. I recognize the driver, one of the Gestapo's senior agents. Tassels, are you sure you followed all our instructions?"

"Of course. As I always do. I noticed no Mercedes following me, or anyone on foot for that matter." Thorn always struggled to believe what Tassels told him. His struggle was intensified by his belief that the lazy Booth had done a half-assed job of validating Tassels's intentions and loyalties. Tangier drew spies from all the major powers like bees to a honey pot. Europe had Lisbon, and Africa had Tangier. With its proximity to Gibraltar, a mere twenty-five miles across the Strait of Gibraltar, and its central location between Casablanca and Rabat to the south, and Oran and Algiers along the coast to the east, Tangier was a mecca for the lawless, who rubbed elbows with military attachés, consuls, reporters, and those passing through the city on their way to Lisbon, the last gateway to America for refugees seeking safety.

"Well, let's see what happens," said Thorn as he turned back around and popped the clutch. The car lurched forward.

"Just pull over and let them pass," Booth said loudly as he fidgeted nervously in the backseat, straining to get a good look at the Mercedes. That's what pissed Thorn off about Booth. He was a trained academic who failed too often to see a developing storm of shit about to rain down.

Thorn stopped the car and looked in his rearview mirror. "They don't want to pass. They want to follow us. They want to see where we take Tassels. We can drive around the city all night, but Tassels here would miss the radio transmission to London that Colonel Eddy has scheduled for"—Thorn looked at his watch—"thirty minutes from now."

Booth leaned forward, sitting on the edge of the seat. "Listen, Thorn, priority one: don't get caught. The scheduled transmission is not the top priority."

"I do not plan on getting caught or missing the scheduled transmission. So hold on."

Thorn put the car back in gear and buried the gas pedal. The tires squealed as they headed toward the end of the street. The Mercedes, caught off guard, reacted slowly. After traveling no more than twenty yards, Thorn slammed on the brakes. Booth and Tassels slid into the back of the front seat. Thorn wasn't sure who it was, but someone had *oof*ed the air out of his lungs when they hit. Thorn threw the Chevrolet into reverse and again stomped the gas. He stopped no more than five feet from the front bumper of the Mercedes and jumped out of the car, leaving the engine running and his passengers scrambling to regain their seats.

"What the hell are you doing?" Booth yelled.

My job, Chester. That's all.

Thorn approached the driver's side of the Mercedes and motioned for the driver to roll down his window. The stunned Gestapo agent complied. Thorn leaned forward so he was eye to eye with the driver—the same driver he saw a day ago—and, shaking his head, began to speak German—much to the surprise of the two Gestapo agents

"*Ihr Motor klingt wie Scheiße. Aber ich werde ihn repariern.*" He sidestepped to his left and sprang open the hood of the Mercedes as the two men in the car shared a look of utter shock and then began arguing. Thorn slipped his knife from its sheath and slit the sparkplug wires. The engine coughed feebly, then died. As he retreated to his car, he resheathed his knife, leaped behind the wheel, dropped the gearshift into first, and popped the clutch.

The two agents jumped out of the Mercedes; the driver raised his gun and squeezed off several shots. Thorn slammed on the accelerator and yanked the steering wheel frantically from side to side to present a more challenging target, throwing Booth and Tassels violently about.

"What the hell are you doing?" Booth managed to scream between grunts.

You got to stop asking that question. It's driving me crazy.

As they neared the end of the street, a bullet smashed through the rear window of the car, shattering it. Tassels screamed, prompting Thorn to grab a quick glimpse in the rearview mirror. The informant cupped his left ear, but blood was flowing through his fingers.

Shit, Tassels is one hell of a lucky guy.

#

Thorn pulled the car into the courtyard of the Italian-style villa, home to Colonel Bill Eddy, and brought it to an abrupt stop. The fountain that dominated the center of the courtyard, its upper portion shaped similar to an oversized birdbath, gurgled with water, the splashing so loud that Thorn could barely hear Booth, who exited the sedan covered in blood and yelling at the figure standing on the whitewashed balcony overlooking the courtyard.

"Colonel, I'm done with him. He's a reckless cowboy, and I won't ever trust him again. He practically got Tassels and me killed."

Thorn reached into the backseat to help Tassels out. The man held a bloodstained handkerchief to his ear while moving his lower jaw in a circular motion. Thorn noticed that Tassels's disguise had soaked up most of the blood that hadn't seeped into the rear seat or onto Booth's linen suit.

"Conor, you better get Tassels to the kitchen and send someone for the nurse right away. Then come to my office," Colonel Eddy said to Thorn, his deep baritone echoing in the courtyard.

"Yes, sir." Thorn took Tassels's arm and helped him into the villa as Booth started up the staircase at a brisk pace, red-faced and breathing heavily.

It had been a typically warm day, but with night falling, Thorn sensed a coolness as it rose up from the terracotta floor in the dimly lit hallway leading to Eddy's office.

As Thorn knocked and entered the office, Colonel Eddy, who was standing behind a large, ornate desk, put his hand up to stop what Thorn was sure was Booth's rant about that evening's escapades.

"Have a seat, Thorn. You too, Booth." They both took seats in dark-mahogany chairs with rounded backs that came up to their shoulder blades. Colonel Eddy, who'd lost his right leg in World War I at the age of twenty-two, took a seat, sat back, and propped his legs on the corner of the desk, his artificial one making a sound when it hit the desk like a car door slamming shut.

"Booth tells me that you took unnecessary risks tonight that could have seen a valuable informant—one that, by the way, took me months to recruit—fall into the hands of the Gestapo. What the hell happened out there?"

"As far as the actual events, I'm sure that Booth covered it, Colonel."

"I am sure he did also. But let me hear it from your point of view, and add a little commentary as to why you did what you did."

Thorn nodded, leaned forward in his chair, and began. It took him close to three minutes to recount the night's events. As he told his story, it all made sense to him: his decisions, the timing of his actions. When he finished, he sat back and gripped the armrests, squeezing tightly.

Eddy sat silently for a moment, then shifted his lean frame in the chair.

"Booth, anything you want to add?"

Thorn glanced at Booth and noticed that he was no longer red in the face.

"No, Colonel. I have made my case."

"OK then, thanks. Why don't you go grab something to eat before you head back to the legation?"

Booth nodded and stood. "I'll wait for you downstairs, Thorn."

Eddy lowered his legs, stood, and ambled over to the sideboard, a persistent squeak coming from his artificial leg. "Conor, you scare Booth. And, if you must know, you unnerve a few other legation staff. Maybe the only one you don't is Heugle, but he's a little off balance too."

Thorn chuckled quietly. Heugle, a longtime friend of Thorn's who had washed out of the academy only to become one of Donovan's new recruits, regularly showed signs that he wasn't right in the head.

"Listen, Colonel, I do what I think needs to be done to get results. I will admit that, since I came to Tangier, I haven't done much to tip the scales in this war in favor of the Allies. Maybe I should have figured out a way to stay in the navy."

"From what I know, it wasn't up to you."

Don't remind me. It was a fucked-up situation. "I was talking about . . . Ah, just forget it. You're right—it wasn't up to me."

"I'd say that Colonel Donovan pulled your bacon out of the fire. Would you agree?"

"Yes. Yes, I would. He's been a great friend of the family's and particularly to me. I'd hate to disappoint him. And I don't think I have . . . up to this point."

Eddy's eyes locked on Thorn. "Bottom line, Conor, I think you acted decisively and boldly. I'll give you that. But we operate as a team here. We have to be able to trust the other fellow. There is no room for men who think with their balls and not their head. Simply put, because you scare the hell out of people, they don't trust you."

Thorn sat silently. There wasn't anything more he wanted to say.

"I have no choice. I am going to ask Colonel Donovan and David Bruce to reassign you. It will be up to them as to where."

Thorn's stomach turned and his mouth fell open. *But I did all the right things, damn it. If they think I can't cut it in this backwater shithole, I'm headed back to the fucking States for sure. Out of the war, with zero chances to repay some debts.* He kept his eyes on Eddy and didn't blink. Thorn began to say something about a second chance but stopped himself.

"Be ready to move on in the next couple of days. I'll arrange for you to meet with the colonel and Bruce in London for your next assignment. And good luck."

Thorn sat silently for a moment before he rose and walked out of Eddy's office. He stood on the other side of the office door and processed his decisions from earlier that evening.

What could I have done differently? Wasn't it better to act than be forced to react? The Gestapo showing up gave me no choice. Thorn shook his head. He decided to check on Tassels and headed down a level to the kitchen.

Ten feet from the doorway, Thorn heard Tassels recount his near-death experience to someone. His voice echoed in the villa. In the hallway, the aroma of lamb and garlic lingered from an earlier meal, and as Thorn entered the room, he saw Tassels flat on his back on a low-slung butcher-block table. His arms mimicked those of an orchestra conductor as he related his story to Bobby Heugle. Heugle's dark hair was cropped high and tight, his round face was tanned from the Moroccan sun, and he looked up as Thorn entered.

"Well, well, here's the hero now. Tassels here says you saved his ass from falling into the hands of the Gestapo. He says he would like to adopt you."

Thorn chuckled and shook his head, happy for the friendly jab. "Will you please pipe down?" Thorn turned to Tassels and placed a hand on his shoulder. "You feeling OK, considering?"

Tassels struggled to sit up, his cotton shirt now stiff with his dried blood. "I am fine, Mr. Lincoln," Tassels said. "Much better than I would be if I had fallen into the hands of those German barbarians. It is quite possible you saved my life."

"Apparently not everyone sees it that way. But that's not your problem," Thorn said.

"Is there something you want me to do? Permit me to vouch for your actions to the colonel."

Thorn chuckled. "No, don't worry about it. He seems to have his mind made up. But thanks anyway."

Thorn and Heugle headed for the courtyard. They approached the Chevrolet Deluxe, and both leaned back on the car's front fender, shoulder to shoulder.

"So . . . I've got some news. Want to hear it?" Heugle asked.

"Only if it's good. Had enough bad news today."

"I'm shipping out. Sunday."

"You're kidding. Where to?"

"London. New assignment. OSS liaison to the navy. Some big operation coming up and Donovan needs eyes and ears close by. You believe that? London. Adios to this stink hole."

"Well, that makes two of us."

"Whoa, what the hell are you talking about? The colonel is sending you to London?"

"More like kicking me out of Tangier. It seems that I am a little too reckless," Thorn said as he looked up at the lights burning in the windows of Eddy's office. The wind, now heavy with humidity, kicked up and brought with it the foul stench from the harbor. The scents from the spice stalls had finally been overwhelmed.

"Kicked out, transferred, reassigned—who cares what you call it, you lucky shithead," Heugle shouted, his eyes lighting up.

"Are you kidding me? I'm far from lucky. Too far," Thorn said while he spun his wedding band around his finger. When Thorn noticed that Heugle was staring at him, he dropped his hands and slid them into his pants pockets.

"Don't you get it? It's London. With no more Blitz, it's the gold ring of postings."

"And far from the front lines. At least here we can mix it up with the Gestapo."

"You're so confused. Give it a day. It'll all sink in." He paused briefly. "Tell me something. Why do you still wear that thing?"

Thorn shot him a hard look. "That . . . thing?" He shook his head in disgust. "I wear it . . . out of respect." *Even I don't believe that. So what is the answer?* he wondered.

"Respect for . . . Ahh, forget it," Heugle said, sliding off the fender, away from Thorn.

"Yeah, good idea."

CHAPTER THREE

Elizabeth wished she had peed before they'd left for the film lab. But the commotion in the office after LCDR Butcher met with the general had distracted her, and before she realized it, she found herself in the backseat of the staff car. The first leg of the trip from Grosvenor Square to the US Army Air Forces Film Lab southwest of London was normally quick, gas rationing having culled the London streets of most civilian vehicular traffic. But once outside London, the narrow roads became choked with numerous types of military vehicles fighting for every inch alongside the brave, bicycle-riding English. Elizabeth customarily took the opportunity to rest her eyes and think of something other than the war. Staff Sergeant Billings, the driver, would take the hint and drive in silence.

Today was different. Billings, a former New York City cab driver, navigated the traffic-clogged roads to the film lab with generous application of the horn accompanied with flashing headlights and an occasional shout of *Move it, Mac!* Butcher slumped in his seat beside Elizabeth, his right hand beating out a silent cadence against his knee.

The satchel that she used to carry documents back and forth to the film lab was handcuffed to her wrist. It didn't need to be, as it contained nothing. She knew that if Butcher asked why she'd brought it along, she would tell him, in no uncertain terms, it was so she could place the missing page inside when it was found. That's how confident she was that this nightmare would soon be over. But as the olive-green Buick Roadmaster with bold, five-point, white stars emblazoned on the front doors darted in and out of traffic, the question did not come. Instead, Butcher sat quietly, staring out the window.

"That lieutenant . . . did you call ahead to make sure that the lieutenant who handled the microfilming was still there?" The question from Butcher startled Elizabeth. It was only then that she realized that she was clutching the satchel so tightly her right arm was trembling.

"Yes, Commander. I asked that he be detained should his shift end before we got there," Elizabeth said, her voice shaky and feeble.

"All right, that's where we'll begin. And tell me, what does *he* know?" Butcher asked in a low voice, pointing with his thumb to the front seat.

"I have told him nothing," she said.

Butcher nodded and turned back to the window.

Billings pulled off the two-lane road onto a narrow one covered in pale, crushed stone that gave up a cloud of dust as each vehicle passed over it. The staff car was waved past the main gate of the bustling camp by sentries who recognized Elizabeth and Billings. They pulled up to a nondescript, two-story, brick building set among a sea of Quonset huts spread out for at least a kilometer in either direction. Billings parked between a Jeep painted with the markings of a military police unit and another that displayed the markings of the US Army Air Forces and had a short trailer hitched to it loaded with several film magazines, of the type used by reconnaissance aircraft.

Elizabeth was the first to jump out of the car as it stopped and the first at the building entrance, where she waited for the others to catch up. The rustling breeze carried the sound of falling leaves from a nearby grove of sycamore trees. Across the road, she saw two uniformed men burning trash, producing a pungent stream of smoke that spiraled into the October sky. At the entrance to the building, two burly guards stood with white helmets and armbands marked *MP* in bright-white letters. Butcher, buttoning his blue naval officer's jacket, approached the guards.

"What's your name, Sergeant?"

"Wright, sir. With a *W*," said the sergeant as he stabbed the stenciled name patch on his chest with his forefinger after snapping off a sharp salute.

Elizabeth noticed that Butcher didn't return the salute. Not the first time. She appreciated that Butcher was more corporate than military.

"OK, Sergeant Wright with a *W*, what's the status here?"

"Per your orders, the lab has been secured. No one in or out for the last hour."

"Good. Right." Butcher headed inside, following Elizabeth and Billings. Butcher, head down, proceeded up a staircase on the right side of the building's foyer.

"Commander. This way," Elizabeth said from the top of a staircase leading into the building's basement. Above her head, on the gray wall, was a stenciled sign that read "USAAF Film Lab" with a hand pointing down the staircase. Bits of flaking paint lay scattered on the steps below. She again went first.

The stairway dropped into a narrow hallway lit by exposed, ceiling-mounted light bulbs every ten feet. The unseasonably warm day and the basement's dampness produced air heavy with humidity. The double doors to the film lab—each door with a twelve-by-twelve piece of glass reinforced with wire—were located halfway down the hall. On either side of the doors, film mags were piled up, waiting to be moved into the lab for processing.

"Why no guard, Sergeant?"

"Sir, I don't have enough personnel to properly man this entrance and the front and back entrances to the building. But I did lock the doors, so no one could get in or out," the sergeant said as he reached for one of the door handles and rattled the doors.

"You mean they're locked inside?" Butcher asked, alarmed.

Elizabeth realized that the more time she spent working for the commander, the clearer it became that he was far from being comfortable with the power of his rank and assignment. She watched as LCDR Butcher's face betrayed a look of honest astonishment that his order to secure the film lab had required incarcerating the lab's inhabitants, who—Elizabeth could see through the scratched glass window—were none too happy.

#

Butcher strode purposefully into the film lab. A lieutenant who appeared to be in charge, a staff sergeant, and two privates stood on the other side of a narrow counter that ran the length of the room as if impersonating statues, all staring at him. Butcher debated whether to tell them they weren't going anywhere until this nightmare was over or not. The lieutenant, with rounded shoulders and hands pushed deep into his pockets, did not look pleased with his circumstances. The enlisted men appeared only slightly more tolerant at being locked up with no explanation from the military police.

Sergeant Wright, who stood at ease with his hands clasped behind his back, cleared his throat, shattering the silence. Butcher suddenly realized that they were waiting for him to address the group. "Lieutenant, my name is Butcher, aide to General Eisenhower. Sorry for this inconvenience, but under the circumstances, there was nothing else we could do."

"Just what are those circumstances, sir?" the lieutenant asked in a melodic, slow drawl as he patted a cowlick on the back of his head. "I must tell you that we are pretty confused, not to mention we're falling far behind in our work." The lieutenant, perhaps thinking he had defeated the stubborn cowlick, returned his hand to his pocket.

"And you are?"

"First Lieutenant Johannson, sir."

"Well, Lieutenant Johannson, let me cut to it because time is something we don't have a lot of," Butcher said, stepping to the counter and heaving his weathered briefcase onto the counter, nearly sending a magnifying glass the size of a dinner plate to the floor. "You, Lieutenant and, I assume, some of your staff are familiar with the type of work that Miss Weddington brings to the lab on a regular basis. Simply put, some of that material has come up missing, and we need to recover it." He paused, the men's gazes still locked firmly on him. "We *are* going to *recover that material*," Butcher said with a raised voice that served to emphasize his own determination. "The film lab is where the material in question was last seen. So this is where we begin our search. At this point, that's all you need to know."

Butcher peeled off his snug-fitting brass-buttoned officer's coat and threw it on top of his briefcase, this time succeeding in knocking the magnifying glass off the countertop. The lieutenant, who stood two feet away, sprang forward with impressive agility and snatched the magnifying glass by its brass handle, almost cracking his head on the sharp edge of the counter.

"Johansson, the first thing I need you to do is to pull together a list of names of everyone who has been in or out of the lab since Thursday, including your lab technicians. While that is being done, Miss Weddington and Staff Sergeant Billings will, with the help of your staff, retrace their steps from earlier this morning. After which, they will go through every trash can, file cabinet, and drawer in this lab." Butcher spun around to face Sergeant Wright. "Sergeant, wait outside for officers from G2, and get them down here as soon as they arrive." Turning back to the lab staff, Butcher said loudly, "All right then. If there are no questions, let's get to it."

"Sir? If I may? I have one question," Johannson said, raising one hand to reengage in the skirmish with his recalcitrant cowlick.

"What is it, Johannson?"

"Well, sir, just what exactly are you looking for?"

Butcher paused for several seconds before he responded. "Lieutenant, let's just say that we're looking for a missing page from Gen—from a report to General Eisenhower from the Combined Chiefs that was to be microfilmed."

Johannson scratched his head. "It must be pretty important to bring you down here. Sir."

"You could say that, Lieutenant."

#

Butcher was pacing along the length of the counter when Johannson approached him timidly. "Commander, here's that list you wanted. Besides my lab staff, there are only four other names on it, so it was easy to pull together. We have a log of everything that comes in and goes out of the lab and who brought it in or took it out."

Butcher started to speak when Sergeant Wright rushed through the lab's double doors with two officers following close behind him.

"Commander, this is Captain Valetta and First Lieutenant Evans from Army Intelligence."

Butcher, who was naval reserve, not career military, opted to shake hands rather than return the salutes of the officers. "Thanks for your help, gentlemen. Captain, follow me," Butcher said as he headed for Lieutenant Johannson's office.

Butcher closed the door to the closet-sized office and sat behind a metal desk that looked as if it was a holdover from the last war. Captain Valetta took a seat in an armless wooden chair in front of a battered, three-drawer file cabinet. A ceiling fan overhead wobbled, causing the pull chain to clink as it danced from side to side.

"Can you please give me a rundown, sir?"

Butcher was pleased to hear eagerness in Valetta's voice. "Bottom line, Captain, we're looking for a missing document. Top secret. And we need to find it—fast."

Valetta hesitated as if he was expecting more. "So . . . I take it you searched the place?"

"My staff is in the process. I need you or your lieutenant to question the lab technicians, and I also need you to track down the people on this list," Butcher said, leaning over the desk to hand the list off.

Valetta slid his index finger down the list.

"It's everyone who has been in or out of the lab since Thursday. We need to get them in here for questioning. My theory is that the document is either still here in the lab or someone walked out with it by mistake."

"Seems simple enough. Just who are these names on the list?"

"I'll get Lieutenant Johannson in here. He runs the lab, so he can tell us. While I do that, can you get your lieutenant to start questioning the lab's enlisted personnel?"

"I can do that, but what do I tell them we're looking for?"

Butcher sat back in his chair and looked up at the swaying ceiling fan. That was the problem with all the extra eyes looking for the diary page. Secrets became less secret. "It's a document numbered *117* in the upper-right corner."

Valetta looked at Butcher for several seconds before nodding. "I get it, Commander," he said, rising from his seat and calling for Lieutenant Evans as he exited.

A few minutes later, Butcher was standing behind the desk and Lieutenant Johannson was in the chair when Valetta came back. Johannson stood up.

"Stay put, Lieutenant," Valetta said, motioning Johannson to sit back down.

"Lieutenant, run down this list for us. Just who are these four people?" asked Butcher, handing the list to Johannson, whose legs swayed back and forth like Butcher's six-year-old son when he needed to pee.

"You OK, Johannson?" Butcher asked.

"Oh, I'm fine, sir. Never better—except for this mess, of course."

"All right, so about the list," Butcher said, knowing that Johannson had no idea how much of a mess this was.

Johannson nodded and pointed to the paper. "The first two names, Betts and Thompson—they're both attached to the Eighth Air Force. They're regulars, and they've been rotating ever since the Eighth started their daytime bombing in August. Good guys."

Butcher was pleased to see Valetta taking notes, the red tip of his cigarette glowing as he stood in a corner of the office, leaning against the file cabinet. The air in the small office, despite the efforts of the ceiling fan, was becoming rank with cigarette smoke and perspiration. "So if they walked out with something by mistake, they would let you know?"

"Oh yeah, Captain. Like I said—good guys."

"Go on," Butcher urged.

"Well . . . there's the guy from that Free French intelligence unit. Name is Toulouse, Captain Toulouse. Tall guy. Never seen arms as long as his. Slicked-back hair, like some old-time actor. He's a nasty type, likes to throw his weight around, is quick to remind us he's a nephew of General de Gaulle."

Butcher and Valetta both looked at each other.

"So an ally, but not a friend?" asked Butcher.

"I don't know, Commander. If I'm honest, I'd say neither. He's become touchier lately, since the Eighth's been hittin' French targets pretty hard, especially Rouen. Likes to complain about the Eighth's accuracy. Guess he's got family around there."

"Anything else?" asked Butcher.

"Just that when he came in on Friday for his set of recon photos of the Rouen raids, we didn't have them ready, so he left without anything. Of course, he let us know General de Gaulle wouldn't be happy," Johannson replied.

"So that would rule him out, I suspect," Butcher said, more to himself than anyone else.

"And the last name?" Valetta asked, coming out of the corner to put out his cigarette.

"That would be RAF Warrant Officer Montgomery. His outfit is the RAF Coastal Command. Been coming in for a few weeks. Seems that the Brits have a few processors down at the RAF base at Mount Farm, lookin' for some spare parts, so's I hear. The RAF has been hittin' the German naval ammo depot at Mariensiel hard."

"What else do you know about him?" Butcher asked, loosening his tie as he silently cursed the fan's inability to cool the room.

"Hardly anything. Doesn't say much. Nervous type. Real jittery."

"OK, Lieutenant. Captain, any other questions?"

"No. Not at this time."

"Thanks, Lieutenant. You're excused."

Johannson rose slowly and shut the door.

Butcher looked at his watch. They had been in the basement lab for hours. No one had had anything to eat or drink. He shook his head and attempted to stretch out the kinks in his lower back.

Weddington and Billings had searched every inch of the lab, in every file. If anything pleased Butcher, it was the thoroughness with which his staff and the lab staff searched. But it was now clear that the missing document was not in the lab. He could confidently report that nauseating news to General Eisenhower.

Butcher went out into the lab to locate Weddington. The fumes from the film processors had given him a pounding headache and successfully torpedoed his appetite. He found Weddington in the back file room, her hair a stringy mess.

"Still at it?" he asked.

"I have been through these file boxes three times now. Nothing."

"Where is Billings?"

Before Weddington could answer, Butcher heard his name being shouted.

"Back here!" he replied above the hum of the processors.

Captain Valetta rounded the corner with a head of steam and almost sent Butcher crashing to the floor. "Let me show you something. Follow me." Butcher and Weddington followed Valetta, who led them to a door in the back of the lab.

"See this?" He pointed to a smashed six-by-eight-inch pane of security glass in the door; it was the pane closest to the doorknob. At least a dozen strands of the wire mesh embedded in the glass were cut. Dried blood was smeared on the door panel below the doorknob and on the deadbolt, though it was clear someone had made an attempt to wipe it clean.

It only took an instant for Butcher's reaction to morph from *so what* to *we've got a major problem here*. Up until that moment, Butcher had worked overtime to convince himself that they were just looking for a misplaced document. But the sight of the smashed pane of glass and the dried blood changed all of that. Weddington covered her mouth with both hands and cowered against the wall. She too understood that the situation had just become bleaker.

"You see a broken pane of glass," Valetta said. "I see someone who wanted to get into the lab without a key."

Butcher ran his fingers through his hair. "Son of a bitch." He looked around for any broken glass on the floor. There was none.

"The door leads to an exterior stairwell that leads to ground level. At night, someone looking to get into the lab wouldn't be seen by anyone," Valetta said, excitement in his voice. He knelt on one knee, putting him at eye level with the smashed pane. "And you can see the blood," he said, pointing to the stains. "If we're lucky, maybe fingerprints too." He rose abruptly; again, he practically knocked Butcher over as he turned and headed to the front of the lab. "Johannson! Johannson!"

"Over here, Captain. I was just about to—"

"I don't care about that. Tell me about the broken glass in the back door. What's that about?"

Butcher, followed by Weddington, caught up to Valetta as he asked the question. The rest of the lab staff, along with Billings, stopped what they were doing to view the unfolding scene.

"Oh, that." Johannson moved his hand to again do battle with his cowlick. "I noticed that when I came in this morning. The door was still locked, and I didn't notice anything missing. All equipment accounted for. Didn't think anything of it, so I didn't report it to base security."

Butcher and Valetta traded looks. Valetta shook his head slowly as he rubbed the back of his neck.

Butcher turned toward Johannson and stood nearly toe-to-toe. He jabbed a finger in Johannson's chest. "I don't give a damn about your equipment. What about the classified materials that this lab handles? How do you know that any of that material isn't missing?"

"Did I do something wrong, Captain?" Johannson said, taking a step back from the fuming Butcher.

Valetta grabbed Johannson's arm and pulled him back. "Answer the question, Lieutenant. The classified materials. How do you know that all of those materials are still here? And think hard before you answer."

"I . . . I . . . didn't think of that . . . stuff, Commander. I just didn't make the connection. I'm sorry."

Butcher shook off Valetta's grip. "You didn't think? Wrong answer." He rubbed his forehead, as if he could calm the anger that was raging inside. "Ever hear of the term *ass in a sling*, Lieutenant?"

No one moved, and nothing could be heard but the hum of the film processors.

CHAPTER FOUR

2200 Hours, Saturday, October 3, 1942
Dean's Bar, 2 Rue Amerique du Sud, Tangier, Spanish Morocco

The Germans were singing again. Another marching song. This one about clearing the streets for the brown battalions and flags on high with ranks tightly closed. Thorn hated the Germans. And the Italians, for that matter. The German bastards always received the most attention and favorable treatment from the Spanish authorities in Tangiers. The Italians did also, but only because the Germans demanded it. It made him crazy. Those national socialists and fascists did stick together—he'd give them that much . . . but only that much.

Thorn had been in Dean's since the dinner hour. He'd had his usual dinner of chicken tagine with onions, honey, and mint. He'd washed it down with a few scotches, which took the edge off the anger that still lingered from the meeting he'd had with Eddy earlier that day.

The bar had been opened by Joseph Anton, an olive-skinned British ex-pat of Egyptian descent, after serving for years as the head bartender at Caid's Bar inside the Hotel El Minzah. Similar to the man himself, Anton's departure from the El Minzah was a bit of a mystery, some saying that he was caught selling his own alcohol on the side to Caid's patrons. A ballsy entrepreneur. Thorn liked that about Anton.

Dean's usual customers typically opted for a late start to their evening's exploits. Nearing ten o'clock, the place was hitting its stride for the night as Anton dragged his five-foot-six-inch frame onto the leather-studded barstool, taking his usual seat near the entrance with his back to the wall, so he could see those who came and went. Given the type of people drawn to Dean's, which included any nationality that had something to gain or lose in the game called World War II, he had to be on his toes all the time. This night, there were Germans, Italians, and a couple of Japanese embassy naval attachés mixed in with some British and American officers and civilians. When there was trouble, it usually signaled that some palooka new to the world of Tangier's international spy trade had recently arrived from parts unknown and let the excitement of rubbing shoulders with their enemies trigger boneheaded behavior.

"So, Conor, where was I?" Anton said.

"You were buying me a drink, I believe," Thorn said, tipping the last few drops of his scotch into his mouth and parking the empty glass on the marble bar.

"I've already bought you two. That is my limit. Why don't you slow down a bit there, Yank?"

"And spoil the fun I'm having? Come on. It's a celebration. Join in, why don't you?"

"Not tonight. Told myself that I needed to stop soaking up my profits for a week or so. And what are we celebrating anyway?"

"I am going on a trip. Back to London." *To get my ass kicked and shipped to God knows where.*

"Ahh, my mother country. I'd love to go with you, but I'm not sure they would let me back in," Anton said as his eyes skimmed the growing crowd in the bar.

Thorn held up his empty glass and motioned to the bartender to signal that his thirst had returned. The table of German officers in the rear of the place, who had been singing since the bar's piano player and singer went on a break, had launched into a beer hall tune that drew stares from the other customers. "Any chance you can get the German opera troop back there to take a break?"

Anton looked toward the back of the bar and located the table with the German officers. He made no effort to move from his seat. "Conor, I have learned by now that the customer, especially the German customer, is always right."

"What about your American customers?"

"Ahh, yes, the Americans, whom I have always admired for their . . . tolerance," Anton said as he continued to survey the crowd.

Thorn shook his head and smirked. He'd taken a shine to Anton mainly due to his finely tuned survivor's instinct. "So, since I am not long for the world of Tangier, clear something up for me. I've heard the rumor that you were a member of the criminal underworld, something to do with drug running? Could my friend Joseph be a gangster?" The squat, dark-complexioned bartender wearing a Moroccan fez on a mop of dark, slicked-back hair delivered Thorn's scotch. "Could you have blood on your hands?"

Anton finally looked directly at Thorn, who saw a glint in his eyes. "If only I had a pound note for every time I heard that story. And the one about being a spy for British intelligence, and about being a military advisor to the sultan," Anton said, wiping his forehead and upper lip with a handkerchief.

Bobby Heugle surprised Thorn with a slap between his shoulder blades, all but knocking him off his stool. "Conor, you son of a bitch. Hey there, Mr. Anton."

"Hello, Bobby," Anton said as he reached into his breast pocket and pulled out a bar tab. "I believe you forgot this last night. I guess you were in a bit of a rush, seeing how eager that lovely, slender Moroccan girl appeared to be."

"I will take care of that. And my apologies. I was a little light-headed, caught up in the moment, you could say." Heugle, dressed in a tailored, blue suit, a loosened tie drooping from his neck, took the bar tab from Anton and waved it at the bartender to get his attention. Thorn saw the bartender turn his back on Heugle, prompting some muttered profanity.

"Where have you been? Said you were going to be here an hour ago," Thorn said.

"I had a few over at Caid's. That place was jumpin'. But I told the ladies I was with that I had to meet up with my ol' pal Conor, to celebrate our grand exodus from their lovely city. Leaving behind a whole crazy bunch of agents, double agents, and maybe some triple agents."

"But that's just it. Something tells me that this part of the world is going to get real interesting. Besides, at least you can see the enemy. Where we're going, the only enemy we'll get close to is a hemorrhoid from sitting on our asses in some backwater shit hole."

"Fine by me. Besides, this war won't be over for at least a few years. You'll get your balls in a fire somewhere before this is over, right, Joseph?"

"Heugle's right about that, Conor. Plenty of shit yet to hit the fan," Anton said.

"'Balls in a fire'? 'Shit hitting fans'? Stop—your efforts to cheer me up are failing miserably."

Bobby shrugged and turned his attention to the bartender. "Hey, sahib, can I get a little action my way?"

The bartender continued to ignore him.

A relative quiet descended on the bar as the German officers disappeared into the head to relieve themselves. It was the first time that Thorn noticed another table near the end of the bar, closest to the piano, contained one uniformed German army officer and a younger man dressed in civilian clothes, sitting erect and still, each with a glass of champagne sitting untouched in front of him. The piano player, a gray-haired, elderly man, returned to his piano and slumped over his keyboard, the tip of his nose hovering inches above the keys.

As he struck up Billie Holiday's "Strange Fruit," two men, also in civvies, joined the German officer and his friend. One man, who Thorn noticed limped to the table, sat facing the piano; the other, tall and fit, sat with his back to the wall, giving him a view of the entire bar, including where Thorn and Heugle sat. Thorn recognized the strapping German and elbowed Heugle, who was talking up two awfully young Frenchwomen who sat to his left.

"Bobby, be on your toes—we could have some trouble here."

"*Un moment*, ladies," Heugle said as he turned around. "What are you talking about?"

"That German who walked in and sat near the piano. I recognize him."

"So? I've seen a lot of these people before. It's a small town. What's the big deal?"

"He and I had a bit of an encounter earlier today in the quarter."

"You mean the Gestapo guy . . . in the Mercedes?" Heugle, his interest piqued, looked for the table of Germans. "Holy shit."

"What?"

"I told you I was over at Caid's, right? Well, that long-legged Gestapo goon over there got into it with a waiter, actually wound up slapping him. He got tossed. And he was pissed. Wouldn't stop screaming about something that I couldn't quite make out—my German is rusty."

"Well, he was the driver."

"OK. So we're simply having a drink. Just relax."

"Well, be forewarned. This was the trigger-happy one that just about killed Tassels. And I'm sure that he's not too happy with me."

It didn't take long for the German to zero in on Thorn, whose face he couldn't have forgotten, given that when Thorn put his head in the Mercedes, they were nose to nose. The Gestapo agent stood, said something to the German officer, and took the quickest route to Thorn. Instead of going through the three-deep throng gathered in front of the bar, the German made a beeline for Thorn that took him behind the bar.

When the bartender held up his hands in protest, the German shoved him into an open cabinet, toppling several bottles stored inside. The crowd quieted, and some of those seated sprang to their feet, no doubt anticipating having to make their escapes if things went too far.

Thorn drained his scotch and wiped his mouth with his hand. He considered throwing his glass at the German but decided to try talking some sense into him first.

With long strides, the German covered the remaining distance to Thorn. Upon facing Thorn, he swatted at Thorn's glass and sent it crashing into the blue-and-white-tiled wall.

So much for talking sense into the crazy German. Thorn jumped out of his stool and took a solid stance, spreading his feet wide.

"You will pay for damaging my car," the German said, his English surprisingly free of an accent. *This guy could've been raised on Park Avenue his English is so good.*

"So we're on speaking terms? I didn't catch your name. Is it Adolph, Hans, Franz, Herman? With one *n* or two *n*'s? What is it?"

"You arrogant shit." The German surprised Thorn by lunging

across the counter, grabbing Thorn's shirt collar, and yanking him onto the bar, grunting as he did.

Out of the corner of his eye, Thorn spotted the two other plain-clothes men shouting in German, moving toward them, while Heugle shoved the two Frenchwomen out of the way. The patrons that stood along the bar cursed the agents as they bullied their way through the crowd. A woman in a low-cut, black dress tossed her glass of champagne into the face of one agent and then screamed when he pushed her to the floor.

As Thorn grabbed the edge of the bar and pushed away from the man, he noticed that the Gestapo agent had an elastic bandage wrapped around his left wrist. He suddenly recalled the accident on the docks a few days before that day's encounter in the Arab quarter.

Thorn went limp and allowed the German to pull him over the bar with his right arm. He hit the floor and heard the crashing of bottles that had been stored under the bar. Thorn, flat on his back, watched the German lift his foot over Thorn's face, as if to stomp on him.

Thorn reached up and grabbed the man's bandaged wrist and bent it downward at a sharp angle. The German emitted a howl and began to lose his balance. Thorn yanked harder. The man doubled over in pain, fell to his knees, and, as he did, knocked a tray of glasses to the floor, inciting screams from the patrons who had begun abandoning the scene.

Thorn snatched a bottle of schnapps from the shelf behind him and christened the German's head. The man collapsed face-first to the glass-strewn, liquor-soaked floor and lay still.

When Thorn popped up from behind the bar, he saw Heugle shoving the two other Gestapo agents back into the throng of cursing bar patrons. Thorn vaulted over the bar and grabbed Heugle by the arm as Anton rushed in from the courtyard at the rear of the bar.

"Sorry, Joseph. He was looking for a little payback and came up a bit short."

"You better leave before the Spanish police over there think they need to arrest someone."

"You don't need to tell me twice. Let's go, Bobby."

Thorn and Heugle moved toward the beaded doorway and were swallowed up by the late, humid Tangier night. With thoughts of a desk assignment in London banging around in his head, Thorn considered that he might actually miss the Tangier nightlife.

CHAPTER FIVE

1100 Hours, Sunday, October 4, 1942
Bureau Central de Renseignements et d'Action (BCRA), No. 10
Duke Street, London

Major Andre Dewavrin straightened his tie and pulled at the bottom of his officer's tunic. His hand passed over the fabric, flicking off any stray cigarette ash. His second-floor office window that overlooked Duke Street was open, to allow the room's temperature to match that of the chilly fall day outside. The ringing of the bells of Saint James Church in Piccadilly drifted into the office, signaling the tardiness of General Charles de Gaulle.

Visits from the general without a previously declared agenda unnerved Dewavrin. He ran his hands over his thinning, blond hair and then rubbed them together to dissipate the pomade. Acting on a presumption regarding the reason for the visit, he studied the notes of his last call from David Bruce, head of the Americans' OSS, about the never-ending discussion of the OSS offering sums of money for intelligence supplied from French resistance units through the BCRA. Frustratingly, it seemed that he could never make it clear enough to the Americans that the BCRA or any element of the Free French would not accept money from Roosevelt or his lackey Donovan. The level of mistrust between his superior and Roosevelt was too high given Roosevelt's support of de Gaulle's rival General Henri Giraud.

Dewavrin reached into his tunic pocket and pulled out a pack of American cigarettes, Chesterfields—a bribe delivered by David Bruce on his last visit. As he lit a cigarette, his aide burst into the office and held the door open for a striding de Gaulle. Dewavrin dropped the cigarette into the ashtray, snatched the pack off the desk, and stuffed it back into his pocket.

"Major. Good morning."

Dewavrin sprung from his desk chair and saluted, then headed around his desk to greet de Gaulle.

"And shut that window. It's damn cold in here."

"Of course, sir." Before Dewavrin could make a move to the window, de Gaulle had settled into his desk chair and dropped his officer's cap and riding crop on top of the desk. "What would the general like to discuss this morning? I am prepared to report on my last conversation with Colonel Bruce if you prefer."

"No, no, no. The only reason I am here is to check on my sister-in-law's son, Remy. My wife will pester me to death if I don't report that I have seen him recently and he is in fine health. So please send for him at once."

"General, that is not—"

"Major, I don't have much time. I am expected at the home of the Spanish ambassador in"—de Gaulle stole a glance at his wristwatch—"fifteen minutes. Now call for Captain Toulouse."

Dewavrin's piercing blue eyes began nervously scanning the top of his desk. Toulouse was an insolent, duty-shirking liability who was, undoubtedly, involved with the recent disappearance of funds from the BCRA's cash box used for the bribing of informants. Toulouse was, indeed, the cross de Gaulle made him bear. An infuriating promotion took Toulouse from lieutenant to captain, only adding weight to his burden. "General, Captain . . . Toulouse is not here. He's been . . . unaccounted for since Thursday afternoon."

"What do you mean 'unaccounted for'? You don't know where a member of your staff is? This is unacceptable," de Gaulle said as he tugged on each finger of the silk glove on his left hand, then removing the glove. "Do you suspect foul play?"

"I do not. At least at this point. He has been very . . . preoccupied of late. I know he has been somewhat upset at the American air force's recent raids over Rouen. His mother and sister—"

"Yes, yes, I am well aware, Major." De Gaulle turned toward

the window and slapped his gloves into the palm of his left hand several times, then stopped and turned to Dewavrin. "So what action have you taken?"

"I have sent Lieutenant Roget to watch his flat. I expect a report from him in short order."

De Gaulle nodded and looked at his watch. "Very well, report to me as soon as he is found." He rose from the desk and approached Dewavrin, stopping well inside Dewavrin's personal space. Dewarvin stiffened and held his breath. "I warned you about him. It seems that you have not listened closely enough. You must . . . have better control of your staff, Major. See to it."

"Yes, sir. But, General, there's one more issue I should bring to your attention. It concerns—"

"Not now, Major," de Gaulle said as he pivoted toward the door. "I must be on my way. Send me a report."

Dewarvin turned to watch de Gaulle exit the office, leaving the door open wide as he passed through. Just as well, he thought, since he knew little about why the Americans wanted the absent and troublesome scoundrel as well. What could he have stolen? Whom could he have impregnated? Whom may he have insulted? The questions hounded him.

#

By the time Remy Toulouse arrived back at No. 10 Duke Street, the brass pendulum clock on the mantel of the bricked-in fireplace was softly chiming one o'clock. He shared what was once a drawing room with Lieutenant Lyon, who was in his chair behind his desk, feet propped up, head tilted back. His Adam's apple pointed directly at the crystal chandelier, and his mouth was wide-open, as if stuck mid-aria. It was not a surprise that the two had become close. They had shared the same rank for most of the time they'd known each other, before the gift of a promotion was bestowed on Toulouse by his uncle. Even though Toulouse knew that it was underserved, initially it annoyed him that Lyon never paid any respect to his promotion. But what sealed their friendship was the shared belief that Dewavrin was nothing but a sadistic bastard.

Toulouse dropped into his desk chair. He'd been on the run since Thursday night. The last two nights in Soho, the warm and supple hands of Chenguang, his healing angel, tending to his wounds. But he had lost two full days he could have been conducting business. All because he'd lost his temper. Their meeting with Chen's boss, the Spanish embassy's press attaché, had gone better than he had hoped. He was a long-time client who, besides being an enthusiastic buyer himself, was also willing to be the middleman with his German contacts, to help Toulouse market certain classified information he had access to. Sitting with Cheng after the Spaniard left their table at the Crown, a celebration had been in order, given their improving fortunes. He should have excused the pig of a barmaid after she dropped a pint of nasty English beer in his lap. Screaming at her and spitting in her face was a mistake—one he'd paid for dearly at the hands of the two English sailors. No one had helped him. Not even the policeman who had stopped to watch them beat him in the alley behind the pub.

He started to roll up his right sleeve to inspect his wounds when the hateful clicking sound from the taps attached to the heels of Dewavrin's boots on the parquet hallway floor stopped him. He whipped a pack of Player's Navy Cut cigarettes at Lyon, hitting him on the side of the head.

Lyon jumped in his chair and his legs crashed to the floor. It took a moment for him to register the clicking.

"Toulouse!" Dewavrin stood in the doorway, posture ramrod straight, clutching a rolled-up sheath of papers.

Toulouse pulled down his right sleeve and buttoned his cuff.

Dewavrin slapped the rolled-up papers against his thigh, the sound echoing off the bare walls and wood floor. "Toulouse! Stand at attention. You too, Lyon."

Toulouse rose and moved from behind his desk, glad now that he'd had Chen press his trousers and shirt—one less thing for Dewavrin to chew on.

"Toulouse. What has happened to ... your face? It's ... Where have you been?" Before Toulouse could begin his tale, Dewarvin turned to Lyon. "Lyon, leave us. Report to Lieutenant Roget."

"Yes, sir. Straightaway," Lyon said as he grabbed his uniform jacket from the back of his desk chair and scurried out of the room.

Dewavrin clicked his way to the center of the room. "I asked you a question."

"I was in a fight two days ago. I sought medical attention." He had worked on his story with Chen since yesterday, in between visits with his clientele.

"With whom?"

"Several Royal Navy sailors."

"What did you do to incite this so-called attack?"

"Nothing. I attacked them . . . sir."

Dewavrin cocked his head and slowly said, "Explain."

"I overheard a British sailor say something about French . . . capitulation. He was joined by one sailor, then another, in their condemnation of the French army. It disgusted me."

Dewarvin stiffened. "Go on."

"After saying something about their faggot king, I was set to walk away when one sailor said that he was glad that the Royal Navy had sunk the French fleet at Mers-el-Kebir. I could not take such a comment in stride. My father and brother were—"

"Yes, yes, I know all about the loss of your father and brother." Dewarvin moved toward the fireplace but stopped and turned sharply back to Toulouse. "But your defense of their memory does not excuse your absence from your post for the last two days. Do you understand me?" Dewarvin's tone had softened.

The worst of the storm had passed. "Understood, sir."

"I shall have to report this to General de Gaulle, as he was here today, asking to see you. I will not lie to protect you. I will never do that."

"I am not—"

"Shut up, Toulouse. I've had enough. Now tell me something, and it better be the truth this time," he said. It took five heel clicks for him to get back to the center of the room. "What would someone from the American army intelligence unit want with you? Have you disgraced yourself and the BCRA in your duties at the American film lab?"

Toulouse's posture relaxed and he turned to look directly at Dewarvin. "I . . . I haven't the slightest idea, Major." *Remember the sound of my voice, Dewarvin,* Toulouse thought. *This is what it sounds like when I'm truthful.*

"Hmmm. I am asking questions of my contacts, and I will get to the bottom of this." Two heel clicks and Dewarvin was inches away from Toulouse. He poked the rolled-up sheath of papers into the middle of his chest two times. "And if I find that you are lying to me, no uncle will save you from my hand. Understand?"

Toulouse noted breath tainted with cigarette and a touch of garlic. "I do, sir."

Dewarvin poked Toulouse once more, this time making him lose his balance. His superior turned on his heels and made for the door. "Get back to work. There is a pile of photos on your desk waiting for analysis. Get busy."

Toulouse stood there until the heel clicks completely faded, then turned back to his desk and settled into his chair. He chuckled under his breath and allowed a smile to appear as he rolled up his shirtsleeves. Satisfied that the cuts on his knuckles and the backs of his hands and wrists had begun to scab over, he reached into his pants pocket to remove a key chain and opened his bottom desk drawer. Beneath a spare uniform was a bottle of cognac and a rectangular tin with a small but stout combination lock. He opened it and glimpsed his stash of deep-black opium pellets, the size of gumballs. He tossed in a roll of British pound notes and a folded, two-square-inch piece of wax paper containing three pellets. This wasn't the bulk of his supply. That resided in a small suitcase safely tucked under the floorboards in Chen's flat.

At the bottom of the drawer sat a manila envelope. He pulled it out and opened it after pausing to see that he was still alone. His collection of photos, lists, and documents was growing. It was time to do something with them.

At the sound of footsteps in the hallway, he locked the tin, slammed the drawer shut, and tossed his key chain on his desk. It slid across the surface and settled at the base of a framed photograph. Lyon reentered and moved toward his desk. He waved at Toulouse, who ignored the greeting. Instead, his eyes drilled into the photo. It depicted his mother and sister, their hair mussed by the wind, sitting in front of an oval wooden sign that read "Village of Ville-Musée, Rouen." The River Seine, in the background, was swelling and white capped. His mood shifted. His chin settled on his chest. "Fucking Americans. A price will be paid."

CHAPTER SIX

1100 Hours, Sunday, October 4, 1942
On Board BOAC Flight 777 to Whitchurch Airport, England

Thorn hated flying as much as Cain hated Abel. The difference was that Thorn couldn't kill the thing he hated. He sat in the first-row aisle seat of the Douglas DC-3, acutely aware that they were eight thousand feet above the Bay of Biscay. Each adjustment in the altitude, whether smooth or abrupt, resulted in a flinch and tighter grip. He hadn't opened his eyes or loosened his viselike grip on the seat's armrests since they'd taken off from Lisbon. Heugle, the bastard, had been lights-out the minute he'd hit the window seat next to him. Thorn groaned when he overheard the stewardess tell the passenger behind him that the DC-3 would land outside London with its full flight of twenty-five passengers in about two hours. His physical misery even kept him from introducing himself to Hedy Lamarr, the last passenger to board the flight, unbeknownst to his slumbering friend.

With his eyes slammed shut, he recoiled when the actress reached across the aisle and touched his forearm. "I didn't mean to startle you, but is there anything I can do for you? Anything at all?" she asked.

"No. Not really," Thorn said, opening his eyes but keeping his grip on the armrests. He couldn't exactly place the slight accent.

Hedy dropped the book she was reading, *Victory Through Air Power*, on her lap, took off her wide-brimmed, floppy hat, and reached for a thermos of coffee she had stored beneath her seat. She poured a cup of the black liquid. "Are you sure? Flying as much as I do, I recognize what a terrified person looks like. And you look terrified. Coffee?"

Thorn raised his hand to decline the offer.

"All right. How about some water, then?"

"No, thanks, Miss Lamarr."

The raven-haired actress smiled. "Call me Hedy. And you are?"

"Conor Thorn," he said, extending his hand, which she took. "And sleeping beauty here is Bobby Heugle, my friend and partner in crime." Her hand was warm from holding the cup of coffee. She locked her gaze on him with her green eyes. There was no denying that the woman was beautiful. "You're as glamorous as my wife said you were, Hedy."

"Conor, any girl can be glamorous. All she has to do is stand still and look stupid."

Even with a sour stomach and a slight taste of bile in his mouth, he still laughed. "I'm sure there's more to it than that."

She held the cup in both hands and blew on the hot brew. "Not according to my agent." She turned to him. "You hate flying, don't you?"

Thorn sat back and gripped the armrests again. "You could say that. Believe it or not, it used to be worse. The fear, that is."

"Well, that's good news. I know one related issue is the feeling of not being in control. Is that something you deal with?"

Thorn gave her an incredulous look. "Why do you know so much about fear of flying?"

Heugle suddenly took in a large, quick breath, his head slumping forward.

"Oh, let's say that I read a lot."

"Obviously more than just scripts."

"Yes. And I'll take that as a compliment. So, if you don't mind me asking, what happened to you?"

"Excuse me?"

"What was the inciting incident that brought all this fear on? Did you lose someone in an air crash?"

Thorn stared at her.

"Oh, I'm so sorry. I've gotten too personal. It's that—"

"It's OK. It's something that I try real hard not to think about. Especially when I'm on a plane." Thorn turned forward and rested his head back, on the headrest. "But, of course, it's all I think about." He shut his eyes. "I was six. It was 1922. My father was invited by an old army buddy to a flying circus out in Mineola, out on Long Island. The whole family went. Our seats were front and center. Could see everything." The churning in his stomach went up a notch. He took in a deep breath and released it slowly.

"After the main event, the planes took up a group of army reserve officers. One plane, a huge two-engine Martin bomber, had five passengers, all in an open cockpit behind the pilot. After a series of figure eights, it went into a nosedive and couldn't pull out. It crashed—burst into flames less than two hundred yards from us. Three died immediately; three others, before they got to the hospital. I can still smell the smoke from the fire."

Hedy drained her cup and replaced it atop the thermos. "That would indeed be difficult to forget. I'm so sorry."

Thorn opened his eyes and took another deep breath. "It's OK. It's not like I fly every day."

"Thank the Lord for that, Conor Thorn."

Thorn nodded, then fell silent for several minutes. He watched Heugle sleep and wondered how mad he'd be when he realized that he'd slept through a flight with Hedy Lamarr sitting across the aisle from him. *Of course, I could wake him. But the guy needs his sleep.* "You're a long way from Hollywood. What brings you to this sinister corner of the world?"

"Well, time marches on. War or not, Hollywood is still in business. My latest film premiered in Lisbon two nights ago."

"I've been in a completely different world the past several months. What film are we talking about?"

"That would be *Tortilla Flat*, or, as I learned at the premier, *O Milagre de Sao Francisco*."

"Steinbeck, right?"

"Why yes," Hedy said, raising her eyebrows in surprise. "My, you are an educated man."

"I am not big on going to the movies, but my wife ... my wife said you were great in *Algiers*." The DC-3 hit a pocket of turbulence, and Thorn sucked in a deep breath; he looked around the cabin quickly, as if he were trying to follow the flight of a darting hummingbird. The turbulence passed, and some of the tension left his shoulders as he slouched forward a little.

"So what are you doing to contribute to the war effort?" she asked.

"What am I . . . ? Well, I was in the navy for a few years—an executive officer on a destroyer pulling convoy duty in the North Atlantic. That is, before the navy said I wore out my welcome."

She shot him a confused look but didn't pursue it, which relieved him.

"Not much since. One thing I do know—I'm not pulling my weight. I want to do more, but I can't seem to figure out where I fit in. Do you know what I mean?"

"As far as fitting in and wanting to do more, yes, I can relate. After all, I'm an Austrian making a living in Hollywood. And I tire of all the people who think all I can do is . . . stand in front of a damn camera." Now it was Hedy's turn to fall silent. She balled up her fists and shook her head slowly.

"If you hadn't become an actress, what would you have chosen to do?"

Hedy relaxed her hands. She slumped down into her seat. "I think of that often. I would say an inventor."

"Really? That surprises me. I would have thought—"

"A housewife perhaps?"

"No, no. I didn't mean to—"

"Would you believe that a little over a year ago, I and a dear friend of mine received a patent for a radio-wave-skipping technology that would make the US navy's radio-controlled torpedoes incapable of being jammed?"

Thorn jerked his head back at her nonchalant explanation of technology she'd invented. The words rolled off her tongue like she was giving a lecture at MIT. While he hadn't assumed anything about her intelligence, she surprised him with it nonetheless. "I . . . I don't know what to say except that's very impressive."

"Well, the navy wasn't that impressed. After rejecting our technology, which was bad enough, they said that I would do more good selling US war bonds. I think they call that a crushing blow."

"But one that you survived."

"You're sweet. But enough about me. Are you feeling any better?"

"Honestly, a little. Thanks for being such a welcome distraction." Thorn sat back and closed his eyes. "You know, Hedy, my friend will be pretty upset that I didn't wake him."

Hedy Lamarr laughed. It was a full-throated, almost bawdy laugh. It made Thorn's head spin. His late wife Grace laughed in the same way.

CHAPTER SEVEN

1130 Hours, Sunday, October 4, 1942
Claridge's Hotel, London

David K. E. Bruce, chief of the Office of Strategic Services in London, was fifteen minutes late. He was generally an impatient man, and slow-moving service staff irked him immensely—and the service staff at the American Club was exceptionally irksome. Why had he agreed to meet Ambassador Winant there for breakfast to begin with? It could have been worse. He'd left after coffee, using his meeting with Donovan as the reason for his escape.

When he stepped through the foyer of Bill Donovan's hotel suite into the main sitting room, he found Donovan seated behind a large art deco–style desk, a phone handset glued to his ear and a cigarette burning away with an inch of ash about to fall. Donovan, who looked to be doing all the listening, acknowledged Bruce with a nod. Donovan scratched out a note on a slip of paper and handed it to Bruce. It read "Menzies!!"

Bruce frowned and nodded at Donovan, silently expressing his sympathies for Donovan having to endure another lecture from Menzies, the fifty-two-year-old head of MI6. Brigadier General Stewart Menzies, also known in Britain's cloak-and-dagger world as *C*, never lost an opportunity to remind Donovan and Bruce that the Brits had been at the spy game long before the thought of fielding a team ever occurred to Donovan. Yet Donovan seemed to take it in stride.

Bruce studied Donovan's full, round face. Although the man's hairline had receded and what hair he did have was light gray, Bruce thought he looked younger than fifty-nine. He dropped his shiny leather briefcase and hat on one of two chairs in front of the desk, flopped into the other chair, and crossed his legs. Placing his elbows on the chair's armrests revealed the monogrammed cuffs of Bruce's gleaming white, custom-made Brooks Brothers shirt. He conveyed the image of recruits that Donovan was drawn to—men with strong personalities, products of the Ivy League. Being rich was a plus.

He had spent many hours with Donovan since the Office of War Information morphed into the OSS. The British intelligence agencies, which had been in the intelligence-gathering business since the late 1800s, scoffed at the efforts of the Americans to bully their way into a game the Brits believed they'd invented.

"Understood. I will communicate that immediately," Donovan said, dropping the handset back into the cradle. "He's not happy with us. Another situation where we 'stepped on his toes,' as he put it. But more on that later." Donovan picked up a brown file. "So you've been through this?" he asked, holding up the file.

"Yes. Thoroughly." Bruce had mixed feelings about Conor Thorn. Was Thorn an asset or a liability? But he did have a clear understanding where Donovan leaned.

"So what do you make of him? Why didn't he work out in Tangier?"

Bruce formed a steeple with his hands and deliberated for a moment before answering. He was aware that Thorn's father had a friendship with Donovan going back to law school, so tact was critical. "I don't have a good answer, Bill. The training he received was thorough. Ciphers, cryptology, hand-to-hand combat. He also requested some additional training in small arms, according to his instructors out at Area F," Bruce said, referring to the OSS training facility also known as the Farm, located at the Congressional Country Club far outside of Washington, DC.

"Top of his class. Still, Eddy wants no part of him. I respect Eddy, but we can't put someone with all his training behind a desk, can we? It doesn't make any sense," Donovan said, setting the file down.

"You know what doesn't make sense? Besides hating to fly, the Farm's psychologist says that Thorn is also afraid of the ocean. So tell me, how does a guy that is afraid of the ocean get into the US Navy?" Bruce asked.

Donovan picked up the file again and took several seconds to peruse through it. "It says, and I quote, 'is not *fond* of the ocean.' I think there's a difference."

"Really?"

"Sure. Besides, in his case, I understand the comment."

Bruce waited for an elaboration, but none was offered. Donovan stood and walked to a window overlooking Grosvenor Street. "When we took him into the organization, we knew what we were getting. Not being on board the *Reuben James* when it was torpedoed was devastating to him. Then to be gut punched again with the loss of his wife and newborn son during childbirth—that nearly killed him. We saved him."

"You saved him, Bill—from himself. I thought Thorn was a . . . risky project to take on. In peacetime, sure, but we don't have the luxury of time. Mistakes cost lives right now. And they very nearly did in Tangier. But I have to agree—those two events seemed to have changed him. If you look closely at his service jacket before both incidents compared to after, it's pretty clear that he was headed in the wrong direction."

"So what do you recommend?"

"Well, I know you have been working on the list of your approved proposals from the joint chiefs."

"I've been staring at it all morning. What of it?"

"I have a suggestion." Bruce sat forward and put his elbows on his knees. "One of the proposals was to assign two agents to the Eastern Task Force commander. Thorn is former navy. Why not put him there? The assignment is based in London, and I can keep a close eye on him." Bruce was intent on keeping Thorn on a short leash, regardless of the assignment—the fewer toes for Thorn to step on, the better.

Donovan stroked a layer of stubble on his chin. "Hmmm . . . that makes some sense. But then there's the bad news that Butcher delivered this morning."

"Bill, wait a damn minute. You're not thinking—"

Donovan raised his right hand and stopped Bruce mid-protest. "I'm still processing things . . . many things. So give me some leeway here."

#

By Sunday evening, there were a few signs indicating a heavy rain had soaked the streets and parks of London late in the afternoon. Lieutenant Kay Summersby, driving the olive-green Plymouth sedan transporting Generals Eisenhower and Clark, plowed through a few sizable puddles before turning sharply off Whitehall, onto Downing Street. As they drove past the barbed-wire fence and the machine-gun emplacement located beneath the street sign, Eisenhower was confident he had mentally readied himself for the evening ahead. He was not fond of the politicking and glad-handing his position as commanding general of the European Theater of Operations called for. He was a military tactician who was at his best when in front of a map in a roomful of officers and their men, not members of the demanding social and political circles of London.

While managing the relations with their British Allies was his responsibility, it paled in comparison to his responsibility to manage their collective efforts to strike back at the heart of Nazi Germany. It did not brighten his outlook knowing that most of the evening that lay ahead would do nothing to push him closer to that goal. As charming and enlightened as Churchill could be at times, the regularly scheduled weekly dinner, filled with cigar smoke and drink, sapped Eisenhower of his patience at times. Not one for talk, he typically found himself a captive listener of Churchill, who could talk the ears off the statue of Admiral Horatio Nelson. But Eisenhower realized that this dinner would be different. Churchill expected Eisenhower to announce the invasion date for Operation Torch. Churchill was certainly not expecting Eisenhower to announce news of a security breach threatening the success of the second front that Churchill, Stalin, and Roosevelt had been clamoring for.

Sliding out of the backseat of the sedan, Eisenhower headed to the front door of the prime minister's residence and headquarters of the British government as a brisk wind swept down narrow Downing Street, snaring pages of discarded newsprint and other debris as it traveled over the smooth cobblestones. Eisenhower stopped on the white stone step several paces from the small, six-paneled, black oak door. The *10* was painted on the door below the top panel, its zero leaning to the left. The iron knocker in the shape of a lion's head dared one to announce his presence.

"What is it, General?" said Clark, who stood behind Eisenhower.

"I wonder if, years from now, I'll look back on this night favorably."

#

Despite his apprehensions about the evening, No. 10 fascinated Eisenhower. It was interconnected with the residences of the chancellor of the exchequer, at No. 11, and the chief whip, at No. 12. Together, the collection of buildings contained more than two hundred rooms that included the Cabinet Room and Churchill's private office, located on the ground floor.

Eisenhower was always taken aback by the small size of the prime minister's dining room. The walls of the room were adorned with portraits of previous prime ministers, all of whom seemed to be staring down on those seated about the table. From where Eisenhower sat, he sensed that Neville Chamberlain's eyes were particularly piercing.

Eisenhower and Clark waited ten or so minutes for Churchill to return. When he finally darted into the room, he looked as if his head would explode. Eisenhower's hopes for a cheerful and sympathetic audience at dinner sank.

"Well, I cannot say that I am shocked—Stalin, that obstinate, pigheaded peasant."

Eisenhower and Clark exchanged looks of surprise and rose from their seats. "Prime Minister, what are we talking about?" Eisenhower asked.

"Ike, this you will not believe. Uncle Joe wrote a letter to a Henry Cassidy, who is the Associated Press Moscow bureau chief."

Red-faced and with bulging eyes, Churchill waved a copy of a letter wildly in his right hand and punctuated his tirade with a cigar he held in his left. "Listen to this. 'In order to amplify and improve the aid from the Western Allies, only one thing is required—that the Allies fulfill their obligations and on time.' That bastard."

Churchill crumpled the paper, tossed it into the unlit fireplace, and began pacing. Eisenhower and Clark stayed standing on the opposite side of the table, giving Churchill his stage.

"I have been summoned to the House of Commons tomorrow morning to address this letter," the Englishman declared.

"What are you going to say?" Eisenhower asked.

"I will tell them not to press this matter unduly at a period that is certainly significant—in other words, I'll say as little as possible."

"Short and sweet. Always a good strategy," Eisenhower said, hoping it would calm the agitated Churchill. "But will that be enough to calm the waters?"

"Who knows? We have a plan, and we will stick to it. But this I can tell you: convoy PQ 19 will not be sailing for Archangel. We, the president and I, have been signaling for the past several weeks that we can't keep the tonnage levels where they have been with Torch around the corner. The president wants to send one or two merchant ships at a time with several warships for protection. But now this ingrate will not be seeing that convoy, large or small, pull into that harbor." The disaster that PQ 17 was had hardly faded when PQ 18 arrived in Archangel with the loss of thirteen out of forty-one ships. Churchill's stance on PQ 19 pleased Eisenhower, as he had pushed hard to have the convoy's war materiel channeled to Torch.

It took several minutes of continued pacing for Churchill to ratchet down his anger, after which, dinner progressed swiftly through a handful of courses. Servants, all elderly, came and went. Churchill continued to handle the conversational heavy lifting, to Eisenhower's relief.

With dinner concluded, the three retired to Churchill's office. It was small, overpopulated with furniture, and cluttered with a diplomat's tools for war in the modern era: phones, Teletype machines, typewriters. The ancient tools for pursuing war, maps, were also present, splayed out over a long rectangular table, their corners held down by small, square-shaped beanbags. Still other maps, some rolled tightly and secured with black ribbons, comingled with maps that were loosely rolled. The office's fireplace was crowned with a portrait of the reigning King George VI wearing a lush, green cape that was complemented by the pistachio green of the room's walls.

It wasn't long before Churchill lit a long Cuban Romeo y Julieta, his favorite cigar, and poured himself a brandy. "Well, Ike, I feel like a young boy who gets to drive his father's car for the first time—light-headed with anticipation. What is the date for Torch?"

Eisenhower hesitated before replying. "November 8, Prime Minister."

Churchill looked disappointed. "I was hoping for a date in late October. As you can tell, I am quite anxious to see this operation underway."

"I understand, but the problem is that, given the recent decision to use American regimental combat teams based in the UK, equipping them so that each team is balanced in materiel and has received the proper amount of training takes time."

Churchill squirmed in his seat. "I will make one more try at this. British commandos are more advanced in their training, so let's put them into American uniforms and get on with it. We would be proud to have our men wear them. Things are desperate in Russia. There is hand-to-hand fighting in the streets of Stalingrad. I've received word that Marshall Zhukov is conscripting civilians to defend the city. Any delay will produce grave results."

"Well, thank you for the offer. And I fully understand the dire circumstances on the Eastern Front. But, as agreed to by all parties, this needs to be an American operation. If we put British commandos in American uniforms, the press would undoubtedly uncover the ruse, and it would destroy the morale of American troops."

"Well, I tried." Churchill took a strong pull from his cigar and released a plume of gray-blue smoke above the heads of his guests. "The eighth it is." He backed off.

It occurred to Eisenhower that Churchill would most likely work the back channels to get the date he wanted. "Prime Minister, there is one more thing I need to discuss," he said as he put his untouched glass of brandy on a side table.

Churchill took a sip from his brandy and slouched deeper into his chair. Eisenhower looked up at the portrait of Chamberlain, whose scrutiny of Eisenhower was undiminished. "Go on, Ike. I'm listening."

"Concerning Torch . . . we've had a bit of a security breach. It occurred a few days ago."

Churchill sat up. "A breach? How serious?"

"Long story short, a message I received from the Combined Chiefs of Staff that outlined the directives of Torch has gone missing."

Churchill sat quietly, clearly waiting for more of an explanation, and put out his cigar in an ashtray.

"It was being microfilmed as part of the process of compiling a diary of wartime events."

"You've searched, I take it?"

"Thoroughly."

"Damn it, Ike. It's . . . it's weeks away. What are you . . . What are we going to do? Without the element of surprise, the losses will be staggering."

Eisenhower looked at Clark, then back at Churchill. "The general here and the rest of my staff must get back to the full-time job of completing Torch's planning. I've brought in Bill Donovan and his OSS and given him the task of finding the document. I have full confidence in Donovan."

"Yes, Bill is a good man. I owe him much. But his OSS is not fully operational, is it? I'm told that it is only now establishing its presence here in England and elsewhere."

"Bill is clear on what's at stake, I can assure you."

Churchill fought his way out of his chair and shuffled to the fireplace, hands clasped behind his back, his eyes locked on the portrait of King George VI for several moments. "Tell Bill Donovan that I insisted he accept some help from us," Churchill said, his eyes still locked on the king. "It would normally be someone from MI5—their mission being domestic counterintelligence—but I have someone in mind from MI6."

Churchill turned to face Eisenhower and Clark. "Emily Bright.

She's a newly minted MI6 agent. I did everything I could to keep her with me. She operated as the secretary for the Joint Planning and Joint Intelligence Committee and general staff. She was indispensible to me during the early years of the war, in the dark days. With time being of the essence, she'll help the OSS navigate the wartime landscape here in Britain, which can be a bit challenging."

Eisenhower nodded in agreement. "That's a good idea, Prime Minister."

"She is known to Bill Donovan. They met when Donovan was sent to England in 1940 by the president, to determine if we were going to survive."

Eisenhower rose from his chair as a clock on the mantel chimed the arrival of the twenty-third hour of the day. "I am sure she will be a valuable asset."

"It's getting late, but let me read something to you before you leave." Churchill stepped to his desk and rummaged through the myriad reports and files, and pulled a single sheet of paper from the mess of paperwork. Eisenhower, his mission of the night completed, was miffed that his hoped-for quick exit was being stymied by the loquacious Englishman.

"When I first read this quote from Herr Hitler's speech a few days ago, I believed it was quite humorous," Churchill said, donning his reading glasses. "The Allied leadership are nothing but, and I quote, 'military idiots who are either mentally sick or perpetually drunk.'" He let go of the paper, and it floated to the desktop.

Churchill looked somber, and it tore at Eisenhower's guts to see him that way, to have disappointed this great man.

"I can't say I find it that humorous now. Good night, General Eisenhower, General Clark," Churchill said, the gloom in his voice palpable.

CHAPTER EIGHT

1500 Hours, Monday, October 5, 1942
Athenaeum Club, No. 107 Pall Mall, London

He passed beneath the Doric portico adorned by a statue of Athena at the Athenaeum Club—Athena, the goddess of wisdom. The statue's surface was gleaming gold leaf. Inside the entrance hall, he glimpsed the shimmering image of a gray-haired man in black tie through the glass door. He stood stoically, hands clasped behind his back as if on guard for any egalitarian-minded people who had ideas of storming the inner sanctum of the private club. His feeling of comfort in these types of exclusive settings ran contrary to his communist-leaning sympathies.

"You must be Mr. Stoker." The statement from the old man rang with condescension. "You're late."

"What gave me away?" Stoker said, removing his raincoat and fedora.

The old man tilted his head back, his eyes narrowing to slits. He didn't like the question. "Mr. Philby said to look for a gangly man, one with abnormally long arms and large hands."

Miles Stoker frowned. It wasn't the first time he'd heard such a description of himself, but that didn't mean he had to accept it from someone who was older than dirt, like this arse. With his lips pursed, Stoker lurched toward the old man, who was unfazed.

The old man pointed to a narrow doorway located along the wood-paneled wall of the club's entrance hall. "Mr. Philby is waiting . . . in the South Library."

Upon entering the library, Stoker was immediately over-whelmed by the sight and smell of so many books. Three levels of books formed a fortresslike structure along three walls of the rectangular room, each level serviced by a substantial iron-and-wood ladder that operated along a rail system. The wall closest to the door hosted a fireplace, free of flame at the moment. Flanking the fireplace, sitting across from one another, were two men sep-arated by a low table. One was Kim Philby, situated deep in a leather armchair, a cigarette in one hand and a drink in the other. Across from him was someone Miles didn't recognize, but a long face, narrow mouth, and elongated, thin nose signaled a privileged background.

Neither man rose to greet him formally, but Philby snuffed out his cigarette and spoke. "Miles, so sorry for the urgent request for your presence."

"Quite all right. At your service, Kim. Apologies aren't—"

"This is Anthony Blunt. MI5. And this is Miles Stoker, my deputy."

Blunt said nothing but gave Stoker a curt nod and reached for his drink.

Stoker dropped his raincoat and fedora on a nearby table and took an armchair across from Philby as Philby continued to speak. "Anthony has shared some . . . rather fascinating news. I believe it is worth looking into."

Blunt drained his drink. "I'll leave the two of you to it. I have pressing issues of my own to deal with," the man said, straining to push his large frame from the cushioned armchair. "Please keep me informed as to your findings, Kim." He continued to ignore Stoker as he headed for the door.

Stoker could detect the scent of Kings Men cologne; men who used cologne bothered him. He shook the thought out of his mind and turned back to Philby. "Your news?"

Philby lit another cigarette. "Yes. Yes. It seems that our American friends are in a bit of trouble."

"Let me guess—another security leak?"

Philby's eyebrows shot up and Stoker guessed that he'd sur-prised the man with his assumption. "My, my, you do have big ears," Philby said, placing his empty glass on the table. "Yes. This time it's somewhat more significant than a big-mouthed American diplomat."

Stoker leaned forward. "What—"

The door to the library opened and the old man moved into the room, a silver tray with one drink balanced squarely in one hand.

"Good timing, Jenkins. I had just come up a bit dry."

The old man nodded his appreciation at Philby's comment.

"So what did the Americans—"

Philby held up his hand to halt Stoker. "That's all, Jenkins." He inhaled deeply from his cigarette and waited as his man took his leave. "It seems they have lost track of a top-secret document containing the details surrounding Operation Torch."

"North Africa?"

"Yes. What's comical about the whole mess is that they lost track of it while it was being microfilmed at their film lab . . . over in Bushy Park."

"Always entertaining, those Americans. But why the interest?"

"Well, think it through some, Miles. I need you to be a sharp thinker. I can't do all the hard work after all."

Stoker took a deep breath. It was a popular refrain of Philby's— one he had grown tired of. "Please, enlighten me."

"We both know how much our friends are displeased with plans for North Africa. They are desperate for substantive help from their allies, no matter how much of their blood would be spilled. An invasion of North Africa is not substantive help."

"Yes. That has been made very clear. What am I missing?"

"What if we recovered the missing document or at least made sure it was never recovered by the Americans? What would happen then, do you suppose?"

Stoker shrugged and paused. "*I suppose* that would be a sizable spanner in the works."

"Indeed. Enough to stop the planning. And what if the recovered document were to fall into German hands? What then?"

"Well, putting aside the question of how that would be accomplished, I would venture to say that the invasion would have to be completely reconsidered. It would be a bloodbath to proceed."

"Ahh, there you go, Miles. You're becoming a critical thinker. I like that."

"You have some assignment for me, I take it?"

"Of course. Head over to Bushy Park. Talk your way in and probe. We need to know more before we notify our friends. And do it quickly."

"Why the haste?"

"Well, for one, the deeper Eisenhower gets into the planning, the more difficult it will be for him to reconsider the operation."

"And for two?"

"We must be consistent in feeding the beast. It craves secrets."

CHAPTER NINE

Thorn had been waiting fifteen minutes in front of Claridge's for the car that was to deliver him to OSS headquarters for his meeting with Colonel Donovan. He was early; he'd slept poorly the night before and had woken before he normally did. While he had no appetite, his stomach churned incessantly, so he attempted to browse the *London Times* for wartime news from North Africa, to distract himself, but gave up when his concentration failed him.

He folded the paper under his arm and began spinning his wedding ring around his finger as he stared out into the traffic on Brook Street. The seven flags representing the governments in exile, plus the flags of Great Britain and the United States that hung above the portico, snapped sharply in the crisp October wind. Among the small black London taxicabs that choked the service drive in front of the hotel, Thorn singled out a black Buick Roadmaster making its way toward the front entrance. The Buick pulled to the curb and a young woman jumped out, ran for the back door, opened it, and snapped her head toward Thorn. "Mr. Conor Thorn?"

"Yes. That's me."

"I'm Anne Hollis, Colonel Donovan's driver. I hope you haven't been waiting long."

"No, not at all. Just enjoying all the commotion."

"Wonderful. Shall we get on to headquarters?" said the willowy young woman dressed in an army-green wool skirt and matching waist-length jacket.

"Mind if I ride up front?"

Hollis, still holding the rear door open, looked surprised. "Wouldn't you prefer to ride in the back?"

"No, never been comfortable in any backseat," Thorn said, making his way to the front passenger door.

"Have it your way, sir," Hollis said as she closed the rear door and slipped behind the wheel.

Thorn settled in for the ride and was quickly impressed with how Hollis handled the powerful sedan in and around the double-decker buses and numerous military vehicles. "I commend you on your driving skills, Miss Hollis."

"Thank you. I do take pride in my drivin'."

Hollis pulled up to a multistoried brick building that was not of ordinary red brick. Its facade had a soft, cashmere-brown hue to it, but otherwise, the building was nondescript.

Thorn got out of the Buick and turned toward the entrance, the American sedan emitting a deep growl as it pulled away. He entered the building and discovered two armed guards flanking the elevator. Standing between them was a grinning Bobby Heugle, raincoat over his arm and hat in hand. Thorn announced himself and one of the guards called for the elevator. Once both were inside, the guard punched the button for the third floor. Thorn looked at Heugle, who looked as if he had just been asked on a date by Hedy Lamarr.

"How'd you sleep?" Thorn asked.

"Like a baby. You?"

"Caught a few minutes here and there. You look pretty chipper for a guy that may get assigned to Iceland."

"Hey, don't joke like that. Cold weather and I don't get along. It's like the army versus the navy, the Yankees and the Red Sox. Like—"

"Stop. Stop. I get it. Jeez. I was joking." The elevator door opened. "Sort of," Thorn said as he stepped off the elevator.

The guard rapped twice on the door of suite 323 and, without waiting for a response, pushed through into an art deco–style living area with lights ablaze despite the time of day and cigarette smoke fully choking the air. Two men seated in the living room looked up as they entered, but only one sprang to attention and moved in his direction.

"Conor, Bobby, good to see you." Donovan approached with a warm smile and shook hands with both men. "Rested after the long trip, I assume."

"Great to see you again, Colonel Donovan. I'm fine, but it is a long trip from Tangier," Thorn replied.

"Yes, it is. And not your favorite mode of transportation, we know. And you, Bobby? You left Tangier in good shape?"

"Yes, sir. I'm fit as a fiddle and ready for my next assignment."

"I actually meant Tangier itself," he said smiling, "but enough of that. Let's get going, shall we?"

Donovan led Thorn by the elbow into the living area, and Heugle followed. "Let me introduce you both. Shake hands with David Bruce—he heads up our London office."

Thorn and Heugle stepped forward to shake the hand of the lanky Bruce.

"Mr. Thorn. An uneventful trip, I hope?"

"Yes, sir. It was. Not a German hostile in sight the whole way."

Bruce looked him over for a moment. "That so?"

Donovan sat down on the couch next to Bruce. Thorn and Heugle settled into club chairs across from the two men. "Bobby, let's start with you. There's been a change in plans. We found a better fit for our liaison with the navy. You need to be on the Friday flight to Lisbon."

Heugle's jaw dropped. "Well I'll be SOL."

Donovan and Bruce glanced at each other, and Donovan cracked a smile.

"Lisbon is a whole lot better than Tangier, Mr. Heugle," Bruce said.

"Yes, sir. It's just that I had my sights set on spending some time here. Can I ask the specifics of the posting?"

"Things are heating up in Lisbon. You've got every country in this conflict staffing up their embassies. And we're running behind. Check in with Larry Hopkins when you get to the embassy. He'll give you the specifics you're looking for," Donovan said.

"Head down the hall to my office," Bruce said. "My assistant, Joan, has your transit papers and some traveling money. She's made arrangements for transportation for you back to Whitchurch Airport. You've got three days to get yourself . . . organized."

Donovan stood and shook Heugle's hand. "Good luck, Bobby. Don't let anyone get the upper hand on you. And stay out of the bars. They're even trickier than the ones in Tangier."

"Ahh . . . yes, sir. I'll do that. I'm not a real bar guy anyway."

Thorn snorted and slapped Heugle on the back. "Wait for me downstairs."

"Keep your head down, Bobby," Donovan said.

"And your ears open," Bruce added.

Heugle, looking like he'd missed the last train home, nodded and headed for the door.

Donovan cleared his throat loudly and rubbed his hands together. "OK, let's get on with it. As you know, we brought you to London for a new assignment. But, before we get to that, I wanted to get into the reason—or reasons—things didn't work out in Tangier."

"I understand. Where do you want to start?"

"Why don't you start with the night you very nearly got a valuable informant killed by the Gestapo," Bruce said, confirming to Thorn who was taking the lead for the prosecution.

"OK. Well, as I told Colonel Eddy, our mission was to get Tassels, the informant, back to Colonel Eddy's villa for a critical broadcast that Tassels was to make to other Berber tribal leaders in the Riff mountain region." Thorn received no verbal or visual reaction from either man. "Colonel, I realize that there is something big about to happen in North Africa, given the type of intel we've been gathering and sending back to London and Washington. And the attitude of many Frenchmen toward the English and now towards we Americans, because we've joined the Brits, isn't heartwarming. We need as many friends in that part of Africa as we can get, including the fighters from the Berber tribes. That's why it was important for Tassels to make that broadcast."

Donovan nodded. Bruce, who had been leaning forward in his chair, sat back, waiting for more.

"Once I recognized the two Gestapo goons following us, I

knew we couldn't make a clean and safe rendezvous at the villa. I had to take them out of the picture."

"You realized they had guns?" Donovan asked.

"I assumed they did. But I confirmed it when I stuck my head in their car."

"So tell me: Why did you do that? I'm not clear on that," Bruce said as he leaned forward again, grabbing a lighter off the coffee table and lighting a cigarette.

"First, I wanted to get a clear ID on them. Second, I wanted to see if I could detect weapons."

"Did you?" Bruce pressed.

"I saw a bulge under the driver's jacket. I assumed at the time that it was a gun."

"Then?"

"I . . . We had two choices if we were going to make it to the villa. I had to either lose them in the quarter or disable their car."

"According to Colonel Eddy's report, you cut their spark plug cables."

"That's about it." Thorn could see Donovan work hard at suppressing a smile. Bruce noticed also and shot Donovan a *you're not helping* look. Donovan shrugged and looked at Thorn.

"So you saw that at least one certainly had a gun. Since you didn't have one, was your action wise?"

"Colonel, I'm glad you brought that up. Colonel Eddy, with all due respect to him, is making a mistake not wanting us to carry guns. I know he doesn't want any of us to get deported by the Spanish police if we get caught with them, but, Jesus, we're not playing tennis with the Germans."

"You may have a point there, Thorn. It might be worth the risk. What do you say, David?"

"I don't know. If one of our agents gets the boot for possession of a gun, it's not as if we have other agents waiting around to take his place. That office in Tangier is understaffed as it is. Colonel Eddy has been requesting additional men for several months. But I get that we're fighting with one arm tied behind our backs."

Donovan nodded and took a moment to gather his thoughts. "Conor, tell me, and be candid, what has been your frame of mind lately?"

You knew this was coming at some point. But are you ready for it?
"Fine, Colonel."

"The first anniversary of the loss of your wife and son is coming up, and—and I apologize for bringing this up right now, but I have to—the anniversary of the sinking of the *Reuben James* is also weeks away."

"Yes, sir. I am all too aware."

Both men stared intently at him.

What do they want me to say? That it's no big deal? It's all in the past? That losing Grace and my son and the Reuben James *hasn't had an effect on me? Shit, it fucked up my head so much it got me drilled out of the navy.*

"Colonel, Mr. Bruce, it's true—it has been a struggle these past few weeks. But I'll get through it. Just like I got through it when it all came down on my head a year ago. I know I screwed up my naval career due to the way I acted after the shit hit the fan, which I deeply regret. And I know you pretty much saved my butt. But I can tell you that I did what I had to do to complete a critical mission. As far as the . . . dustup at Dean's is concerned, that Gestapo agent was off his reservation, looking for trouble. And he found it. But I'm not running from any Nazi goon. Never."

Bruce rose from the couch. "Sounds as if you have something to prove, Thorn."

Thorn turned abruptly to Bruce and nodded. "Yes. Maybe I do, sir."

"What's that?" Bruce asked.

Involuntarily, his hands balled into fists. "I need to prove that there's a good reason I'm still alive and not on the bottom of the North Atlantic with most of the crew of the *Reuben James*."

Silence filled the room. Donovan spoke first. "Sit down, David." Bruce, his eyes locked on Thorn, hesitated, before moving back to the couch.

"I need to assign someone to be a liaison between the OSS and the commander of a task force, Admiral Burrough. This task force will be a part of a major Allied operation called Torch—the invasion of North Africa."

Thorn's mouth fell open. "Ahh, of course. Now it all makes sense," he said, slowly nodding. "What will my role be?"

"Well, you're about as qualified a person as I have, given your naval background. Essentially, you would listen to the admiral as he readies his task force and help him iron out any disagreements or issues that he may have with the US Navy and Army."

A glorified referee. Caught between big egos. A peacekeeper. Shit. He leaned toward Donovan. "Colonel, I received extensive training at the Farm, but I'm not a good peacemaker or politician. Can I request another field assignment?"

"Let me finish." Donovan's response drew a quick look from Bruce. "I have received an assignment directly from General Eisenhower."

"Bill?" Bruce interjected.

Donovan held up his hand, stopping further comment.

Bruce settled back and rested his head on the back of the couch.

"I'll get to the point. A top-secret document that outlines key directives of Operation Torch has gone missing. That missing document puts the security of Torch at stake, as well as the lives of thousands, if it is not found. I'm giving you the assignment to find that document before task forces sail from the States and England."

Thorn stole a quick look at Bruce, then looked back at Donovan before he leaned back in his chair again. "When do the task forces set sail?"

Donovan paused and looked away. "The eastern and center task forces set sail on the twenty-second of this month; the western task force sails from the States on the twenty-third. At the outside, you have sixteen days. Don't use them all," Donovan said.

Bruce was quiet as he slowly shook his head.

"You will have whatever you need," Donovan continued. "Stay in communication with me and David."

"Wow," Thorn muttered under his breath.

"Indeed." Donovan leaned toward Thorn. "Find it."

"Yes, sir. Are there suspicions that it has been stolen or passed on to—"

"That isn't clear. That's for you to discover. And one last item: you will not be working alone. General Eisenhower told me this morning that the prime minister has insisted that you work along-side an MI6 agent he has great confidence in, as do I, by the way.

Someone to help you deal with the maze that the British military and intelligence community has become."

"Who, sir?"

"Emily Bright. She's waiting for you over at MI6."

"Wait. A woman?"

"Don't be fooled, Conor. Before her transfer to MI6, Emily was Churchill's right hand. She was the secretary for Joint Planning/Joint Intelligence Committee and the general staff. She practically lived in the underground Cabinet War Rooms during the Blitz. She is a selfless patriot."

"Understood, sir."

"Be at General Eisenhower's headquarters tomorrow morning. Commander Butcher will brief you." Donovan rose from the couch and started for the door, Thorn and Bruce following suit.

Thorn walked with Donovan, who again took Thorn's elbow. "Conor, this is one of the biggest assignments the OSS has received thus far in the war." He stopped at the door and squeezed Thorn's elbow with a strength that surprised Thorn. Then he whispered, "Do not fuck this up."

CHAPTER TEN

1600 Hours, Monday, October 5, 1942
No. 28 Queen Anne's Gate, London

When Warrant Officer Quinn Montgomery emerged from the Saint James Park underground station scarcely feet away from the intersection of Broadway and Petty France, he stopped at the top of the stairs and looked up at the sky. The bright October afternoon sun was momentarily blinding. The exhaust of a double-decker bus idling nearby made Montgomery's eyes water, making it more difficult for them to adjust. Before starting down Queen Anne's Gate to Henry Longworth's home, he patted his uniform's right breast pocket to ensure his cigarette case hadn't been nicked on his underground journey. As soon as he realized he hadn't been a victim of London's nefarious legions of pickpockets, he held out his left hand and found it was still trembling—a perfect match for the queasiness he'd suffered since the moment he'd awoken early that morning, which was the last time he'd lit up.

Trudging down Queen Anne's Gate, he passed two men in dust-covered overalls working behind a line of wooden barricades, salvaging bricks and stacking them ten tall in front of a home that had been destroyed in the Blitz of '41. The men jabbered back and forth, one man constantly shouting "rooobish" at the other.

The street, which was wide for a London street, was lined with four and five-story Georgian mansions whose porches still had boot scrapers and gas lamp snuffers. Montgomery approached the statue of Queen Anne located halfway down the street. It was inside a brick enclosure that had been built before the Blitz to protect the statue of the United Kingdom's 1702 ruler. Montgomery hated what they'd done to the queen. It looked like a damn coffin sitting on its end. She had been bricked up so long that Montgomery's memory of the statue's appearance had begun to fade.

He stopped in front of it and noticed how quiet the street was. Only a couple of lone people strolling by on the far ends of the street were in sight, so he ducked into the shadow of the brick coffin. After double-checking for any curious onlookers, he pulled his silver cigarette case from his breast pocket and opened it. There were eight cigarettes inside—six were Woodbines, two were hand rolled. He took a hand-rolled cigarette out and lit it with a shaky hand, inhaling deeply and trapping the smoke in his lungs. Five seconds passed and he exhaled in a well-practiced, deliberate fashion. The mixture of Woodbine tobacco and opium produced an incense-like scent that he swatted away lest it settle in his clothes. He stared at the wall, which was so close he could see droplets of moisture running down the seams of the brickwork, and realized he couldn't smell the dampness.

Earlier that morning, what had most concerned him was his meeting with Longworth and passing along more information about the upcoming convoy to Russia. But now, he didn't much care about that—what concerned him most was whether Longworth would be able to help replenish his dwindling supply of opium.

Montgomery approached No. 28, Longworth's home. It was a five-story, brick structure with a black-painted, carved wooden canopy over the front door. The keystones of the arches were carved stone, providing howling, wild-haired men in the middle of them on the ground and first floors. The heavy, varnished wood door creaked open, revealing Longworth standing in the doorway. He was dressed in a blue, double-breasted, pinstripe suit, and he twirled a pair of glasses by an earpiece.

"If you are coming in, then, damn it, get on with it," Longworth said, his face twisted in annoyance.

Montgomery stepped inside the entrance hall; the wood-planked floor creaked under his feet. Longworth had already disappeared into his study, off to the left of the hall. As Montgomery entered the room behind Longworth, the long-case clock on a landing halfway up the stairs chimed two o'clock. He took a seat in front of Longworth's desk, which was laden with papers, files, and books. Most of the books, Montgomery remembered from his previous visits, were about the 1917 Russian Revolution and current histories of the Catholic Church.

"So, Quinn, before I share some news, what news have you? Any movement on the next convoy to Archangel?"

"Sir, there's a lot of confusion at Coastal Command."

"Confusion? Explain."

"One day PQ 19 is on; the next, it's off. Then the next day it goes from forty merchantmen with an escort of seventeen warships and twenty B-24s as air cover to thirteen merchantmen and two warships with five B-24s."

"Well, that makes some sense. I told you about a big offensive coming up. We've been told that there are only so many ships. Mounting large convoys and supporting a major offensive is too much of a strain. But whatever size is finally decided on, I need to get a sailing date. You can get that for me, right, Quinn?"

"Oh, right, sir. That shouldn't be too difficult, as long as my duties won't change."

"Don't worry on that front. I arranged for your promotion to warrant officer and had you assigned to Coastal Command for good reason, so I have a handle on that." Longworth rose from his chair with a glass of whiskey in hand, came around the desk, and sat on a clear patch. "Speaking of duties—they still include occasional trips to the Americans' film lab, right?"

"Right, sir. At least until the film processors at Mount Farm are fixed," Montgomery answered, patting the flask in his breast pocket, surprised by the question.

"When was the last time you were there?"

"Friday last week. Why, sir?"

"While you were there, did you notice or hear anything unusual?"

"No, don't think so. Just the usual."

"The usual meaning what?"

"Oh, you know—the Yanks like to pull our chains a bit. Think their shit don't stink, that sort of thing. Excuse the language, sir."

"That's all right. But no talk of something gone amiss? A crisis?"

Montgomery hated all the questions. It reminded him of his younger days when he was running wild in the West End and getting pinched for breaking into mansions in Mayfair. The coppers from Metro Police held him for two days. Question after question for two days. The bastards.

"No. No, not that I remember." It was then that something kicked in. A message from his superior officer that he'd received Saturday. He had been dipping heavily into his fresh stash of cocaine. It had been a long day, and much of it wasn't real clear. "But now that you mention it, there was one thing that happened."

"Go on." Longworth returned to his desk chair and topped off his drink.

"Warrant Officer Haldane told me that an American lieutenant came around looking for me. Said he wanted to talk to me about something that happened at the US Army film lab a day or so ago. I wasn't around at the time. Said he'd come back."

"What unit was the lieutenant from?"

"He told Warrant Officer Haldane that he was from the film lab."

"Did he come back?"

"He did, but I was in the infirmary. I went there in the middle of the night with a nosebleed that wouldn't stop. I didn't wake Warrant Office Haldane, because it was so late."

"Were you going to tell me about this?"

"Never crossed my mind, sir. But now you mention it, do you think it could be about me passing along convoy information to you? Because if it is, you know I don't—"

"No, no, no. It is not about that. They'll never discover that, so calm down and get a grip," Longworth said. He sat back and propped his elbows on the chair's armrests and spun his glass in both hands. Montgomery couldn't see his whole face. "Churchill revealed in today's cabinet meeting startling news of a security breach concerning the next Allied offensive. The Americans are looking for some top-secret document, something the film lab had in its possession . . . until recently." It seemed as though Longworth wasn't speaking to Montgomery. He was talking to himself in a hushed tone.

Longworth drained his glass and slammed it down on the desk, but the paperwork muffled the sound. Nonetheless, Montgomery jumped in his chair. "You need to smarten up, Quinn." Longworth stood up behind his desk and leaned halfway across it, his hands spread far apart. "I have told you time and time again to tell me when anything out of the ordinary happens—that includes anyone from any unit, American or British, wanting to talk to you."

"I thought it was about something I left at the lab or some order I dropped off. Some Coastal Command requests are real doozies . . . real complicated, I mean."

"You need to be more careful and aware." Longworth calmed down as a quizzical look crossed his face. "How much opium are you smoking? Last time, you said that you were cutting back."

"I have, sir. Believe me, I have," Montgomery said with his hand over his heart, feeling the outline of his cigarette case. He realized, to his dismay, that it might be a bad time to ask for cash to replenish his supply.

CHAPTER ELEVEN

1700 Hours, Monday, October 5, 1942
MI6 Headquarters, No. 54 Broadway, London

Thorn, with Heugle in tow, followed the directions he'd received, including the instruction to ignore the brass plaque on the front of the building that announced it as the location for the Minimax Fire Extinguisher Company. After announcing his name and whom he was there to see, Thorn and Heugle waited for several minutes in the lobby for someone to tell him where to go next.

"What if this Bright is some decrepit battle-ax of a woman? You said she lived underground after all."

"Bobby, maybe you should leave and bone up on your Portuguese."

"Not on your life. I want to meet this 'right hand' of Churchill's. I might want to drop her name while I'm in London, in case I get in a bind."

Thorn was about to tell Heugle to leave when the elevator door opened and revealed a dark-haired young woman. Her off-white blouse was pulled tight across her ample chest. She held the doors open and leaned out of the elevator, stretching her blouse to the breaking point. "Are you Thorn?"

Heugle elbowed Thorn indiscreetly and loudly cleared his throat.

"I am. And you are?" asked Thorn.

"Never mind that. Who's this fella? I only had one name."

"He's my partner . . . for now, at least. We work for the same outfit."

"Heugle. The name's Heugle," he said, piping up.

"Hmmm." She looked them both up and down. "Come with me," she said, ducking back into the elevator.

They joined her as she poked a button marked with a faded *B*, and the elevator descended begrudgingly. It was marginally bigger than a phone booth, which made it possible to hear the young woman's breathing. Thorn couldn't help but stare at her. Her charcoal-colored skirt covered her shapely rear as snugly as her blouse, slightly straining the zipper that ran up the back of the skirt.

Heugle's eyes were glued to her backside. He took a deep breath and exhaled loudly, which drew no reaction from the woman, probably something she had grown used to—or more likely tired of. Thorn missed being around Western women, especially those who weren't afraid to show their curves. Maybe he had been in Tangier too long.

"You wouldn't be Emily Bright, would you?" Thorn asked, worried that he sounded too hopeful.

"No, dear. Not me."

"Oh . . . too bad."

She cocked her head at him, smiled playfully, and raised one thin, dark eyebrow in his direction. With his luck, Bright would turn out to be exactly like Heugle had described. "So where are we headed?"

"You'll soon find out, you lucky bastard," she said, smiling when she said *bastard*.

"OK then." *What a shame. Working with her would have been . . . fun.*

Heugle couldn't hold back a laugh. "Will you be joining us?"

"It's my greatest hope, sweetie. It truly is," she said. The sarcasm was a sure sign that she'd dealt with men for far too long, Thorn thought.

The elevator door opened to reveal a dimly lit, smoky space that, to Thorn, looked remarkably similar to a bar. "So what's this?"

"It's a pub, silly boy." Thorn and Heugle carefully squeezed past the woman, who made no effort to stand aside. "Have fun, boys," the woman said as the elevator doors squeaked shut.

Thorn looked around and saw a group of men grouped along a long, dark bar that ran the length of the room. There were several tables that entertained other men, but Thorn didn't see any women.

"I'll be dipped in shit. Do you believe this? A bar in the basement of MI6. No wonder the Brits are losing the war," Heugle said.

"Bobby, shut the hell up. And behave yourself, at least for the next few minutes."

They headed to the bar and ordered drinks.

The barman cocked his head. "I don't recognize you. Who are you with?"

"Well, I'm supposed to meet someone."

"Ahh, a Yank are ya. So who'd that be?"

"Bright, Emily Bright."

"Oh, Miss Bright. Lovely woman. She'd be over there," said the barman, pointing to a table that was partially blocked by the three men who flanked it. A moment later, one of the men stepped away, revealing a woman holding court alongside a naval officer. Her light-brown shoulder-length hair contrasted somewhat with her fair skin, which glowed. Her cheeks were highlighted by a light-red hue. Hedy Lamarr had nothing on Emily Bright.

Easy, boy. You've got your chance to prove yourself. Don't let a pretty face cloud your vision.

"Well, so much for working with a battle-ax, you lucky dog."

Thorn backhanded Heugle in the arm and made a move to the table. As he got closer, he heard Bright laugh. It was a full laugh—one that, by the look on her face, she never apologized for. Getting closer, he could now see that her blue eyes, even through the haze of cigarette smoke, had a sparkle to them that set off her warm smile.

"Hello, everyone," Thorn said. "I'm Conor Thorn. Excuse the interruption. You must be Emily Bright." He leaned over the table and extended his hand.

"I am. Hello, Conor. Welcome to MI6 and the Broadway Club," Bright said as she accepted the handshake. Her hand was warm and her grip firm.

Thorn held on to it a little too long, and he was pretty sure everyone at the table took note. When he finally let go, he took a seat.

Heugle cleared his throat. "And I'm Bobby Heugle. Just protecting my friend's flank. Nice to meet you, Miss Bright."

"A pleasure, Bobby. Please, join us."

"No, no, thank you. You two have business to discuss. I, on the other hand, need to track down our tour guide. She's about five foot three and—"

"That would be Prudence, Mr. Heugle. And don't let her name throw you off." The three men standing around the table all laughed. Bright shook her head.

"Try the third floor," said the only man seated at the table, who also happened to be the only uniformed man at the table.

"Thanks . . ."

"Fleming. Ian Fleming."

"I'll be off, then. Thanks, Fleming. Keep your head down, Conor." Heugle headed for the elevator, high hopes written across his face.

Bright introduced the three men who were standing at the table, who then all drifted off. "And, as you heard, this is my dear friend Ian Fleming," she said, nodding to the man seated with them.

"That's Lieutenant Commander Fleming, Miss Bright," Fleming said with mock sincerity. "A pleasure to meet you, Conor." Fleming was sitting with his legs crossed, his chair angled toward Bright. He had a cigarette holder in his right hand and was in the process of inserting another cigarette into it.

"Lieutenant Commander Fleming works at the Naval Intelligence Division, although he seems to spend quite a bit of time here at Broadway," Bright said, turning toward Fleming.

"Only so I can feast my eyes on you, my dear," Fleming said in the exaggerated tone of someone who was flirting.

It was obvious to Thorn they enjoyed each other's company, which made him feel like a third wheel. "I take it you know why I'm here?" he asked.

"I do. The prime minister has given me a bit of a briefing. I imagine we'll get a full picture once we meet with Commander Butcher tomorrow morning."

"Just what are the two of you up to? Some dangerous undercover assignment for Winston? Let me guess—you are going to be dropped deep in German-held territory in France to whip the French Underground into fighting shape."

"*Oui*. But you must tell no one. Do you hear?" said Thorn.

Bright smiled broadly, and Fleming chuckled as he lit his cigarette.

"So tell me, is it just me, or is it strange to you that there is a bar in the basement of MI6?" Thorn asked.

"Actually, it makes great sense," Fleming said as he pocketed his gold lighter, which was emblazoned with the crown-and-anchor symbol for the Royal Navy. The two columns of brass buttons on his double-breasted royal-navy-colored jacket sparkled in spite of the dim light of the bar. "Intelligence agents are going to drink and gossip no matter what, so let them drink where they can discuss matters of critical importance to the Crown with complete freedom. I think it's brilliant, don't you?"

"I'll have to suggest that to Colonel Donovan," Thorn said, turning from Fleming to Bright, whose eyes were focused on Thorn's hands as he wriggled the wedding band on his finger.

"Yes, you should. And tell him that Ian sends his warmest regards, will you?" Fleming replied.

"So you're acquainted, I take it?"

"Yes, yes. Not as close as Emily here, but Wild Bill and I go back to early '41, when we initiated efforts to coordinate our intelligence organizations. He's been a great friend to the British."

Thorn nodded, then turned to Bright, who was staring at him. "I understand from Colonel Donovan that you were the right hand of the prime minister. He went so far as to call you a 'selfless patriot.'"

Bright looked down at the table and folded her hands. A wisp of her hair fell across her face. "Praise that I certainly don't deserve, not in light of the sacrifices that so many others have made," she said, looking a bit less cheery than she had when Thorn first arrived.

"Emily, how is your mother getting on?" Fleming asked.

"She's strong, Ian. You must be to have a husband in the Merchant Navy all these years," she said, draining her glass. "Can I bum a cigarette?"

"Yes, my dear." After lighting Bright's cigarette, Fleming turned to Thorn and offered him a cigarette.

Thorn waved it off. "Your father's a man of the sea?" he asked, turning back to Bright.

"Yes. Or *was*. We lost him only a few weeks ago. He was the captain of the SS *Empire Stevenson*. A cargo ship carrying munitions that was part of the last convoy to Russia. Torpedoed by a U-boat." Bright looked off in the distance as she spoke and took a strong drag on the cigarette.

"I'm so sorry," Thorn said.

"Thank you. It still hurts. But my work has saved me."

"I hate to lay it on so thick, but what word of Richard?" Fleming probed.

"None. All I can do is hope, pray, that he is alive. All we know is that his ship made it through."

Fleming leaned toward Thorn. "Emily's brother, Richard, followed in his father's footsteps and joined the British Merchant Navy several years ago. He was aboard the merchantman *Rochester Castle* on convoy relief to Malta. His ship was strafed and bombed but made it through. No word on Richard, unfortunately."

Thorn's gut filled with a hot sense of sadness at the suffering that Bright was enduring. He caught his breath for a moment. *You are not alone, Emily Bright.*

Fleming turned back toward Bright. "Don't look now, Emily, but the ever-popular Kim Philby is fast approaching, and he looks none too happy for some reason."

Fleming put out his cigarette and readied another as Philby approached, wearing a blue pinstripe suit with a bright-white shirt. He had his hair slicked back with a sharp, long part on his right side. He took an empty chair and placed his drink on the table.

"And here I thought the Broadway was for senior officers," Philby said, stressing the S in *seniors*.

"Tonight, Emily is an 'evening member,' with a powerful benefactor, I might add," Fleming replied.

"Let me guess—none other than our intrepid prime minister."

"You know, Kim, people who don't know you—such as Conor Thorn here—don't know when you're being sarcastic and when you're being serious," Fleming said as he locked eyes with Philby.

"Well then, I should get to know Conor Thorn. So, who are you?"

"Conor works for Bill Donovan," Fleming offered.

Philby turned sharply to Thorn at the mention of Donovan's name. "Ah, Wild Bill Donovan. So tell me, Conor Thorn, why are the Americans so inept at keeping secrets?"

Thorn immediately saw where Philby was coming from—and going to. "Well, I'm not sure what the hell you're talking about, but I'll say this: we're new to this spy game. But give us time. You'll be learning from us one day."

"Well, bloody good for you and Wild Bill Donovan."

Thorn realized that throwing a punch in another bar, particularly one in the basement of MI6, would result in him being sent to an OSS outpost in the Aleutian Islands. But he would remember this conversation with the overserved Philby.

"I do have one question for Miss Bright though" Philby said, pressing on. "Why is an MI6 operative, a new and untested one at that, and not an MI5 operative assigned to clean up what is a domestic mess for the Americans?" Philby asked as he drained his highball.

How much does this asshole know?

"I trust the prime minister knows what he's doing," Bright said.

Philby pushed his chair back from the table, his legs a bit wobbly. "Well, good luck cleaning up the mess." He stumbled as he headed back toward the bar but regained his balance before crashing into a table occupied by three huddled together, grayhaired men.

Fleming grunted. "Well, that was pleasant."

"Ian, he's just miffed that his section five isn't involved. Pay him no mind." She waved off the interaction with Philby as she spoke.

"Involved in what?" he pressed.

"Can't say. But knowing you, you'll pry the lid off someone and find out—it won't be my lid though." She smiled.

"Just tell me one thing," Thorn interjected, still following Philby's progress through the room with his gaze. "Whose side is he on?"

CHAPTER TWELVE

0900 Hours, Tuesday, October 6, 1942
Office of Commander Harry Butcher, Headquarters ETOUSA, No.
20 Grosvenor Street

A grim-faced woman held the door open to Commander Butcher's office and with a practically inaudible voice announced Thorn and Bright's arrival. When Thorn passed by the woman, he noticed that her eyes were red and swollen. She clutched a dingy handkerchief in her hand.

What the hell is going on here?

Thorn entered the office first. The air was fouled with stale cigarette smoke, and Thorn's glance snagged on the six or so cigarettes in the glass ashtray on Butcher's desk. But he also detected the smell of something else he couldn't put a name to. Butcher was standing behind the desk, looking out a twelve-by-twelve-inch window, which overlooked Grosvenor Square.

"Did you know the British call the square Eisenhowerplatz?" Butcher said, his back to his guests. The engines of several vehicles could be heard through the second-floor window. "I am told that the square used to be beautiful: lush, green lawns and dense gardens. Now it looks as if the entire US Army has been training on it for the past month." Butcher turned and approached Thorn and Bright. "Please, sit."

"Thank you, Commander," Thorn said. Butcher's face was drawn and pale, and Thorn knew from his own days of standing long watches on the bridge of the *Reuben James* that it was from lack of sleep—Butcher looked as if he had pulled a few midwatches himself.

Butcher shook a cigarette from a pack of Lucky Strikes, which he tossed onto his desk, and proceeded to light up. "Well, let's get on with it. I believe you have both been given a general idea as to our situation. Is that right?"

Thorn and Bright looked at each other and nodded.

"Good. I have a file here for you both to review. It contains notes on all the interrogations of the film lab's staff and a copy of the report filed by Army Intelligence. There's some background information on the lab's staff. No red flags with the staff, except maybe the officer in charge, a Lieutenant Johannson. Not the sharpest tool in the shed."

Butcher opened the file, pulled out a report, and pawed through it until he found the page he wanted. "As far as the break-in is concerned, based on a statement from Johannson, the lab had been broken into sometime between late Friday night and early Saturday morning."

"What was taken?" Thorn asked.

"That's just it—apparently nothing. That's why Johannson didn't report it. No equipment, no files, nothing, at least according to Johannson."

"Has the lab been a target before?" asked Bright.

"No. At least not that we're aware of. It's only been in operation for four months."

"Fingerprints . . . footprints?" Thorn asked.

"Don't know. A team from MI5 has been sent to the lab. G2 doesn't have the resources. We'll know something soon, but I do know there was some blood found on the door that was used to gain entry."

"Who from MI5 is handling it, Commander?" Bright asked.

"A Trevor Hightower. Reach out to him and get briefed."

"Will do," Bright said.

"One thing you should know though. We couldn't locate two of the people who visited the lab. One is an RAF warrant officer by the name of Montgomery. He's attached to Coastal Command and—"

"Coastal Command?" Thorn asked.

Bright nodded, her attention riveted on the commander. "Their primary responsibility is to provide air cover and defense of convoys heading to the Soviet Union," she recited to Butcher and then glanced at Thorn.

"Where is he based, Commander?" Thorn asked.

"Northwood, southwest of here."

"Sounds like a good place to start, but you said two people," Thorn said.

"I did. The other is a Captain Toulouse, attached to the BCRA, Free French Intelligence. They're over on Duke Street. You need to know that this Toulouse happens to be a nephew of General de Gaulle. And that could be a big problem for us."

"Yes. I get it," Thorn said. "A question, sir: We know where the diary page was last known to be, but why was it being microfilmed?"

Butcher shrugged. "It's part of the process of compiling the general's wartime diary. We've been doing it for months. Why do you ask?"

"Just filling in some missing information. Whose responsibility is it to handle the day-to-day diary work?"

"Well, by my direction, Elizabeth Weddington handles the brunt of it."

"By any chance is Weddington the woman who let us in?"

"Yes."

"Has she been questioned?" asked Thorn.

"Yes, by me, very early on."

"She was the last person to possess the document?" Bright asked.

"Yes."

Butcher squirmed in his chair somewhat. "Listen, both of you. You're barking up the wrong tree, so don't waste your time, which you don't have much of."

Touchy. Thorn stole a quick glance at Bright, who nodded at Butcher.

"Before we leave, I'd appreciate it if Bright met with Miss Weddington for a moment, if you'll allow it. I can't help but wonder if she would be more comfortable talking with another woman instead of a man. We might learn something."

"Ahh, suit yourself." Butcher closed the file and handed it to Thorn. "We're done here."

Thorn and Bright began to stand, but Butcher held up his hand to stop them.

"Let me add to the picture. General Eisenhower has orders from the highest Allied levels that the French, free or otherwise, be rendered blind and deaf as to what may or may not be happening in French North Africa. You understand what 'orders' means, Mr. Thorn?"

"Yes, sir. I have my own set, and I have every intention of following them."

"Good. Now we're done."

Thorn and Bright stood.

"Remember." Butcher tapped the face of his watch with his index finger to finish his thought.

"Understood, Commander." *Don't worry. The clock in my head doesn't tick; it pounds with each passing second.*

#

Miles Stoker stood outside the brick building that housed the film lab, his neck tilted back, his face to the gray sky, his wide-brimmed hat in his hand. A fine mist settled on his face as he watched a white-bellied, two-engine, twin-tailed plane making a very low approach to the nearby runway. The sound from the plane's engines filled the air around him and rattled in his chest. His good ear was overwhelmed with engine roar.

"Are you lost, sir?"

Stoker continued to track the plane's approach.

"Sir?" Someone was tapping him on his shoulder.

He spun around and saw a US Army private jump back a step. The man held up both hands in a surrender pose. "Sorry . . . sorry, sir. You looked a bit lost. I was just asking—"

"No, no. My apologies entirely. Bad ear, you see. Just taking in the scenery. Quite impressive."

"Very good, sir. So you know where you're going?"

"Yes. Right in there, if the guards at the front gate were correct. This is the Eighth Army Air Forces film lab, right?"

"That would be right."

"Thank you, Private. I'll be on my way then." Stoker replaced his black felt hat on his head and moved toward the building. After a minute of orienting himself, Stoker found himself at the double doors to the film lab. Another army private, a rifle slung over his shoulder, was there to greet him.

"Your business, sir?"

"Ahh, I'm with British Intelligence. I'm here on official business."

"Identification?"

"Certainly." Stoker pulled a leather wallet from his raincoat pocket and flipped it open. The private leaned over and squinted. As he silently read the identification card, his lips moved.

"OK, Mr. Higgins. You may pass," the man said as he opened and held the door for him.

He removed his hat and entered.

Inside the lab, the first sensation was the intense, sinus-clearing chemical odor followed by the loud, low-bass hum of machinery. The only person in sight was a lieutenant, stooped over a counter, examining a stack of photos with a magnifying glass, deeply engrossed.

"Leftenant?" Stoker said, moving closer to the counter.

The officer didn't move. "What?"

"My name is Higgins. Attached to MI5, British Intelligence. May I have a word?"

"About what? And it's *lieutenant*, Mr. Higgins, Lieutenant Johannson," the officer said, raising his upper body to a standing position. He placed the magnifying glass on the counter and, with both hands, smoothed some errant hairs on the top of his head.

"Yes, of course, Lieutenant Johannson. I'm here—"

"About the break-in . . . the missing document, whatever the hell it was. Am I right?"

"I'm sorry, Lieutenant. What did you say? I've a bit of trouble with my hearing, you see."

"I said," the lieutenant said, drawing out his words, "the missing document—you're here about that."

"Ah, yes, Left—Lieutenant. Correct. So what can you tell me?" Stoker drew closer to the counter and placed his fedora on it.

Johannson stared at the wide-brimmed hat for a moment. "Listen, Mr. Higgins. Been through this with a whole bunch of other muckety-mucks. I've got a lot of work to do. Why don't you talk to Commander Butcher from Ike's office? He'll fill you in."

Stoker's confidence in his ruse was growing. "Already done, Lieutenant. But I've got bosses like you and Commander Butcher, and I need to form my own picture about this tits-up situation."

"What the hell did you say?"

It was the first time that Stoker clearly picked up on the slight drawl.

"Sorry, Lieutenant. I meant to say that I was looking into just what went wrong."

Johannson began shaking his head, smirking as he walked down the counter toward Stoker.

"Lieutenant. The missing document. Is there anything that you haven't already reported to the other . . . investigators?"

Johannson scratched his head and looked up at the ceiling. "Well, can't say there is." He massaged his chin and looked down at the floor. "I . . . can't think of anything." He shook his head slowly. "Oh, there was one thing." Johannson's attention turned to the lab's doors as a young woman in her midtwenties entered along with an American sergeant. The woman, with auburn hair and light-bronze-colored skin, had a briefcase that was handcuffed to her wrist. She approached the counter. "Excuse me, Mr. Higgins," Johannson said, scurrying down the counter to meet the woman.

Stoker took the opportunity to take some notes while Johannson fussed over the woman. When he looked up, he saw them both looking at him. They broke off their staring almost immediately followed by a high-pitched laugh from the woman. Johannson took the briefcase from her and disappeared into the rear of the lab, returning quickly with another briefcase, which the woman cuffed to her wrist. She turned toward the door, which the sergeant held open. Before passing through it, she turned briefly and shot a look at Stoker, complete with a wry smile.

Johannson returned, and Stoker could discern the remnants of a blush on his cheeks.

"So who was that, Lieutenant, if you don't mind my asking?"

"That's Miss Weddington. She works for Commander Butcher

. . . in Ike's office. She comes here a lot."

"She's quite . . . pretty."

"I'll say. I can't keep my staff in line when she's here. That's why I'm her point man," Johannson said, the tenor of pride unmistakable.

"You mentioned there was something else. What was it?"

Johannson looked blankly at Stoker. At that moment, Stoker knew he could waste no more time in this tomb. "I don't rightly remember what it was, Mr. Higgins. Sorry. If I remember—"

"Listen, Lieutenant Johannson." Stoker motioned Johannson closer to him, and the man complied, leaning over the counter. Stoker went nose-to-nose, which made Johannson noticeably uncomfortable. "The missing document. It is critical that it be found. If you or any of your staff should come across any information . . . *any* information at all concerning its whereabouts, I can say that British Intelligence would pay dearly for it. I personally will see to it. Am I making myself clear, Lieutenant? We will pay. I will *personally* see to it."

Johannson backed up a step. He nodded solemnly as if he had just heard a dying man's confession. Stoker reached into his breast pocket and pulled out a small card. "Here is where I can be reached. Call anytime. If not me, someone will answer. Trust me."

CHAPTER THIRTEEN

1030 Hours, Tuesday, October 6, 1942
The Berghof, Hitler's Mountain Headquarters, Berchtesgaden,
Germany

The overnight train trip from Berlin to Munich drained Admiral Wilhelm Canaris. Normally, Canaris, the fifty-five-year-old head of the Abwehr, the German military intelligence organization, needed eight or more hours of sleep a day. But those badly needed hours of rest proved elusive on the private railcar that carried Canaris and his adjutant, Captain Herbert Wichmann, to Canaris's meeting with Hitler and Heinrich Himmler, head of the German SS. One needed to be at his best when dealing with the führer and Himmler, Canaris's personal adversary. Today, he was not at his best. But he was not at his worst either. Knowing the reason for the hastily called meeting—the Allied plans for a second front—was helpful.

As his driver inched the staff car up the narrow road to the main entrance, Canaris spotted the Berghof, Hitler's residence, perched high above them to the right. The sky brimmed with light-gray, low, fast-moving clouds, but blue patches of sky were beginning to take over. Canaris took it as a good sign. It took a moment to pass through the gate security and a few more moments before they arrived at the stone steps of the entrance. Two SS Leibstandarte guards stood at attention and waited for the staff car to come to a stop, their Mauser pistols tucked away in their holsters as their hands tightly gripped their Maschinenpistoles.

It had occurred to Canaris that he might have been summoned to the meeting to be sacked. The idea that he would be unseated as head of the Abwehr when his country most needed him had made sleep impossible. He had to keep both Hitler and Himmler at bay.

As Canaris and Wichmann ascended the front steps of the Berghof, the sight of the residence's bright, gleaming walls could be seen supporting a long, peaked roof that jutted out toward the mountainous landscape, some of which was already dusted with snow. A slice of Austria, Hitler's birthplace, could be seen in the background, through a notch in the Bavarian mountains.

A tall, strapping SS lieutenant, his blond hair slicked back and his blue eyes radiating, bounded down the entranceway's interior staircase, stopped abruptly, clicked his bootheels together, and raised his right arm in the Nazi salute. "Heil Hitler."

Canaris raised his right hand no higher than his stooped shoulder and nodded.

"Admiral Canaris, Captain Wichmann, please follow me. Admiral, the führer will meet you in the main salon."

#

Dressed in black trousers, a double-breasted gray-blue tunic over a white shirt, and a black tie, Hitler greeted Canaris warmly. Heinrich Himmler stood quietly nearby, resplendent in his SS uniform, a row of ribbons running across his left breast and rectangular epaulets on his collar flanking his black tie. His boots reflected the bright sun streaming in through the fifteen-foot-long window that stretched to the vaulted ceiling. Canaris's deep dislike of Himmler—who was bald and flabby and whose main facial feature was a receding chin—had grown exponentially over the past year.

"Shall we sit and get on with it?" Clearly bored and antsy, Himmler motioned Hitler and Canaris over to a couch and group of chairs surrounding a low table with a vase of mountain flowers in its center. "Admiral, please sit here," Himmler said, pointing to the long, green divan situated along the wall. Himmler and Hitler took chairs on the other side of the table. Canaris, a short man at five feet three inches, sank deep into the soft cushions, looking as if he were a young boy being questioned by two headmasters. Canaris could see that Himmler had given much consideration to the meeting's staging.

"If I may begin, Führer?" Himmler nodded toward Hitler, who gave his approval with the wave of one hand as he stroked his loyal German Shepard Blondi's head with the other. "Winter is approaching in Europe. If the English and the Americans are planning a major offensive, it must come soon. The Allies talk and talk of a second front, but, I must say, there is severe disappointment that the Abwehr, your Abwehr, has produced little to no reliable information as to where the English and the Americans plan to strike next."

Hitler nodded slowly, his lips pursed in an antagonistic frown.

Canaris sat back and let Himmler go on, knowing that interruptions irritated the man.

"The Abwehr's list of achievements is short and unacceptable. Its list of failures is growing, and that too is unacceptable. My God, the miserable failure of Operation Pastorius has made your Abwehr a laughingstock."

Canaris could not argue that the Pastorius failure had damaged the reputation of his intelligence organization. He had argued, without any success, that there were too many operations being asked of the Abwehr to be able to properly staff it with well-trained agents. The caliber of men available to the Abwehr was shockingly deplorable.

"Your—"

Hitler stopped Himmler with a fist pound to the armrest of his chair. "Admiral, these are serious accusations. Yet you have no reply?" Hitler shouted.

Canaris sat calmly; he never let Hitler's outbursts rattle him. "It is true—Pastorius was a failure. It was mounted hastily." Canaris knew that taking strong adverse positions with Hitler and Himmler was a poor strategy. Taking a cue from the temperature and temperament of his audience had served him well over the years, and most certainly with Hitler. "And we have learned from it."

"Learned from it? Preposterous. I see no indications of a more effective Abwehr, if that is what you are implying." Himmler was incensed. In the rays of sunlight that peeked in, Canaris could see Himmler launch spittle across the table, toward him, as he spoke. "Your Abwehr has failed, again and again, to produce accurate assessments of enemy activities both in the east and the west. You failed miserably in detecting the Russian buildup in the Stalingrad area, which cost us dearly. How do you explain that, Admiral?"

Canaris remained calm as he answered. "At this point in time, the Allies are producing a large amount of contradictory information concerning their operations. That includes the Russians. It takes time to confirm exactly what is the wheat and what is the chaff."

"Oh, stop with your cute little sayings," Himmler shouted. "They disgust me."

Canaris decided to not engage with Himmler, instead, allowing him to settle down. "Führer, yes, there have been setbacks. But there have been successes."

"Yes, Admiral. But not enough recent successes." Hitler stood and walked over to a low, long table in front of the massive window.

Canaris believed it was time to remind Hitler how effective the Abwehr—his Abwehr—could be. "I shall remind you, the Abwehr did present intelligence regarding the British and Canadian raid on Dieppe."

Himmler sat back in his chair and stole a look at Hitler, who, at the mention of Dieppe, turned and pointed at Canaris.

"Admiral, that was, indeed, a great victory for the Reich. The Abwehr's role has not received the attention that it deserved. Himmler, do you agree?"

Himmler's pudgy hands, resting on the arms of the club chair, were balled into fists, the knuckles white. "The führer is generous with his praise, I feel."

Hitler shook his head at Himmler's lack of generosity and moved back to his chair. "Admiral, where will the Allies strike next? It is imperative that we pin down their next target. What have your agents been reporting?"

"Führer, again, we are sifting through a large amount of intelligence. The Allies have become experts at generating indications that they are considering multiple targets."

"Such as?" Himmler asked.

"Targets range from as far south as Dakar, off the west coast of Africa, to the Cherbourg peninsula, to Norway."

"Ach, Norway. This target has been reported on in American newspapers for days. Surely you have more sophisticated means of gathering intelligence than reading the enemy's newspapers, Admiral."

Canaris had had enough of the probing, the insults, and the insolence from someone who had never seen active military service on behalf of Germany. He jumped to his feet and looked at the führer, who appeared startled by his sudden movement. "I can assure you both that every effort is being made to discover where the Allies will open a second front. Reporting intelligence that is not vetted is worse than reporting no intelligence at all. I will not provide the führer with guesswork. Now, if it pleases the führer, I must return to Berlin and get on with the Abwehr's work."

"Admiral, a display of hurt feelings will not persuade me to relieve the pressure on the Abwehr to fulfill its mission to the Reich," Hitler stated.

Canaris stood motionless.

"I expect accurate and irrefutable intelligence from you regarding the second front in a week. One week. Do you hear me? Sift through all your intelligence and find the wheat, as you say. Am I . . . clear?" Hitler said, his face a glowing shade of red.

"Yes, Führer, you are exceedingly clear, as usual."

#

Canaris and Wichmann sat in the rear of the staff car in silence as it drove though the Bavarian countryside. Canaris was brooding after his encounter with Hitler and his sycophant Himmler. Unless he produced some reliable intelligence, his sacking may have been only delayed. A disaster for the German people.

"Herbert, what have we heard from Longworth of late?" Canaris asked, staring at the forest greenery as it whisked by his window.

"Nothing since he reported that convoy PQ 18 would have enhanced RAF air coverage. That was at least a month ago. Why, Admiral?"

"Can we apply some pressure on him to provide . . . a higher class of intelligence?"

"Regarding?"

"Regarding where the Allies plan to open a second front."

"I gather that was the subject of your meeting."

Canaris didn't respond.

"Admiral, may I suggest that I reach out to Major Kappler in Rome and have him communicate with Longworth through our friend Bishop Heinz in the . . . usual manner? I think it's time that we remind Longworth that his future as an English statesman is completely in our hands. Maybe we should send a specific reminder of that?"

"What do you mean?"

"I would ask Major Kappler to include a copy of a picture of Longworth's last night with his Italian mistress when he was stationed in Rome—the night he asphyxiated her."

"I struggled with this from the beginning. I am not comfortable with being so heavy-handed. We are not the Gestapo."

Wichmann leaned toward Canaris and spoke in a hushed tone. "Admiral, if you are to remain as the head of the Abwehr, where you can do the most good for Germany, you must prove your value to Hitler and those around him. Besides, to not use the photographs given to us by the Italian secret police would be . . . wasteful."

Canaris went back to his silent study of the wooded landscape. He abhorred the darker art of spy work. It was not how he wanted the Abwehr to conduct itself. But he needed to get back into Hitler's good graces.

"Admiral, maybe a mention of the poor woman's name?" Wichmann asked. Several moments passed, during which a heavy rain began to fall.

"Do what you think best," Canaris said without turning his head.

CHAPTER FOURTEEN

1300 Hours, Tuesday, October 6, 1942
Regent's Park, London

There was a bracing chill in the air as Miles Stoker strolled through York Gate into Regent's Park as if he were a prewar tourist, stopping occasionally to stare at the birds as they soared overhead. He never feared being seen or that he might have been followed on his regular jaunts into various London parks to meet his comrade. He was always exceedingly careful to follow all the protocols that he was instructed to follow when meeting with fellow conspirators.

He enjoyed his meetings with Otto just as much as Philby did, especially their initial meetings, when they were probing each other to determine the other's suitability for the tasks that lay ahead. Their conversations ran the gamut from music and art, to the politics of Marx and Lenin.

As Stoker strolled over York Bridge and approached the Inner Circle that encompassed Queen Mary's Gardens, he spotted a group of young women chatting away as they clustered about a metal drum with holes drilled into the sides, to help diffuse the warmth from a fire that burned within. Nearby were the lashings that kept a large barrage balloon tethered to the ground. There was a mountain of sand beyond the barrage balloon that had been dumped at the start of the war for sandbags. Three young boys—with their mothers nearby pushing baby carriages back and forth—played war games on the pile of sand with broomsticks standing in for rifles and a faded, tattered Union Jack flying from a sycamore branch that had been downed by a strong fall wind. Stoker could smell the damp sand—the only scent on the slight breeze, as the blooms of summer had long since vanished.

He tightened the scarf around his neck and adjusted his fedora. As he did, a compactly built man passed behind him, bundled up as if he had recently arrived from Murmansk. Stoker held his ground and fumbled with a set of binoculars as the man took a seat on a bench twenty yards down the path. He searched the nearby trees for birds. He couldn't tell a ruddy duck from a sanderling, but no one would know that. He finished his bird gazing several minutes later and, now confident that neither man was followed, joined the man, being sure to sit with his good ear facing his handler.

The man's gray hair was combed straight back off a large forehead that featured eyebrows arched as if in perpetual surprise. His matching gray beard was unruly, with hairs splaying in all directions, and his large hands showcased long, slender fingers with bony joints.

"I am sure you know winter is months away," Stoker said.

The man grunted. "Yes, yes. But I am not as hardy as our comrades who are valiantly defending Stalingrad." The man's English was stiff and proper, delivered in a deliberate fashion.

"Hardiness fades with age. Didn't anyone tell you that?"

Otto could only grunt at Stoker's pronouncement. He noisily blew into his tightly cupped hands while he watched a mother of one of the young boys box the child's ears for throwing sand in the face of his now-wailing friend. Otto began to cough, at first lightly, then more forcefully. Each successive cough lingered longer, until he finally stopped and spit into a handkerchief, then wiped his mouth. Stoker could see dark-colored phlegm staining the cloth. They sat in silence for another minute.

"I am cold and tired. And, if I am not mistaken, it was you who signaled for this meeting," Otto said.

"I was only being polite, waiting for the black lung episode to pass."

"Your humor at my expense is shameful. Now what do you want to tell me?"

Stoker surveyed the area and spoke quietly. "Philby has been made aware that the American's have . . . misplaced a top-secret document that details key information regarding the Allied invasion of North Africa. This document has great value to us."

"Why are you so interested in an operation that we have known about since before Churchill's visit to Moscow? He himself gave Premier Stalin key information about the operation."

Stoker shifted in his seat to face Otto. "Answer this question: Does not Premier Stalin want the Allies to launch a second front in Western Europe and not in North Africa?"

"A second front in Western Europe . . . yes, that is true, Comrade."

"So tell me—if the directives, the specific details of this North African operation—were to fall into the hands of the Germans, what do you think the Allies would do?"

Otto shrugged. "You are the expert on the Allies. You tell me."

"Gladly. Philby and I—" Stoker stopped and pulled a handkerchief from his coat pocket and blew his nose, allowing a woman pushing a baby carriage to pass by. His attempt to take credit for Philby's strategy was risky. But without risk, there was no reward. "We believe that with the element of surprise gone, the Germans will, to some extent, fortify the Vichy French. But it will be half-hearted because the Germans firmly believe the Allies will strike somewhere on the Continent. Norway or possibly the Cherbourg peninsula. Even they know that to give proper relief to their Soviet ally, a major attack must be mounted on the Continent."

"Yes . . . yes. You make some sense."

"Some? It is more than some. It is assured that if Roosevelt and Churchill know the directives are in the hands of the Nazis, at best, the North African operation would be canceled, or at the least postponed to allow for a different set of objectives and time-tables to be determined. Neither Roosevelt nor Churchill would risk the success of the first major Allied offensive in the European Theater." Stoker beamed at Otto, which only appeared to confuse Otto more thoroughly.

"A postponement only brings us back to where we are now. So what good—"

"It will give Premier Stalin more time to convince the Allies to mount an invasion of France and will give the Americans and the

British more time to build the necessary forces to launch such an operation. Only then will Hitler move enough troops and arms to the West, and only then will the Soviet Army reclaim land lost to the Nazis and expand beyond."

"Fine. Fine. But unless you have the document, you are wasting my time."

"We don't have it. Yet."

Otto's head snapped around to face Stoker. "Yet? What do you mean?"

One of the young women tending the barrage balloons threw more wood into a drum, which threw off a thick, black cloud accompanied by some sharp cracks and pops. Several women screamed and backed away.

"I received a call this morning. It was a woman. Cockney accent. She made it clear that she was representing someone. This someone has the document. I don't know this woman. I don't know how she got my phone number. All I know is that if this person has this document, we can put it to great use."

"This person, she or he . . . they are—"

"Selling it for five thousand pounds. And with your ability to provide the necessary funds, it can be ours."

"If we did . . . provide these funds, what do you plan to do with it?"

"I . . . We . . . plan to put the document in the hands of our friend, the Abwehr agent."

"Longworth," Otto spat, his face pinched. "The man I said long ago we should expose to the British."

"No. The information he was passing to the Germans about convoy activities was always intercepted and altered by our agent in the Hamburg Abwehr station, making it worthless. No, Philby's decision to leave him alone until he could serve a greater good was the right decision."

"And you believe that this 'greater good,' as you call it, is a second front on the European continent?"

"Philby does. And so do I. But, more importantly, Premier Stalin does also."

"We shall see, comrade," Otto said as he stood and stretched his back. He studied the women gathered around the smoking drums for a long minute. "I will report to Moscow Center to see if they agree with your plan. If they do, I will provide the necessary funds."

"One last thing. This woman has started a clock. She gave me forty-eight hours to find the money. Will that be a problem?"

Otto snorted.

"I'll take that as a no."

Stoker rose from the bench and smoothed out the wrinkles in his trousers.

A thin smile formed on Otto's face as he rubbed his chin for several moments. He pulled down his hat, covering most of his forehead as a chilly breeze swept though Queen Mary's Gardens. After looking around to see that no one was near, he shoved his hands deep into his coat pockets. "Enjoy your walk back to MI6, Mr. Stoker."

CHAPTER FIFTEEN

1330 Hours, Tuesday, October 6, 1942
RAF Coastal Command, Northwood Headquarters, Eastbury,
England

Thorn and Bright waited in their staff car near the front entrance to the Quonset hut that acted as sleeping quarters for Quinn Montgomery's Coastal Command unit. Thorn was behind the wheel, and Bright sat beside him. It had taken some serious arm-twisting to get Hollis to give up the wheel, but she now sat nervously in the rear seat. On the way to Northwood, she had protested several times that it was against regulations for her not to be driving. If she was found being driven by superiors, she could be disciplined. Thorn assured her that wouldn't happen.

Montgomery's superior officer had told them that Montgomery was on an assignment but would return soon. Bright studied a photo of Montgomery that had been included in the file that Butcher gave them. It showed a dark-eyed, balding man with a blank expression.

"You didn't mention whether you learned anything from your heart-to-heart with Weddington," he said.

"I didn't learn anything significant. Or at least, I don't think I did."

"What do you mean you don't think you did?"

"Just that her opinion was that the lab staff always took their jobs seriously. They gave the impression that they were always working on something. She said they niggled a bit about the workload. And—"

"They what?" Thorn heard Hollis giggle in the rear seat.

"Oh, sorry—they complained a bit."

"And what else?"

"She did say that the newest member of the staff was a bit of a nuisance."

"How so?"

"Weddington said he kept asking questions about the material she was bringing to a Lieutenant Johannson at the lab. The lieutenant told him to mind his own business, but he kept at it when the lieutenant wasn't around. She simply began ignoring him after a while."

"Hmm . . . anything else?"

"Actually, yes. She told me that there was someone in the lab yesterday talking to Lieutenant Johannson. The lieutenant told her that he was from MI5. Went by the name of Higgins."

"What did he want?"

"He was asking about the lab break-in."

"I wasn't aware that anyone else was working on this. Were you?"

"No. But that's just it. When I checked with MI5, they said they weren't aware of any break-in at the film lab, and to top it off, they hadn't heard of a Higgins either."

Thorn shifted in his seat to look at Bright. "Someone with a false name . . . false identification, asking about a break-in of the lab where a top-secret document goes missing. Do we have a description of this phantom agent?"

"Weddington gave a murky description at best." Bright lurched forward in her seat. "Look, there he is." Bright held the photo of Montgomery up to eye level as she looked out the windshield of the staff car. As the man walked, Thorn saw that his right foot twisted to the left, forcing it to land on the edge of his shoe, producing a slight limp. "Yes, that's him," Bright said.

"Let's go. Miss Hollis, we won't be too long," Thorn said.

Thorn and Bright intercepted Montgomery at the entrance to the Quonset hut. "Warrant Officer Quinn Montgomery?"

"That's me. Who's askin'?" said Montgomery, who gave each of them a good once-over.

"My name is Thorn, and this is Bright. We need to ask you a few questions."

"About what? I haven't done anything."

"No one said you did, but that is an interesting response," Thorn said calmly. "Let's step inside and get comfortable."

"Just who are you with?" the man asked, blinking rapidly.

"Let's say we work for the prime minister and General Eisenhower," Thorn said.

"Ahh, don't we all," Montgomery retorted, a smirk appearing on his face.

He entered the hut first. There were two rooms on either side of the entrance. Standing in the doorway, you could see a spacious room that featured rows of cots lining each wall. There was little light inside, as it was empty of personnel. The smell of disinfectant hung in the air. Montgomery opened a door to a cramped room located to the left of the main entrance. The deficient lighting in Montgomery's quarters was at least aided somewhat by the sunlight coming from a small window cut into the hut's corrugated metal.

Montgomery sat down on his cot after he tossed his hat onto an undersized, six-drawer dresser. His right foot turned in and rested on its side. The stink of chemical cleaners became stronger, so Thorn shut the door. Bright stood in the corner, near the dresser, while Thorn stood by the door.

"So tell us what you do here at Costal Command."

Montgomery's eyes narrowed. "I work at headquarters. The command provides air cover for convoys coming from the States and for convoys headed to Russia."

"But what do you do?"

"What do you think? I'm a warrant officer." Montgomery snickered. "I do whatever they tell me."

"That include visiting the US Army Air Forces film lab at Camp Griffiss?" Thorn asked.

Bright was moving about the room, looking at pictures pinned to a corkboard on the wall above the dresser. Her movements distracted Montgomery, who watched Bright bend over to retrieve something from the floor on the other side of the dresser.

He refocused his attention on Thorn. "Yeah, a couple of times.

Our own lab had been down for a few days. So what of it?" Thorn noticed Montgomery's right eye twitching. He had lost what little color his face had.

"You all right, Montgomery? You look as if you saw a ghost or something."

"Yeah, I'm all right. Get on with it." Montgomery nervously folded his arms, then unfolded them.

"The film lab. You ever walk out with anything that didn't belong to you?"

"What? Like what?" Montgomery took a deep breath and rubbed his eyes.

"Like anything you weren't ordered to pick up. Like someone else's recon photos or any type of paperwork."

"No, nothing like that. I picked up what I dropped off for developin'."

"You said Costal Command's lab had been down. Is the lab back up yet?"

"Yeah, just yesterday."

"We were told that someone came here to ask you some questions on Sunday, but you weren't around. Where were you?" Bright asked as she took a photo off the corkboard and looked at it intently.

Montgomery fixed his eyes on her. "I was in the infirmary."

"How come your superior officer didn't know where you were?" Thorn asked.

"I had a bad nosebleed real late on Saturday night. I left on me own. Didn't want to wake him."

Thorn stared at the man. "Ever hear of leaving a note?"

"Warrant Officer, is this you in this snap?" Bright asked, interrupting the questioning as she handed the black-and-white photo to Montgomery.

"Yeah, that's me. Why you askin?"

"Is the man in the middle Henry Longworth?"

"It would be. Why you lookin' at me things?"

"How do you know him?"

Montgomery shifted into defense mode. Bright seemed taken aback for a moment, and Thorn made a mental note to find out why. A moment later, Montgomery began blinking rapidly.

"He's . . . he's . . . a family friend. That's all." There was a knock at the door, and an RAF flight lieutenant stuck his head in. Montgomery rose to his feet.

"Montgomery, is this about finished?" The lieutenant turned to Thorn. "He's not in trouble, is he?"

"These people were askin' some questions about the film lab at Griffiss Park, sir."

"Just trying to track down some information on suspicious activity, Flight Lieutenant. Just routine, really," Bright said.

"Well, are you 'bout done?" the flight lieutenant asked.

"Yes, I believe we are. Right, Mr. Thorn?" Bright asked, buttoning up her coat.

"Yes, I think so."

"Montgomery, get over to headquarters. It looks as if PQ 19 is on again."

"Yes, sir."

Thorn and Bright walked out of the hut, and Thorn saw Hollis in the driver's seat. He gave her a *what the hell are you doing* shrug, and she got out of the car, slipped into the backseat, and slammed the door.

"Did you see what he was doing with his eyes?" Thorn asked Bright.

"I did. A classic nervous tic. There was something about the photo that got under his skin for sure."

"So what's the significance of it?"

"Montgomery is standing next to Henry Longworth. He's a member of the war cabinet." Bright directed her gaze toward the gravel-covered ground and shook her head. "It was something I didn't expect to see, I guess. I don't think it necessarily means anything."

"If you ask me, Montgomery doesn't seem the type to be hanging around high society."

"Yes, that is odd. The family friend response has me thinking a bit. But there was something else."

"What?"

"This." Bright pulled a small square of brown wax paper, folded over several times. Inside was a single black ball, smaller than a marble. "It was on the floor, wedged behind a leg of the dresser.

I'm not sure what it is." Bright raised the contents to her nose. "It smells kind of like incense and looks like tar. I can only guess."

"Well, go ahead."

"Opium. But here's a potential problem—I think Montgomery saw me take it."

"If it's what you think it is, isn't it a problem for Montgomery? And maybe Longworth?"

Bright paused for a moment. "Montgomery? Yes. But Henry Longworth? That's too outrageous to think about."

CHAPTER SIXTEEN

1530 Hours, Tuesday, October 6, 1942
No. 28 Queen Anne's Gate, London

The more Longworth read, the quicker his pulse raced. His disgust rising like poisonous phlegm in his throat, he tossed the week-old edition of the Soviet newspaper *Pravda* across the study, its pages floating to the floor after it hit the wall below the portrait of Pope Pius XII. It was the news that Soviet forces had beaten back the Germans from the ancient burial grounds of Mamayev Kurgan overlooking Stalingrad, if it could all be believed, that had done it. It was *Pravda* after all. But he chose to believe the news that the Soviet government had stopped distribution of the antireligious publications from the League of the Militant Godless, but not because of the reported reason—a shortage of paper.

Stalin was no fool. He needed to curry favor among his new allies and garner the support of the religious people who occupied the newly annexed territories of Eastern Poland, the Baltic states, and part of Finland. Longworth's thoughts drifted back to his days as a midlevel Foreign Office diplomat in Moscow in 1925, when he saw firsthand the religious oppression Stalin meted out. Longworth failed to keep from thinking about his arrest and abuse at the hands of communist thugs when he'd been paying a visit to the archdiocese of Mohilev.

He rubbed the four-inch reminder that ran across his chest above his heart; the jagged scar tissue was still firm to his touch.

Longworth was ripped away from his dark recollections by the booming of the front door opening and quickly slamming shut.

Montgomery stood in the study's doorway with his coat collar pulled up tightly around his neck and sweat dripping into his eyes.

"Damn it, man! What's gotten into you? You look as if you've been fighting the devil himself," Longworth shouted.

Montgomery flopped into a chair in front of Longworth's desk and took a few moments to reclaim his breath.

"Well, come on, man—get a grip." Longworth grabbed a letter opener made to look like a Royal Scots Fusilier sword and began to fiddle with it as he watched Montgomery wipe the sweat from his eyes.

"Some investigators questioned me today. They came to Coastal Command headquarters. They were waiting for me. I couldn't get—"

"Slow down, man! Tell me who they were, these investigators."

"One was called Thorn, and the other, the woman, her name was Bright."

At the sound of Bright's name, Longworth dropped the letter opener, the hilt of the miniature sword clanging loudly against the oak floor, and bolted upright in his chair.

"Bright? Emily Bright?"

"She didn't say her first name, just Bright."

"The Bright I know is now with MI6. What did she look like?"

"I don't know . . . between five and six feet, brown hair . . . I think. Maybe in her late twenties."

"Close enough," Longworth mumbled. He rose from his chair and picked up the letter opener. He walked over to a large map of Europe on the wall adjacent to his desk and stared at it for several moments, then placed the tip of the letter opener directly on Moscow. "What did they want?" Longworth asked, still staring at the map.

"They asked what I did at Coastal Command. And they wanted to know about me going to the Americans' film lab. They're snooping around, lookin' for something about me gettin' you convoy information—it's got to be. They were—"

"No, no, no. They have other problems. And this Thorn, he didn't say who he was with?" Longworth turned around and tossed the letter opener onto his desk.

"Just that he worked for General Eisenhower. And he was the one who asked the questions, or most of them." Montgomery slumped forward and rested his head in his hands.

"What did Bright want to know?"

"She was the one who asked about a photograph of me and you. I had it pinned to the wall in my quarters."

Longworth's eyes widened as he strode over to Montgomery and shoved him into the back of his chair. "What the hell are you talking about?"

"That photo of you and me and my mum at her birthday party last year. It's a photo my dad took."

"Damn it!" Longworth said, returning to his desk chair. "What did you tell them?"

"That you were a family friend, that's all. Nothing more." Montgomery was fidgety; his right leg began bouncing.

Longworth closed a book on his desk and shoved it out of his way. He sat back and stared up at the ceiling. "So they've made a connection . . . a weak connection between you and me. So what?" he said softly, as if Montgomery weren't in the room. "As long as they don't inquire further about your activity on my behalf at Coastal Command, all should blow over. As I said, they have other problems."

Montgomery's rapid blinking only served to further confirm the young man's rattled state. "There's one thing, sir," he managed. "At the end, I saw the woman, Bright, pick up something off the floor. She slipped it into her pocket."

"What of it?"

"I think it was an old packet of opium."

Longworth slammed both hands on the desk, sending several sheets of paper to the floor and making Montgomery cower. "Goddamn it, man. Now they have a link from you to me, *and* they can link you to illegal narcotic use. That will invite ever more scrutiny. Don't you see? If they can pin that on you, there will be no way for me to keep you assigned to Coastal Command. I couldn't get involved."

Montgomery again buried his face in his hands, and Longworth reached for a decanter and poured himself a drink, then downed it in one smooth motion.

"Go back to Coastal Command. Tell them you need a few days' leave for a family emergency. Then come back here." He poured another drink and looked at the younger man, whose face was resting in his hands.

"Look at me!" Longworth shouted.

Montgomery jerked his head up, still blinking fast.

"Get ahold of yourself. And heed my words—if your carelessness goes unchecked, it will lead to my ruin."

CHAPTER SEVENTEEN

1600 Hours, Wednesday, October 7, 1942
Bureau Central de Renseignements et d'Action (BCRA),
No. 10 Duke Street, London

After requesting to see Toulouse and presenting their identification at the front entrance of the BCRA headquarters, Thorn and Bright were immediately escorted by a silent French lieutenant to a windowless room located at the rear of the ground floor. The room, which reeked of bleach, contained four chairs around a small table that sported several deep gouge marks and a dozen or more burn marks lining its edges. It was dimly lit by a frosted-glass, domed ceiling fixture. Insect carcasses littered the bottom of the dome.

As soon as they were alone, Thorn began to closely examine the room, pacing slowly along its perimeter.

"Checking for bugs?" Bright asked.

"Yep," Thorn said. "Remember where we are."

Bright nodded and sat down as Thorn continued his sweep.

"Clean . . . as far as I can tell."

"In more ways than one, I suspect," Bright said.

"What are you talking about?"

"That smell. It's bleach. You use it to clean up bloodstains."

"Huh?"

"Well, it's not just my imagination running wild. There have been plenty of rumors in intelligence circles about this place."

"Fill me in."

"Rumors about torture mainly," Bright said.

The door handle slammed downward and the door swung open. The sound of tapping heels announced a strutting, tall man with thinning, blond hair. His knee-high, black boots glistened even in the low light of the room. Another uniformed man, dark haired and equally tall but broader shouldered, followed him into the room, but his gait lacked the crispness of what was clearly his superior. He stood at ease in a darkened corner behind the booted officer.

Thorn and Bright rose from their chairs.

The boot clicker spoke first. "I am Major Dewarvin. Why have you come here?"

Thorn, realizing that a relaxed conversation among allies was out of the question, pushed his chair back under the table and remained standing. "We have a few questions for Captain Toulouse. This shouldn't take long."

"Questions about what?"

"About his recent visits to the film lab at Bushy Park," Bright said. "There has been some unusual activity there of late and we—"

"What type of unusual activity?" Dewarvin asked, not once taking his eyes off Thorn.

"We're looking into an incident that involved some materials being passed along to the wrong people," Thorn said. "Captain Toulouse was singled out to us as a person who may have received these materials."

"Materials? What do you mean?"

"Photos, possibly some documents," Thorn said. He looked at Bright, seeking some signal that he had handled the question with enough care. There was no signal. Bright's gaze was locked on the man in the corner.

Dewarvin tilted his head back and gave them an exaggerated frown. "Careless. How can we win this war if the Americans are so careless, Mr. Thorn? Ask your questions, but make this quick." He stretched his right arm behind him and, with his index finger, motioned the man in the corner, who must have been Toulouse, forward.

As Toulouse moved toward the middle of the room, into the light, Thorn took in the look on his face: his eyes in a piercing stare, his lips pressed firmly together, his jaw jutted out—Toulouse hated them, but Thorn couldn't have guessed at why. The captain's arms hung at his sides, his hands resting below midthigh. Dark, dried blood marked the location of cuts and scratches on the back of his hands.

"Have you received anything from the film lab staff that wasn't meant for the BCRA?" asked Thorn.

"No," Toulouse said, the word choked off by a collection of phlegm in his throat.

"Speak up, Captain," Dewarvin said.

"No, I said."

"Where were you late Friday and early Saturday morning?" Bright asked as she took a step closer to the two French officers.

As Toulouse unraveled some farfetched story about getting drunk with his girlfriend and a press attaché from the Spanish embassy named Jorge Alba and then getting into a bar fight with some Brit sailors, Dewarvin studied Thorn intensely, as if he was trying to learn something from Thorn's reaction to Toulouse's story.

Bright continued with more when, where, and why questions, and Toulouse answered in short spurts. At Toulouse's mention of the word *capitulation*, Dewarvin became more rigid and Toulouse feigned spitting on the floor.

"What's your blood type, Captain?" Thorn asked.

Dewarvin reacted as if Thorn had slapped him in the face and quickly jumped in. "Do not answer that . . . insulting question. This is finished, and you will now leave."

CHAPTER EIGHTEEN

0700 Hours, Thursday, October 8, 1942
Regents Park, London

Stoker tapped his right foot on the gravel path, the tempo getting faster the longer he sat alone. He had waited in Queen Anne's Garden past the arranged time for his meeting. Daybreak had not yet finished unfurling its warming rays upon the frost-covered grass, and the barrage balloon minders had begun to stir near their hut. It was now fifteen minutes past the target time. He had never had to contend with a tardy Otto before. There must have been a good reason. Maybe Otto had been followed and did not want to lead his tail to the park. This possibility alarmed Stoker. Not connecting with Otto and collecting the payment would sabotage Philby's plans.

He instinctively felt for the five-inch knife, its leather scabbard stitched under the overcoat lapel in a manner to give him quick access to the knife's handle. The weight of the .32 caliber Colt against his leg comforted him—somewhat. He got up to take his leave, but he had taken no more than ten paces when a tall man who looked to be in his early sixties, a cigarette dangling from his compressed lips, approached him.

"Come back," the tall man whispered as he passed by.

Stoker stopped in his tracks and turned to see the man sit down on the bench that Stoker had just deserted. He didn't recognize the man, which elevated the risk in approaching him. But if he brought word of Otto, it would be worth the risk. Besides, his weapon gave him the edge over the old man.

"Pardon me. Did you say something?"

"Yes. Sit down. Please."

Stoker surveyed the park in all directions. Nothing appeared unusual or out of place for an early morning in a public park. He took a seat on the bench again.

The stranger's hands protruded from the sleeves of a black wool overcoat; they were large, but not in a beefy way; the palms were wide, his fingers long, and the knuckles like tight knots of twine. "I was looking to meet someone. Perhaps you know him."

"He was called back to Moscow. I am your new handler, as well as your boss's. My name is Shapak," the man said, his tone clipped and words precise. His Russian accent was detectable but not distracting. Stoker could tell that his new handler had been in England for some time. But this did nothing to quell his concerns. Breaks in routines were always unwelcome, and being called back to Moscow was never a welcome development. He was aware of Stalin's purges. But Philby drilled it into him to always focus only on matters he could control. Nevertheless, Stoker liked Otto.

"What is the reason for his callback?"

"What reason will make you comfortable?"

"He was . . . he *is* a loyal communist. Never did he utter a word against Premier Stalin."

Shapak lit a cigarette and looked up at the cloud-filled sky.

"Did he go willingly?" Stoker asked.

Shapak answered with a shrug. Philby had decided long ago that they would not allow internal Soviet political matters to deter them from doing what they could to aid in communism's fight against fascism. Stoker willingly accepted Philby's belief that capitalism was fated to fail, leaving communism the only true safeguard against fascist world domination. That must be his only focus. But, at that moment, it was not. "I don't understand. Why go back to certain horrible fate? Why not simply drop out of the battle and stay here?"

"It's simple: kill him there or kill him here. What's the difference? It is better that it happened there. In his homeland."

Stoker lowered his head, as if in prayer, even though prayer was foreign to him. The news of Otto's demise angered him, but he was more disappointed at Shapak's blunt and callous way of delivering the news. He struggled to keep himself in check. He nodded, not showing his new handler any emotion. "He was a good man."

"Meh. There are many good men . . . on our side. And some . . ." Shapak trailed off with a flourish of his hand.

And with that coldhearted motion, Stoker regained his focus. He zeroed in on the women across the way who were handling the barrage balloon tethers. "Did you bring the money?"

"What have you heard from the woman?"

The nonanswer annoyed Stoker. He jerked his eyes back to Shapak. "She, or they, are ready to deal. Tonight at twenty-three hundred hours . . . in Trafalgar Square." Stoker turned back to the barrage women. "Are *we* going to make the deal?"

"Your plan. I don't see the sense of it. Giving secret documents to the fucking Germans? Whose side are you on, Stoker?"

"There are many ways to win a war. Some are not so obvious."

Shapak laughed. "Oh, I see now. What you are saying is that I lack the intelligence to see the brilliance of your plan?"

"No. No, of course not. But maybe your briefing was not so complete as to see the full picture."

"Ahh, bullshit." Shapak flicked the stub of his cigarette across the path, into the grass that glistened with the melting frost.

Stoker sat silent for a moment, to allow the other man's annoyance to dissipate.

"For some reason unclear to me, Moscow Center thinks your plan has a chance of altering Allied invasion plans. If that happens, maybe Premier Stalin's skills of persuasion will convince them to invade France sooner rather than later. That is what they think. That is what you think. Apparently, it does not matter what I think."

Stoker decided not to engage Shapak on his opinion. "Then all I need is the money. I assume you have it?"

Shapak had been staring at the group of women, who were gathered about their campsite, feeding scraps of wood into the metal drums for their morning fire.

"Pretty girls. But what a stupid thing to be asked to do—watch a fucking balloon all day."

"The money, Shapak?"

Shapak rose slowly. Stoker heard the dry cracking of knee joints. Shapak lit another cigarette and took a deep drag; it was pinched tightly between his thumb and index finger. He took another pull from the cigarette, this one quicker.

"Shapak—"

"Quiet. After I leave, wait at least five minutes, then head down the path to a bench with a chalk mark X on the left armrest. Reach under the seat. The money you requested is there."

"This is a great thing we are doing, Shapak."

His new handler dropped his cigarette to the ground and twisted the sole of his shoe over it. "Get caught with that document, and you die a traitor. Like Otto."

Stoker stared at Shapak, a man that would take some time to like. "I know what a traitor is, Shapak. And Otto was not a traitor."

CHAPTER NINETEEN

1900 Hours, Thursday, October 8, 1942
Savoy Hotel, Victoria Embankment, London

Thorn had barely started the long climb out from his hellhole that was his life when he'd last seen his father. They'd had dinner at the Old Ebbitt Grill in Washington, DC, with Thorn's older brother, Johnny. A lieutenant in Patton's II Corps, Johnny was on leave, spreading his wings in Washington, bedding, it seemed, anyone he wanted—and he wanted a lot. Their father, Jack, was in town visiting the Federal Communications Commission on regulatory business that impacted his Republic Broadcasting Service. It was the last night before Thorn was to begin his training at the OSS's Camp F, formerly the Congressional Country Club. He remembered little from that evening. His brother hadn't stayed long before he'd headed over to the Mayflower Hotel bar. His father had talked at length about the confounding actions of the FCC.

What Thorn did remember was that it had been four months after the death of his wife and son and the sinking of the *Reuben James*, and only one month after washing out of the navy. He had been circling the drain then.

When Thorn entered the Savoy's Grill Room in London, it was easy to spot his father. As usual, he was center stage, encamped at a table in the middle of the room, a location that could be easily seen from anywhere in the place. Two men sat with Jack, all of them having drinks.

The Savoy Hotel was a popular choice as a base of operations for US journalists covering the war in Europe, and Thorn easily recognized both men with his father. One was Bob Trout and the other was Ed Murrow, both from CBS. Thorn assumed his father was doing one of two things—either gathering inside information about CBS management, or trying to poach them for RBS. Thorn watched his father, a drink in his right hand, tick off one item at a time with the fingers of his left hand as if in the middle of a sales pitch. Trout and Murrow were nodding politely.

It took Thorn less than a minute of weaving through the sea of white-cloth-covered tables to arrive at his father's. In that span, Thorn's father no longer resembled an enthusiastic pitchman but more a stunned recipient of bad news after a medical checkup. His father hadn't noticed Thorn approaching the table. Both Murrow and Trout had though; they looked as if they appreciated his timing.

"Hey, Dad."

Thorn's father, rousted from his stupor, rose and gave him a bear hug. Even when it was too tough to love anyone, Thorn loved his father.

"Damn great to see you. Looking sharp as ever. You remember Ed Murrow and Bob Trout, don't you?"

"I sure do. Gentlemen, great to see you again. So let me guess, you turned down my dad again?"

Both men laughed. "Not yet, Conor. We thought we could get a few more highballs out of him before we did," Murrow said.

"And we're waiting for Jack to throw in a country club membership to Burning Tree," Trout added.

"Sit down, Conor, sit, sit," his father urged. "Ed here was just delivering some ... some startling news about your sister."

"Jack, listen, I'm sorry. I assumed you knew. I didn't mean to—"

"Ed, Ed. Relax. While I didn't know, I'm sure not surprised," Jack said before he polished off his drink.

"Hey, let me in on this big news," Thorn said. "Did Mags find some guy in a uniform to finally make an honest woman out of her?"

"Tell him, Ed," Jack said, searching for a waiter.

"Maggie landed in London yesterday. She's supposed to meet Bob and me here tonight."

"What? I thought she was working back in the DC bureau for RBS. Is she on assignment?"

"It looks like it, but not for RBS."

"She's working for CBS, Conor," Trout said. "We thought your father was aware."

Thorn, with raised eyebrows, looked at his father and shook his head.

"I was in the bureau two weeks ago, and she cornered me again and asked—no, she demanded to be assigned to London to cover the war. I, for the tenth time, said no. I told her I had enough of my children in harm's way."

"And?" Thorn asked, not surprised by his sister's heavy-handed tactics.

"She quit. On the spot. And just stormed out of the office. As her mother would have done. I haven't heard from her since."

Thorn choked down a laugh. "So Bill Paley finally pulled one over on you. How 'bout that?" Thorn said. Both Murrow and Trout sprouted smirks while Jack shook his head.

"Jack, we'll leave you to your son here and catch up with you later. Maybe in the American Bar, upstairs. Who knows? We might run into Hedy Lamarr. I saw her in the lobby on my way here," Trout said.

"Bob, she's not your type. I'll see you later, gentlemen," Jack said, slumping back in his chair. Neither spoke for several moments as other patrons passed by, going to and from their tables. A five-man ensemble had appeared and began to play Lena Horne's "Mad About the Boy." It had been his wife Grace's favorite song. He hadn't heard it in a long time. Thorn was glad no one was there to sing the lyrics. It would have been too much.

"Son, it's damn good to see you. How long has it been?"

"At least . . . six months—you, me, and Johnny in DC."

"Yes, that's right. It's been too long. But I get it—the war and everything."

"How's Uncle Mick doing? Life getting any easier for him?"

"Not a chance. In fact, after the Madison Square Garden case, the higher-ups in the NYPD seem to have it in for him. I call him every week. But it's always a bit of a one-sided conversation."

It pained Thorn that his uncle couldn't catch a break even if it had been gift wrapped and dropped into his pocket. The other detectives on the NYPD called him an odd duck right to his face. But Uncle Mick never lost his cool—a trait Thorn was still working on. Jack looked across the bustling room and then turned back to Thorn. "So how are you doing?"

Thorn realized his dad wasn't merely making conversation. He was digging for information, as Thorn assumed he had been doing earlier with the CBS guys. "Fine . . . I think." He took the napkin and dropped it into his lap.

Jack, looking intently at him, nodded slowly and appeared satisfied.

"So, what brings you to war-torn London, Dad?"

"Ahh, well, the main reason is the First Lady's trip here. Eleanor is due in a few days. It's a big deal for the people back home."

The band struck up "When the Lights Go On Again"; this time the bandleader covered the vocals with a sad, soft voice. The room grew still; the waiters, normally buzzing full-tilt about the room, stopped and listened briefly. As the room sprang back to life, Thorn looked at his watch.

"You expecting someone?"

"Actually, yes, someone who works for the British government. She said that she'd meet me here. Do you mind?"

"She? Absolutely not. It would be nice to have the company of a woman for a change. What are the two of you working on?"

"Can't say much. Something that both governments want . . . taken care of."

His father listened but looked above and beyond Thorn, and then stood.

Thorn turned around and saw Bright standing behind him wearing a snug-fitting, red-and-white, long-sleeved dress with a coat draped over her arm. Her face was glowing. She had taken the time to put on a modest amount of makeup, and he detected the scent of lavender following her to the table. She was simply striking.

Easy. You're not ready. And you've got a mess to untangle.

Thorn rose from his seat, and the napkin on his lap fell to the floor. "I was beginning to think you weren't coming. This is my father, Jack. Dad, this is Emily Bright."

"So nice to meet you, Mr. Thorn," Bright said. She walked up to Jack, hand extended. Jack took her hand with both of his and gently shook it. Thorn noticed an identification bracelet dangled from her right wrist.

"Oh, please, Emily, call me Jack." He released her hand and Bright took her seat, which had been pulled out from the table by Thorn. Unseen by Bright, Jack raised his eyebrows and, with wide eyes, shot an approving look at Thorn. "Can I order a drink for you?"

"That would be wonderful. A pink gin would check the box."

As his father busied himself with flagging down a waiter, Thorn leaned into Bright. "You look . . . uh, look . . ."

Bright turned to Thorn and tilted her head. Several strands of her light-brown hair fell across her face, covering her left eye.

" . . . like you have some news." *Well, that was a little clumsy.*

"Really, and what look would that be?"

"Like . . . you can't wait to tell me something."

"Well, actually, I do have something. I did a little digging and found out that Quinn Montgomery's mother is Henry Longworth's only sister."

Thorn sat back in his chair. "Hmm . . . that fills in a few blanks."

The drinks arrived, and his father was the first to move to the toast stage. "To my son, to his friend, and to the brave British people."

"Hear, hear," Bright added.

Over dinner, his father told the story of an old family acquaintance. Thorn listened but was more focused on his female dinner companion.

"So . . . Hey, are you listening, Conor?"

"Yes. The Sullivans. What about them?"

"Well, it turns out that the Sullivans' oldest son, Sean—do you remember him?"

"Dad, I think I was six when he babysat Maggie and me."

"Maggie?" Bright asked.

"My younger sister. More on her later. Dad took the family over to Dublin for a few years when we were all fairly young. Mr. and Mrs. Sullivan did the driving and housekeeping. My dad was the US vice-consul."

"Mostly trade and other economic matters," Jack said. "It was an exciting time to be there, the civil war and all." His father leaned into the table. "Conor's mother believed otherwise. Too dangerous for her liking." He leaned back in his chair and grabbed his drink. "So, as I was saying, Sean became a . . . priest!" he said, slapping the linen tablecloth. "And he's right here in London, at Westminster Cathedral. I hope to get time to see him before I leave."

"When is that, Dad?"

"Not sure. I'll most likely stay at least until the First Lady returns to the States."

"Yes, isn't that exciting news? My mother hasn't stopped talking about the visit. Will you get to meet her, Jack?"

"Already have. I went to law school with Franklin, see them both whenever I get to Washington. She is a dynamo, unmatched by most of us."

As the waiter cleared the dinner dishes, a quiet fell over the table. Thorn stared at Bright. She was radiant; her blue eyes sparkled. When Bright turned and saw that Thorn was staring at her, he abruptly stopped, as if he were back in eighth grade, getting caught looking at Joyce Petrementi's burgeoning breasts. When Thorn looked back at her, Bright tilted her head slightly and smiled. *What woman doesn't like a little attention? But don't get carried away, mister.*

"Oh, before I forget, Conor," Jack said in more of a whisper. "I noticed this past Sunday that there were no flowers on Grace's and Timothy's graves. So I called the flower shop near the cemetery and found out there are new owners. I straightened out the confusion. They'll start taking flowers to the cemetery every Sunday starting this week."

Thorn didn't want to be taken back—not to the cemetery, not to the hospital, not to the bedside of his wife. "Thanks," he muttered. He saw Bright's gaze was locked on him, but he did not engage her and instead took a sip of his coffee. Over the brim of the cup, he spotted his sister darting in and around the tables. A guy was at least four steps behind her, trying to keep up. Maggie's blue dress was cinched at the waist with a bright-white belt that accented her shapely figure. Her wavy, red hair bounced on her shoulders with each step she took. She had a head of steam built up as she approached the table. Thorn was the only one who noticed her and her old boyfriend, who pulled up the rear—none other than Bobby Heugle.

This could get interesting.

"Batten down the hatches, folks. There're rough seas ahead," Thorn muttered.

"Father. Good evening," his sister said, announcing her surprise attack on the table. Jack choked on a swig of coffee. Bright smiled as if she were watching a family drama unfold on the stage of the Old Vic.

"Conor, you big lug, come here and give your little sister a hug. She could use one from a friendly family member."

Jack sighed deeply.

"Mags, we just heard you were in London. And I'm sure you can imagine Dad's surprise," Thorn said, wrapping his arms around his green-eyed sister. She had yet to look their father directly in the eye.

Jack screwed up his face but got up to kiss his only daughter on the cheek and hug her, patting her on her back as he let her go.

"Mr. Thorn, good to see you again," Heugle said, his hand outstretched.

"Bobby, it's good to see . . . that you're not in jail. What brings you to London?" Jack asked, coolly accepting Heugle's handshake.

"Just picking up an award for exemplary service in Tangier, just like Conor here, except it's in the form of a new assignment." Heugle winked at Thorn before turning his attention to Bright. "Miss Bright, great to see you again. You look . . . stunning."

"Hello, Bobby," Bright said, clearly enjoying the scene. "Please, call me Emily."

"So, Emily, don't you know that London is a dangerous place? Or so my father says." Maggie extended her hand to Bright. "Doesn't look too dangerous to me. What do you think?"

"I'd say don't let the lovely confines of the Savoy fool you. I'll show you the hotel's bomb shelters later if you like."

The comment triggered a broad smile from Jack that Thorn did not miss. Maggie lit a cigarette in surrender, but not before she also smiled at Bright's quick response.

"Maggie, Emily and Conor are working together," Jack said as

Thorn and Maggie took seats. Heugle scrambled and pinched a chair from a nearby table, ignoring a protest from a blue-haired older lady.

"Working together. Hmm . . . and what exactly would you two be working on together?" Maggie asked, shooting quick looks at her brother and Bright.

"Can't really say," Thorn said.

"You could say matters of security, Maggie," Bright said.

"I see. I know the outfit that Conor works for, but who do you work for?"

"Military intelligence essentially." Bright's smile faded a bit.

"Well, I'm impressed. That's a man's game for sure. And it says a lot about you if you're playing that game. If I had a drink, I'd raise my glass to you."

"Message received," Heugle said, signaling to a passing waiter.

"I have a question, Maggie. How do you and Mr. Heugle know each other?" Bright asked.

"We were an item—"

"For a week, no more than three, if I remember," Jack said.

"Father, it was ten days."

"News flash, Bobby told everyone it was at least a year," Thorn said.

"All right, all right. I'm obviously outgunned here. But . . . never say die when it comes to true love."

"Oh boy. You delusional man. Someone change the subject. Please," Maggie said. "And where's that waiter?"

Jack leaned into the table. "So it had to be CBS? It couldn't have been Life or Colliers? CBS . . . that hurts."

Maggie rolled her eyes, then pulled a cigarette from a silver case. Thorn leaned over and lit it, shaking his head. She shot him a *so what?* look and blew a long stream of smoke into the air above the table.

"Father, get over it. It's a chance to do some real reporting for a change. I'll be interviewing Clementine Churchill tomorrow at 10 Downing Street. I already have a slot on Sunday's *World News Today* broadcast."

Jack's eyes widened, and his mouth fell open. Thorn was sure it was the reaction Maggie was looking for. Thorn himself was never surprised by his sister's bravado, but he was surprised that his father didn't protest more.

"That's quite a get, Maggie. Congratulations," Bright said. "She's a wonderful woman, beloved by many Britons. Please extend my greetings."

"Oh, you know her, I take it?"

"Yes. I spent a good deal of time with her when I worked for the prime minister."

"My, my. You are an interesting woman. We should compare notes sometime."

Thorn noticed a uniformed man sauntering toward their table.

"Good evening. Sorry for barging in on you. I'm First Mate Trevor Shockley of the Merchant Navy." The right sleeve of his officer's jacket climbed up his arm as he stretched out his hand to Bright.

"Hello," she said. "This is Jack Thorn; his son Conor; and daughter, Maggie; and her . . . friend Bobby."

"A pleasure, I'm sure. I came by to tell Miss Bright that all the Merchant Navy is pulling for positive word of your brother. We served together on the *Rochester Castle* last year. He was . . ."—the first mate tossed his head back and momentarily frowned—"*is* such a good man and one of the ablest sailors I have ever seen."

"Thank you very much, Mr. Shockley," Bright said as she nervously rotated the glass in front of her. "He is just like his father."

Thorn looked at his dad, whose face betrayed his confusion.

"Well, I must be off. A pleasure meeting you all and seeing you again, Emily."

As the officer retreated, Jack leaned forward and placed his hand on Bright's forearm. "Tell me about your brother," he said.

"Dad . . . not now," Thorn protested, hoping to spare Bright the pain of relating her story.

"That's all right, Conor. It's no trouble," she said, then took a deep breath and looked at Jack. "My brother, Richard, is an officer in the Merchant Navy. He's been missing ever since his ship was torpedoed in the Mediterranean. The ship made it to Malta, but I don't know if he's alive, wounded, or . . ." Bright's voice trailed off.

"I am so sorry to hear that," Jack said. "You mustn't lose hope. Promise me that."

"I haven't and I won't," she said. "And thank you—you're very sweet." Maggie handed Bright a handkerchief, which Bright acknowledged with pursed lips and a nod of her head.

Jack settled with the waiter and pushed away from the table. Maggie collected her cigarette case and lighter, and Heugle pulled her chair from the table. She was still watching Bright as she spoke. "Well, I'm off. I would prefer to think we could do this again, but I suppose that's not likely."

Jack and Thorn stood and Maggie hugged them both, lingering with her brother a moment longer.

She dug into her purse and pulled out a calling card and handed it to Bright. "Emily, call me, if you just want to talk to another girl—someone who doesn't have a thick head like these guys."

"Hey, I resent that," Heugle said in a mock indignant manner.

Bright chuckled. "Maggie, I may do that. Thank you. And good luck at CBS."

"Thanks. It'll be interesting, I'm sure." Maggie turned to her brother, winked, and was swallowed up by the crowd of other grill patrons who were taking their leave. Heugle was, again, several steps behind her.

"Oh, wait, Conor. I forgot to tell you," Jack said. "I heard from Johnny. He told me that his unit has been practicing amphibious landings in Chesapeake Bay. He says the chatter is that they're close to a deployment. All sorts of targets have been mentioned—Norway, Africa. It sounds as if he could be in the thick of it soon."

Thorn looked at Bright, and from the startled look on her face, she understood what he was thinking. *Johnny in the thick of the invasion of North Africa. Shit.* "Oh, and he also wanted to make sure I told you he recently received his captain's bars."

Thorn stood motionless, staring at his father. He shook his head slowly.

Jack laughed as he turned to Bright. "Those two guys, always competing."

Not quite, Dad. Johnny's headed into a meat grinder if we don't find that fucking document. Thorn shook hands with his father, who then surprised Bright with a soft kiss on her cheek, which, Thorn noticed, brought a warm smile to her face.

"Well, if you two want to join me later, I'll be in the American

Bar. I need a shot of war gossip. And I think those guys from CBS owe me a drink for stealing my daughter," he said as he turned and began to wind through the maze of tables.

"Let's take a walk," Thorn said. The news of Johnny's unit's involvement in Torch did nothing but tighten and twist his guts.

"Where?"

"Somewhere. Anywhere."

CHAPTER TWENTY

2100 Hours, Thursday, October 8, 1942
Victoria Embankment, London

With his shoulders hunched and his head slumped forward, Thorn stopped in front of the hotel, under the massive, stainless-steel *Savoy* sign that was topped with the medieval-style gold-clad statue of the crusader Amadeus VI, Count of Savoy. The count was holding his shield and lance and peered past Savoy Court, to the Strand; blackout curtains shrouded the windows above the statue. Bright stood by Thorn's side, her concerned look trained on him. There were two taxis and a sedan parked along the inside curb of Savoy Court. Thorn helped Bright with her coat and waved off one of the taxis.

"Let's go down to the river. I need to clear my head," Thorn said, turning up his trench coat's collar against the chilled, damp nighttime air.

"All right, let's do that," Bright replied.

Thorn took the lead and headed down Savoy Court toward the Strand. They passed the second taxi, its driver fast asleep, and then the sedan, a dark-gray Rover with a dark figure slumped behind the wheel—maybe asleep, maybe not.

As they neared the Strand, Thorn heard the Rover's engine turn over. He stopped and turned toward it, listening as the driver revved the engine. They continued down the narrow, sloping Carting Lane, which dropped them in the darkened Victoria

Embankment Gardens. Thorn continued his swift and silent march with Bright a short step behind. Once on the Thames side of the gardens, he took a right turn onto Victoria Embankment, avoiding a walk along the riverside and its accompanying brisk wind that rolled off the river. The full moon created thousands of tiny, glistening sequins on the river's surface, heightened by the gusting wind.

"Conor, who are Grace and Timothy?"

Thorn looked at the river, his hands buried deep in his coat pockets. "Grace was my wife. Timothy . . . our first child." Thorn heard Bright's soft gasp. *Here it comes.*

"I can't express how sorry I am. I . . . I really don't know what else to say."

"That's OK. I've heard all the expressions of sympathy I want to hear."

Bright crossed her arms against the chill wind. "Will you tell me what happened?"

Thorn could recall every argument he and Grace had ever had over having kids. "Doctors told her she shouldn't have children due to a serious bout of rheumatic fever as a teenager. It severely weakened her heart. But she wouldn't listen. Damn stubborn woman. I was at her bedside when she died." He paused. The wind swirled around them. Every time he told the story, he hoped the ending would be different—could be different. "The baby just didn't have a chance. He was too premature. But, in a strange way, it may have saved my life." *Saved. Again.*

"How do you mean?"

Thorn turned toward Bright. "I . . . don't . . . know. Maybe that was a stupid thing to say. We'll talk about it later. Enough sharing for tonight."

They resumed their walk, abreast and slower this time, each entertaining their own thoughts. They headed toward the Hungerford Rail Bridge, and it was several minutes before Thorn broke the silence. "Before the dinner developed into a family drama, I couldn't stop thinking about your news that Quinn Montgomery's mother is related to Longworth. What does that mean?" Thorn asked.

"Maybe nothing. Could just be a coincidence."

"No, there has to be more to it. It's too big of a coincidence."

"So you're trying to connect the missing diary page to the film lab, then to Quinn Montgomery, then to Henry Longworth, a member of the prime minister's war cabinet and a friend of Winston Churchill's for virtually thirty years?" Bright stopped and grabbed Thorn's arm. "You can't be serious, Conor."

"Well, I am. And *if* it can be connected, we have to follow it up. We can't ignore anything just because it may involve a cabinet member. Don't you agree?"

She freed his arm. "Must I remind you that time is of the essence? And any time spent 'following up,' as you call it, on a member of the war cabinet is a damned waste of time." Bright stormed off.

"It's not as if we have a lot of other directions to go in at this point," he called to Bright as she continued walking.

The Victoria Embankment hosted sparse pedestrian and vehicular traffic as the nine o'clock hour ticked on. What little traffic there was moved slowly. Thorn couldn't help but notice a delivery truck coming toward them, the driver leaning on his horn as he stared straight ahead. Thorn looked over his shoulder and spotted a sedan in the wrong lane—speeding toward him and Bright. The sedan's right-side tires scraped against the curb. Its three outsized headlamps formed the shape of a triangle, emitting a faint amount of light through lamp covers that featured horizontal slits.

It wasn't until the sedan had pulled closer that Thorn noticed that the front driver's side window was lowered. He could clearly see the driver had his right arm outstretched. The blare from the truck's horn grew louder.

"Son of a bitch," Thorn hissed.

He sprinted the fifteen feet to Bright and lunged, taking her to the ground and landing on top of her. The breath rushed from her lungs as two gunshots rang out, followed by the sound of the sedan's tires squealing as it swerved back into the left lane, missing the skidding truck's front end by inches.

"Bright . . . Bright, are you okay?" Thorn asked, putting his hand on her cheek. As he lay on top of her, he was hit again by the scent of lavender and could hear her struggle to fill her lungs with air. He began to pat her down, searching for a gunshot wound. His hands slid across her chest. He felt her firm breasts through her coat and lingered too long. Just then, she shoved him off her and onto the sidewalk.

"Had enough?" Bright asked, her voice raspy and starved for air. She rolled onto her side toward Thorn, who was on his back now, looking up at the night sky.

"Sorry, I was just—"

"I know . . . I know, just playing doctor. I get it. But what just happened?"

"That was an out-and-out murder attempt. And it certainly wasn't random," he said.

Bright began to stand, but she wobbled on weak legs.

The driver of the delivery truck ran toward them. He wore a bloodstained apron over a dark wool coat. "My Lord, are you both all right? Should I get some help? That crazy arsehole almost done us all in!"

Thorn stood and helped Bright to her feet. He noted that the side of the truck was painted with the name *Borden's Fine Meats*.

"Thank you, sir. We're fine," Bright said.

"Were those gunshots I heard?" asked the driver as he wiped his forehead with the bottom of his bloody apron.

"Oh no, I don't think so. I guess you could say we were . . . caught off guard," Thorn said ruefully. "But I do think that Rover needs a tune-up." The explanation appeared to satisfy the rattled driver, and he returned to his truck, muttering to himself.

"How do you know that it was a Rover?" Bright said as she brushed off her coat, her voice having reclaimed its strength.

"That was the same car that was parked in front of the Savoy when we came out."

"There are plenty of Rovers in this city—"

"The Rover in front of the Savoy had a bad cylinder; it was misfiring," Thorn insisted. "You could hear it a mile away. The car that just tried to mow us down had the same exact problem."

"You could actually hear a bad cylinder? I—"

"Trust me. I'm good with engines."

They resumed their walk and soon found themselves staring up at the Hungerford Bridge.

"Bright, you OK?"

"Recovering, I'd say. I'll be fine. And . . . thank you."

"For what?" Thorn asked, smoothing back his windblown hair.

"I think you saved my life."

He turned to face her and looked at her face intently. He waited several moments, then turned away and looked down the embankment. "Well, whoever that was, he was after the both of us—not just you. And I couldn't be happier," Thorn said, smiling broadly.

"Are you a madman? A minute ago, someone tried to kill us. Right out in the open." She beat off some leaves that clung stubbornly to her coat. The thumping sound reverberated in the night air.

"Think about it," Thorn said. "If we weren't getting close, no one would want us dead."

CHAPTER TWENTY-ONE

2200 Hours, Thursday, October 8, 1942
Trafalgar Square, London

The newspaper-strewn train car was nearly empty. Four seats away from him, a couple was engaged in a tight embrace, tonguing each other sloppily. *Yet another couple, living for the moment*, he thought with disgust. Fortunately, Stoker was minutes away from ending the third leg of his serpentine trip from Broadway to Trafalgar Square. One stop from Saint James Park to Westminster on the District Line, followed by a brisk walk, with two stops along the way to look over the moonlit Thames, ensuring that no one was tailing him; to the Charing Cross Underground Station's Bakerloo Line for the train to Piccadilly Square, purposely bypassing the stop for Trafalgar Square. All very tiresome but necessary.

He exited the train and walked down the platform, toward the stairs that led to the surface. The train he left, now on its way to Tottenham Court, picked up speed as it passed him. Inside the train, he glimpsed the couple still tightly stuck to one another. Once the breeze created by the passing train lessened, he smelled the sharp, foul odor of the chemical toilets at the far end of the platform that had been put in place during the Blitz. There were still areas where bedding belonging to escaping and homeless Londoners was laid out. Since the threat of German air raids had subsided, only an occasional person lay sleeping, their shoes standing at attention close by, worn socks and stockings sticking out from threadbare blankets.

Stoker arrived at the surface winded from the climb. He headed down Haymarket, toward Trafalgar Square, cursing the night's robust moonlight and unseasonably warm weather. On his trek down Haymarket, despite his compromised hearing, he still heard the voices beckoning provocatively from dark doorways and alleys. He checked his watch—it was ten thirty. He was right on schedule.

#

It was Toulouse's first time in Trafalgar Square. He stood at the top of the stairway to the Trafalgar Square Underground Station to get his bearings. The woman's instructions said to meet at the base of the statue of King George IV. Sitting on a "bloomin' humongous horse" near the backside of some bomb shelters, she said. Ten thirty, she said. He spotted the statue and trotted toward it. Don't be late, she said. He was five minutes late.

The weighty revolver bounced inside his waistband as he trotted, and he began to make out the woman up ahead. She was blond, with short legs. Her calves were large, rounded masses of muscle. She had her head on a swivel—back and forth it went, looking for someone. For him.

#

Stoker took a hard left off Haymarket onto Pall Mall and walked another three hundred feet and entered the north side of Trafalgar Square around 10:40. As he passed through the square's entrance, he walked by a Royal Navy warrant officer who was leaning against a red postbox, a woman was proudly showing him the backs of her legs. Stoker overheard her say that her flat mate drew the seams of her phantom stockings with a black eyebrow pencil. The sailor mumbled his approval.

He moved deeper into the square, which was eerily quiet for a moonlit and balmy night. As he passed the brick bomb shelters hastily erected aboveground between Nelson's Column and the

National Gallery, he counted five women, all decked out in their showy black-market outfits, conducting business. He stopped and turned his head slightly back toward Pall Mall. If he was being followed, they were good. One woman mistook his glance behind him with an interest in becoming acquainted. He pressed on to the base of Nelson's Column.

#

"You're late, you bloody Frenchman."

"Yes, yes, I am French, what can I say? And you, you look . . . so beautiful, my dear."

"Don't 'dear' me. I'm on a tight schedule."

"And your poodle, a French poodle. He, she?" Toulouse extended a friendly hand toward the dog, who wasted no time in nipping at it.

"He's a he. And keep your hands to yerself. Do you have the money? The six thousand pounds?"

"Ahh, the money. Yes. How do I begin to explain?"

"Explain what? You either got the money or you don't. Either way, I don't want any bloody explanation."

His attempt to befriend her was only serving to unnerve her. "I have the money—"

"So give it here."

"I have four thousand pounds. The rest after I . . . transact some business. I only need—"

"*You* only need? Aren't you the cheeky one? I *need* the six thousand pounds. So no deal tonight, dearie. Now move on with you. I've got appointments." The woman turned toward Nelson's Column and gave a thumbs-down signal to a lone man standing near the large monument.

"Please, madam," Toulouse said, grabbing her elbow.

She tugged it from his grasp and turned. A small gun pointed at his gut. "We'll give you two seconds to turn around and disappear."

Toulouse looked back at the monument. The man hadn't moved. "Or *we* will do what?"

She smiled coolly. "Or I'll start screamin' me head off. Something about rape."

Toulouse gave the man one last look and nodded, held up his hands in surrender, and started to backpedal. The blond spun on her heels and bolted toward Nelson's Column. He could see her calves wiggle as she marched off. He headed for a small grove of trees that bound the east side of the square and kept his eyes on her as she moved to the east side of Nelson's Column. The man, at least a foot taller than her, came out of the shadows to meet her. She talked as the man paced.

Toulouse looked at his watch. Their failed negotiation had taken eight minutes. He waited, not knowing what his next move would be.

#

Nelson's Column, a monument to the British naval victory at Trafalgar, was 145 feet tall. Stoker approached the monument and chuckled to himself, thinking about the intelligence uncovered the year before that the Nazis had developed plans to transport the monument to Berlin after their planned invasion and occupation of England.

He stopped and stared at the square base of the column; it was wrapped by a picture of an Avro Lancaster bomber on fire and under attack. A sign beneath proclaimed "The Sky's the Limit— This Is Wings For Victory Week." Another effort by the Churchill government to squeeze another few pence out of broke Britons.

Stoker checked one more time for his lapel knife and Colt. He unbuttoned his overcoat to give himself a bit more freedom of movement. As he did, a small flock of pigeons moved toward him. One pigeon a bit braver than the others jaunted near his feet and pecked at his shoe. Stoker punted the bird ten feet into the air, where it then took flight. The rest of the flock followed suit. It was 10:55. Heeding the instructions he'd been given, he moved to the south side of the base of the column, between two of the Landseer bronze lions, where he was to wait until five minutes after the hour. He was certain someone was going to make sure he was alone. He took a moment to glance toward Cockspur Street for the Sunbeam saloon. It was right where Shapak said it would be, cigarette smoke drifting out of the lowered driver's side window. He checked his watch again; it was 11:05. He eased the semiautomatic Colt from his pocket and pulled the slide back, chambering a round before returning it to his pocket. It was time to move. Stoker walked south about 150 feet, to the site of the exchange—the edge of a bomb crater just north of a statue of Charles I. Wooden barricades were placed haphazardly around the crater, with large gaps between them. A dilapidated truck was parked on the sidewalk near the crater, half-filled with cracked concrete, bricks, and dirt. Several shovels rested in the debris, blades down, looking like the stems of decapitated flowers. Standing alone at the edge of the crater, Stoker looked back at Nelson's Column. A woman emerged from between the Landseer lions on the east side of the column, and a tallish man, in dark clothing and a wide-brimmed hat, remained behind, leaning against the base. She walked with purpose toward Stoker. His watch said eleven o'clock.

The strong scent of a perfume preceded the woman by at least two feet. Her black felt jacket was complemented by a matching hat that was perched jauntily at an angle. Stoker was taken aback by the sight of a French poodle sitting snuggly in a cloth shopping bag she was carrying. He took another look at her partner—the man's features were obscured by shadow.

"Are you Higgins?" The poodle started to bark the moment Stoker opened his mouth. The blond shoved the dog back down into the bag and zipped it closed. She didn't appear nervous; she was in her element, dealing one-on-one with a man. Stoker looked again at her partner. She saw the look. The man inched away from the base of the sculpture toward them.

"Yes. And who is that?" Stoker asked with a quick tilt of his head toward the man. "Wouldn't be the other half of the act, would it?"

"Oh, aren't you the smart one? Cambridge, isn't it? Well, you're right, dearie. I'm the messenger and that one, the shy one, he's the brains . . . if you call what's inside that melon of his brains. Just tell me that you have the five thousand."

Stoker looked back at the "shy one." He stood about five feet from the base of the sculpture and had pulled his hat down over his face more. Their section of the square was empty except for the three of them.

"Right down to business. Well, that's quite all right." Stoker reached inside his overcoat but stopped. "Why don't we invite your shy boyfriend over? I'd like to meet him."

The woman signaled with her index finger for him to handover the money. "You two wouldn't get along. Oil and water. Trust me. Just hand it over."

Stoker pulled the envelope from inside his overcoat and handed it to her. Her eyes grew wide as she snatched it from his hand. Peering into it, she began counting, whispering the numbers as she flicked through the stack of notes. With the money now in his partner's hands, the shy one started to back off, inching toward Nelson's Column again.

"The package?"

She reached inside her jacket, then down her blouse, and yanked out an envelope.

"Here you go, dearie. Have a look. It's the real thing."

One side of the envelope was moist from her perspiration. Stoker pulled the document out and held it in front of him, so the waning moonlight could fall on its surface. The official-looking document had all the markings and signatures of an original. Satisfied, he placed the envelope in his breast pocket; he saw the woman eagerly stuff the wad of notes into her shopping bag.

The shy one was now back to leaning against the base of the lion sculpture. Stoker's next moves had to be quick. He wrapped his left arm around the woman's head and, with his hand covering her mouth, twisted her body, so her back rested on his chest. His right hand moved for the lapel knife, another swift flick, and the five-inch blade pierced her jacket and blouse, plunging into her heart. He gave the knife a sharp twist and then yanked it out. As her legs gave out, blood gushed through the wound with each heartbeat.

The blond fell to her knees and started to topple over. He held her up while he rifled through the shopping bag for the money. The dog snapped at his hand. He grabbed its neck and snapped it. A shot hit a cracked slab of concrete five feet from Stoker, the sound echoing into the night. He'd expected some reaction from the shy one, so he was prepared. He shoved the woman into the crater with his foot and turned away; he could hear her roll down the side, smashing into large chunks of concrete. Up ahead, the driver emerged from the Sunbeam, gun drawn. He fired one shot at the shy one, but the man kept advancing. Stoker took up a shooting stance and shot twice. The shy one dropped, his hat falling off and a breeze carrying it several feet away.

Stoker waved at the driver, then pointed at the body of the man. The driver ran to the lifeless body as Stoker sprinted to the Sunbeam. Another shot echoed in the square—not from Stoker or the driver. Stoker felt wet warmth in his left hand. He looked down. A round had grazed the meaty part of his palm. The driver, who was dragging the man's body, dropped it and fired off two rounds in Stoker's direction. Stoker heard the rounds zip past him as they headed for a target behind him. He stopped, turned, and attempted to find the interloper. A body was lying on the ground, but a moment later, the body sprung up and retreated into the night.

Stoker jumped into the backseat of the Sunbeam as the driver shoved the body of the shy one in through the other door, which landed in a heap beside him. The driver put the car in gear and raced out of the square. Stoker wrapped a handkerchief around his hand.

"He's alive," the driver said over his shoulder.

Stoker turned the man's face to him. He was breathing unevenly, producing bubbles in the blood trickling from both sides of his mouth. Stoker recognized him.

"Ahh, yes. Leftenant Johannson. That makes so much sense. Obviously a man with no worthy belief system—except for money." Stoker placed the muzzle of his Colt on Johannson's chest, which began to heave rapidly. "Such a waste. For that, I'm sorry to say, you forfeit your life, or what's left of it." He fired once into his heart.

The driver jerked around in his seat and swerved into the opposite lane before quickly recovering. The crack of the Colt was near deafening inside the Sunbeam. Soon, the cabin filled with the acrid smell of discharged gunpowder. The driver lowered his window as Stoker shoved the body to the floor of the saloon.

"We have to dump the body somewhere it won't be found," Stoker stated.

"Leave that to me. The lions in the London Zoo never get enough meat . . . not since the war started, or so I'm told by my friend the night watchman."

He struggled to understand the driver's English; his Russian accent strangled each word. Stoker's hand started to throb, so he rewrapped it, tighter this time. "Who was the other shooter? And where the hell did he come from?"

"From the trees on the edge of the square. I missed him by a mile. But . . . he still ran." The driver snorted. "That man. No conviction."

CHAPTER TWENTY-TWO

0800 Hours, Friday, October 9, 1942
Ministry of Works and Planning, No. 3 Whitehall Place, London

"Mr. Longworth is attending Mass at Westminster Cathedral as he does daily and is not expected until fifteen minutes past the hour," said a sour-faced, fiftyish woman whose gray-streaked hair was pulled into a bun that sat atop her head. "Have a seat and wait." Thorn's dislike for the woman was immediate.

Thorn and Bright had no other place to be, so they sat. The outer office that served as a waiting area was the size of a small hotel lobby. It was furnished with soft armchairs covered in a deep-red felt, which made sliding into and out of them difficult.

"How well do you know this guy?" Thorn asked.

"Address him that way and the only thing we'll get is relieved from this investigation. And I will say it again: this is not the best use of our time. In fact, this will only cause problems that we do not have time for." Bright turned away from Thorn, who could clearly see that she was peeved by the flush on her cheeks.

"We'll be brief and tread lightly."

"I want to believe you, but—"

Henry Longworth, Minister of Works and Planning, one of several "constant attenders," as Prime Minister Churchill called them, to the war cabinet, burst through the door to the outer office. Not noticing his visitors, he marched up to his assistant's desk and picked up several messages.

"Mr. Longworth, you have two guests, and no, sir, they do not have an appointment," the assistant said, leaning to her left to look around Longworth at the intruders sitting across the room.

Longworth turned and saw Bright and, with eyebrows raised, registered a moment of muted surprise. "And what do you want, Miss Bright?"

Bright struggled to pull herself from the chair that seemed to have a hold of her dress. Once erect, she had to smooth and pull her dress back into place. "Sir, excuse the unannounced visit. This is Conor Thorn, who works for William Donovan and General Eisenhower. We have a few brief questions to ask you—"

"About what?"

"Can we talk to you in private . . . sir?" asked Thorn.

Longworth appraised Thorn fully, his stare starting with his face and traveling down the length of his body to his shoes and back again. "You both will have to wait. I have some matters that I must attend to immediately. So take your seats."

#

While Bright picked up a copy of *The Daily Mirror* and mumbled something about wasting time, Thorn watched Longworth's secretary, her head bent over a ledger, tap a pencil on the rim of a teacup. The incessant clinking seemed to go unnoticed by Bright. Thorn was up to a count of fifty-five clinks when the door to Longworth's office opened.

When Thorn and Bright entered the office, Longworth was standing behind his desk chair. "So, tell me—what is the purpose of your visit?"

"May we sit?" asked Thorn.

"No. I am sure this won't take long. Besides, I have much to do. Now, what is it you want?"

"Sir, Mr. Thorn and I have been investigating a security breach at General Eisenhower's headquarters," Bright said.

"Yes, I am aware. The prime minister has informed the cabinet of the breach. But why are you talking to me?"

"Our investigation—"

"Do you know a Quinn Montgomery?" Thorn interrupted.

Bright shot a look at Thorn, her lips pursed.

"I do. What of it?"

"How do you know him?"

"He's my nephew. The son of my only sister."

"We've spoken to him about a break-in at the Army Air Forces film lab and—"

"Wait one minute here, Thorn. You think he has anything do with this break-in? You think he is a criminal? What a preposterous—"

"He was in and out of the lab at the time that a top-secret document was reported missing. We're just—"

"You're just carelessly and recklessly accusing my nephew of involvement in the theft of a top-secret document. You're accusing him of treason! Do you realize that?" Longworth shouted. He pounded the top edge of his desk chair.

"We're only following up on our meeting with your nephew, sir," Bright offered. "Nothing more. It was merely surprising to see a picture of a war cabinet member in his quarters. And we—"

"Well, get over your surprise, Miss Bright. You of all people should know to respect the position and authority of a cabinet member. And to think you have in any way connected my nephew and, therefore, me to this traitorous break-in is audacious, impudent, and totally unacceptable. The prime minister will hear about it—mark my words." Longworth pulled a pocket square from his breast pocket and mopped his glistening forehead.

"Sir, do you own a car?" Thorn asked, drawing an incredulous look from Bright.

"What?"

"Do you own a car, and if so, what type?"

Longworth marched to the door and opened it wide. "Get out of my office. Both of you."

Bright rushed from the office, leaving Thorn alone, standing in front of Longworth, doing all he could to not ask another question.

#

When Thorn caught up to Bright, she stood by the staff car, her arms folded; Hollis sat comfortably in the backseat, flipping through a newspaper.

"Well, that went exactly the way I believed it would. Horribly," Bright said, refusing to look directly at Thorn.

"I . . . I was polite," he said.

"Not enough. You could have been more . . . more deferential."

"He was a little too pompous for that. Anyway, what did Shakespeare say? 'The man doth protest too much, methinks.'"

"First off, it was 'the lady doth protest too much,' and second . . ." She paused, took a deep breath, and quickly released it. "We *need* to head in another direction instead of harassing cabinet members. We need to get on with a more effective investigation. It is critical that we find this document as soon as possible. The sooner we do, the fewer people will have seen its contents. The clock—"

"Is ticking. No one knows that better than me. No one. Not you, not Eisenhower or Churchill," Thorn said loudly.

Bright, wide-eyed, unfolded her arms and took a short step back.

He paused and took a deep breath. "Listen, humor me a little longer. I want to talk to a family friend. The one my dad was talking about at dinner last night—Sean Sullivan. Remember? He's assigned to Westminster Cathedral. The same church that Longworth goes to—every day, according to his warmhearted secretary. Just a quick conversation to get his opinion of Longworth. OK?" Thorn could appreciate that his pigheaded persistence was not his most endearing quality.

Bright glared at Thorn, unblinking. "OK. Then we're moving on."

Thorn made a move toward the driver's side door of the staff car. "Yes . . . unless, of course, we find something."

CHAPTER TWENTY-THREE

1100 Hours, Friday, October 9, 1942
Westminster Cathedral Clergy House, No. 42 Francis Street, London

Thorn loved being behind the wheel. He was in complete control. With Bright sitting beside him, he deftly piloted the Buick Roadmaster as Hollis shouted directions to the cathedral's clergy house from the backseat. They careened through the London streets, swerving in and out of traffic and around mounds of rubble that had been undisturbed since the end of the Blitz. The mounds of detritus had sprouted weeds and, in some cases, flowers that were now losing their seasonal life. Thorn slowed to a stop in front of a four-story, rectangular, brick building, its entrance at the top of a stairway on the short side of the building. Then, he and Bright made for the entrance as Hollis settled back and unfolded a copy of the *London Times*.

Thorn rapped on the door and waited alongside Bright, who had talked little on their drive from Longworth's office. He had trouble reading her. *Is she still fuming, or is she just ticked off? I'd settle for just a little ticked off.*

The door creaked open, and the aroma of boiled potatoes and cabbage escaped into the October morning air. A short woman in her sixties stood in the doorway, drying her reddened hands on a dingy apron. Her thinning hair was pulled back behind her ears. "And what can I do for you two lovebirds? Wouldn't be lookin' to ask for a banns of marriage, would you? Too bad, but there's—"

Bright laughed, just like she had that evening in the Broadway pub—a hearty, rambunctious laugh that seemed to underscore the ridiculousness of the possibility.

Thorn shot her a look. *Shake it off, Conor. It's not time yet anyway.*

"No, no, ma'am. Actually I . . . We're looking for a Father Sean Sullivan. Would he be around?" Bright asked.

"Father Sean? Sure he is. Just got back from hospital. Doin' his rounds. Come in. Come in."

"If you're the cook, you should be commended. It smells wonderful," Bright said, taking in a full whiff of the scents emanating from a nearby kitchen.

"Oh, aren't you the kind one? Head straight ahead down this hallway to the sitting room, and I'll fetch Father Sean. If I know him, he won't be far from the kitchen. Who should I say is calling?"

"Conor Thorn and Emily Bright."

"Thorn and Bright. Very well. I'll be back."

In the sitting room, three walls were adorned with pictures of the cathedral at various seasons. Hanging on the remaining wall, prominently in the center, was a sizable but solitary and washed-out reproduction of the Sacred Heart of Jesus. The blood dripping from the flaming heart had faded to a light pink. A vase of fresh lilies, flanked by two flickering devotional candles, sat on a small stand immediately below the painting.

"Here they be, Father Sean. This is—"

"God bless us all, Conor Thorn, as I live and breathe," a beaming Sean bellowed. Sean, topping six feet with a barrel chest, surprised Thorn with a bear hug that made his back crack.

Thorn wasn't sure exactly what he'd expected to see when he met up with Sean. He only vaguely remembered his boyish face from eighteen years ago. But the looming mass of a man with a warm, welcoming demeanor wasn't on the top of his list.

The black-haired, green-eyed priest extended his meaty hand to Bright. "And you must be Miss Bright. A pleasure. Please sit," Sean said, guiding them to a couch located across from the painting of the Sacred Heart.

"Father, they aren't here askin' for a banns of marriage announcement. I already asked that."

"Oh, that so, Edith?" said a smiling Sean. "Well then, I'll have to have a talk with these two lovely people." He broke into an even wider grin.

Bright shook her head at Sean's playfulness.

"I'll call you for supper when it's ready," Edith said as she took her leave.

"Ahh, yes, supper. Can't wait." Thorn could see that Sean didn't miss many suppers. "So, Conor, it's been, what? Nearly twenty years, right?" Sean said, leaning forward, his elbows on his knees and hands clasped together, genuinely interested in what his old friend had to say.

"At least. And tell me—your mother and father, are they well?" Thorn asked despite being unable to recall their faces.

"Ahh, they've passed. Several years ago, I'm afraid. And your father and mother? Are they in good health?"

"Dad is fine. In fact, we had dinner with him last night." Thorn stopped and cleared his throat.

"And tell me, how is your dear, lovely mother?"

"She . . ." Thorn stopped and looked over at the painting. Bright shifted her gaze from Sullivan to Thorn. "She drowned, Sean. She jumped in the ocean to save me from a riptide and didn't make it back to shore. I was ten years old." The words formed quickly, surprising Thorn, who didn't speak of the circumstances of his mother's death.

"Oh my Lord. Bless her soul," Sullivan said as he made the sign of the cross.

Bright's jaw dropped. She didn't take her eyes off of Thorn as she raised her hand to cover her mouth.

"I'm so sorry. It's such a small gesture, but tomorrow's Mass will be said in her name."

"Thanks, Sean," Thorn said, clearing his throat again.

"So, what brings you to the cathedral's doorstep?"

"We wanted to ask about one of your parishioners. A man named Henry Longworth. Do you know him?"

A furrowed brow betraying Sullivan's concern quickly replaced his initial wide-eyed look of surprise. "Why yes. Is he all right? I just saw the man this morning at seven o'clock Mass."

"Yes, he's fine, Father," Bright said. "What can you tell us about him?"

"I see him about every day at Mass. And I often see him in the clergy house, dropping mail off. But what is this about?"

"We're involved in an investigation. I work with General Eisenhower's headquarters, and Bright works with the prime minister's office. We can't tell you much more than that right now. Longworth is—"

"A high-standing member of the prime minister's war cabinet, as I am sure you know," Bright interjected. "It seems that a family member of his may have put himself in an awkward position."

"Well, that is unfortunate. But what does this have to do with Mr. Longworth?"

"It seems that Mr. Longworth has a strong relationship with this family member," Bright responded.

Sean sat quietly, head bent toward the floor. He wrung his hands several times. "Is Mr. Longworth guilty of a crime?" he asked as he sat upright.

"You tell me. Are you his confessor?" Thorn asked.

Sean tossed his head back and chuckled. "Ah, what a sense of humor you have. What I can say is this—he has, on occasion, come to me and not by chance, because our names are on the doors of our confessionals. But, beyond that, I can say no more."

"So what can you tell us?" Thorn asked as he took a small notebook from his pocket.

Sean shrugged and stared into space for a moment, then began to speak. "I have known him for some time now, since my days in Rome. I was assisting Cardinal Massy, who oversaw the Supreme Secret Congregation," said Sean, both of his hands moving about as if he were conducting an orchestra. "Mr. Longworth was working in the office with Sir D'Arcy Osborne, the British minister to the Holy See."

"Was there much contact between the two of you?" Thorn asked.

Sean turned his attention to Thorn. "No, not much. But the Vatican is much like a small Irish village. You didn't have to see someone often to know their business."

"And what business of Longworth's did you know?"

"Well, there was a story that floated around the Vatican for years about Mr. Longworth and several priests being kidnapped and tortured at the hands of the communists while he was on a tour of Russia in the late twenties."

Thorn and Bright exchanged glances. "Well, that is a story," Bright said. "He's alive, so it ended well, right?"

"I suppose as well as can be expected. The story goes that he escaped and made his way into Turkey."

"Commendable," Thorn said, looking down at his notes. "But, Sean, you said something about seeing him regularly here, in the clergy house. Tell me again what brought him here."

"Well, from his years of service at the Vatican, he and Cardinal Massy became close. And they picked up their friendship when Cardinal Massy and I were assigned here, at the cathedral. They talk often. They're close friends."

"You said something about dropping mail off. Mail for whom?" Thorn pressed, looking down as he jotted more notes.

"Given their friendship, Mr. Longworth was permitted access to the cathedral's diplomatic pouch by Cardinal Massy. The pouch is how the cathedral, the seat of the Catholic Church in Great Britain, communicates with the Vatican."

Thorn shot a look at Bright. *Does his access to that pouch mean that—*

"Father, diplomatic pouches are for official state business," Bright said. "It's absolutely a violation of its diplomatic immunity to use it for personal communication. Isn't Cardinal Massy aware of this?"

"I am sure he is, Miss Bright. Cardinal Massy, was, I am sure, taking into consideration his friend's long years of service at the Vatican when he allowed him to use the pouch to communicate with his Vatican-based friends."

Thorn sat back in his chair and mulled over the special nature of Longworth's surprising privileges afforded him by the cardinal. "Who are his friends in the Vatican?"

"He has several, but most letters are addressed to a Bishop Augustus Heinz, who runs the German College."

Thorn sprang forward. "The German College? What's that about?"

"It is a pontifical college where they educate future priests of German descent. There are several pontifical colleges."

"That's interesting. Bright, ever heard of that?" asked Thorn. *Longworth has a friend in, of all places, the German College. I'll be damned.*

"No, I haven't. But given the worldwide reach of the church, I certainly understand the need for such colleges. But, Father, I have to ask—does this college or Bishop Heinz have any contact with anyone inside Germany?"

"Certainly, the Catholic Church is allowed to operate inside Germany. Of course, the relationship between the church and the German government, from what I remember from my days in Rome, is somewhat tenuous," Sean said, then paused for a moment. He began to speak but stopped and looked across the room, his forehead creased and his eyes narrowed. "And, as I said before about knowing the business of others, it's known that Bishop Heinz had fallen out of the Holy Father's favor."

"Really? Politics inside the Vatican? I'm shocked," Thorn said, his eyes open in mock wide-eyed surprise.

"You shouldn't be," said Sean, oblivious to the sarcasm.

"You said out of favor. Why?" Bright asked.

"It had become clear over the years that Bishop Heinz's opinions were exceedingly favorable toward . . . the German regime. In fact, he was called the 'Brown Bishop.'"

"The Brown Bishop as in the German Brownshirts?" Thorn asked.

"Yes."

"Are you telling me he's a Nazi?" Thorn asked.

"Or at least...favorable," Sean repeated, "to the Nazis, yes."

So Longworth is in direct contact with an acquaintance who is a friend of the Nazis. How the hell does a cabinet member explain that? Thorn turned to Bright. *I hope you're getting this,* he thought.

Suddenly, Edith appeared at the doorway. "Father Sean, Cardinal Massy would like a word, if you please."

Sean rose abruptly, the interruption triggering a look of relief. "Of course, Edith. Conor, Miss Bright, it was a pleasure. And I hope I was somewhat helpful."

Thorn and Bright stood.

"More than helpful, Sean." Thorn's extended hand was engulfed by Sean's massive grip, the pressure of which was eyebrow raising.

"Wonderful," Sean bellowed. "I must go. God bless you both."

Thorn and Bright headed for the front door. Thorn put his hand on the doorknob but stopped before opening it and turned to her. "Where does MI6 have files on known enemy agents?"

"The Central Registry, down on Ryder Street. What would we be looking for?"

"A file on the Brown Bishop. I have to believe that a Nazi sympathizer inside the Vatican must be on someone's list."

CHAPTER TWENTY-FOUR

1130 Hours, Friday, October 9, 1942
No. 10 Downing Street, Westminster, London

A plainclothes guard answered the knock at the door of No. 10, and upon being recognized, Henry Longworth was immediately shown into the entrance hall. Elizabeth Nel, Churchill's personal secretary, soon hurried down the corridor linking the entrance hall with the offices in the rear of No. 10. Nel's condescending attitude and her intense, ruby-red lips always irritated Longworth. He stood motionless as she approached, his hands resting on the top of his brass-handled umbrella. Nel greeted Longworth with a tight smile, her blazing lips framing her teeth, some of which were stained with her lipstick.

"Mr. Longworth, what a pleasure. What can we do for you?"

Longworth took two steps toward the oncoming Nel, forcing her to stop abruptly. "Where's Winston? I must speak with him."

"I am afraid he's not here at this moment," she said.

Longworth noted her familiar patronizing tone. Before he could respond, she turned toward the sound of footsteps on the marble floor and voices bouncing off the walls in the corridor. Clementine Churchill's personal assistant led a striking redhead holding a leather valise under her arm toward the front door. The redhead wore a wide-brimmed, white hat that set off her hair.

"Ahh, Miss Thorn, I trust your conversation with Mrs. Churchill went well?" Nel asked.

Longworth's lips parted and his brow creased as he shot a look at the redhead then back at Nel.

"Oh, yes, Miss Nel. She was exceptionally generous with her time," Thorn said. "I am very thankful, as is CBS. My technicians will be out of your hair quickly."

Longworth regrettably took note of the coarse American accent. "You are . . . ?"

"Oh, forgive me, Mr. Longworth," Nel said, grabbing Maggie's forearm and guiding her toward Longworth. "This is Maggie Thorn, a reporter for an American radio network. Maggie, this is Henry Longworth, minister of Public Works and a member of the prime minister's war cabinet."

"A pleasure, Mr. Longworth," Maggie said, extending a gloved hand.

Longworth did not move.

Maggie retracted her hand and looked at Nel.

"Are you related to Conor Thorn?" Longworth asked.

Maggie smiled. "Yes, that would be my brother. I assume you've had the pleasure of meeting him?"

"I've met him. And it was not a pleasure. He's an impudent pest."

Nel and Maggie exchanged wide-eyed looks.

Longworth turned to Nel and jabbed the black-and-white floor with the tip of his umbrella. "When will the prime minister return?" he snapped.

"I can't say. I should think soon."

"Then I'll wait."

Maggie reset her hat and extended her hand to Nel, who received it with both hands. "Well, I'll be heading back to the Savoy to work on my scripts. Thanks so much for your help."

"Oh, think nothing of it, Miss Thorn. And remember—seven o'clock Sunday night. Mrs. Churchill is so looking forward to introducing you to the cabinet wives at her table at Oddendino's Imperial," Nel said.

"A date with Clark Gable couldn't keep me away. I shall be there seven o'clock sharp." Maggie smiled broadly. As she walked past Longworth, she gave him a curt nod.

He eyed the redhead with the hard look of a hunter focused on his prey.

"Mr. Longworth, let me show you to the library. You will be more comfortable there."

But Longworth continued to watch Maggie as she neared the front door.

"Mr. Longworth," Nel said, raising her voice.

He turned toward Nel, who then escorted him through the inner hall and into the sun-filled library.

"What shall I tell the prime minister the subject of your visit is when he arrives?"

"That is private, Miss Nel."

"Very well." Nel closed the pocket doors to the room and started back to her office. Longworth was, in fact, pleased that he had to wait, as he needed a few more moments to pull together his thoughts, which had been jolted by the revelation that Thorn had a sister who was close at hand. He strained to focus on what was most critical for him—to convince Churchill to exert his power to put an end to Bright and Thorn's investigation.

When Churchill entered the library, Longworth was standing before the middle window on the north wall, his hands stuck in his vest pockets as he observed the blustery skies growing ever darker. "Henry, to what do I owe the pleasure?"

Longworth was jerked from his reverie and turned to face Churchill. "Mr. Prime Minister, good day to you." Longworth made no attempt to shake Churchill's hand. "I am here to register my deepest and sincerest complaint about the treatment I received today at the hands of Emily Bright and her insolent accomplice, Thorn."

Churchill's brow furrowed deeply, and he tilted his head as if perplexed.

He can be so annoying, Longworth thought.

"I know nothing of this. Please go on."

Longworth scowled. "It appears that they are looking into the security breach at General Eisenhower's headquarters that you spoke of in Monday's cabinet meeting."

"Yes, I'm aware that they have been assigned to that. But what does that have to do with you?" Churchill fumbled for something in his breast pocket and appeared concerned that he couldn't find it.

"Exactly why I am here."

Churchill pulled a cigar from inside his suit coat and then occupied himself with finding something else in his pockets.

"I'll wait, Prime Minister?" Longworth said.

Churchill abruptly ceased his search, his hand still in his pocket.

"My nephew, a warrant officer in the Coastal Command, has had occasion to visit the US Army film lab of late. Why, it is not clear to me, but that is beside the point."

"And the point is, Henry?"

Longworth was annoyed by the question from a seemingly unconcerned Churchill. "The point is, Mr. Prime Minister," Longworth said loudly and slowly, "they think somehow—brazenly, I might add—that because of my relationship with my nephew, who recently frequented the lab where this breach may have occurred, that I may be involved."

"Really, Henry? I find that difficult to believe."

Longworth took two quick steps toward Churchill and reclaimed his umbrella that leaned against a nearby couch. "Do you? You don't appear to, Mr. Prime Minister. Must I remind you that I am a loyal servant of the king? I am a minister in your government. At your urging, I joined your war cabinet because of my, using your words, 'expertise in Soviet political and military behavior.' Your cabinet, Mr. Prime Minister. I shall not be insulted, suspected, or disrespected by anyone. I have served my king and country unfailingly, as I now serve you. I have suffered at the hands of our enemies—the IRA and most notably the communists. I have done my share."

"Henry, while I don't understand your indignation, I promise to look into the matter and, if called for, do what has to be done to properly address it. I hope that is satisfactory to you."

"The vagueness in your response is not satisfactory," Longworth said, punctuating his protest with a jab of his umbrella onto the oak floor. "You must tell Thorn and Bright to step back and cease their ridiculous and insulting probing of my nephew and myself."

"As I said, Henry, I will do what has to be done." Churchill lit his cigar, and a cloud of blue smoke began to fill the space around him.

Longworth, stone-faced, was careful not to display his utter shock that he was unable to sway his longtime political associate. "That is all you will promise?"

"Yes. That is all."

As he stared at the unyielding Churchill, Longworth's chest began to tighten as if a clenched fist was lodged deep inside. A clamminess overcame him. He reached for his chest with his hand and struggled with his breathing. "Good day, Prime Minister," Longworth said, his voice weak and raspy.

CHAPTER TWENTY-FIVE

As they walked up to the ordinary-looking entrance, Thorn saw that the brickwork and limestone window casements of the Central Registry were becoming stained with the cold rain. The lower level windows were fogged over. The cold, damp air easily penetrated Thorn's trench coat, and he cinched its cloth belt around his waist.

In the entrance hall, Thorn and Bright showed a uniformed security guard their identity cards and were pointed in the direction of the elevator. They waited five minutes for it, which then announced its arrival with a general racket that was highlighted by metal-on-metal shrieks, then a thud as it landed. Thorn struggled to push aside the elevator's wobbly gate.

"I didn't think there was a more primitive elevator in England than the one at Broadway, but we've found it. Jeez, what's that smell?" Thorn asked, waving away the air in front of his nose.

Bright placed her hand over her mouth and giggled, which brought a smile to Thorn's face. "That is the odor of coal. As you've noticed, this is a historic building. Many of the rooms are heated by small coal fires."

"Historic? Isn't everything in this country historic?"

"Yes, that's true, but given the destruction wrought by the Blitz, in many places, we have become buried by our history." The elevator announced its arrival at the fourth floor with an unsurprising cacophony that could have drawn the attention of anyone within a three-block radius—that is, if there'd been anyone around. The high-ceilinged, narrow hallway the elevator opened onto was vacant.

"So tell me about this place. What goes on here?" Thorn asked as he fought to close the elevator gate.

"It may not seem like it, but this is the heart of the Secret Intelligence Service. It's where case histories and individual dossiers are stored. Believe it or not, most of the records are kept on cards."

Thorn shot Bright a look of disbelief, which she returned with a shrug.

They walked down the hallway to an unmarked door. Bright pushed through, and they found themselves in a large room with row upon row of floor-to-ceiling oak shelves. Some shelves held card catalogues and some file drawers. There was an L-shaped counter inside the door that kept visitors from entering the rows of shelves. Thorn rapped his fist on the counter to attract some attention. A moment later, a squat and bespectacled middle-aged man hurriedly emerged from the shelving; remnants of his dark hair surrounded a patch of baldness on the top of his head.

"Mr. Woodfield. Excuse me, sir, but I didn't expect you," Bright said.

"And you shouldn't. It's Miss Bright, isn't it?"

"Yes, sir. And this is Conor Thorn, with General Eisenhower's headquarters."

Woodfield eyed Thorn in the manner of a protective father taking the measure of his daughter's suitor. "Can I see Mr. Thorn's identification, please?"

Thorn looked at Bright but gave his identification to Woodfield.

"Conor C. Thorn. Hmmm. Very well then." Woodfield passed the identification card back. "As I was saying, I would not be behind this counter if they would just send me the additional staff that I requested—several times now. It appears that there are many deaf ears back at Broadway." He sighed loudly as he noticed a wire bin on the counter that was overflowing with files. He began to empty it in the loudest possible fashion. "As you can clearly see, I have much to do, so what is it you want?"

"We're here for a dossier on a Bishop Augustus Heinz," Thorn said as he read from his notebook.

"*If* one exists," Bright added.

Woodfield looked confused. "Country?"

"Vatican City. He supposedly runs the German College," Bright said.

"Hmmm, that's a shame. If you can't trust a priest, who can you trust? Well, if he's up to no good, we undoubtedly have something. Go across the hall to office 402 and wait there. It'll take a few minutes."

Thorn and Bright entered the hall and could hear the sound of a BBC broadcast from a nearby office. It was a report from Washington stating that FDR had announced there would be a commission set up after the war to judge those guilty of committing atrocities and mass murder. Thorn found a door marked No. 402 and held it open for Bright. "Hmm ... after the war. Have you even had one notion about life after the war?" Bright asked as she walked past Thorn.

"No way. There're far too many battles to fight. What about you?"

Bright nodded. "I share your thinking. After-war planning is an indulgence that I won't allow myself. That seems to be true for most of those I know, I'm afraid."

The small office was sparse, furnished with a battered desk and three armless chairs. The desk was marked along its edges by cigarette burns. An empty, crumpled package of Player's Cut cigarettes lay beside an ashtray that overflowed with spent ashes. It was cold, but Thorn welcomed the absence of a coal fire. A portrait of King George VI hung on one wall, directly opposite a portrait of Winston Churchill that was a tad cockeyed. Bright straightened it and took a seat. Thorn leaned against the wall, inches away from the brooding Churchill.

"Did you get through to that guy Hightower yet?" Thorn asked.

"No, unfortunately. But MI5 warned me that he's notorious for being a bit of a ghost."

"Meaning?"

"He's never at his desk. Always out somewhere. He's a bit of a problem they—"

Before she could finish, Woodfield came into the room with a dour look.

"Well, the good news is that I found your man Heinz." Woodfield dropped a file marked *SIS—Secret—Not to Leave Central Registry.* "I don't know if this is good news or bad news, Miss Bright, but your man . . . the bishop, is dead."

"What? That can't be," Thorn said as he flipped open the file that revealed a large, white index card with a grainy, black-and-white photo stapled to the top left corner. There were several fields on the card containing information concerning physical description, background, suspected activity, and a list of German National Socialist organizations that Heinz had ties to. Stamped boldly in red across the card on a diagonal was the word *DECEASED* with the date of *September 1942* written in by hand beneath the stamp. "Long—" Thorn caught himself. "He was writing letters to a dead man? That makes no sense."

"Could Father Sullivan have it wrong somehow?" Bright asked as she reached across the table to slide the file toward her.

"I don't know. But I doubt it. He seemed pretty sure of himself."

"Look here." Bright had turned the card over and began to read from it. "According to sources inside the Vatican, Bishop Heinz is suspected of being an informer for German intelligence organizations—the Abwehr and possibly the German SS. It should be noted that Heinz is the author of a book published in 1937 titled *The Foundations of National Socialism.*"

"It seems the name 'Brown Bishop' suits him. But if he's dead, who's receiving the letters?" Thorn turned to Woodfield, who was standing next to Bright, stroking his chin. "Can you tell me who last looked at this file?"

"I can. It's right on the back of the file. Let's see . . ." Woodfield turned the file over. "Well, isn't that a curiosity? It was last seen by Reggie Bullard a week ago yesterday. Look here, Miss Bright." He showed the back of the file to Bright.

"Bullard, Reginald, Section Five. What makes that odd?"

"Well, first off, Bullard is also dead. A train killed him three days ago. A sad coincidence for sure."

Thorn looked at Bright, doubting the existence of coincidences in the world they lived in, sad or otherwise.

"And before Bullard, when was the file last checked out?" Thorn asked.

"Ah, it hadn't been checked out for some time...January 1941."

The room fell quiet except for Woodfield's raspy breathing. Thorn turned his gaze to the picture of Churchill, which he noticed had again become lopsided. He slapped his hand on the table; the ashtray bounced, spilling ashes onto the file. "Let's go. Mr. Woodfield, thank you. We may be back to see you again soon."

Out in the hallway, the burning-coal stink was more evident than before, but it didn't seem to affect the few people that now roamed the hall. As they neared the elevator, Thorn stopped abruptly and turned, nearly pinning the reeling Bright to the wall. His face was mere inches away from hers, and he felt her warm breath on his face. He heard her breathing quicken. Her blue eyes were open wide, as if in anticipation of an advance. Several seconds passed.

"Section Five—isn't that where Philby works?"

"Conor, don't go there," Bright said as she waved a finger in his face, practically touching his nose.

"Well, isn't it?"

Bright shook her head, pushed him away, and kept on toward the elevator. But she stopped and turned back. "Yes, it is, but there's something you must understand," she said softly but firmly, looking over her shoulder. "Philby is one of MI6's golden boys. He has risen up the ranks quickly, and he has many supporters, not the least of which is my boss, C."

Bright's tone made it clear she was losing patience with him. *It seems the Brits don't like to point fingers at their own.* "Here's what I think—there are a lot of moving parts to British intelligence—MI5, MI6, SOE, naval intelligence. And if it's anything similar to the relationship between our military and intelligence services, no one trusts one another. So it makes sense to me that a bad apple might not be seen for what it really is."

"Listen to me. I'll grant you that there are disturbing revelations concerning Longworth that we need to get to the bottom of. But don't waste your time chasing Philby. You'll look like a fool." With that, she spun around and headed toward the elevator.

"So do me a favor," Thorn said, trailing behind. "Get me the home address for this guy Bullard. I want to check out his place."

Bright stopped again and turned to him. "Just what are you looking for?" she asked, her tone only slightly less frustrated.

"I don't know. I may not know until I find it," Thorn said.

CHAPTER TWENTY-SIX

1600 Hours, Saturday, October 10, 1942
OSS Headquarters, No. 70 Grosvenor Street, London

As Thorn grabbed the doorknob, he heard Bill Donovan's raised voice through the door.

"Take a seat, Thorn," David Bruce said without looking up when Thorn entered the office. Bruce's tone was eerily similar to the Naval Academy's superintendent when Thorn had been called on the carpet for removing the University of Virginia's bus's engine the night before the academy took them on in football. Removing the engine alone was enough to get Thorn in hot water, but convincing the offensive line to dump the engine in the Severn River had nearly made the superintendent's head explode. That hadn't ended well. *Get ready, Conor*, he thought.

"Yes, sir."

"Hello, Conor," a red-faced Donovan said. He was seated on a brown leather couch with several files in his lap.

Thorn swiveled a club chair so he could see both men and took his seat.

"You or me?" Bruce asked, looking at Donovan with wide eyes and raised eyebrows.

"You've been chomping at the bit for the last few hours. Have at it."

Bruce turned his attention to Thorn but sat back and appeared to order his thoughts before he spoke. "The colonel is right. I have been 'chomping at the bit' ever since he received a call from General Eisenhower, who, in turn, received a call from the prime minister that was prompted by a visit from a Henry Longworth. Does that name ring a bell, Thorn?"

"It does, yes, sir." *Shit does roll downhill.*

"Well, that's a good start. Because it seems Longworth certainly remembers you." Bruce sat up straighter. "People tend to remember those who accuse them of betraying their government."

"Sir, I did not accuse him of anything. I asked some questions about his nephew, who had been seen at the film lab after General Eisenhower's missing document was taken there. He took offense to his relationship to someone who might know something about the missing document. He pretty much wrote his own script about our meeting."

Bruce held up his hands to stop Thorn. "Listen, Thorn, it's no secret to anyone over here that we are new to this wartime intelligence game. We work hard, every day, to build a reputation as an effective, trustworthy organization. We need to cultivate support among the British to be able to tap into their experience. Pissing off a member of the prime minister's war cabinet isn't helpful. In fact, it's plain stupid."

Thorn's anger simmered. "We were following the few clues we *did* have. We wouldn't have been doing our jobs if we hadn't. It was just odd that someone who might have walked out of the film lab with the missing diary page was the nephew of a cabinet member."

"That might be a reason to trust the nephew. Did that occur to you?" Bruce said, his scoffing tone not lost on Thorn.

"I think it makes no sense to trust anyone until we find the missing diary page," Thorn said in Donovan's direction. *I could use some help here, Colonel.*

Bruce sat back in his chair but kept his gaze locked on Thorn.

"Did this nephew give you straight answers when you talked to him?" Donovan asked as he stood and put his files on Bruce's desk.

"He was the nervous type. Maybe not the brightest member of Coastal Command, and Bright did notice something odd."

"Odd? Meaning?" Donovan asked.

"While I was asking Montgomery questions, Bright looked around his quarters. She found a small packet containing a tarlike substance."

"What was it?" asked Bruce, lighting a cigarette.

"We're not sure."

"So what the hell are we talking about?" Bruce asked as he tossed his lighter onto the desk.

"Bright thinks it might be opium."

"So now you're investigating illegal drug use by some low-ranking RAF officer? What the hell does this have to do with finding the missing diary page?" Bruce fumed.

Donovan glared at Thorn, and Thorn realized if he couldn't convince Donovan that they were on the right track, he couldn't convince anyone.

"Most likely nothing. But it paints Longworth's nephew as someone who isn't on the up-and-up. Maybe someone to keep our eye on for a few days."

"And what about Longworth?" Donovan asked as he paced the floor, his hands in his pockets. Thorn heard the sound of coins jingling.

"Well, that's where it gets interesting. We've found out that he's been communicating with a bishop in Rome on a regular basis. He's using the diplomatic pouch that goes back and forth between Westminster Cathedral and the Vatican."

Donovan stopped pacing and exchanged glances with Bruce.

"That has to be a violation of the Vatican's neutrality, isn't it, Bill?" Bruce asked.

"I'm not sure, but it does violate the pouch's diplomatic immunity."

"Colonel, that's the least of it. It turns out that this bishop has a reputation for being an informer for the Abwehr."

Neither Bruce nor Donovan responded. Thorn looked at each man. Bruce was first to move, quickly putting out his half-smoked cigarette in the ashtray. Donovan then dropped into the chair beside Thorn.

"You have to be joking. Where did you learn that?" Donovan asked.

"Something a friend of mine mentioned led us to MI6's Central Registry. They have a file on this Bishop Heinz. He even has a nickname: 'the Brown Bishop.'"

"Jesus H. Christ," Bruce said under his breath.

Thorn leaned forward. "But there's something screwy going on. His file at Central Registry says he's dead—just last month."

Bruce threw his head back. "Aww, come on. You're telling us you're chasing a dead man?"

Thorn twisted in his chair to face Bruce. "That's just it. I don't think he's dead."

Donovan and Bruce shared bewildered looks "How the hell do you figure that?" Donovan asked.

"Well . . . the last guy to check out the file, just a week ago . . . is dead too."

Bruce slammed his desk with the palms of his hands and shook his head. "Bill, this has gone too far. We—"

Donovan halted Bruce with a raise hand. "Go on, Conor."

"Colonel, I'm convinced that we're onto something. I can't explain why the last guy who read the file is dead. Maybe . . ." Thorn rubbed his forehead with his fingertips, then stopped suddenly. "Maybe he doctored the file to knock us off track. And them someone took care of a . . . . . .loose end. I don't know. But I *do* know you've to back me on this. We're stepping on someone's toes."

"Why are you so convinced?" Donovan asked, his face knotted with doubt.

Thorn sat back. "Thursday night, someone took a couple of potshots at Bright and me."

Donovan sat bolt upright. "Good God. Was Emily hurt?"

"No." *And I'm OK too, Colonel.* "We hit the dirt just in time."

"And you think all of this is connected somehow?" Donovan asked.

"After learning about Longworth's relationship with Heinz and seeing his file, I don't think—I know it is. That shooting incident wasn't random. At that point, we hadn't accomplished much. Actually, we had only seen Longworth's nephew. He was the one person that Commander Butcher and G2 hadn't questioned because they couldn't find him. We rattled him, and . . . I think Longworth too."

Donovan and Bruce fell silent for several moments. "Do you have any leads that don't point to Longworth?" Bruce finally asked.

"Well, we did track down the Frenchman Toulouse. That led

nowhere. Just some hothead that has it in for us and the Brits. He's just an errand boy, running back and forth from the BCRA to the film lab."

"That reminds me," Donovan said. He reached back toward the desk and snatched a notepad. "Who's Lieutenant Johannson?"

"Ahh, he's in charge of the lab. Supposedly the point man for Miss Weddington when she drops off material to be microfilmed. Why?"

"I got a call from Commander Butcher and according to Weddington, he's been AWOL for the last two days. No one knows anything. What's that mean to you?"

Thorn was quiet as he thought, and Donovan threw the notepad back on the desk.

"It could just be some guy shacked up with some woman or someone on a bender, but it seems too coincidental," Thorn said. *Damn, you were making some headway in rough seas there for a minute. Until this newsflash.* "I'll dig into this Johannson character. And I want to look into Longworth's background some more. I need to understand the relationship between him and Heinz. That relationship seems to loom larger than anything this Johannson might be involved in."

Bruce grimaced and shook his head. "Bill, the prime minister needs a heads-up on Thorn's . . . thinking," he said.

"Agreed. I'll handle that as soon as I make this clear: Conor, I do not want any further direct contact with Longworth unless you get my approval. Your ass shouldn't be the only one on the line with General Eisenhower or the prime minister."

Thorn took a deep breath and exhaled slowly. "Understood, Colonel."

"Now, get going. I need to reach out to the prime minister and try to convince him he may have a spy in his cabinet."

CHAPTER TWENTY-SEVEN

1800 Hours, Saturday, October 10, 1942
Caxton Bar, Saint Ermin's Hotel, No. 2 Caxton Street, London

The bar was filled with men, some in uniform but most in civilian attire. What few women there were in the bar soaked up the rapt attention of the men. Cigarette smoke swirled above the heads of the bar's patrons, who were predominantly English, and glasses were raised to survival. Thorn stood in the bar's entry, off the lobby of the hotel, and spotted Bright looking at the crowd of celebrants while seated on a small cream-colored sofa in a window alcove.

"There you are," she said, a cup and saucer resting in her lap.

"How did your meeting go?" Thorn asked as he sank into an armchair opposite her. Before she could reply, a middle-aged woman approached and, without taking notice of either of them, noisily closed the window shutters behind the sofa and then turned and left.

"As expected. I was able to fit in at least two words while he paused for breath. I didn't realize that he and Longworth shared some history."

"So you didn't lay it out for him, the connection between Longworth and Heinz?"

"No, I did not. I must be absolutely sure that there are reasons to suspect he's involved in something nefarious. His station demands that."

Station my ass. "Listen to me—we're onto something here. And I think I convinced Colonel Donovan of that fact."

"That's just it. It's not a fact in my mind; it's only a theory."

Thorn shook his head. *I don't understand why she won't at least try to connect the dots.*

"Any luck connecting with Hightower?" Thorn asked.

Bright sighed heavily. "No. I'm quite confounded by it all. But there is something else I need to tell you," she said. "You have to promise me you won't overreact."

If she defends Longworth any more . . . Thorn hesitated, then nodded.

"About five minutes before you arrived, while I was ordering my tea, I caught sight of Maggie. She was in the lobby talking to someone. But before I finished ordering, she had already left."

"Oh. That's too bad." He looked at her questioningly. "Why would I overreact to that?"

"It was who she was speaking to."

As long as it wasn't Bobby Heugle. "Go on."

"Special Operations Executive . . . they do their recruiting upstairs."

The SOE? Another one of Britain's clandestine organizations, this one set up by Churchill to "set Europe ablaze." "Maybe she's doing some research for a story," Thorn said.

"Conor, few people in Britain even know the SOE exists. They don't talk."

"Wait a minute. Don't tell me they recruit people who aren't Brits."

"That's what I'm not sure of. I'd have to reach out to someone."

"All right. And I'll track down Maggie. I'm sure there's an explanation for it." *Maggie, talk about pushing Dad's buttons.* "By the way," he said. "I understand that a who's who will be at Paddington Station in a couple of days to meet Eleanor Roosevelt, including members of the cabinet. I was thinking of heading out there to—"

"To do what? To badger Longworth yet again?" Bright rolled her eyes.

"No, no. Just call it an opportunity to observe."

"Or an opportunity to annoy?"

Thorn heard footsteps close behind him and turned to see Ian Fleming approaching their table.

"You two look way too serious to be in a bar, so I come bearing gifts." Fleming placed a tray with three martinis on the table between Thorn and Bright and, with a quick move, snatched one and plunked down on the sofa next to Bright. "And what are the two of you conspiring about? And if you can't tell me, just say, 'Oh, shut up, Ian.'"

"Thanks for the drinks. I believe we both could use them. Oh, and shut up, Ian," Thorn said, snatching a martini from the tray.

Fleming snorted into his drink and managed to spill most of it on his trousers.

Bright smiled at Thorn and turned to Fleming, who was sopping up his martini with his handkerchief. "On a different note, tell me something. How well acquainted are you with Henry Longworth?" she asked as she took the last martini.

Fleming shot a quizzical look in her direction. "Hmm, that's a question out of the blue. Well ... he has history with Winston. And Winston is, among his many laudable qualities, exceedingly loyal to his friends. But Longworth does have a growing reputation for being a bit of a ... crackpot."

"A crackpot? That's rather harsh," Bright said.

Thorn sat back and nursed his drink, letting Bright dig a little bit.

"Maybe, but it looks as if it's deserved. He seems to be unrestrained when it comes to voicing his disdain for our Soviet ally."

"What's the reason for his attitude toward the Soviets? They seem to be pulling their weight and then some," Bright said.

Fleming drained what was left of his drink. "Emily, it comes down to plain hatred for the communists—a hatred once shared by Winston himself, by the way. That was when Longworth and Winston were of like mind."

"There's a distrust of Stalin in a lot of places, including among many in the United States," Thorn said.

"Yes, but it goes further for Longworth. He couldn't care less about providing the second front that Stalin is screaming for. In fact, at Naval Intelligence Division, we heard that Longworth told Winston in a cabinet meeting that he should put off Torch until some security breach the Americans are dealing with is contained."

Thorn and Bright exchanged quick glances. Fleming stopped talking, and Thorn saw that Fleming had taken note of the exchange. *So Longworth wants to put off Torch. I hope Bright heard that.* Fleming fed a cigarette into a silver holder.

"You were saying, Ian?" Bright said.

"Yes . . . well, according to a school chum of mine who is our naval attaché in Moscow—or should I say, NID's man in Moscow—calling off Torch wouldn't bother the Russians too much." Fleming's eyes darted from Bright to Thorn, looking, Thorn thought, for any reaction.

"Why is that?" Thorn asked.

"Word is they think that Torch is a horrible idea that will achieve little strategically."

"So where exactly do you get all this information?" Thorn asked.

Fleming snorted and squinted through the haze of smoke he blew across the table. "Ah, Conor, you will soon learn that the British intelligence community resembles a big, happy family—a family that shares."

Thorn polished off his drink. "A family of spies. Hold on to your wallets, everyone."

Bright nailed Thorn with a look of disapproval, but Fleming roared with laughter.

"So, it's your turn. Tell me—why the interest in a member of Winston's cabinet?" Fleming asked.

"I wish we could get into that, but we can't. Not now," Bright said, looking at Thorn. "In fact, we've said too much already. Can I trust you not to mention our interest in Longworth to anyone?"

Fleming nodded, smirking slightly. "I am the most trusted man in England. You should know that by now, Emily." Fleming, his smirk now a wide grin, was reloading his cigarette holder when a youthful, petite woman in an olive-green wool jacket and skirt approached the table and pulled a small envelope from a cloth satchel that hung from her shoulder.

"Mr. Fleming, message for you. I'm to wait for a reply."

Fleming, his cigarette holder at an angle between his pursed lips, tore open the envelope and read the short note. "Ahh, it seems that my boss is in a bit of a snit with the admiralty and is looking for some . . . creative solutions." Fleming turned to the young woman. "Tell him I will be along momentarily."

"Yes, sir," the messenger said as she saluted and turned on her heels to exit the bar.

Fleming gathered up his lighter and cigarettes from the table and donned his officer's hat. "Well, I must be off. Duty and all that."

"Ian . . . can you tell me if the organization upstairs recruits people from . . . say the US?"

"Well, my impression is that they'll take anyone crazy enough to join them. Cheers to you both."

A moment later, Thorn and Bright were alone. Several of the bar's customers began to leave, allowing a lull to descend on the space.

"I'll get to Maggie. She'll clear this up. But you heard what he said about Longworth telling the prime minister to put off Torch?" Thorn asked.

"Yes. That is news. But not his stance on the communists."

"This guy becomes more interesting to me by the day."

Bright frowned and looked away.

Thorn stood and picked up his trench coat. "By the way, we need to follow up on one piece of news that Donovan spilled today." Bright ignored him. "It seems the lieutenant that ran the film lab has flown the coop."

"Excuse me?"

"AWOL, absent without leave. Probably holed up in some—"

"Mr. Thorn?" The voice was raspy—a smoker's voice. Its Boston accent was familiar. Thorn turned, and a face as recognizable as his own stared back at him. "It is you. Conor Thorn."

Abe Fellows. The man standing before him was in his midthirties, short with a stocky build, and dressed in a US naval officer's uniform; the single silver bar noted his rank—lieutenant junior grade. He squirmed inside the uniform as if it belonged to someone else. He was a crewmate from the *Reuben James*.

People in the bar seemed to move in slow motion. Their chatter became a low buzz as Thorn stood staring at what he assumed was a ghost.

Bright got up and went to him, touched his forearm; he flinched.

"Yes, it's me, Abe," Thorn managed to say. "I'm . . . surprised to see you."

"You're telling me! No one ever told us what happened to you."

Thorn looked at Bright, his mouth open but not forming any words.

"Hello, my name is Emily Bright. I'm a . . . friend of Conor's."

Fellows extended his hand. "Abe, Abe Fellows. Mr. Thorn and I served togetha on the *Reuben James*. I was a chief petty officer then. That is, before they made me a ninety-day wonda," Fellows said, nervously twirling his cap in his hands.

"I'm sorry. I don't understand, Mr. Fellows," Bright said.

"It's wartime. The navy is hungry for experienced officers. They're tapping the ranks of non-coms to fill their needs," Thorn said.

"Yeah, you got it, Mr. Thorn," Fellows said. "Hungry, they are, if they're tapping me on the shoulder." Fellows chuckled, then sniffled. He ran the back of his index finger under his nose.

"Abe, you were one of the best. You saved my ass a couple of times, if I remember correctly."

"Thanks, Mr. Thorn. We all looked up to you. You kept us together. But . . . what happened? One minute you were there; the next you were gone. We sailed without an XO."

Thorn chewed the inside of his cheek. His right hand balled tightly into a fist. He saw Fellows looking at Thorn's academy ring. A shameful malaise swept over Thorn. He shifted his trench coat to his right arm to cover his hand. "I was called away by a family emergency. I couldn't get back in time. I'm sorry. I truly am. I think about the *Reuben James*, the crew . . . every day."

"That's OK, Mr. Thorn. I do too. You couldn't have helped. It was a real—"

"Tragedy. A gut-ripping tragedy," Thorn said, his eyes lowered to the floor.

"You've got that right, Mr. Thorn." Not a word passed between the men for several seconds. Fellows was the first to speak. "Well . . . it's time I shoved off." Fellows, who stood directly under a pool of soft light, saluted Thorn, then turned quickly and walked away. Thorn stared at the man as he exited the bar, then returned his old shipmate's salute. He was still saluting when Bright grabbed his forearm and stood on her toes. She softly kissed his cheek. "It's in the past, Conor. Nothing you can do now."

CHAPTER TWENTY-EIGHT

1900 Hours, Saturday, October 10, 1942
Saint George's Hospital, Hyde Park Corner, London

The white dress shirt that had been drenched when Longworth arrived at Saint George's one hour earlier was now dry, but it was stiff to the touch. The trigger for his chest pains—the early morning call from Churchill with his earsplitting expressions of disappointment and scorn—still rang in his ears like an air-raid klaxon. Longworth's protestations and claims of a massive misunderstanding were, at first, ignored but had gained traction by the end of the call. Calling upon his shared history of serving with Churchill in the Sixth Battalion of the Royal Scots Fusiliers in the Great War calmed the prime minister. But it was clear the threat level had risen and something needed to be done.

As he slipped his shirt on and pulled it across his chest to button it, a residual tightness in his chest remained. The private room that he now stood in was on the second floor. Looking out the window, Longworth had a clear view of Wellington Arch. The view of Green Park beyond the arch was slightly obscured by low clouds that had dampened the grounds of the park with a soft mist. The pleasing view of the park contrasted starkly with his current surroundings. He believed that the small, harshly lit hospital room with its pale-yellow walls was the perfect place to receive bad news.

Longworth finished dressing, sat on the edge of the bed, and waited. The call to Quinn had been made when he had first arrived at Saint George's. He had expected Quinn at his bedside thirty minutes ago. Longworth had begun pacing when the door to the hallway burst open. His doctor, Algernon Smith, a frail, squat man, stared at the empty bed, his mouth agape. He fixed his gaze on Longworth, who stood by the window fully dressed.

"What exactly are you doing?" Smith asked in a voice much less frail than the body that it came from.

"I told you I felt fine. It was solely an exaggerated case of . . . indigestion."

"Oh, I see. Just indigestion, is it? Is that why you asked me to call your nephew to your bedside?"

Longworth expected the push back from Smith, who never lost an opportunity to scold Longworth for ignoring his warnings about his weak heart. "It is none of your business why I asked that you call him. Now, what is it you want to tell me?"

Smith slammed shut the door and tossed a medical chart on the bed. "You're a sick man, one who just suffered a heart attack. Yes, it was a mild one, but if you don't properly respond to it, the next one may be much more severe."

"Properly respond?" Longworth asked as he stole a look at his watch, silently damning Quinn for his tardiness.

"You need bed rest. Plain and simple. No more ministry work for four weeks at the least."

"Out of the question. In peacetime, maybe. But not now."

Smith sprang toward the bed, snatched the medical chart, and slammed it on the foot of the bed. "Peacetime? You have the heart of a ninety-year-old man. And frankly, if you don't listen to me, you won't see peacetime. You'll see the underside of a coffin lid."

"Oh, stop with the dramatics," Longworth said as the door opened and Quinn meekly poked his head through the narrow space. "Well, don't just stand there. Come in. And where have you been?"

Quinn, his uniform rumpled and his tie loose about his neck, shut the door behind him. "They couldn't find me right away. I came as soon as I got the message."

Longworth shook his head in disgust. He slipped on his gray wool suit coat and began to button it. "Doctor, I must speak to my nephew in private."

Smith's bony shoulders sagged. He shoved the medical chart under his arm and pursed his lips. "Mark my words: you will do severe harm should you continue to ignore my advice. Good day," Smith said, turning and heading through the door, leaving it wide open.

"Shut the door, Quinn." Longworth reached into his breast pocket and pulled out a small, cream-colored envelope. "This is why I had you called." He held up the envelope, walked over to the window, and placed it on the windowsill.

Quinn followed and stood behind him. Longworth leaned against the sill with outstretched arms and stared out onto Green Park. "Tomorrow night, Clementine Churchill will be hosting a dinner for the wives of the cabinet members at Oddendino's on Regent Street, right off Piccadilly Circle. One guest will be a woman who is a reporter for an American network."

"So?"

Longworth snapped to attention and spun around to face Quinn. "Shut up and listen to me."

Quinn recoiled.

"Get to the restaurant at half past eight. No later. It should be dark then. Ask the maître d' to get this note to the reporter." Longworth reached around for the envelope. "This note says that there is someone from General Eisenhower's office waiting outside in a car who has important information concerning her brother."

"Who is she?"

Longworth held his hand up to stifle Quinn. "When she goes outside with you, it will be dark—no streetlights, no electric signs. Get her into the car. I don't care how, but do it quickly and quietly." Longworth pulled a small, dark-colored glass bottle from his suit pocket. "If she struggles, use this." He passed the bottle to Quinn, who studied its white label. "It's chloroform."

"Where did you get this?"

Longworth turned back to the window, still clutching the envelope. "From an underpaid and overworked nurse." Quinn held the bottle up to the faint sunlight that came through the window and shook it.

Longworth turned around at the sound of the anesthetic swishing about. "Quinn, pay attention!"

His nephew slid the bottle into his tunic pocket.

"Take her to your flat in Norwood and make sure she goes nowhere until you hear from me."

"You going to tell me who this bird is?"

Longworth paused, then handed the envelope over to Quinn. "Maggie Thorn. The sister of Conor Thorn."

Quinn's expression morphed from *bored errand boy* to a *prize-fighter waiting for the bell*. "Shite." His face broke into a smile. "What's the plan?"

Longworth moved past Quinn and headed for the door. "For now, just a distraction for this pest Thorn, something to take his mind off of you . . . and me."

"I got it. Knock him off the scent, right?"

Longworth reached the door and turned back to Quinn. "Yes, in a manner of speaking. But, Quinn, don't cock this up. Is that clear?"

Quinn took several big strides toward the door. "As a cloudless, blue sky."

#

His freshly lit cigarette dangling from his lips, Toulouse stripped off his tunic and flung it over his shoulder. It was his fifth cigarette since he'd watched Montgomery enter Saint George's Hospital. The midafternoon traffic on Duke of Wellington Place headed toward Hyde Park was thick with military trucks and double-decker buses. Toulouse watched as a young woman behind a pram, holding the hand of a squirming and bawling blond-haired boy, stood on the curb across the street, looking for a break in the traffic. The woman, also a blond, was rattled. Each time the boy took a step away from her, she yanked firmly on his arm to bring him crashing into her leg. Toulouse took his eyes off the woman to gaze back at the entrance to the hospital. A steady flow of people, many in uniform, traveled under the four-columned portico, through the hospital's front entrance. There were a dozen or more patients in wheelchairs parked on either side of the entry. A few patients had their heads bowed, chins resting on their chests. Several others smoked and chatted up other patients.

Toulouse lit his sixth cigarette with the end of his nearly spent fifth as he spied Montgomery exiting the hospital, stopping and shielding his eyes with his right hand. As Toulouse flicked his cigarette to the curb, he put his tunic back on and looked back at the street and the blond, pram-pushing mother. She had begun to cross the street, taking a chance on a gap in the traffic that was shrinking fast as a military truck tried to speed past a lumbering double-decker. She pushed the pram, struggling to steer it with one hand across the pitted street. The boy's wailing became louder as they approached Toulouse. Nearly across the street, the boy jerked his arm from his mother's grasp and stepped backward only to trip on the pavement, falling onto his back and hitting his head as the speeding truck, laboring to pull in front of the bus, bore down on them.

Toulouse looked back at Montgomery and spotted him now more than half a block away. Toulouse took a short step toward the woman, who had left the pram to retrieve the stunned and now-silent boy. The pram began to roll into the truck's lane, and Toulouse stopped and looked again at Montgomery, whose figure was growing smaller as he walked down Duke of Wellington Place.

What was he thinking? This Englishwoman and her brat of a boy meant nothing to him. Montgomery had his money. He began to run toward the withdrawing man, and five steps into his sprint, he heard tires squealing and the woman's scream. Toulouse didn't look back.

He followed Montgomery down, then across Duke of Wellington Place, into a stand of trees adjacent to the Royal Artillery Memorial, with its limestone replica of a massive howitzer targeting the cloudy southeast sky. As he approached Montgomery, he slowed to a trot. The man was crouched over tying his shoelaces.

"Thank God. I thought I'd never catch up to you . . . you son of a bitch," Toulouse said joyfully.

Montgomery, still in his crouch, spun around and almost lost his balance. He spread his arms wide, touching the unkempt grass to steady himself, like a sprinter at the start line.

"Toulouse! Shite! What . . . Why are you following me? What do you want?" Montgomery asked, rising to his feet.

Toulouse, bent over with his hands on his knees, chuckled, and took a few deep breaths. Finally, he stood and took several paces toward Montgomery, who was creeping backward. He smiled but kept advancing while Montgomery continued slinking backward until he tripped on a tree root and tumbled to the ground, breaking his fall with his extended arms.

Toulouse surveyed the grounds around the war memorial. There were a few people traversing the far corner of the Palace Gardens, paying little attention to the two men gathered under the shade of the trees. "You owed me two hundred pounds."

Montgomery strained to stand, but Toulouse jammed the sole of his shoe into his chest and sent him back to the ground, grunting. "Owed? What do you—"

"You owed me two hundred pounds yesterday. But you've been making me wait for over a week, so you now owe me three hundred pounds."

Montgomery rolled over to one side, his face twisted.

"Where is it?"

"I don't have it."

Toulouse pulled his right leg back, as if to kick him again.

"Wait. I'll have it . . . all of it . . . in a . . . in a few days," Montgomery said, his arm raised in a feeble defense.

Toulouse paused momentarily, then quickly followed through with a solid kick to the other man's rib cage. "I let you go too long. That was my fuckup." Toulouse wedged his foot under the gasping Montgomery's chin and transferred his full weight onto the man's neck. "Where's all that money—*my* money—coming from, Quinn?"

Montgomery's mouth formed words, but he was soundless.

Toulouse backed off the pressure.

Montgomery clutched his neck. "My uncle . . . he'll spot me the quid."

Toulouse removed his foot from the man's neck. "Ahh, right. Your uncle the minister. Should have thought of that days ago."

Montgomery rolled over onto his hands and knees, but Toulouse kicked him in the ribs again, flattening him.

"When?" He waited as Montgomery regained his normal breathing; then he nudged him with the point of his shoe.

Montgomery jumped. "Give me a few days. Wednesday at the latest. My uncle won't be an easy mark."

If it meant getting the extra hundred pounds, Toulouse could wait; he wasn't going anywhere. "One week. But not any longer. And, for the wait, it's an extra thirty pounds. You hearing me, Quinn?" All Toulouse could hear was Montgomery's labored breathing and a throaty gurgle. He landed another blow to Montgomery's midsection with his right foot and said, "I'll take your silence as a yes."

Before he turned back toward the war memorial, he stomped on Montgomery's face and twisted his foot back and forth a bit, as if he were putting out a cigarette. "That's for my father and brother, you fucking Englishman."

CHAPTER TWENTY-NINE

2000 Hours, Sunday, October 11, 1942
Oddendino's Imperial Restaurant, Regent Street, London

Clementine Churchill was chilled. Her request for more heat, made an hour earlier, had resulted in making the private room on the second floor of Oddendino's a sweatbox for everyone else, but no one complained. Maggie Thorn wondered if anyone else had beads of sweat running down their necks.

The multicourse dinner was accompanied by several heartfelt speeches from the cabinet member's wives. Some speeches extoled the bravery of the Allied forces, but most praised the dogged determination of the British people. When it was Clementine Churchill's turn to buck up the gathering, she stood. Five minutes into her disjointed speech, the maître d' slid silently into the room, handed an envelope to Maggie, and bent down close to her ear.

"Miss, please excuse the interruption. But the officer was quite insistent that you receive this right away. He says that it is urgent." The man's breath was warm and carried the overpowering smell of cigarettes. As he left, Maggie concealed the envelope beneath the table, on her lap, and opened the flap. She read it once and then again, her breathing quickening.

Miss Thorn:
Apologies for interrupting your evening. Please meet me outside the restaurant as soon as possible. I have urgent news concerning your

*brother, Conor Thorn. I am waiting in a parked car near the restaurant.
My adjutant, who will be waiting downstairs, will show you the way.*

The typed note was signed illegibly. Maggie fumbled with the
paper, trying to get it back into the envelope. She placed her
napkin on her plate and quietly exited the room. She found the
maître d' waiting in the hallway to escort her downstairs.

When she arrived at the maître d's station at the front of the
restaurant, she noticed a man in an RAF uniform leaning against a
dark-paneled wall. One side of his face was swollen; the other side
featured a black eye. It momentarily baffled her that a member
of the RAF had been sent to get her, but her concern for Conor
overrode the oddity.

She approached the officer, who, upon seeing her, straightened
and leered. "Are you the messenger who dropped this note off?"
Maggie asked, waving the envelope at him.

"That's right. I'm the messenger. Warrant Officer Montgomery,"
he said, not shy about giving Maggie a thorough once-over. "Are
you ready?"

"First, tell me who sent this note. I can't make out the name."

"I'm sorry. That's not for me to tell. He'll tell you himself."
Montgomery put his officer's hat on and tugged on the bottom of
his tunic. "Are you ready now?"

Maggie's unease mounted. She looked at the maître d'. "I'll be
back in a moment." The maître d' nodded, and she turned to exit.

Montgomery grabbed her upper arm. It was not a gentle
gesture.

"Hey, bub. I can walk on my own two feet," Maggie said, twist-
ing her arm from his grasp. "And here I thought the English were
all gentlemen."

"Apologies, ma'am," Montgomery said, half-heartedly offering
a shallow bow. "This way."

Outside on the sidewalk, it took Maggie several seconds for her
eyes to adjust to the darkness; it was as if she were staring directly
into a well of India ink. Her damp dress cooled her when it came
in contact with the chilly night air, and she made out the red glow
of a cigarette next to the building. She heard the scuffle of shoes

on the sidewalk, and a blond woman with a wide-brimmed hat emerged from a dark alcove. She was close enough for Maggie to smell her gin-soaked breath.

"Hey, dearie, this is my turf. Don't bring your sorry arse around here again, hear me?"

Montgomery shoved the woman backward. "Shut up, bitch. She's no tart, so stop your worryin'."

"Bugger off, you wanker. I wouldn't let you near me privates with a queen's escort." The woman sneered as she retreated into her murky nook.

Maggie's breathing became quick and short. One minute, she had been dining with the prime minister's wife; the next, she was being dragged into a scene from *Oliver Twist*—except she wasn't on a stage. "Now tell me where we're going."

"Not far, miss. Not far. The car's just around that corner, on Air Street," Montgomery said, pointing ahead.

Maggie quickened her pace, turned the corner, and stopped. The street was only wide enough for a single car, and where it intersected with Regent Street, it passed under an archway that protected anyone under it from being seen by passersby on Regent. She could just make out the shape of a car parked close to the archway.

"Let me get the door," Montgomery said, lurching ahead of her. He bent forward to reach the door's handle but then reared back.

Maggie saw his hand rushing toward her face, and she braced herself for the blow, squeezing her eyes shut. It landed on the left side of her head, and she crumpled to the ground, a blast of tiny, bright lights assaulting her vision before everything went black.

#

A bolt of pain had shot up Quinn Montgomery's hand to his shoulder when he struck the redhead. He let the two-centimeter lead cylinder drop to the floor of the sedan, opened and closed his hand several times, then rotated his wrist. He winced, regretting hitting her so hard. He pulled the small bottle of chloroform from his tunic pocket and twisted off its cap. The pain in his wrist exploded, forcing him to drop the bottle to the ground, where it burst into pieces.

"Ahh fuck!" Montgomery hissed. He opened the back door of the sedan and bent over, grabbing the woman under her armpits. He dragged her the two feet to the back door, his injured wrist searing with pain. He fought against the dead weight of her body as he shoved her onto the backseat. He leaned over and ran his hand down her face and found her mouth; it was open, and her shallow breath blew against his palm. He moved his hand down her neck, to her chest, and her breast filled his hand. His breathing accelerated, and his groin ached as he squeezed and smiled, his eyelids drifting closed.

The sound of a truck crunching its gears on Regent Street startled him, and he jerked up. After tying her hands and feet with heavy twine, he backed out of the car and closed the door. "Plenty of time for fun later, Miss Thorn."

CHAPTER THIRTY

1000 Hours, Monday, October 12, 1942
Paddington Station, London

The sun streamed through the slits in the curved roof of the enormous rail station and poured down onto the platforms, revealing the dust particles and smoke that rose from several locomotives sitting on the tracks. After entering the station on Eastbourne Terrace, Thorn and Bright proceeded through the waiting area, toward the main concourse.

Thorn looked up and down the platform and noticed that there were several groups of children without any adult supervision. They were waiting patiently for someone, the boys dressed in dark-colored shorts and jackets with knee socks and the girls in knee-length coats and berets. Each child carried a battered suitcase and a light-colored, rectangular box draped over their shoulders.

"What's with all the kids? And where are the parents?" Thorn asked.

Bright surveyed the throngs of children and sighed. "Many of these children were sent to the towns outside of London during the Blitz. They've been returning over the past several months. Unfortunately, some are returning to single parents or aunts and uncles."

"That's sad." Thorn saw that, regardless of their circumstances, the kids looked carefree. "What are the kids carrying in the boxes hanging off their shoulders?"

"Those would be gas masks. Fortunately, things never got that bad," Bright said as she reached out to muss the hair of a passing redheaded boy, who looked up at her and smiled. As the boy stepped past Bright, he dropped a cloth hat he was holding on to.

Thorn bent over and handed it to him. "Hey, don't forget this, buddy. It's chilly outside."

"Thank you, mister," the boy said.

Bright smiled warmly at the exchange, but her smile faded. "Conor, where's your academy ring? Did you lose it?"

He stole a look at his right hand. There was a pale patch of skin on his ring finger, where the ring had been for the past four years. "No. I didn't lose it." *You have to earn the right to wear it every day. And I haven't done that. Running into Fellows reminded me of that.* "Lost some weight, and it got a little too loose. Just took it off for safekeeping, that's all."

Bright nodded and let it drop.

They stood on the platform for track number one and hugged the wall between a newspaper kiosk and a tearoom. Metropolitan Police had begun to clear the platform, pushing stragglers toward the waiting area near the Pared Street end of the station. One elderly, portly officer, who looked as if he had been plucked out of retirement, approached Bright, who flashed her identity card.

"Ahh, a woman in the intelligence service. Now I've seen everything. Stay if you like, but don't get too close to the important people. Understand?"

"Understood, Officer," Bright said, putting her card back in her pocket. "Is the First Lady's train on time?"

"How the hell do I know? They tell us nothing. We're just the police." The officer proceeded down the platform, taking his frustration out on four teenage girls who had most likely gathered to get a look at the king and queen. "Move along, move along. Nothing for you girls to see here."

As travelers and onlookers were steadily pushed off the platform, members of the official greeting party replaced them, which included Churchill and his wife, along with Eisenhower and additional members of the Metropolitan Police, who lined the platform with their backs trackside. The greeting party had entered the station through the main entrance on Eastbourne Terrace and congregated on the platform adjacent, allowing for the shortest walk from the train to the waiting line of cars.

The greeting party dramatically grew in numbers as King George VI, Queen Elizabeth, and their party arrived. As soon as King George, resplendent in an olive-green army officer's uniform, noticed General Eisenhower, he pulled him aside and dove into a deep discussion. Churchill occupied Queen Elizabeth, who was dressed in a dark dress and matching coat, her three strings of white pearls dramatically offset by the dress. Her hat was rakishly tilted to the side, and she clutched a small purse, her hands clad in black gloves.

Churchill's war cabinet members were spread out along the platform, among attendees that included SHAEF staff members and members of the press, their cameras and notebooks at the ready. Thorn picked out Bob Trout from CBS, but did not find his sister, Maggie.

Strange. Why would she miss this?

"I expected to see Maggie with the press, but it seems she's not here. Give me a minute. I want to talk to Trout."

"Sure. But she could be outside with the rest of the crowd of onlookers."

"Yeah. Maybe," Thorn said. When he approached Trout, the tall, thin journalist, his hair parted in the middle and slicked back, flicked his cigarette to the ground, and stamped it out under his shoe.

"Conor. How the hell are you?"

"Hey, Bob," Thorn said, taking Trout's extended hand in a firm handshake. "Any chance you've seen Maggie around here? I expected this would be an all-hands-on-deck event for CBS."

"Well, you'd be right," Trout said, stroking his neatly trimmed moustache. "She's supposed to be here, but we haven't seen her."

"Really?" *Is there any chance she could have already been pulled into the SOE? Nah.*

"She was supposed to be here thirty minutes ago. And she's not."

Thorn shook his head. "Bob, she always seems to operate on her own clock. But she'll show. This is too big of a deal."

"Well, she's cutting it a bit too close, if you ask me."

Thorn spotted Longworth, a newspaper folded under his arm, standing off to the side of the platform in front of a refreshment cart loaded down with pastries, an urn of hot tea, and small drink bottles. "Right. I'm sure she'll pop up sometime. I have to go," Thorn said, patting Trout on the shoulder.

Thorn rejoined Bright, who wrapped up a conversation with a plainclothes member of the king's security team.

"Look who joined the party," Thorn said, tilting his head toward Longworth, who stood fifteen yards away. When Longworth turned away from the refreshment cart, Bright saw him clearly, the sight of him evoking a heavy sigh.

Don't worry. Donovan told me hands off. For now.

Thorn watched as Longworth unfolded the newspaper and skimmed its pages. A moment later, another man, this one wearing a dark overcoat and a large, brimmed hat, emerged from the Eastbourne Terrace entrance and walked toward Longworth, his back to Thorn and Bright. Longworth lowered the newspaper and acknowledged the man, who brusquely took Longworth's elbow and escorted him farther down the platform, past the refreshment cart and away from the thickening throng of people. Several minutes passed, then Longworth and the other man returned. Thorn couldn't see enough of the other man's face to be able to recognize him.

"Can you make out who Longworth is talking to?" Thorn asked.

"No. Not clearly."

Thorn turned to face Bright, whose eyes were locked on Longworth and his companion. "Well, it's someone with a high clearance level to get this close to the First Lady's train."

#

The bleary-eyed Longworth was already preoccupied with his vexing dilemmas and didn't need some low-level MI5 operative bending his ear about who knows what. "Higgins, whatever you are rambling on and on about, I can't fathom. I suggest that if you have something to say, then get to the point, man. And what are you doing here anyway? This was to be for top-level members of the government and the king and queen."

"Yes, perhaps I haven't been direct enough. Your—how shall I put it?—dangerous habit of communicating with a known Nazi informant attached to the Vatican has not gone unnoticed. Is that pointed enough, Longworth?"

The blood drained from Longworth's face. He began to turn from the much younger Higgins, but a firm grip on his elbow stopped him. If MI5 was going to pull him in for questioning, they wouldn't do it in a public place with members of the press swarming about the station, and this middling agent wouldn't dare make that move on his own. It would happen at his home, in the dead of night, with the streets deep in darkness and clear of traffic.

"I will dignify your comment only by saying, yes, I do stay in touch with old friends at the Vatican. Why should I not? I was stationed there for many years. But I know of no Nazi informants, and if I did, I would have turned that information over to British intelligence immediately." Longworth yanked his elbow from Higgins's grasp. "And must I remind you that I am a trusted member of the war cabinet?" he asked in a harsh tone. "Are you here at the direction of your superiors, or are you acting on your own? Which is it? Could you possibly be an agent of the Germans yourself?" Longworth pressed, looking to set Higgins back on his heels.

"Oh, please, Longworth. Stop with the stupid accusations. And no need for the reminders. We know who you are. Perhaps better than anyone in London." Higgins took Longworth by the elbow again, this time with more force, and directed him into a shadowy area close to the brick wall of the platform. "You're a bloody anticommunist who has been feeding convoy logistics to the Germans for months. You would applaud a dead communist with more gusto than a dead Nazi. And that disgusts me. And as for my superiors . . . they know what I tell them."

Longworth again twisted his elbow from Higgins's grip. "You impertinent bastard. Who are you to level these outrageous claims against me?"

"Calm down." Higgins adjusted the brim of his hat. "The German Abwehr is filled with Russian agents. For months, they've been monitoring your efforts to 'stay in touch,' as you so inanely call it. And yes, we know of your use of the Vatican's diplomatic

pouch. Clever. Certainly not the first misuse of the pouch system."
Higgins grabbed the lapel of Longworth's suit coat and pulled him
closer. "Let's talk in simple terms, shall we? Longworth, you have
betrayed the British government."

Longworth stood motionless and peered down the track. He
bit his bottom lip. Higgins's last words echoed in his head. His
only recourse was to continue to deny—strongly. And to threaten
even more forcibly. A locomotive made slow progress toward the
platform, the lantern mounted on the nose of the massive engine
undulating from side to side as if shaking its head.

Longworth turned abruptly to face Higgins. "Rubbish. You
talk of complete nonsense. I will not stand for this."

"Oh really? Nonsense, you say? I don't think so. Not in the
least. Bishop Heinz has a dossier at Central Registry. And your
old boss, D'Arcy Osborne, has been keeping an eye on him for
many months. He has done a splendid job of providing a wealth of
information on the Brown Bishop."

Longworth's heart raced faster at the mention of Heinz's mon-
iker. Denials and threats would not suffice.

The sound of the slow-moving locomotive on its approach
echoed about the semicircular steel trusses of the station's ceiling.
Higgins leaned in toward Longworth. The smell of coffee filled
the little space between them. "I'll get to the point. It is clear to
us that you have strong feelings about Operation Torch—feelings
about the need to have it canceled or postponed."

The mention of Operation Torch confused him. What did
Higgins want from him besides a confession? Was he looking to
make a deal? "I have expressed those feelings. What of it?"

Higgins looked at him as if confused. "What did you say?" He
turned his head slightly, directing his left ear toward Longworth,
obviously struggling with the mounting sound of the approaching train.

Longworth repeated himself.

"There are some in Moscow who also believe that Operation
Torch should be . . . rethought. Rethought, that is, in favor of
an invasion of the Continent, directly on the coast of France.
Preferably this year."

"Impossible." Longworth noticed Higgins focused on his lips
as he spoke.

"Oh no, that's not true. The American military has believed for some time that it would be possible. But they chose to be manipulated by their British ally."

"What do you want? And who the bloody hell are you working for?"

The locomotive discharged a blast of steam, forcing Higgins to pause before replying. "The latter is simple—I work for the defeat of fascism. As to what I want, I want you to get a document, a very important document, to your . . . friends in Rome," Higgins said as he pulled the collar up on his overcoat.

"What document?"

Higgins blew into his folded hands. "It is the missing document from General Eisenhower's diary that contains the directives of Operation Torch." He studied Longworth.

Longworth swallowed past the knot in his throat. It was the unassailable intelligence that Kappler was demanding. "My God. Where . . . where did you get it?"

"Unimportant. What is important is that if you follow my instructions, you will get what you want—a canceled second front. And our allies the Russians, in the aftermath of the canceled Torch, will have a renewed opportunity to push for what they want—a second front where it was promised it would be: France. Maybe not this year, but certainly by spring of next year."

Longworth processed all this—it sounded unfathomable. He stood silently as the massive locomotive and its load of passenger cars crept past. The platform rumbled under his feet, vibrating up through his legs.

"And if I comply with your"—Higgins cupped his left ear as Longworth spoke—"outrageous demand, what then?"

"Ahh, we seem to be getting somewhere." Higgins motioned Longworth closer and spoke directly into his ear. "Listen carefully. At the end of this platform, near the Pared Street entrance, you will see a bookstall. Go to the travel section. On the bottom shelf, there is a book titled *The Delights of Morocco* hidden behind the other books. Inside the book, you will find an envelope with the document in question. I'd suggest you retrieve it after the king, queen, and Roosevelt have left for the palace." Higgins looked at a passenger car that was now stopped abreast of the two men. The engine let off a last gasp of steam that rose to the steel girders above and dissipated quickly. "*The Delights of Morocco.* Do you understand?"

Longworth nodded.

"You will send a letter immediately to Heinz via the diplomatic pouch that is scheduled to leave for Rome this afternoon. It will state that you have come into possession of an intelligence windfall concerning the Allied second front, but, as a result of your intrepid spying, you have been exposed as an agent for the Abwehr."

Longworth's jaw muscles flexed as he ground his teeth.

"You will also say that once you are safely inside Vatican City, you will hand it over to the Abwehr."

"What are you saying? *I* will hand it over? Inside the Vatican?"

"Yes, of course. You see, Thursday, you will be on a KLM flight that leaves for Lisbon."

Longworth shook his head vigorously. "I am going nowhere, I tell you. Besides, you idiot, they would just take it from me in Lisbon. This is madness," he said.

"Shut up and listen. In addition to the letter you send to Heinz, you will also send a letter addressed to yourself care of D'Arcy Osborne. In the envelope, you will enclose the document. In the letter to Heinz, you will demand that, in exchange for the intelligence, the Abwehr provide safe passage from Lisbon to the Vatican."

Send it to himself? Then he realized that Osborne had been in London for the past few weeks and would not be there to wonder about the letter, but Longworth would get there and, as it was essentially sent to himself, he'd have the document in Vatican City via the diplomatic pouch.

"This should ensure that the Abwehr and Heinz will get you inside the Vatican, where you will hand over the document to the Abwehr and personally vouch for its authenticity."

\#

Thorn left Bright with the greeting party and moved down the platform, closer to the two men. He hugged the wall, obscured by a pile of luggage stacked on a cart. He could not hear what was said but could see that the man in the dark overcoat did most of the talking.

What are they jabbering about? Thorn grabbed the handle of the luggage cart, which was top-heavy and overloaded, and tilted it toward his chest. He began to move it slowly down the platform. Just then, the wheels of the cart hit a wide seam in the concrete platform, jolting it. Two battered suitcases crashed to the ground. He bent to collect them and stayed crouched, while he continued to watch Longworth's meeting play out.

#

The sound of luggage crashing to the ground momentarily startled both men, who turned toward a luggage cart fifty feet down the platform. After a moment, they turned away from the man who was stooped over, collecting the spilled contents of one suitcase. Longworth pulled back from Higgins, his mouth open.

Higgins yanked him back toward his face. "I'm not finished." He turned from Longworth for a moment to look at the crowd pressing toward the railcar just behind the hissing locomotive.

Without looking back at Longworth, he continued. "You have two days before the flight leaves to pull your affairs together. When we are assured that you are in the hands of the Abwehr, I plan to deliver a report that will prove you are a traitor."

Longworth stopped breathing. He was never going to return to England. His own actions had sealed his fate.

Higgins locked his gaze on Longworth's. "Yes, I see you now understand. You will be leaving England—for good, leaving us for the bosom of the communist-hating Catholic Church, with the help of Bishop Heinz, of course."

Longworth's head snapped back, his eyes bulging. "You . . . you don't understand. I will be—"

"Missed? Yes, of course. But, you see, the Churchill government will make up some story to explain your . . . absence, making sure that word of a traitor in the cabinet will never be uttered. Ever."

Longworth's shoulders slumped. He looked down the platform

at the throng of greeters. He spotted Churchill, a cloud of blue smoke from his cigar gathering over his head. "There is the issue of the agents that have been investigating—"

"Oh yes. That would be Thorn and Bright. May I suggest that your goon of a nephew take care of that matter? Maybe with a little more effectiveness than the last time?" Higgins smirked. "So, are we done here, Mr. Longworth?" asked Higgins who, not waiting for an answer, retook Longworth's elbow and led him back toward the greeting party.

"I am a dead man," Longworth mumbled.

"That's not how I see it. I see you as a man who stood for something and sacrificed for it. Even if it was the wrong thing."

Higgins let go of Longworth's elbow and headed down the platform, away from the crowd.

#

Thorn stood and got Bright's attention. He pointed to Longworth and then to Bright. She nodded as Thorn spun around and raced down the platform. The overcoat man was fifty yards ahead of him, walking rapidly alongside the First Lady's train. Ahead of Thorn, the platform was clear except for his target. He was closing the distance, wondering where the overcoat man was going as he saw the end of the platform looming ahead.

Thorn heard the near-deafening hiss of the locomotive sitting on the track adjacent to the First Lady's train. The shriek of metal fighting metal mixed with the sound of hissing steam, overwhelming the announcements of departing trains. Thorn had him in his reach, but as the overcoat man reached the end of the platform, he didn't stop but dropped down onto the tracks behind the last car of Roosevelt's train.

Thorn could hear nothing but the engine purging itself of steam as he reached for the tail of the man's coat and yanked it. The man was no more than a foot from the nose of the locomotive when he twisted around and saw Thorn. Steam obscured Thorn's sight, so when the man's right arm swung at him, he was slow to react. He caught a glimmer of light off a small-bladed knife before it cut the sleeve of his trench coat. Thorn lost the grip and the man slipped across the track inches ahead of the engine. Thorn stumbled as the locomotive moved between the two men, blocking any further pursuit. He fell onto the gravel between the two rail lines, steam laced with the stench of grease blowing in his face.

\#

First to exit the railcar was a porter who placed a wooden step on the platform. Eleanor Roosevelt was dressed in black shoes and a matching long coat adorned with a thick fox fur that she clutched tightly with black-gloved hands. She followed the porter and smiled broadly at the king and queen as flashbulbs popped and a smattering of polite applause rippled through the crowd of dignitaries, each of whom was introduced to the First Lady by Churchill.

Longworth stood on the perimeter of the crowd, unsure exactly what to do. He was reeling from his encounter with Higgins. His mouth was dry, and his hands became clammy. The chattering and tumult that swirled around him dissolved into a dull buzzing in his head. But a moment of clarity broke through, and he turned toward the Pared Street entrance.

"Henry, Henry, please join me." Churchill's command could be heard across the platform. Longworth stopped and immediately understood that to ignore the prime minister at this moment would create unwanted attention. He turned back and joined Churchill and Roosevelt.

"Eleanor Roosevelt, this is Henry Longworth, minister of Works and Planning and a member of my war cabinet and, I might add, a longtime associate."

"First Lady, it is indeed a pleasure." Longworth formed his words slowly, fighting through dry mouth. "Welcome to England." Longworth's stomach was roiling. He had to get out of there.

"Thank you so much. I haven't slept for what seems days due to anticipation. I fully expect to be impressed by the resolve and determination of the people of Great Britain."

"You are too generous with your praise, First Lady," Longworth said. Higgins's voice banged around in his head: *I know who you are—you are a traitor to the British government.*

"Yes, indeed. We do make a great team."

"Eleanor, it seems that the king and queen are a bit anxious to whisk you away to the palace," Churchill said.

"Ahh, yes. Good day, Mr. Longworth," Roosevelt said as she took Churchill's arm and joined the king and queen. The scrum of photographers moved in lockstep with Churchill and Roosevelt. Longworth turned and headed for the bookstall at the end of the platform.

Slightly out of breath, he waited inside the bookstall for a group of tittering teenage schoolgirls to leave, then located the travel section. The book, *The Delights of Morocco*, was right where Higgins had said it would be. Placed inside the book, as if bookmarking a section of beach photographs, was a brown envelope. Longworth shoved the envelope into his breast pocket and exited the station onto Pared Street. The contents of the envelope were pulling him deeper into a dark and treacherous morass.

#

When Thorn returned to where he'd last seen Bright, she was gone. He waited for her return while watching lingering dignitary staff and security people make their exits from the station. He spotted her a minute later, dodging through the exiting crowd toward him.

"I lost him. I'm so sorry, Conor," Bright said, her face reddening as she glared back toward the Pared Street exit. "Bloody hell. I saw him head for the Pared Street exit, but I couldn't get through a swarm of photographers fast enough to keep up with him."

"That's OK. Let's follow the swarm."

"What happened to the man he was talking to?"

"Lost him too. He definitely didn't want to talk to me, and I still didn't get a good look at him." They set out through the Eastbourne Terrace doors. At the top of the concrete steps that dropped down to Eastbourne Terrace, they surveyed the crowd. The mass of people that flanked the steps on both sides, held back by wooden barricades bolstered by a glut of Metropolitan Police, cheered as the king, queen, and First Lady took their time loading into a gleaming, black Rolls Royce that sat at the bottom of the steps, its doors wide-open. Two motorcycle escorts boxed the limousine in, front and back.

"Are you still looking for him?" Bright asked.

Thorn knew that seeing Longworth and his friend together was significant. But he couldn't put his finger on why. "Don't need to. We know where to find Longworth."

CHAPTER THIRTY-ONE

0800 Hours, Tuesday, October 13, 1942
No. 28 Queen Anne's Gate, London

Longworth smelled. Slumped in his chair, he rubbed his eyes with his uninjured hand and stroked the stubble of two days' beard growth. He hadn't left his study since the afternoon before. The air in the room was foul. He needed to sleep, but it had eluded him.

A knock at his front door roused him. Looking out the study's window, Longworth saw a young boy, one of Westminster Cathedral's altar boys. He finally left his study and opened the front door a crack, peering though the narrow opening.

"What is it, boy?"

"Father Sullivan told me to give this letter to you. He told me to say it arrived yesterday afternoon from Rome."

Without uttering a word of thanks, Longworth took the over-sized envelope from the boy and shut the door. When Longworth entered his study, he locked the doors and closed the heavy drapes. He poured himself a finger of single-malt whisky and dropped into his chair. After he threw back the drink and poured another, he opened the large envelope.

Inside were two smaller envelopes. One envelope—addressed to "Mr. Henry Longworth, Minister of Public Works and Planning, London, England"—was in the familiar hand of Bishop Heinz. He opened the envelope, picked up his drink, and began to read.

My friend Henry:

I shall not be long-winded. It is due to the level of my concern that I feel compelled to tell you that, over the past several months, our close mutual friend has experienced a drastic change in demeanor and has suffered a demise in his spirits. I believe the enclosed letter from him goes into great detail as to the reasons for his emotional and mental setback. I sincerely hope that you can suggest a strong remedy to his troubles, as I am at a loss. Given his current state, a timely response from you is of utmost importance.

Yours in Christ,
Bishop Heinz

Longworth tossed the ambiguously written letter on his desk. He knew who the "close mutual friend" was, and to hear that he was distressed filled him with dread. He finished his drink, poured another, then picked up the second envelope. It was addressed simply to "H. Longworth." He slit it open and found bold handwriting that filled each page; the edges of each stroke of the pen became jagged as the soft, porous paper absorbed the black ink.

Longworth:

I am at my wit's end, and I turn to you for guidance. Alas, I am damn tired every time misery and apathy comfortably nestle inside the empty heart of any nation that . . .

Longworth quickly surveyed the rest of the letter. It contained a dreary account of an excursion across Rome to take in historic religious sites. A series of examples of access being denied or drastically limited due to Italian and German security concerns ended with news of a relative being detained by the Italian secret police, OVRA, under suspicion of antifascist activities. Longworth snorted at the backhanded cleverness of the letter's creator, Abwehr Major Kappler, whose last line begging for Longworth's help in freeing the relative incensed Longworth. Kappler was playing with him—Longworth knew it. Thankfully, their communication was infrequent.

Three full handwritten pages of single-spaced dribble would take Longworth at least two hours to decipher. The painstaking task of composing his own ciphers regarding the logistics of northbound Allied convoys always drained Longworth. The task of breaking down Kappler's acrostic code, in which the first letter of every other word from every other sentence would reveal Kappler's true demands was equally laborious.

The clock chimed half past the hour of ten when Longworth raised his head from Kappler's letter. It took another twenty minutes for him to break up the string of letters into words. As he unmasked each successive word, he began to pant; his breath was hot and dry. He slumped in his seat when he read the complete message.

I demand that we receive by 25 October definitive, unassailable intelligence as to Allied plans for second front. Your position as member of Churchill's cabinet puts you in position to accomplish this and more. It is disappointing that we find it necessary to write a letter that expresses our deep disappointment in the quality of intelligence that we have received from you since your arrival in England. The single focus of your information—northbound convoys—leaves us underwhelmed.

Our disappointment will force us to take action with photographs that we have concerning the murder of your mistress.

The clock ticks toward one of two events: our smashing of the Allied second front or the end of your career and, quite possibly, your life.

We await your response.

He sat motionless; his head fell to his chest, his right hand gripping the letter. Had he received this letter the day before his meeting with Higgins, he would have been able to clearly see his demise. But he now had the "unassailable intelligence" his keepers wanted. It would keep them at bay for a while. A forgiving God was watching out for him.

His thoughts drifted back to the night in Rome, the last night with Maria, his lustful, daring, and beautiful mistress. Her dreams of some day leaving her disappointment of a husband and following Longworth back to England, of having his child, kept her alive. Her dismissiveness of anyone who would oppose her dreams, including the Italian military police, had emboldened Longworth. But the last night, Maria had pushed him—pushed him to take their lovemaking to ever-greater heights of ferocity, and Longworth, in one moment, saw Maria struggling in ecstasy, then plunging the next moment into a breathless silence—a moment that changed both their lives forever.

As Longworth sat staring at Kappler's flamboyant signature, he suddenly felt a sharp pain in his hand. When he looked down, he saw he was clutching the blade of his letter opener so tightly he'd drawn blood. He dropped the letter opener and wrapped his hand in his handkerchief and then snatched a lighter off his desk. After setting the letters afire, he dropped them into a wastebasket. The ashes turned from a searing, angry red to a gray black and then crumbled.

Yes, Kappler would soon be satisfied—but then there were Higgins and the blasted Thorn and Bright.

CHAPTER THIRTY-TWO

0900 Hours, Tuesday, October 13, 1942
Underground War Rooms, No. 2 Storeys Gate Building, London

Thorn was confused as to where they were to meet with Churchill, but his confusion took a backseat to the distraction of Bright's shapely legs. She was wearing a dress that was a bit shorter than she typically wore, and it settled a few inches above her knees as she sat across from Thorn. She wore a bit more makeup than usual as well and had decided to wear nylon stockings for their meeting with Churchill. The result thrilled and distracted Thorn.

As to his confusion, they weren't anywhere near 10 Downing Street. Instead, following Bright's directions, he had taken a left turn onto Horse Guards Road, placing Saint James Park on his left. "Hey, where the hell are we going? Is this the long way to number ten?"

"We're headed to the Cabinet War Rooms, 'the hole in the ground,' as we used to call it."

Thorn gave Bright a confused look.

"The short of it is, during the late 1930s, war seemed so assured that the British government believed it would be prudent to establish an underground haven for the prime minister, his cabinet, and the chiefs of staff. I've spent many a day and night in the hole, and I cannot say I miss it."

They entered a nondescript government building and were met immediately by a dark-haired woman with blazing-red lips.

"Emily, so good to see you. We miss you so," the woman said, her voice warm and sincere.

"Elizabeth, what a pleasure. This is Conor Thorn. Conor, this is Elizabeth Nel, the prime minister's saving grace."

"That's some title, Elizabeth." Thorn smiled. "Nice to meet you."

Nel chuckled. "Well, Yankee humor. We can use some of that down here. Come, the prime minister is expecting you. He is talking to the president at the moment, whom he roused out of bed, mind you, so I am sure he will be done in short order." Nel headed to a door marked *Staircase 15*, and the group began their descent. The dreary atmosphere in the staircase was bolstered by low light, peeling paint, and a frosty dampness that made Thorn consider what it was like in the deep winter.

At the bottom of the staircase, Nel hit a buzzer mounted on the wall alongside a massive wooden door that prompted someone on the other side to slide open a four-by-four-inch speakeasy door. The guard peering through silently approved the guests and slid open the door that sat on rails embedded in the concrete floor. They entered a hallway, narrow and low ceilinged. Thick wooden support beams that sustained the weight of the building above sprouted in every direction. Aiding that effort were sporadically placed steel girders, each painted a bright red and stamped with the name of its fabricator: Dorman Long & Co. As they moved down the hallway, Thorn noticed a middle-aged man dressed in a gray, double-breasted suit with a trench coat draped over his left arm, leaning against the wall at the far end. As they approached, he stood, his head barely clearing a wood support beam. Nel came to a halt and placed her hand on the gentleman's shoulder.

"D'Arcy Osborne, this is Emily Bright and Conor Thorn. Also here to see the prime minister. D'Arcy is Britain's minister to the Vatican."

Bright's look of surprise was not lost on Thorn.

We need to buttonhole this guy about the Brown Bishop, he thought. *But when?*

"A pleasure to meet you both," Osborne said as he shook hands while adding a slight bow. "Elizabeth, I was just about finished with the prime minister, or I should say he was just about finished with me, when his attempt to reach the president succeeded. I simply would like to bid him farewell, as I am not quite sure when I will see him again."

Thorn found it difficult to understand Osborne's heavily accented speech. He spoke in a formal, restrained, upper-crust manner.

"I'm sure he won't be long," Nel replied. "The only item on today's list was a review of the first day of Eleanor Roosevelt's visit."

"Excuse me, Mr. Osborne, but would it be correct to assume that you are acquainted with Henry Longworth?" asked Thorn.

"Oh, quite so. We worked together for several years before the war began. Rather interesting years, I must say." Before Thorn could ask Osborne about Bishop Heinz, the door to Thorn's right opened and revealed Churchill with his cigar wedged tightly between his fore and middle fingers. The room Churchill exited was not more than five feet wide and ten feet deep. A desk sat at the far end of the room, and olive-green metal shelves were anchored to the wall. On the desk were a green, hooded banker's lamp, a black Bakelite phone, and an ashtray overcome with spent tobacco ash.

"Well, I see that I have merited a greeting party. Not entirely as big as the First Lady's, but it will do." Churchill smiled warmly at Bright and gave her a lingering hug, deftly avoiding stabbing her with his cigar.

Thorn noticed Bright blush a bit.

"And you must be Conor Thorn. I've heard much about you from Emily here and, of course, Bill Donovan. They both sing your praises."

Thorn saw that Churchill's comment deepened Bright's blush.

"And your call with the president? It went well?" Nel asked.

"Oh, yes. Quite so. He is happy with the grand start to Eleanor's trip, as am I. It will go a long way to further cementing our strong relationship," Churchill said, waving his cigar and dispatching ash to the concrete floor.

"Prime Minister, I must take my leave," Osborne said. "So thoughtful of you to spend time with me. I hope my briefing was found useful."

"Oh, D'Arcy, of course it was." Churchill turned toward Bright and Thorn. "D'Arcy is to be commended for his service at the Vatican." Churchill began poking the space between him and

Thorn with his cigar for emphasis. "A rat's nest of spies if there ever was one. His work there has, indeed, been impactful, so much so that he will be knighted in a week's time."

"So kind, Prime Minister. I am sorry to say that I am running late for a lunch that is being given by your war cabinet. Good day to you all."

"Certainly, you shouldn't be late for your own lunch," Churchill said.

"Mr. Osborne, might we meet with you to discuss a Bishop Heinz?" Thorn asked. "I believe he runs the—"

"German College," Osborne finished for him.

Churchill, his brow furrowed, looked at Bright and cocked his head.

"I'd be happy to. Quite a scoundrel, that man. Certainly can't be trusted. I'm staying at the Savoy," Osborne said as he pulled on his trench coat.

"D'Arcy, I'll walk you out," Nel offered.

"Then let us move into the Cabinet War Room, shall we?" Churchill ushered Thorn and Bright down the hall, to a square-shaped room. In the ceiling, red-painted steel girders crisscrossed above a blue-felt-covered table that mirrored the shape of the room. Churchill took his seat with his back to a world map that spanned ten feet of the wall. A box covered in red leather that rested directly in front of the prime minister mesmerized Thorn. It was too big for a cigar box and too small for a toolbox. Thorn supposed it was the perfect size for a gun box, in case Churchill wanted to calm the dissension among his cabinet members.

Churchill settled into his chair and relit his cigar. As he did, Thorn and Bright took seats side by side, near the door to the hallway. A small fan adjacent to the map and above Churchill's shoulder whirled and oscillated, dispersing the cigar smoke throughout the room.

"Hopefully, you both bring good news."

For the next fifteen minutes, Thorn and Bright switched off briefing Churchill. Thorn led the charge when it came to explaining the suspicions about Longworth, his behavior at Paddington Station, and his connection to the Vatican and the Brown Bishop Heinz, something that Churchill seemed to take particular note of.

"He's a fascist?"

"To the extent that he earned the name 'Brown Bishop,'" Thorn said.

"And his own file at MI6's Central Registry," Bright added.

Churchill lost the pinkness in his cheeks as he pulled another cigar from his breast pocket. Thorn waited for him to light his cigar, but he just continued to scowl at Thorn.

Churchill turned his attention to Bright as she gave details about Montgomery, Toulouse, and MI5's tailing of Toulouse that led to information concerning his involvement with the Spanish embassy.

Churchill dropped back in his chair. "And what do you make of all that?"

"Unclear, Prime Minister," Bright said. "It's a neutral country, but one governed by fascists being visited by a low-level member of the French intelligence. It's concerning."

"It may all be connected," Thorn said.

The room fell silent except for the sound of the fan. Churchill cocked his head toward the two agents and took a moment before he responded. Thorn looked at Bright, who gave no indication she might know what was coming.

"What you've done—what you both have done—is, to my mind, not make much headway in actually finding the missing document. That alone will make me lose sleep. There appears, at this point, no direct connection from the document to Longworth, his nephew, or this BCRA chap. But what disturbs me more is this information about Longworth's correspondence habits." Churchill stood and leaned on the table. "Tread as heavily as is necessary with Longworth, with no concern as to my feelings. Do so quietly, but get to the bottom of this bloody Frenchman. And above all, do not lose focus on locating the damned missing diary page. That is ultimately the paramount mission. Understood?" Churchill moved away from the table.

Thorn was the first to rise from his seat, followed by Bright. The reply, "Understood," uttered crisply and in unison, echoed off the steel girders above.

Thorn and Bright were not quite out the door of the cabinet room when Elizabeth Nel entered through the door behind them.

She handed Churchill a note that he unfolded and read. He fell back into his chair. Thorn heard the air in the seat cushion as it was quickly ejected by Churchill's girth.

"Please sit again. Both of you," Churchill said in a low voice. Nel stood stoically beside him as he stared at the note. Thorn and Bright exchanged glances as they retook their seats. A list of possible complications raced through Thorn's mind.

Churchill leaned over to Nel and whispered something. She raced from the room.

"Emily, we have received news of your brother."

Thorn turned and studied her. She sat on the edge of her seat, hands folded in her lap. He could not detect her breathing. "It is not good, I'm afraid." It took a moment before her shoulders slumped and she let out a long breath. She continued to stare at Churchill.

Nel returned, approached Bright, and laid a white handkerchief embroidered with the initials of E. C. N. before her. Bright didn't touch it.

"Yes, sir. I . . . What happened to—"

"He succumbed to wounds that he received in the attack on his ship. I am told he is credited with saving the lives of several men during the attack. That is all we know. I am deeply sorry and . . . entirely sad."

Thorn reached for Bright's hand and squeezed it. He felt her hand tremble and she grasped his tightly.

Churchill and Nel quietly left the room.

"I'm so sorry. Good, decent people losing family. God knows I wish it weren't the case." Thorn understood too well loss and sacrifice and the unfairness of heaping so much of it on one person. He questioned if Bright too needed to seek justification for the sacrifices made by others.

"It's war. And nothing about it is fair, Conor." Her voice was soft and choked by emotion. With her free hand, she grabbed the handkerchief from the table and dabbed at the corners of her eyes and slowly rose from her chair. Thorn stood and pulled her to him, slipping his arm around her waist. The look of surprise quickly dissolved into one of relief. He felt her heart pounding. Or was it his?

As her green eyes brimmed with tears, he kissed her. She didn't resist, giving herself to him. It was one kiss, lasting no more than a few seconds, but when he broke it off, she stared at him.

"I'm . . . I went too far," Thorn said, setting her free.

She looked down and dried her eyes with the handkerchief, then looked up at him. "I'll be the judge of that."

CHAPTER THIRTY-THREE

1030 Hours, Wednesday, October 14, 1942
Office of Field Marshall Keitel, Wunsdorf, Germany

The hour-long drive south to Wunsdorf from Berlin went by quickly, this primarily due to Canaris's last-minute decision to take his two wire-haired dachshunds along with him. The playful and loyal dogs kept him occupied physically and, thankfully, mentally. When he had been summoned the day before to a meeting with Wilhelm Keitel, chief of the Supreme High Command of the German Armed Forces, he'd inquired as to the purpose. He was not given the courtesy of a reply.

Upon exiting his Mercedes, he gave instructions to the driver and to take his dogs for a long walk and take note of their bowel movements, as he would want a report when he returned. The driver took his leave, and Canaris turned to look up at the massive bunker complex that housed the OKW—Oberkommando der Wehrmacht.

On Canaris's first visit to Wunsdorf in the summer of 1939, Keitel had gushed with praise for his "fortress," explaining that the bunkers, walls, and floors, which were composed of concrete and iron reinforcements, were more than three feet thick. He was especially proud of the fact that the bunkers were designed to look similar to houses from the air, so they had sloping tile roofs and chimneys that concealed air filter systems. At Keitel's urging, German efforts to mask the bunkers went so far as to have fake windows painted on the walls. Nothing was as it seemed, mused Canaris.

Canaris was met by an SS guard who took him to Keitel's office located in one of the two floors below ground level. Canaris found Keitel seated comfortably behind his desk in an ornately designed throne-like chair, its seat back rising well above the head of the field marshal. Keitel made no move to greet Canaris.

"Your trip was uneventful?" Keitel was in full dress uniform. His collar, buttoned tight, was decorated with the Knight's Cross of the Iron Cross. Two rows of campaign and service ribbons adorned the area above his left breast pocket. Canaris heard the drone of a ventilation system as it spewed a metallic-smelling flow of air.

"It was, Field Marshall. It is good to see you. You look well."

"Well then, why do I feel like shit?"

"I am sorry to hear that. Is it the Eastern Front that makes you ill?"

Keitel looked slyly at Canaris, who realized that he made Keitel a bit nervous. "It is a factor. One hour ago, I received an order from the führer. He wants the suspension of all activity on the Eastern Front except for Stalingrad and the Terek River in the Caucasus."

"The führer is right, of course."

Keitel again surveyed his visitor carefully. "Admiral, I will tell you what the führer is—he is deeply disappointed and dejected over your inability to provide any reliable material intelligence on where and when the Allies plan to establish a second front. When will you have the intelligence we are asking for? And I don't want a question thrown back in my face. I want a direct answer."

It provided no comfort to Canaris that Keitel wasn't acting on his own initiative. The field marshal, who had a reputation as Hitler's lackey, was clearly doing the bidding of his master, which put Keitel in the class of spineless desk warriors.

"My direct answer, Field Marshall, is soon."

"That is all you have to say? What are you waiting for?"

"The Abwehr has uncovered intelligence regarding multiple targets for the second front. As I have told the führer myself, inaccurate intelligence serves no purpose. With much satisfaction, I can say that, any day now, I am expecting specific intelligence directly from inside Churchill's inner circle."

"His inner circle—what does that mean? Whom are you speaking of?"

"I can say no more other than to say that it is someone close to the prime minister himself."

Keitel leaned over his desk and stared down at Canaris, "If he's so close to Churchill, why doesn't he shoot the *Schweinhund*?"

Canaris sat motionless, silently hiding his amusement at Keitel calling Churchill a pig-dog.

CHAPTER THIRTY-FOUR

1100 Hours, Wednesday, October 14, 1942
Westminster Cathedral Clergy House, No. 42 Francis Street, London

Even the cool day couldn't keep Longworth from sweating through his linen shirt. He was running late. The courier would be leaving with the pouch in less than fifteen minutes.

He steered the battleship-gray Humber around a double-decker bus that spewed a thick cloud of exhaust as it lumbered down Victoria Street, and picked up speed as he turned onto Ashley Place, leaning hard into the curve that connected to Morpeth Terrace.

Longworth eased the car alongside the curb in front of the clergy house. He jumped out and squinted at the early-morning sun. The chilled air against his damp shirt made him shiver.

While Longworth waited for Edith, the housekeeper, to answer the door, he took out the two envelopes he intended to drop into the pouch. His only concern was that no one see the letter that was addressed to himself care of D'Arcy Osborne, for it would certainly arouse suspicions.

The door opened and Edith stood there, short of breath. "Ahh, good morning to you, Mr. Longworth. Sorry to keep you waiting. Not movin' so well this morning. It's me joints that be botherin' me. You're here to see the cardinal? He—"

"No, no, Edith. Not today. I only wanted to drop a couple of letters into the pouch before it left this morning. The pouch hasn't left yet, has it?" Longworth asked as he pushed past the house-keeper into the foyer.

"No, no. Father William hasn't come downstairs yet—running late as usual. I believe he was packin' a few things for the trip. The pouch is right there in the office." Edith pointed down the far end of the foyer. "You was here Monday with a letter, wasn't you? A lot to talk about, right, Mr. Longworth?"

"Yes, indeed. I'll just drop them in if you don't mind."

"I'd be happy to do that for you, Mr. Longworth." Edith extended her hand.

"No need, Edith. I'll do it myself." Longworth bolted for the far end of the foyer. He found the office door open and the pouch sitting on a chair beside the desk. The black valise had a gold-colored chain attached to a stout buckle on one end and a handcuff on the other. It sat open, filled with numerous letters of various sizes. He slipped his letters into the pouch, making sure they made it to the bottom.

He turned to exit the office, then stopped in the doorway. He suddenly became aware that with his letters now in the pouch, he had set something quite momentous in motion, the outcome of which would not be completely in his control. This notion unsettled him.

"Thank you so much, Edith. Tell the cardinal that I'll stop by soon to catch up," Longworth said as he passed the housekeeper, who stood by the still-open front door.

"I will, Mr. Longworth."

He headed down the stone steps, toward the Humber. Thirty feet from the car, Father Sean Sullivan approached, his windswept, black cassock trailing behind him as he briskly walked toward the clergy house. Priest or not, the ever-smirking Irishman was not someone Longworth was fond of.

"Good morning, Mr. Longworth. Missed you at Mass today. Everything is well, I hope?"

"Yes, Father, all is well. But I must be going. Cabinet business, you see." Longworth opened the door and eased himself behind the wheel.

"Of course. Good day, Mr. Longworth."

Longworth grinded the Humber into gear and sped from the curb, making a sharp turn onto Francis Street.

#

Sullivan studied the car until it disappeared from view, noting that Longworth had appeared a bit jittery. When he entered the clergy house, he looked for Edith and found her in the kitchen cutting two slices of toast in half.

"Father Sean. You're late . . . as usual."

"So I am. Edith, tell me, what did Mr. Longworth want?"

"Nothing much. He wanted to catch the pouch before it left this morning, so he could add a couple of letters. Would you like some toast and a hot cuppa, Father?"

Sullivan leaned his broad frame against the doorjamb. "No, thank you. Tell me, is the pouch still here?"

"You just missed it. Father William stormed out of here like a whirling dervish. Said he was running late as he headed out the back door to the garage."

"Hmmm . . . that's unfortunate. By the way, any chance you saw who the letters were addressed to?" Sullivan asked, the memory of his conversation with Conor Thorn still fresh in his mind. The idea that a friend of Cardinal Massy might be conducting nefarious affairs that went beyond merely conversing with old friends at the Vatican troubled him.

Edith took a bite out of a slice of toast. "Oh, no," she said with a shake of her head, her mouth full of toast. "Strange though—he was quite insistent he place them in the pouch himself."

"Hmm. As if he was hiding something?"

"Oh no, Father. He's a good man. Just ask Cardinal Massy. He'll tell you."

Sullivan believed that was a good idea.

#

Maggie Thorn's fear after coming to had shifted into a raging and riotous desire to see the psycho lying lifeless in a growing pool of his own blood. If he had meant to kill her, he would have done so after he dragged her up a staircase, which had scraped the skin from the back of her lower legs. The blood that had run down her legs and into her shoes had dried. The gag in her mouth created a pulsating pain in her jaw that had worked its way down her neck. Turning her head in any direction triggered bolts of pain that added to her nausea. The rope that bound her hands behind her back and her feet to the legs of the chair cut into her skin, killing any sensation.

He continued to lean on a dresser in the corner of the room, a cigarette dangling from his mouth. She remembered little from when she had first set eyes on him at Oddendino's. The citywide blackout and her preoccupation with her concerns about Conor had conspired to make her captor a faceless entity.

He picked up a tray from the top of the dresser and approached her, his footsteps muffled by a tattered rug that covered most of the floor, which, given the steep slope to the ceiling, she assumed was an attic. When he was no more than six feet from her, the light from a ceiling fixture captured his face.

The man was in his thirties, with full cheeks and a high forehead. His left hand was wrapped with gauze. His smile revealed crooked, yellowed front teeth. He knelt on one knee before her and placed the tray on the floor. It held a single bowl filled with a brownish mush, a spoon, and a glass of water. He looked up at her, and his smile faded.

"Are you hungry, little lady? You'll be here awhile, so you've got to keep your strength up," he said, his eyes falling from her face to her legs. "Wouldn't want you to faint from weakness, now, would we?"

The thought of food only stoked her nausea, but removing the gag would provide some relief. She nodded slowly at first, then faster, with wide eyes.

"Well, all right, then." He stood and reached around her head to untie the gag. His chest was inches from her face, and the smell of cigarettes and perspiration filled her nostrils, spiking her queasiness. The gag loosened, then fell from her mouth.

She waited until he took a step away, so she could see his face. "You bastard. You fucking bastard," she screamed. Her hair, previously held back by the gag, now fell forward and covered her cheeks. "You—"

He reared back and slapped her with such fury that the chair she was tied to nearly toppled. Before the chair finished righting itself, he had the gag back in her mouth. The left side of her face burned and throbbed.

"Now that wasn't smart, you twat," he said, his face flushed. "You can starve for all I care, you stupid bitch." He walked to the dresser and stared into an oval mirror that hung above it, then fiddled with something on the top of the piece of furniture. He wiped his face with his bandaged hand and stood motionless, staring in the mirror for a long minute.

When he finally turned back to Maggie, she saw that his eyes were half-closed. He came and knelt before her, his chest heaving and his mouth open. He pushed the hem of her dress up her thigh, exposing the top of her stockings and her garter straps. Maggie tensed. He lifted one garter with his finger and let it snap back onto her thigh. She jumped. His laugh fought through a phlegmy buildup in his throat.

"Hope that didn't hurt . . . too much," he said without looking her in the face. His hand traveled up her thigh, reached for the soft cotton fabric of her panties, and yanked it aside. Maggie's legs struggled against the rope that bound her feet to the legs of the chair. She tilted her head back and visualized her feet landing deep in his genitals, sending him flying backward and crashing to the floor on his back. But the image was short-circuited by the movements of his fingers.

Maggie convulsed in a fit of rage. She pulled and kicked against her bindings, which only cut deeper into her skin. Her hands and feet that were once numb now tingled. The man kneeling before her laughed gleefully—but this time he was looking straight into her eyes.

CHAPTER THIRTY-FIVE

1115 Hours, Wednesday, October 14, 1942
Embassy of Spain, Belgrave Square, London

Thorn pointed the Roadmaster northwest along Belgrave Place. The numbers of leads to follow up on were dwindling. Thorn expected little from their meeting with the press attaché, but he needed to keep Bright on the move and focused on something other than her brother.

As they crossed Eaton Place, a full block from the embassy, she pointed up ahead. "There seems to be a bit of a commotion."

At least six cars had converged on the front of the embassy from multiple directions; several of them still had their driver's side doors open. An olive-green ambulance, its rear doors wide-open, had backed up to the chest-high, spiked front gate. A handful of people flanked the ambulance's rear doors. Thorn steered the Buick toward the curb on the Belgrave Square Garden side of the street, a short distance from the ruckus, and watched along with the others as two middle-aged men carried a stretcher with a fully covered corpse from behind the three-story embassy toward the waiting ambulance. Another man, much older than the stretcher-bearers, followed. The right sleeve of his coat was ironed flat, the end stuffed neatly into the pocket.

Hollis, who had been reading a book in the backseat, slid over to the driver's side rear window. "Oh, dear. What could have happened, I wonder."

"Well, we missed all but the last act of the main attraction," Thorn said.

"I can see our MI5 contact standing off to the side," Bright said.

"Let's go see what we missed," Thorn said, yanking on the door handle. "Hollis, you—"

"Stay in the car. Right, sir. I'll be fine. I've got my Wodehouse to keep me company." She waggled her book at him.

As Thorn and Bright crossed Belgrave Place, the windswept tree branches behind them rustled, sounding like subdued applause. A tall man, at least six and a half feet, leaned against the black-iron fence in front of the embassy. The collar on his suit coat was turned up against the blustering wind. His fedora was pulled down tightly over his head, distorting the shape of the hat.

"I think I see our contact." Bright picked up her pace and was the first to approach him.

"Are you from MI5?"

It took several beats before he responded. "Yes. Hightower, Trevor Hightower," he said without shifting his line of sight from the approaching stretcher. "And you would be?"

Bright's jaw dropped. "Ahh, finally, the ghost appears."

Hightower snorted. "Not like I haven't heard that before."

"Well, this is Conor Thorn and I'm Emily Bright. I've been trying to reach you for . . . quite some time. What do you have on the Army Air Forces film lab break-in?"

Another series of beats accompanied by no eye contact. "Not much. No fingerprints. Blood type O positive. Most common in the UK . . . and the US, by the way. Pretty much a dead end." Still no eye contact. Bright, her lips pinched, shrugged at Thorn.

The bearers lowered the stretcher to the ground, the hands of one bearer covered in blood. The old man with one arm gently lowered himself beside the stretcher. He pulled back the now-crimson sheet revealing a man with wavy, dark hair and a sharply trimmed moustache. A light-blue shirt betrayed a large patch of still-wet blood just below his sternum. Trickles of now-dried blood had drained from the man's nose, mouth, and ears. The one-armed man reached into the dead man's breast shirt pocket and pulled out a small object, studied it, and put into a brown paper bag. Several people gathered on the embassy side of the fence. Three women stood closest to the fence. Two were weeping. Thorn noticed the third, a young Asian woman, her arms folded across her chest, was glaring at him, her face pinched in a concentrated look of anger. Thorn turned back to Hightower, waiting for him to finish. Five more seconds passed before he realized that wasn't going to happen.

"Tell me that the press attaché is inside and not on that stretcher."

Hightower turned to Thorn. "You're here to see Alba?"

"Yes. Jorge Alba. Know him?"

Hightower turned back to the stretcher. "Never met the man, Yank. But there he is, in all his gory glory. Jorge Alba, the late press attaché for the Embassy of Spain. The press shall miss him, I'm sure."

"What in God's name happened?" Bright asked.

"All I can tell you is that our man inside the embassy saw Alba meet a French captain, a Remy Toulouse, in the reception area of the embassy yesterday morning." Hightower wouldn't look at Bright, but anchored his gaze on Thorn. "Our man didn't see Alba the rest of the day and neither did anybody else. About an hour ago, a secretary looking out a back window saw our Mr. Alba draped over this iron fence like wet laundry."

"That's it? How did Alba know Toulouse?" Bright asked, her voice rising with each question.

Hightower finally turned to Bright. "Toulouse has been a regular visitor. At least every two weeks. We haven't made a connection beyond that yet." Hightower pointed at the gathering at the rear of the ambulance. "Go ask him. Detective Chief Inspector Archibald Lawton. Fresh from the ranks of the retired Metropolitan Police detective corps. The Met's finest. Maybe he can do better, Bright." Hightower pivoted on his heels; Thorn and Bright watched him disappear into Belgrave Square accompanied by a low rumble of thunder.

"Well, that didn't end well," Thorn said. "I think he needs a nap, don't you?"

"Sorry about that, Conor. A bit embarrassing that."

"Ahh, forget it. Let's go talk to the detective chief inspector. Maybe he can brighten our day."

Thorn and Bright approached the ambulance as Clark strained to get to his feet.

"DCI Lawton, I'm Emily Bright. This is Conor Thorn. We're with . . . Allied intelligence," Bright said.

Lawton dusted off his knees and straightened his jacket. "That so? Well then, you can show me some identification to that fact, I'm sure."

Thorn and Bright flashed their identification to Lawton's begrudging satisfaction.

"I guess that will do. And what brings you here to this grisly scene?" Lawton's large, roundish eyes were supported by half-moon puffs of skin that complemented his sagging jowls. Thorn detected the strong scent of pipe tobacco.

"We came here hoping to talk with your victim," Thorn said.

"About what, may I ask?"

"Someone he was seen with recently," Bright said.

"And that would be?"

Bright looked at Thorn, who returned her look with a shrug.

"A French captain named Toulouse. Heard of him by chance?" asked Thorn while he stared at the body. The chest wound was still weeping blood.

"No. Not sure why I would. I don't even know this sorry bloke," Lawton said with a head toss toward Alba's body.

"Right. Well, can you share what you do know?" Thorn asked.

"You're an American. Knew some from my service in the Great War. Good chaps. Lost my best friend at the Somme. My right arm, I mean." Lawton motioned to the stretcher-bearers who began to load the body into the ambulance.

"DCI Lawton?" Bright prompted.

"Right. Our man here, he's been dead twelve to twenty-four hours. I'm not the expert on that. Have to get him back to the city morgue and have the doc look him over."

"How did he die?" Thorn asked.

"Bloke was impaled on the rear fence. Facedown."

"Pushed from the roof?" Thorn asked.

Lawton glanced at Thorn. "Mister . . . Thorn, was it? Pushed or . . . possibly thrown. The fence is too high for anyone to lift the body."

"You're saying he didn't jump?" Bright asked.

"It looks like he had help, meaning he was pushed or thrown. Probably a bit of both, as the fence is at least twenty meters from the base of the building."

"And nobody heard him scream or yell?" asked Thorn.

"Not possible."

"Why?" Thorn asked. *So this is what pulling teeth is like.*

Lawton stretched for the paper bag that sat in the rear of the ambulance and handed it to Bright. "Hold this, please, miss." Bright complied and Lawton reached in and pulled out a kerchief and what looked like a dark-colored sock. "Nobody heard anything because he had this stuffed in his mouth and his hands were tied."

Bright's jaw dropped.

Thorn shook his head. "I'll be damned," he muttered.

"As I said . . . grisly."

"What did you find in his shirt pocket?" Thorn asked.

"Ahh, yes. Something I hadn't seen in a while." Lawton reached into the bag again and retrieved a small wax-paper packet. Bright's eyes lit up. "Opium if I'm not mistaken."

Bright took the packet and opened it, then nodded. "You're correct, DCI Lawton—it's opium, in black-tar form. Just like we found before." The sky rumbled more loudly and a light rain began to fall. She closed the packet and returned it to the evidence bag.

"Well, thank you for confirming. Helpful, that is," Lawton said, taking the bag back.

Thorn looked up at the dark sky. Low clouds moved quickly northward. The rainfall became heavier. *What the fuck are we doing? Wasting our time chasing a drug dealer?*

#

When Elizabeth Nel showed a dejected-looking Winston Churchill into the ground-floor dining room, General Eisenhower was already seated at the table. A butler stood quietly alongside a serving cart holding two large dishes topped with silver cloches. Eisenhower stood as Churchill approached the table.

"Nel, a whisky, please. And bring the bottle." Churchill shook

Eisenhower's hand and took his seat. He signaled the butler to begin service, then waited for the man to leave before he continued. "General, I come from the underground Cabinet War Rooms. There, I experienced an enormously pleasant conversation with your president. He was absolutely thrilled to hear about the first day of Eleanor's visit to England."

Nel returned with a tray that held a glass, an ice bucket, and a bottle of Johnnie Walker Red. As soon as she placed it on the table, Churchill filled his glass. He swirled the whisky as Nel closed the door behind her.

"But I also experienced a somewhat disturbing briefing given by Emily Bright and your Conor Thorn. It seems they have uncovered some significantly damning information concerning the activities of a member of my cabinet."

"Your cabinet? Don't tell me. This isn't about Henry Longworth, is it?"

"I'm afraid so, Ike." Churchill polished off the whisky and placed the glass on the table, but he didn't let it go. "It appears that we may have been too quick in chastising them for ... questioning Henry."

"What exactly has Thorn briefed you on that has you so concerned?"

Churchill informed Eisenhower of the latest developments, including the use of the Vatican's diplomatic pouch.

"Do we have any idea what he has been passing along to this Heinz?"

"No. But members of the war cabinet are privy to a sizable amount of classified intelligence. Any of which, if communicated to this suspected informant, could be devastating on many levels." Churchill shakily refilled his glass, spilling some of the whisky onto the white linen tablecloth. "If the worst-case scenario concerning Longworth is true, the revelation that a selection of mine, to my own war cabinet, was consorting with a German informant would ... It would most assuredly shake my government to its core." Churchill's face flushed. "The king would be compelled to ask that the ruling party form another government. And that would put Allied efforts to finally and aggressively confront the Nazis behind schedule at least a year."

"Another government? Now? Is that possible?"

"Yes, General. As much as it sickens me, another government would need to be formed. On the eve of Operation Torch." Churchill buried his face in his hands. "After I tendered my resignation," he muttered, his voice beleaguered and weary.

CHAPTER THIRTY-SIX

0900 Hours, Thursday, October 15, 1942
Claridge's Hotel, Brook Street, London

How did Trout put it? It wasn't like her to just head out on her own. She was headstrong, but she played by the rules. Yeah, that's Maggie—headstrong.

Thorn stood next to a waist-high side table, his hand still resting on the handset of the hotel lobby phone, recalling the few details of his conversation with Bob Trout about Maggie's disappearance. The anxiety Thorn detected in Trout's voice rattled him and made him think that he had underreacted when he'd first learned of her absence. He needed to take action.

As he moved through the lobby toward the revolving doors, head down, he mulled over what steps he could take. When he emerged from the lobby of the hotel, the sound of the flags that jutted out from above the portico snapping in the crisp, spirited October air stole his attention. He leaned against the sandbags piled high near the entrance, seeking what little shelter there was from the stiff breeze. There were four cars parked in the front drive, none of which was the Buick Roadmaster Hollis and Bright had ridden in. Dressed in a thin, warm-weather suit, Thorn decided to retreat to the lobby to wait for them. No sooner had he turned to do so than he spotted Quinn Montgomery emerging from one of the cars that was parked in front of the hotel. *What the hell is this guy doing here?*

As Montgomery approached, Thorn could see that the man's face was distended on one side and his left eye looked like it was sitting on a dark-purple sack of flesh.

"I have a message for you," Montgomery said, his tone past ninety percent on the threat meter.

"Whoa. Looks like you walked into a wall, Montgomery. Or maybe someone's fist?"

Montgomery's jaw muscles tightened. "It's from Mr. Henry Longworth." Montgomery handed him a small envelope with "Mr. Thorn" scrawled across it in black ink, the letters of his name formed by a broad-tipped fountain pen guided by a shaky hand.

"So how is Uncle Henry? Still a prickly bastard?" Thorn opened the note and read its brief message. "Ahh, an invitation to a meeting today." Thorn looked up at Montgomery. "But no reason is given. So what gives, Montgomery?"

"Just be there and don't be late."

"Or what?" Thorn asked, now well beyond annoyed.

Montgomery snorted and looked away. "You Yanks—all of you too big for ya boots." He turned back to Thorn. "Just don't keep Mr. Longworth waiting. He's a busy man."

Thorn gave Montgomery an exaggerated nod. "By the way, shouldn't you be up at Coastal Command, doing your part to win the war?"

"I'm on leave."

"Lucky boy," Thorn said.

"Bloody wanker," Montgomery mumbled, turning back toward his sedan. He got behind the wheel, and as he pulled away from the curb, he stared Thorn down.

Thorn walked back to the sandbags. Thoughts of meeting Longworth collided with those of his missing sister. *What is Longworth up to? What does he want from me? And where the hell is Maggie?*

A blaring horn jolted him from his trance. The Buick Roadmaster sat in the drive with Hollis waving her arm frantically out an open window. Thorn raised his finger to signal he saw her, then took out his notebook and jotted down Trout's phone number and a message asking him to check Maggie's room at the Savoy and then contact him at Colonel Donovan's office with anything of interest.

He stepped toward a waiting doorman who stood stoically near the curb, his long greatcoat flapping in the breeze.

"Hey, buddy, a favor for a friend?"

The doorman, pushing sixty, turned on his heels, exhibiting a broad smile. "My pleasure, sir. What'll it be?"

Thorn handed him the note. "Please call this number and give this message to a Mr. Trout. Can you do that for me?"

"A message for Mr. Trout. Like the fish. No problem, sir. Consider it done."

Thorn handed the doorman a pound note and headed for the waiting Buick. "Much appreciated."

The doorman beamed with satisfaction. "Anything for a Yank!"

Thorn hurried over to the car to open the driver's side door for Hollis. "I brought the newspaper for you to read."

"Why, thank you, Mr. Thorn," Hollis said as she slipped into the backseat and settled in.

"Good morning, Conor," Bright said, her voice wispy.

Thorn slid behind the wheel and looked over at her. His heart sank. Her eyes were puffy, and she held Nel's handkerchief.

"How did you sleep last night?" he asked.

"Sporadically at best. Thanks for asking." Bright quietly cleared her throat and took a deep breath. "So, what were you so deep in thought about?"

"Well, it has been an interesting morning to say the least." Thorn shut down the idling engine and shifted in his seat to face her.

"Oh, really? Please explain," Bright said.

"I put a call in to Bob Trout, the reporter for CBS. Just to check on Maggie. He tells me there's been no sign of her since Monday. Not a word from her."

"That's deeply troubling," she said. "Who does she know here in London?"

"As far as I know, no one," Thorn said. "Trout should be getting a message from me soon asking him to check her room at the Savoy for anything out of the ordinary."

"It's been over two days now. I think it's time to file a missing-persons report with the Metropolitan Police. I'll do that after we meet with Cardinal Massy."

Thorn shook his head vigorously. "Nope. I mean, OK to the report, but we can't meet with Massy this morning. Maybe this afternoon."

"Why? What changed?"

Thorn gripped the steering wheel and looked in the rearview mirror. Hollis's head was buried in the newspaper. "The other thing that made it an interesting morning. While waiting for you, I received a message from none other than Longworth delivered by his loyal nephew."

Bright perked up and put away the handkerchief. "Go on."

"He wants to meet with us today," Thorn said, looking at his watch, "in a little more than an hour from now, at his home. And before you ask, no reason was given."

Bright looked out the windshield and chewed on her lower lip. "What do you think that's about?"

"I was hoping you could tell me. You know the man."

"I haven't the slightest. But it may be more informative than our planned talk with Cardinal Massy."

Thorn began slowly drumming out a beat on the Roadmaster's steering wheel, lost in thought.

"What is it?" she asked.

"I have an uneasy feeling about this, especially after what we saw at Paddington Station. This guy is up to his eyeballs in something bad. We shook him up, and people who have been spooked can be unpredictable."

"I think your mind is racing too fast. He's a cabinet member and a longtime friend and confidant of the prime minister."

Thorn turned the engine over and put the car into gear. "Longtime friends and confidants can change their tune . . . if they're not getting their way," he said as he popped the clutch and shifted smoothly through the gears down Brook Street. "I need to get to Donovan right away." He glanced at his watch. "I need some help with my backup plan."

Bright shot Thorn a curious stare.

"I don't trust the bastard." *And neither should you.*

She put her hand on the dashboard to steady herself as the Buick darted in and out of traffic.

Ten minutes later, Thorn pulled up to 70 Grosvenor Street. He jerked the parking brake on as the sedan was still moving; the Buick lurched to a halt. Thorn was first out of the sedan, leading Bright to the front entrance. As they were about to open the door, David Bruce burst through, briefcase in one hand and struggling to put on his trench coat.

"Thorn! What are you doing here?" Bruce asked as if he had just discovered a thief in his home. "We weren't supposed to meet today."

"I know, Colonel. But I need to see Colonel Donovan. It's extremely urgent."

Bruce shook his head. "Sorry, can't be done. He's on his way to Casablanca." He looked at his watch. "And I'm running late for a meeting at Broadway."

"Then I . . . we have to brief you. It's about Longworth."

Bruce ran his hand through his hair and deliberated. "OK, let's get off the sidewalk."

Three minutes later, Thorn and Bright sat in Bruce's office on the third floor. Thorn took note of the amount of antique furniture in the spacious room and formal paintings mounted in ornate frames that adorned the walls. It wasn't the office of a spy.

Bruce sat behind his desk but kept his coat on. "So, what's so urgent?" he asked, pulling a pack of Camels from his breast pocket and shaking free a cigarette.

"I'll get to the point. I received a message from Longworth less than an hour ago. He wants to meet with us. We don't know why, but he has no other reason to see us than our questioning of his nephew, the one who had been seen in the film lab in the days before the diary page was reported missing."

Bright raised her right hand to stop Bruce. "Colonel, in a briefing two days ago, Prime Minster Churchill told both of us to pursue the Longworth connection with all due haste, which is what we must do, given this development."

"The point is, this smells like a setup," Thorn added. "I haven't forgotten that after we met with the nephew, we got shot at."

"So why go? It makes no sense."

"Why?" Thorn sat back and took a deep breath. "Because the clock is ticking on the launch of the task forces." Thorn let that sink in. "I have a backup plan, in case this meeting is what I think it could be."

"Explain."

Thorn sensed he might have hooked Bruce. "First, I drive us to Longworth's house, leaving our driver behind, just in case. Second, we each need a weapon. We can't go in unarmed. I should have asked a while ago. Third and most important, I want a team of two agents to be outside the house when we go in. We'll be early, and so should the team, so we can coordinate. If we don't come out in, say, thirty minutes, they kick the door in. If we need more time, I'll signal the team to stay put for another thirty minutes."

Bruce sat silently for several moments, his elbows on the desktop, his chin resting on his clasped hands. "I'm surprised you aren't planning on busting in as if you were Errol Flynn and swashbuckling your way through like you did in Tangier."

Thorn glared at Bruce and said nothing.

Bruce blinked first. "OK, I can take care of the weapons. But it will take me a little time to round up a backup team. They'll have to meet you there." He reached for a notebook and a fountain pen. "What's the address?"

Thorn took the message from his breast pocket and read the address to Bruce. As Bruce was writing it down, his phone rang, startling him. He picked up the handset and said, "No calls, Joan," and hung up. He finished scribbling the address.

Thorn looked at Bright and capped a smile with a wink. Bright nodded.

"Get down to the basement armory and get outfitted with some hardware. I'll get a couple of agents to Longworth's home."

#

The walls of the basement armory sweated. The building's boiler was located in an adjacent room, and it kept the basement warm and humid. A gray-haired man with the sleeves of his dingy-white shirt rolled up to his elbows laid out two 1911 Colt .45 caliber automatic pistols for Thorn to inspect and several different types of smaller guns for Bright. The armorer stood there and wiped his oily hands on an apron.

Thorn played with the slides on each. "One of these will work. What about some mags?"

"How many are we talking about?" the man asked.

Thorn took a rag from the counter and wiped down one of the Colt's grips. "For now, three should do it."

Bright handed a Walther PPK to the man. "This one will do."

"OK, I'll get some magazines and be right back."

As Thorn continued to play with one of the .45s, Bruce's secretary, Joan, appeared, out of breath, her blouse untucked. "Here you are . . . My, it's hot down here."

"What is it?" Thorn asked as the armorer came back and laid the magazines on the counter.

"Colonel Donovan's office received this message for you. They sent it over to me since you were meeting with Mr. Bruce." Joan handed a folded note to Thorn, who tucked the Colt into his waistband. "I'm so glad I caught you."

"Thanks, Joan."

Thorn read the message as Joan left the basement. "Shit."

"What is it?" Bright asked.

"It's from Trout. He checked Maggie's room at the Savoy. He found nothing unusual except an invitation to a dinner this past Monday at a place called Oddendino's." He crumpled up the message and tossed it in a wastebasket. "So the night before Roosevelt's arrival, she was at a dinner thrown by Churchill's wife. What the hell happened at that dinner?" He looked at his watch and shook his head. "We're running out of time. We need to get to Longworth's."

Thorn led the way out of the basement, taking two steps at a time. *Maggie, where the hell are you?*

CHAPTER THIRTY-SEVEN

1040 Hours, Thursday, October 15, 1942
No. 28 Queen Anne's Gate, London

Thorn and Bright parked several doors down from No. 28. They were twenty minutes early, giving them some time to coordinate with the backup team. He was nervously looking out his side and rearview mirrors for that very team. Bright peeked at her watch for the second time.

"Well, well, would you look at that?" Thorn was the first to spot Toulouse heading down Queen Anne's Gate toward them and No. 28. Dressed in dark-colored civilian clothes, he was walking at a brisk pace. Two steps behind him and to the side was the Asian woman from the Spanish embassy.

"Not who I expected to see," Bright said, sliding down farther into her seat. "What's your guess as to why he's in the vicinity?"

"Could only be two reasons. Our drug-dealing murder suspect is here to collect from Montgomery, assuming he's inside with Longworth, or to make a delivery. Maybe both. But, even from this distance, he doesn't look too happy."

Toulouse stopped suddenly and turned around as the Asian woman caught up to him. He flicked a cigarette into the street. Thorn saw the woman's mouth move rapidly. She reached out and shoved him backward. Toulouse responded with a backhanded slap to her face. The force of it caused her to stumble.

"Good God," Bright said. "He's such a brute. Should we do—"

"Nothing. Not now."

The woman regained her composure and dabbed at the corner of her mouth with the tips of her fingers. She examined her fingers, then, without looking at him, turned and walked away from Toulouse and No. 28.

"There's more to that lover's spat than we know," Thorn said.

An indifferent-looking Toulouse turned and headed toward No. 28. Reaching the front door, he ignored the brass doorknocker and banged on the door with a fist. The door opened slowly, creating a narrow opening of several inches. Toulouse shouldered the door open and went in.

Thorn looked at his watch. "Eight minutes to the hour. That team should be here by now." He pounded the steering wheel with his fist, which made Bright flinch. "Jesus, Bruce had one job—to get the backup team here early so we could brief them." He pulled out his 1911A1. He pulled back the slide and released it, letting it click back into place. Seconds later, a single gunshot rang out.

"Son . . . of . . . a . . . bitch," Thorn said. "Damn it! We can't wait any longer. We've got to get in there."

"Conor, let's leave. There's no backup team in sight—this just doesn't feel right."

"No, we can't. Not now. Listen, the task forces sail ten days from today. If I'm wrong and this Longworth lead points to nothing but a drug ring, then we're back to square one. And if that happens, we need as much time as possible to regroup." Thorn's adrenaline was pumping. He grabbed her forearm. "You OK?"

"I . . . Yes, I believe so." Her voice trembled.

"Then let's go." *Don't worry. I won't let anything happen to you.* Thorn released his hold on her arm.

#

The heavy pounding on the front door startled Longworth. He looked at his watch. It was too early for Thorn and Bright.

"Quinn, get rid of whoever that is. Thorn and Bright will be here any minute."

Quinn rose and went into the foyer, followed by Longworth.

He opened the door slowly and only a few inches. His jaw dropped, but before words could form, the door flew open and crashed into the wall. The man slammed the door shut while grabbing Quinn by the throat and pinning him against the wall. Longworth retreated several steps back into the study.

"Hello there, Quinn." Toulouse's eyes bugged. "Such a surprise to see you here. But you look terrible. Like you've been in a fight—on the wrong end of it."

Quinn began to struggle, prompting the man to draw a gun and fire it into the plaster wall just inches from Quinn's left ear, ceasing Quinn's efforts to free himself. The gunshot echoed.

Longworth stood in the doorway to the study. "Take your hands off him. Don't you know who I am?"

"Pfft. Of course. I'm with the Free French Intelligence. I know all I need to know about you, Henry Longworth." Toulouse released his grip on Montgomery, who immediately crumpled to the floor, his hand cupping his ear. "You're a cabinet minister and a man with some wealth, no doubt."

"Who are you and what is it you want?"

"I am Toulouse. Your nephew here owes me three hundred thirty quid, which I have been waiting too long for, so I've come to his banker. Believe me when I say that I'm not leaving without my money. Now where is it?"

Longworth looked at his watch. Five minutes to the hour. The lout before him was fixated on money—a fixation he would use to co-opt his services. "That much money . . . I don't have it. Not here."

"That's . . . unfortunate. It seems that I—"

"I will double what Quinn owes you."

Quinn's mouth opened, forming a perfect circle.

Toulouse registered no reaction.

"I will pay you seven hundred pounds. That's over—"

"I'm not stupid, old man." Longworth stole a glance at his watch. "When do I get it?"

"After you help me with a personal matter."

"Go on."

Longworth needed to quickly reel in his catch, one that would make dealing with Thorn and Bright that much easier. "Two people will be arriving here in a matter of minutes. They . . . have created much trouble for me, and they must be . . . I must put a stop to it."

"Ahh. A man of action, you are. I'm surprised. Not an English gentleman at all, are we?"

"Enough. Do we have an agreement or not?"

"Just who are your guests?" The study's clock chimed softly, announcing the eleven o'clock hour.

"Investigators . . . a man called Thorn and a woman. Bright's her name."

"I know these people. They are looking for something to do with the American film lab. Is this right?" Toulouse pulled his hand from his pocket.

"Yes," Quinn said.

"Shut up, Quinn."

Toulouse studied both Longworth and Quinn for a long moment.

"Will you assist us or not? If you don't, you must leave and come back later."

"No, no, no. I trust no one. Especially Englishmen. Even less when they're related to a lowlife like him," Toulouse said, tilting his head toward Quinn. "I will help you—I despise that American— for one thousand quid."

"Agreed. For your help and . . . your silence."

"Agreed."

Whether Toulouse agreed to and actually followed his terms didn't concern Longworth. He would personally ensure the man's silence later.

#

Thorn and Bright stood on the doorstep of No. 28. Thorn gave one last look up and down the street for any sign of the backup team. He shook his head.

"Here we go, and don't worry—I'll watch your back," he said, as he lifted the knocker and let it drop. He could hear it echo inside the home.

"Come in, Miss Bright, Mr. Thorn." Longworth stood beside the open door, his arm extended in greeting, his other hand stuffed in his suit coat pocket. "Come in, come in."

Thorn and Bright walked past the surprisingly chipper Longworth.

"Thank you, sir. I apologize for being late," Bright said.

Thorn saw the bullet hole in the wall as he walked by Longworth. *Where's the Frenchman?*

"We heard a gunshot. What was that about?" asked Thorn.

"Just an accident. I'll explain. Let's get comfortable in the study, shall we? Right through there." Longworth pointed the way through an oak pocket door. Bright took the first steps toward the study door; Thorn followed close behind.

Bright turned toward the sunlit end of the room, and as soon as Thorn entered the study, he spied a figure that had emerged from the darker side. The man grunted as he brought his raised arms down and smashed a weapon on the back of Bright's head. She crumpled to the floor.

"Emily!" Thorn yelled. He threw his body at the attacker before he could raise his arms again, but Thorn never made it that far. One step into his attack, Thorn was grabbed from behind, two arms wrapped tightly around his neck; the foul odor of cigarettes filled his nostrils. The weight of a body on his back forced him to the floor, his arms tangled beneath him. The hard landing drove the air from his lungs. He tried to take a breath, but the grip around his neck kept his lungs from expanding. The weight on his back reminded him of the late-night competitions in Bancroft Hall to see who could do the most push-ups with their roommate on their back. He just needed one this time.

Thorn untangled his arms and fired off. The body on his back bounced off once his elbows locked, but the arms around his neck tightened their hold. As he pulled his knees under him, he felt a hard kick to his ribs. He strained to turn his head, to look where he'd seen Emily fall. It was then he saw Montgomery sitting astride her body. The hold around Thorn's neck tightened, followed by a harder kick. The little air that was in his lungs escaped.

I'll watch your back. That's what I told her. A lot of talk and no action. I'm so sorry, Emily.

"Let him up, Toulouse." Thorn saw Longworth move into view, a German Luger trained on him. Montgomery stood and hovered over Emily's body.

Toulouse released his hold and jumped to his feet, pulling a small pistol from his coat pocket. His face was red from exertion; his forehead glistened with sweat.

"You fucking bastards," Thorn said, his voice raspy.

"Search him," Longworth barked. Montgomery approached Thorn, knelt, and ran his hands up and down Thorn's body. Thorn winced when Montgomery's hands slid over his rib cage. He pulled the Colt from Thorn's waistband, then tossed the gun to Longworth, who dumped it in his suit coat pocket.

"Thorn, sit in that chair," Longworth said, pointing to a wooden chair with his pistol. Thorn moved slowly to the chair and sat. Montgomery searched Emily's prone body and produced her PPK, which he pocketed, then began the process of gagging her and tying her hands and feet.

"Help him, Toulouse. And make sure the hands and feet are bound tight," Longworth said.

"He's doing just fine. I'll watch. Just like you," Toulouse said, his breathing labored.

Montgomery finished with Emily and turned to Thorn and began to tie his feet.

"So you *are* the leak. No, that's not really accurate, is it? You're a traitor, working inside the cabinet."

Longworth's jaws clenched.

Toulouse's eyes bore into Longworth. "What did he say? You're working for the Germans? Or is it the Russians?"

"Stay out of this. You'll get your money," Longworth said.

"Oh, you can be assured I will. But maybe now it will have to be double our agreed amount."

"Is that what this is all about, Longworth? Money?" asked Thorn.

"There is no time now to explain everything. But there will be time later. Come on, come on, Quinn. Get a move on, and shut this man up."

"My pleasure." Montgomery pulled a white cloth from his shirt pocket. As the gag was being set, Thorn smelled, then tasted furniture wax on the tattered cloth. The fumes were overpowering. He heard Montgomery's labored breathing as he finished with the gag and then moved to tie Thorn's hands and feet. Toulouse lurked in the corner of the room, his arms crossed, gun in one hand. The man smirked—it was the same smirk Thorn had seen when he'd first questioned the man.

Thorn looked down at Emily's bound-and-gagged body. Blood had pooled around her head and seeped into the rug.

I failed you, Emily. But that won't happen again.

"Toulouse, move them to the back of the house. And, Quinn, you get rid of their car. Park it a block or so away from MI6 and leave it."

Thorn could hear Longworth speaking, but the words were nothing but a buzzing in his head. His eyes were locked on Emily. He tried to break his gaze from her, but he couldn't. Another example of his failed attempt to protect someone lay on the floor before him, bloodied and unconscious. He fought to stop his trance; he needed to focus on what they were doing and saying. He needed to spot their mistakes and weaknesses. He needed to save Emily.

Montgomery nodded and searched Thorn's pockets for the keys. "When you get back here, you and Toulouse dump the three of them into the trunk of the car, along with that rug," Longworth said.

Three? What other sorry-ass guy fucked up like me?

"I'll move the Rover to the rear door, so no one will see you load them in."

Longworth stepped toward Thorn and crouched down to look into his eyes. "And make sure you put in the shovels. We'll put them to work digging their final resting places."

Longworth turned and left the study, Toulouse giving him a deliberate nod of approval.

Montgomery followed Longworth into the front hall. Toulouse pocketed his gun and stood with the toes of his shoes nearly touching Emily's shoulders. He bent over her body and shoved his hands under her arms to lift her. He struggled with his grip, and as he lifted her, he fumbled and she crashed to the floor again.

Thorn roared a string of profanities, all stifled by the stinking gag. He lunged forward in his chair, tipping it in Toulouse's direction, landing a head butt in Toulouse's rib cage before falling to the floor.

Toulouse grunted as he dropped. "Fuck . . . you," he hissed, not able to give full voice to his words.

Thorn, lying on his side, watched Toulouse snag a smallish bat-shaped cudgel from the floor near Emily. Toulouse's eyes bulged and nostrils flared. A thin rivulet of saliva ran down his chin. He raised the bat over his head with both hands and lowered it in a fierce motion toward Thorn's head.

Before the blow landed, Thorn felt a brief waft of air on his sweaty face caused by Toulouse's arms as they moved swiftly toward him.

CHAPTER THIRTY-EIGHT

1400 Hours, Thursday, October 15, 1942
Wooded Area Near Whitchurch Airport, Bristol

When Thorn regained consciousness, the pounding inside his head confirmed that he had fucked up. *I let my guard down, and it cost us.*

He sensed he was in a vehicle; there was the muffled sound of an engine, and the vehicle bounced and swayed. His mouth was dry and his jaw ached from the gag. His body was stiff.

How long have I been tied up? Where the hell is Emily? His hands, bound behind his back, throbbed from a restricted blood flow. His feet were numb. His sense of smell was not affected though, as the combination of the odor of gasoline and the stink of damp, moldy canvas was overpowering. He lay on his left side, and there was something covering him. Using his right shoulder and his bound feet, he gradually knocked it off. When that was accomplished, the smell of petrol became stronger. It also helped him see, as a few slivers of light seeped in from around the edges of what appeared to be a trunk lid, where the rubber seals had begun to rot.

As his eyes adjusted, he made out Emily, lying on her right side. She was facing him with her eyes closed, her hair covering the upper portion of her face. Her arms were pulled behind her back. His relief at seeing her soon changed to fear, as it was impossible to tell if she was still breathing. Thorn struggled to confirm her condition, bringing his knees up to his chest and nudging her once and then again.

He breathed a sigh of relief when she stirred and began to open her eyes. Thorn's mouth fought to form a smile, straining against the gag. *Stay with me, Emily. We're not done yet.*

He nodded at her. All she could do was look at him, her eyes barely open. Her eyelids fluttered, then closed. He decided to let her rest.

#

It had been close to forty-five minutes since Thorn woke. The car was traveling over rough roads, as evidenced by the bouncing the car was doing. Something hard and sharp poked him in his side. He groped with his restricted hands and found a pole. He could only move his hands a few inches down the shaft, where he touched smooth, cool metal. *Well, they didn't forget the shovels.*

He shifted his body in order to use the edge of the shovel to saw at the material that bound his hands. He grunted through the gag as he pushed himself to free his hands, ignoring the numbness creeping into his left side. *If I don't get my hands free, we're not going to make it.*

The car slowed and jerked to a full stop. Thorn had run out of time, but he managed to get in a few more high-pressure strokes on the edge of the shovel before the engine switched off; then Thorn heard Longworth shout instructions. He shifted to his right side.

"Untie their feet, then walk them up into the tree line. If they're still out, we'll have to drag them. And here, take these," Longworth said.

Thorn heard two doors open, then slam shut. An instant later, he heard a third door open.

"Come on, you bitch. You're comin' with me," Montgomery said between grunts.

The third door slammed shut. "Here. Open it." More instructions from Longworth. A moment later, a key was inserted into the trunk's lock. As the lid was raised, afternoon sun flooded in and blinded Thorn. He could make out three shadowy forms, their features obscured by the sun's strong backlight. While his eyes adjusted, Montgomery reached in and untied his feet, then reached over Thorn and untied Emily's. Montgomery shifted his attention to Emily's face. He hovered over Thorn, sweat dripping from his chin onto Thorn's cheek, which then ran into his mouth. Montgomery slapped Emily's cheek three times to get a rise out of her.

When Emily began to stir, Montgomery backed away from the trunk. Thorn made out Longworth, his Luger in his right hand, and Toulouse, standing a step behind Longworth and holding his own gun at his side. *That's two guns. There're two more. Longworth gave something to someone. What? And to whom?*

Cracking and popping sounds emanated from under the car as the engine began to cool. A slight breeze dispersed the smell of petrol, leaving only the odor of furniture polish from Thorn's gag to fill his nostrils.

"Thorn's awake. So is she," Montgomery said, wiping sweat from his forehead with his coat sleeve.

"Then get on with it," Longworth said.

Montgomery grabbed Thorn's belt and wrapped an arm around his neck, then yanked him out of the trunk and dropped him on the ground facedown. All Thorn could see were Longworth's black shoes, not more than two feet from his face. He struggled to get his knees pulled under his body, pushed off the ground with his forehead, and then he eased his upper body to an erect position. On his knees, his hands still bound tightly and the gag still in place, he saw another body on the ground: Maggie, bound and gagged.

Relief took seconds to collide with boiling rage. His breathing ramped up. Longworth had attacked not just him and Emily, but also an innocent member of his family. Someone he loved dearly.

Maggie was five feet away on her back, her head turned toward Thorn. She blinked, releasing tears that streaked down the side of her face. Her long, wavy, red hair was a tangled mess. One side of her face showed signs of bruising.

His gaze zeroed in on Montgomery, then Longworth, who smiled.

I swear to God, you'll fucking pay for this.

And for a moment—at least that—he fully believed he would. And he did his best to hold on to that feeling, because it was that, that would get him through this.

Toulouse spotted Thorn looking intently at Maggie. He walked over to her and crouched, his eyes never leaving Thorn as he began stroking Maggie's hair. She pulled as far away as she could; emphatic but garbled words carried on the light breeze. Toulouse swiped a hand at Maggie's head, snared a handful of her hair, and yanked her back toward him, lifting her off the ground. She screeched. Toulouse looked back at Thorn, who made no effort to hide his seething hatred. Toulouse snorted and released his grip, and Maggie fell back to the ground. Muttering something in French, Toulouse returned to a position behind Longworth.

Stand in line, you French motherfucker.

Thorn scanned his surroundings. They were in a secluded area, parked on the edge of thick woods.

"Get Bright, Quinn," Longworth ordered.

Montgomery bent over, reached into the back of the trunk, then wrapped his arms around her waist and hauled her out. When he planted her on her feet, her stance was unsteady. Her auburn hair still covered her forehead and eyes, and when she tossed her head back, uncovering her gaze, it darted about. It was clear she was in shock. Then her eyes fell on Maggie's prone body. She stared for several moments, then looked at Thorn. Her eyes locked on him in a harsh squint.

Montgomery untied the bindings around Maggie's feet, then grabbed her around her waist and helped her stand. But once she was on her feet, he didn't let go; his hands slid up toward her breasts. She forcefully twisted her shoulders to free herself, and Montgomery stepped back, grinning. Then Maggie let loose with a sharp kick that landed deep in his groin, dropping Montgomery to his knees. Thorn's smile was short-circuited by his gag.

Toulouse cackled loudly, his head thrown back, thoroughly exposing a pointed Adam's apple dancing up and down his throat.

Longworth fired a round into the dirt inches away from Maggie's feet. "I'd kill you all now, but we have to take a little walk first." He walked over to Montgomery and bent down toward his face. Thorn's view was blocked, but when Longworth rose, Montgomery was nodding.

As Longworth held the Luger on them, Montgomery hobbled to the car, pulled two shovels and a pickax from the trunk, and slammed it shut. He then pulled Thorn's Colt from his coat pocket. Thorn knew one thing—graves were to be dug. Their graves. *And that means hands have to be untied. But if they expect me to pull anything, it will be once my hands are freed, so I need to make a move sooner.*

"Get going," Longworth said, waving his Luger toward a narrow dirt path that led into a forest of elm and oak trees. They walked for several minutes, Montgomery in the lead, Emily and Maggie in front of Thorn, followed by Longworth, with Toulouse pulling up the rear. As they continued their march, the path sharply inclined. Trudging along, Thorn continued to consider the timing of his move.

He turned to look at Longworth and noted the man was breathing heavily. They began a slow descent into a shallow gully as the growing wind whistled through the tree branches and triggered a shower of leaves. The path leveled out as it entered the gully, which was boxed in on three sides by tall limestone formations. Montgomery stopped near the base of the far wall and dropped the tools, then circled Maggie, Emily, and Thorn as they entered the gully, stopping at the base of the far wall. Near them were the remnants of a campfire; rimmed with small rocks, a charred tree branch that hadn't burned through laid half-buried in ash. Thorn moved to a position between Maggie and Emily and nodded to Emily. She blinked several times and nodded back. Thorn turned toward Longworth and grunted loudly to get his attention. Thorn sent a confusing message by gesturing wildly with his bound hands, pointing at Emily and Maggie, then himself.

"Go ahead, take their gags off. We're too deep for anyone to hear them," Longworth said.

"Don't. You're asking for trouble," Toulouse said as he leaned against a small rock outcropping several feet from the group.

Longworth nodded at Montgomery, who took off Emily's gag first, followed by Maggie's, then Thorn's. Thorn worked his jaw in a circular motion, and it didn't take long for Maggie to summon the saliva to spit at Montgomery. She missed, but it didn't seem to bother her. And it didn't bother Toulouse either, who failed at stifling a laugh.

"This isn't over, you pig," Maggie snarled. Montgomery, Thorn's Colt in his hand, made a move toward Maggie.

"Quinn, not now!" Longworth yelled.

Thorn smiled at his sister's penchant for standing up for herself. "Maggie, you OK?" he asked.

Maggie, still looking intently at Montgomery, clenched her jaw, then turned her head slowly to Thorn. "Much better, but there's room for improvement. Any chance you know what the hell is going on here?"

Thorn shuffled his feet. Longworth didn't see Emily inch away from Thorn. "Well, that's quite a story, isn't it, Longworth? Emily and I have most of it, but maybe you can fill in some details?" he said, noticing that Toulouse was making his way toward them, his pistol dangling at his side. "As for you, Maggie, I'm not sure why you're here."

He said "take these" earlier. The two guns? Who has the PPK?

"Oh, I'd be glad to tell you, Thorn. You see, it's quite simple really. At first, I took her to merely knock you off your guard, to slow you down. But as you persisted, I decided it would be so much more satisfying to make you watch as I killed her."

Thorn's entire body tensed, and his spine became rigid.

Longworth smiled.

You prick. Time to knock you off your guard and onto your ass. "I can't begin to tell you how happy I am right this minute," Thorn boasted.

"What are you talking about?" Longworth asked. "Do you think I'm naïve enough to fall for your bravado as we prepare to kill you all?" He said it mockingly, but Thorn saw a hint of fear. The man may have been a traitor for a long time, but he looked unsure of himself. He operated in offices and cabinet meeting rooms. Snatching intelligence agents was new territory for him. He couldn't be entirely sure that Thorn didn't have something up his sleeve.

Montgomery was aggressive, closing the distance on Maggie, his arms dangling in front of him, the Colt in his right hand.

"Emily will tell you that Colonel Donovan, among others, didn't believe me when I said that you had something to hide. 'Oh, no. Not Henry Longworth. Longtime friend of the prime minister's. A member of his cabinet. You're crazy, Thorn,' they said. Well, I can't wait to see their faces when I get back to London and tell them all about our trip to the English countryside."

Longworth took several steps closer to Thorn, the Luger trained on Thorn's chest. Toulouse, a short step behind Longworth, matched Longworth's strides but drew closer to Emily.

"You cocky bastard," Longworth said. "To think that you will live past this day is a testament to your American arrogance." But Thorn still saw the slight doubt in the man's eyes.

"And stupidity," Toulouse added.

"Oh please," Thorn said, warming to his approach. "That the best you two morons can do? I've been called worse and by my own family, right, Maggie?" he said, turning to look at his sister. He winked before turning back to Longworth. "But I'm dying to know, Longworth—how is Bishop Heinz feeling these days? Someone at MI6 thinks he's not doing so well. He is alive, isn't he?"

Longworth didn't make an effort to hide his shock. He opened his mouth to speak but stopped, looked briefly at Emily, then back to Thorn. "I don't know what you are talking about."

"We found out about Heinz. So—"

"How long have you been passing information to Heinz? To the Germans?" Emily asked through a clenched jaw, her voice low and controlled.

Thorn could see that she was seething.

"Shut up. You're no different than Churchill and his other minions." Longworth inched toward Emily, waving the Luger back and forth as he spoke, spittle shooting from his mouth. "All of you refuse to realize England's true adversary. So myopic that you can't fathom that Stalin and the savages that put him in power will turn on us the moment he sees the time has come—unless the Germans are allowed to continue their offensive undeterred by a second front."

Stalin? This guy is crazy. Fleming was right. He does want to blow up Operation Torch. Thorn threw his head back as he was hit with an epiphany. "*You* have the diary page," he said slowly, stressing each word. He looked at Emily. "He has the page. Do you believe that?"

Toulouse's gun arm dropped. "What did you say?" He was looking at Thorn and then he suddenly grabbed Longworth's upper left arm and spun him around, causing him to nearly lose his balance. "You have the document? It was you that bought the document from that bitch and then killed her?"

Longworth attempted to retrain his focus on Thorn, but Toulouse's outburst was making it difficult. Longworth looked rattled. "I don't know what you're talking about. I didn't kill any bitch. Not yet. Now please shut up."

Toulouse stood down, but Thorn was as confused by his reaction as Longworth was. The missing diary page was a valuable commodity. In the hands of someone who hated the Brits and the Americans, it could go far in helping them seek a measure of revenge, not to mention putting some money in someone's pocket. *Time to plow that field and see what sprouts up.*

"So, Toulouse, Longworth's left you in the dark. Not fully a part of his plan possibly. Maybe you won't make it out of the woods either." Thorn turned back to Longworth. "How the hell you pulled off getting your hands on it is a mystery. But another thing I can't figure out, at least for now, is what the hell you're going to do with it…or maybe you've already sent it to Heinz through the cathedral's diplomatic pouch."

Longworth couldn't suppress a smirk, which told Thorn he was headed in the right direction.

"No, Thorn. I still have it. And when I put it directly into the hands of the Abwehr, Operation Torch, its element of surprise destroyed, will have to be canceled; otherwise, it would be doomed to be a bloody failure," Longworth said, his voice growing louder as he spoke. He continued to bounce the Luger around like a metronome.

"So you're just going to hand it over, a gift for Hitler." It wasn't a question the way Thorn said it.

"Yes, that's right. With no second front to be concerned with, the Germans can continue their valiant struggle against Stalin, against the spread of communism." Longworth was becoming red-faced; a vein in his neck bulged. He stepped within a foot of Thorn just as Toulouse sprang toward the man.

"Don't!" yelled Montgomery.

Longworth turned in time to block Toulouse's attempt to pistol-whip him. Toulouse, denied his revenge on Longworth, backed away a step.

"You're just going to give it to the Germans? Don't you know what it's worth to them? What it's worth to—"

Longworth's hand shook, but the short distance between him and Toulouse made it easy to place a round in Toulouse's gut. The Frenchman fell back, landing in the fire pit, his arms and legs spread wide, making an *X* in the dirt. The pungent smell of discharged gunpowder drifted on the wind, mixing with the billowing ashes.

"Then there were two," Thorn said.

"He served a purpose."

"So where were we? Oh yes, the Germans and their valiant struggle, Stalin the bad guy. Do go on," Thorn said.

Longworth reclaimed his position within inches of Thorn's face. "You are too smug for your own good. You have no idea that one day, all of Britain, America, and Europe will thank me for saving them from the clutches of that savage." Longworth's spittle hit Thorn's face. "Have you ever been tortured, Thorn?"

One more step, Longworth. Just one.

"What do you know about torture, you pampered traitor?" Thorn said, firmly setting the hook.

Longworth took one more step. "You bloody, miserable bugger. At the hands of communists, I—"

It took less than a second for Thorn's head butt to land on the bridge of Longworth's nose. Longworth grunted in pain as his cartilage snapped. Blood gushed from his disfigured face, and the Luger fell to the ground. Longworth's head slumped forward, his hands cradling his nose as his knees buckled. Thorn's raised knee met Longworth's face on the way to the ground.

Thorn, adrenaline pumping, lunged at the slow-reacting Montgomery, landing a cross-body block on his midsection, knocking the wind from the man's lungs and sending him to the ground. Montgomery landed on his back, gasping for air. The Colt flew from his hand, landing in nearby low brush. Maggie saw her chance and planted another swift kick in the man's groin but lost her balance, tumbling to the ground into a pile of leaves.

Montgomery, holding his groin with both hands, rolled over to his side. Thorn grunted as he snapped the partially slashed rope binding his hands, grabbed a shovel, and, with a home run swing, drove the side of the shovel's blade hard and fast into

GLENN DYER

Montgomery's neck. The shovel sliced deep, and blood spurted in rhythm with his heartbeat. Montgomery pawed at the wound with his hand for a fleeting moment before his body went limp.

Shovel still in hand, Thorn spun around; Longworth thrashed about in the dirt, holding his face in blood-soaked hands as Thorn rushed past him. His gun couldn't have been far away, but Thorn couldn't see it. Ash from the fire pit was still floating thickly in the air, and Thorn heard nothing but the sound of a moaning Longworth as Emily emerged through the floating ash, her face and clothes coated in gray-black soot. In her still-bound hands, she held a rock.

"Emily, good God, are you all—"

Emily's face froze in fear. She awkwardly raised the rock above her right shoulder and, with both hands, heaved it at Thorn. He dropped into a defensive crouch and twisted his body to track the rock. Its trajectory took it as far as the feet of Longworth, who now stood, Luger back in his hand, staring at Thorn.

His heart hammering in his chest, Thorn dove at Longworth, swinging the shovel. Longworth fell backward. The gun fired. A bullet smacked Thorn's shoulder, and he cried out. Pain seared hot and deep through his body, and he dropped to his knees, his vision blurring, sweat stinging his eyes. Then, all went black.

#

Maggie and Emily watched Conor collapse to the ground; the sound of the shot echoed in the gully. Screaming, Maggie began to crawl to her brother's body.

Longworth, his hands slick with his own blood, rose from the ground and turned to Emily, leveling the gun at her chest. Her eyes widened in horror as she lunged at a nearby shovel. She snatched it from the ground, wheeled around, and swung it wildly at Longworth, missing him as he squeezed the trigger twice; metal clicks filled the air, but there was no discharge.

Hope raced through Maggie's veins as Emily sprang at Longworth; Emily swung the shovel again, this time at the Luger, but Longworth stepped back to avoid it, clenching the gun's grip

246

with one hand as he worked the action with the other. He squeezed the trigger again.

Still jammed, the gun was tossed to the ground as Longworth turned toward the path. Emily tossed the shovel and slid feet first toward the escaping Longworth, who easily avoided the attempt to trip him. A moment later, he was gone.

The breeze died down, plunging the gorge into a quiet that was interrupted only by the call of a lone crow. A coppery odor filled Maggie's nostrils as Emily stood and stumbled over to Conor, joining Maggie. Emily bent down and grabbed Conor's shoulders, rolled him over, then shook him.

"Is he breathing?" Maggie asked. "Tell me he's breathing, please. Please!"

"Conor!" Emily shouted.

Conor's eyes fluttered briefly, then stopped.

Emily began to cry. "Conor! Talk to me Conor, please ... please, just talk to me."

Conor began to stir. His eyes opened slowly as he groaned.

Emily caressed his face with her bound hands and squeezed his cheeks. Something seemingly occurred to her as she quickly released his face and turned to Maggie.

"Maggie, untie me ... quickly," Emily said.

The woman tugged at the knot that bound Emily's hands but couldn't loosen it.

"Maggie, please ... hurry."

Again, she tried, but when nothing happened, Maggie placed the knot between her teeth and pulled. It began to loosen. A few more tugs with her fingers, and Emily's hands were free. She lifted Conor's blood-soaked shirt to see the extent of his wounds and tore at the hem of her dress, ripping off a swathe of cloth, which she used to dab at the shoulder wound. "Maggie, lift his shoulder ... gently."

Maggie placed her hands under Conor's shoulder and lifted. Emily reached back, below his shoulder, but it took a moment before she smiled. Then she pulled her hand from under Conor's shoulder and lowered him to the ground.

"What? Tell me," Maggie said.

"It went through." Emily lowered her face to Conor's. "Oh

thank God. Thank God. I thought I lost you!" she practically yelled.

"You don't have to shout, Emily. I can hear you," Thorn said quietly.

Emily sat back up and laughed.

"Where's Maggie?" Thorn asked.

"Right here, you . . . you dope. Someone had to save your butt. And thank God Emily was here." Maggie looked at Emily, and both women collapsed in laughter. Emily wiped away tears of both relief and joy with the back of her hands.

Thorn moved onto his side to get up, winced, and grabbed his shoulder. "What the hell happened? I thought it was all over when he shot me."

The tears streamed down Emily's face now. She wiped her nose and grinned. "Stupid luck, just stupid luck. His gun jammed and . . . and . . . he ran off. I don't understand. He could have killed me with a shovel or a rock, but he simply took off."

Emily buried her face in her bloodstained hands and began to sob, her shoulders heaving. Conor drew her to him and stroked her blood-caked hair.

"It's OK, Em. We made it through. It wasn't our turn. And we know exactly where we stand. No more guessing. We know who our man is. We just don't know where he is or where he's going."

Conor continued to stroke her hair, and her weeping slowed. She hugged, then kissed him.

"Don't let me go," she said. "Not yet."

"Not a chance."

Maggie rose, her eyes on the embracing couple. She smiled warmly at them before going over to Montgomery's body and kicking him in the groin one last time.

CHAPTER THIRTY-NINE

1715 Hours, Thursday, October 15, 1942
The Shield & Sword, Whitchurch

When they arrived back at the area where they had been off-loaded from Longworth's car, Thorn noticed shallow ruts and spewed gravel that indicated tires were spinning when Longworth pulled away.

Their trek from deep in the woods had been painfully slow. Maggie had twisted her ankle twenty minutes into what was now approaching a two-hour hike. Even with Thorn helping her, the ordeal had left Maggie drained, and Thorn and Emily close to it.

Trudging along a path due west from the gorge, Thorn strained to bring his focus back to his pressing goal—chasing down Longworth. His emotional encounter with Emily made his head swirl with feelings of guilt and passion that crashed into one another and almost squeezed out thoughts of his shoulder wound. Images of his past life with Grace, her warm smile and sparkling eyes, flickered in his head and then faded—Thorn didn't know if it was sad or if it was simply time to let those memories go. He wondered what Emily was feeling. She hadn't said a word the entire journey from the gorge. What images flickered in her mind?

During their hike, the wind had kicked into a high gear and the skies had darkened rapidly. The rain had fallen lightly at first and then built in intensity. Thorn, his reclaimed Colt tucked in his waistband, cradled his right forearm as if it were in a sling.

It throbbed with each step. Their clothes, already covered in dirt, quickly became caked with mud. They stood on the gravel road, looking for any activity. Thorn spotted someone on a bicycle at least a mile down the road. Too distant to get the biker's attention.

"Do you have any idea where we are? Or how long we were in Longworth's trunk?" Thorn shouted above the storm.

Emily, massaging her wrists and leaning into Thorn, finally broke her silence. "No, no idea where we are."

"Let's head down the road and see what we find. A road this wide should have some traffic at some point. That biker has to be headed somewhere with shelter in this storm," Thorn said. They headed down the road, Maggie gingerly walking on her swollen ankle, and for a few moments, the rain lightened.

"How's the shoulder?" Maggie asked.

"It's stiff. Like the rest of my body."

"Is it still bleeding?" Emily asked.

How lucky am I? Not one but two nursemaids.

"I don't think so." Thorn realized it had been a long time since someone actually cared about how he was feeling—or at least a long time since he'd recognized it. He stopped suddenly and turned to Emily. "How are you . . . how are you feeling?"

She turned to Thorn and smiled before replying. "Actually, considering what just happened, quite good except for a splitting headache. But I must be a sight."

"That you are, and I mean that in a good way," Thorn said, eliciting a laugh from her.

The wind abruptly increased, whipping the rain into a frenzy.

"I see a light up ahead," Maggie shouted.

"Ahh, civilization," Thorn yelled. Between blasts of the wind, he heard the intermittent sound of an engine—an airplane engine. It grew louder until it sounded directly overhead. Thorn looked up but could see nothing but low, dark clouds. "I don't know who's luckier—that bastard, because he's sitting in a dry cockpit, or us, with our feet on the ground."

"Look, Conor. That sign up ahead—looks like a pub." Emily pointed.

Thorn made out the sign that was nestled beneath the over-hang of a peaked roof —The Sword & Shield. It swung in the stiff wind, generating high-pitched squeals that grew louder as they stumbled closer to the pub's bright-red door.

Emily was the first one in. Thorn turned sideways to pass through the narrow doorway with Maggie's arm still clamped on his good shoulder and his left arm wrapped securely around her waist. They entered a cramped, low-ceilinged room with a blazing fireplace that filled the small space with a golden glow. Two windows flanked the doorway but were shuttered on the inside. Emily approached the bar, where a short, heavyset man was drying a pint glass with a dish towel. Two older men in overalls topped with tweed jackets leaned on the bar. The barman's jaw dropped when he glimpsed his new customers.

As Thorn led Maggie toward a booth and eased her into the seat, Emily spread her hands wide on the bar's surface and hung her head. Her soaked hair dripped on the bar as the three men stared at her. The barman passed his towel to her without saying a word. Thorn slipped into the booth beside his sister. Resting even for a moment lessened the throbbing in his shoulder.

"We need a doctor...right away. Is there one nearby?" Emily asked, her voice reedy and her head still hanging low. She picked up the towel and began to pat her drenched hair.

The barman looked at the two men, then back at Emily.

"I said, we need a doctor," she repeated as forcefully as she could.

"Ahh, that'd be Dr. Mike. He's . . . he's just down Bishopworth's Lane a bit. I'll call him. What should I tell him the reason, if you don't mind me askin'?"

Emily raised her head. "My friend's been shot."

The barman fumbled the pint glass into a sink, and it sank to the bottom of the soapy water. "Shot? Bollocks!"

The two old men drained their pints, ducked into a dark corner of the pub, and emerged with bicycles, each with a basket attached to the handlebars. As they made their way out the door, Thorn could hear the pub's sign swinging in the wind. It was clear they thought trouble was following the new arrivals.

But the barman was willing to help. "I'll ring him up straight-away, miss. And I'll fetch some steamin' hot tea and some biscuits." As he retreated to the end of the bar to make the call, Emily snatched two more towels and joined Thorn and Maggie in the booth.

Maggie turned to her brother. "Conor, I need to use that phone. I need—"

"Maggie, we need to call in too, but first things first," Emily said.

"Yeah, phone calls after we figure this out," Thorn said. He stuffed a towel under his shirt, to staunch his gunshot wound.

"You don't understand. I really need to get a call through to Trout. I can't sit on this story," Maggie said, keeping her voice low.

Thorn and Emily shot a look at her.

"No one will believe that a cabinet member would—"

"Whoa, Maggie. Hold your horses. That's *exactly* what you need to do—you have to sit on this, possibly for a long time," Thorn said.

"You're joking, right?" Maggie was building up a head of steam. "I get kidnapped, slapped around—among other things, I might add—all because of a traitorous British cabinet member who is handing over intelligence to the Nazis, and I have to spike my story? No way. You're asking too much . . . way too much."

Thorn opened his mouth to argue, but the barman returned with a tray of three steaming mugs and a plate of biscuits. His gray woolen pants were supported by a set of wide suspenders, and brown rubber boots noisily scuffed the plank floor as he approached. Maggie snagged a biscuit from the plate and tore into it.

"Doc Mike will be here straightaway, miss. As soon as he's done puttin' the Wyndham kid's leg in a cast. I will say, by the look of the lot of you," the barman said as he gave Maggie and Emily a good once-over, "it looks as if the storm chewed you up and spit you out." He turned to Thorn and spotted the blood-soaked shirt Thorn was trying to cover with his right hand. "And you look quite a bit worse for wear, mister."

"You should see the other guy," Thorn mumbled.

"In worse shape, I take it." The barman turned to Emily. "Can I get you anything else?"

"You're so kind. What is your name?" Emily asked.

"Benjamin. Folks around here call me Benny."

"Benny, where are we exactly?"

"You're in the village of Whitchurch, about five kilometers south of Bristol."

Thorn quickly put it together: *Shit. Whitchurch Airport...with flights to and from Lisbon each week.* He looked at Emily and saw that the gears in her head were spinning as well. "But that's a strange question, not knowing where you are."

"Long story, Benny," Emily said.

"Oh boy, that's an understatement. It's a long and unbelievable story," Maggie said, wiping crumbs from her lips.

"Maggie, pipe down," Thorn said. He turned to Emily and nudged her leg under the table. "You're thinking the same as me," he said to her quietly. "Lisbon. That's why he came here—to get to Lisbon."

Emily nodded.

Maggie's wrinkled brow betrayed her confusion. "Lisbon? What are you talking about?"

"That's right, mister," the barman interjected. "That Dutch airline, KLM, operates flights to Lisbon, and British Overseas—"

"Thanks, Benny. Can we use your phone?" Thorn asked.

"Sure. Help yourself." An explosion of shattering glass from a room behind the bar sent Benny scurrying, mumbling under his breath about a ditsy bird in the kitchen.

Thorn leaned into the edge of the table. "Emily, get a call in to KLM and find out about flights to Lisbon and ask if anyone that fits Longworth's description showed up in the last couple of hours. If that bastard made a flight, we have to get them to recall it."

Emily started to slide out of the booth, clutching the towel she'd been using to dry off. "Right. And we can meet it when it lands back in Whitchurch."

"Right after we reach out to MI6 Section Five and Donovan," Thorn shouted at Emily as she darted behind the bar. He took a slug of tea and closed his eyes, lost in the warm sensation of the hot liquid as it traveled down his throat into his chest. His head started to slowly bend forward.

"I stink," Maggie said.

"Hmm," he grunted, not surprised by Maggie's confession. "You sure do, but you're in good company. How's the ankle, Mags?"

"Sore as hell and, if you want to know, throbbing at the moment."

"I'll go ask Benny for some ice," Thorn said. As he turned to get out of the booth, he saw Emily headed toward him, the panic clear on her face. "What's wrong?"

Emily dropped back into her seat and buried her face in the bar towel. "Longworth made the flight. It left close to three hours ago."

"They're sure it was Longworth?"

"Yes, yes, they're sure." She lifted her head. "He had no space reserved, so he had to use his special travel permit allowing ministers priority if traveling on government business. And he fit the description," she explained. Her face was drawn; only her bloodshot eyes showed any sign of color. "The flight left forty-five minutes early. The pilot wanted to get ahead of a fast-moving storm that was headed east into the Bay of Biscay." Emily leaned back and shook her head slowly. "And that's not the worst of it."

"What—"

"KLM has been trying to reach the flight by radio, but there was too much interference."

"They must be in the middle of the storm then. Shit," Thorn said, trailing off into a mutter. "Electrical interference." *That marathon hike out of the woods cost us.*

"They told me the flight is just over two hours out from Lisbon."

Thorn's shoulders slumped. "Damn it. This is getting worse by the minute." They couldn't put it off any longer. "Emily, time to call MI6."

"OK. Right after you call Donovan."

CHAPTER FORTY

1800 Hours, Thursday, October 15, 1942
Regents Park, London

Philby should have left his friend Tomás Harris's home earlier. But the wine flowed too freely, and the home hummed more than normal with the sound of the empire's best spies guardedly sharing stories but typically extracting dated intelligence from one another. Philby arrived at Queen Anne's Gardens five minutes late, his head buzzing from the excellent Syrah that came from Harris's impressive cellar.

He took a seat on a bench and wrapped his long, green overcoat with red-fox-fur lining around his legs to combat the blustery wind. The barrage balloon support team was nowhere in sight. The balloon tugged at its mooring cables and bounced about in the rambunctious airstream. Shapak walked up to Philby's bench and plopped down in a heavily bundled heap. He made no move to speak.

"Good evening," Philby said, breaking the ice.

"Where is Stoker?"

"Ahh, yes. Stoker. It was decided that given the aftermath of his meeting with Longworth, it would be advisable to"—Philby shrugged—"shall we say, assume a lower profile. I sent him up to Saint Alban's to conduct some training. Away from prying eyes."

"He got sloppy. Maybe he should stay there for quite some time as long as he's training MI6 agents to be sloppy. That we can accept."

"Yes. But that's not why we're here. Is it?"

Shapak remained quiet for three more beats before he spoke again. "The two agents assigned to follow Longworth have finally reported back." Shapak rearranged his neck scarf.

"And?"

"The lead agent reports that late this morning, Longworth was first visited by an RAF officer, his nephew, and then just minutes later by a French captain. We also know him—he's with the BCRA. We do not know why he was there. Several minutes later, two people that match your descriptions of Thorn and Bright entered the house," Shapak said, choosing not to look directly at Philby. "They never saw Thorn or Bright leave the house. But he did see Longworth's car with a driver and two passengers leave from the rear of his flat."

Philby needed an extra moment to process Shapak's report. He lit a Woodbine. "Did they follow the car?"

"The lead agent did. He left the other agent behind to see if Thorn and Bright ever left. The lead agent lost the car about three kilometers south of Whitchurch Airport. He thinks they must have pulled off somewhere, but he doesn't know where."

"But Thorn and Bright—did they ever leave the house?"

"No. The agent waited another hour."

Philby sat silently for several minutes, smoking the Woodbine down to a nub.

Shapak stamped his feet and blew into his cupped hands. "What are you thinking?" he asked.

Philby waited a beat and flicked the cigarette into the grass. "Well, first, Longworth either has Thorn and Bright with him, or they're back at his home tied up or possibly dead. Second, I think Longworth is following our instructions. He's tying up loose ends before he heads to Lisbon to link up with the Abwehr. And third, and this is most critical, our plan is on track."

"What of the Frenchman?"

"That's a complete mystery. One I'll look into further."

Shapak grunted, then abruptly turned to face Philby. "Your conclusion regarding your plan . . . how do you come to that?"

"I am assuming that Longworth has harmed in some way—kidnapped or killed—Thorn and Bright. If so, he has played his final hand. That and the fact that flights leave from Whitchurch Airport to Lisbon on a regular basis. The closing act of the Longworth saga has now begun," Philby said. His last few words rolled off his tongue slowly, as if he were the narrator of an Elizabethan drama.

"Fucking crazy Englishman."

Philby pulled the last Woodbine from his pack. He lit it, crushed the pack, then tossed it over his shoulder. "Maybe not so crazy. He must have known that Thorn and Bright were getting close to figuring out what he was doing. Longworth didn't have many options."

"Speaking of crazy, your plan for this document—will it still work?"

"I think it can." Philby tapped an ash that curled off the tip of his cigarette and took a long drag. "Here is what I am going to ask that you do. First, get into the house. If you find Thorn or Bright, get back to me. Then, when Longworth lands in Lisbon, make sure that he is . . . undisturbed by MI6 or American agents. Assist him in his efforts to contact the Abwehr. Can you do that?"

Shapak blew warm breath in his cupped, chilled hands. "Of course. But tell me—when does word get out of this traitor Longworth?"

"Maybe never. Churchill has too much to lose. He will ask for a cover story at some point. The truth would be disastrous. No, Longworth will die in his sleep one night and be buried in a private ceremony."

Shapak breathed into his clasped hands again and shook his head. "This plan of yours—a lot can go wrong. Especially in a place like Lisbon."

Philby tossed the spent cigarette across the path. "I'm feeling lucky, comrade. Let's roll the dice on this one, shall we?"

CHAPTER FORTY-ONE

1830 Hours, Thursday, October 15, 1942
On Board KLM Flight 777 to Lisbon

Longworth would have killed for an aspirin. Resetting his broken nose in the loo at the airport had given him a dull, throbbing headache. He sat quietly and stole glimpses at his watch every two minutes or so. The KLM Royal Dutch Airline owned DC-3 flew at an altitude of twenty-four thousand feet. Its unpainted sheet metal was stamped with the Dutch flag on its tail and the letters *KLM* on either side of the nose, along with the name *Ibis*, after the long-legged wading bird. Longworth sat in the second row of the cabin, beside the rectangular window. The fully occupied cabin was quiet except for the drone of the plane's two radial engines. The Royal Navy commodore who sat to his right now slept soundly, after Longworth had rebuffed his attempts to engage in a conversation.

He put his head back, rested his eyes, and listened intently to the drone of the engines. Concern as to how much of a lead he had on his remaining pursuer, Bright, gnawed away at what little focus his weary mind could generate. Knowing he had put a bullet into Thorn provided some relief, but he had many miles yet to travel.

His breathing slowed, and he finally became restful. Then, unexpectedly, the plane banked sharply to the left, and his body was pushed deep into the cushioned seat. Several passengers awoke and began shouting questions. The DC-3 banked hard to the right, then downward, sending hats, umbrellas, and newspapers scurrying throughout the cabin.

Just as the plane began to level out, engine sounds unlike the sound of the DC-3 engines began to fill the cabin. Longworth peered out the window on his left and made out the silhouette of a smaller two-engine plane on a perpendicular course to collide with the airliner.

He bolted upright in his seat and gripped the armrests, awaiting the attack. Shouts of panic erupted behind him. Longworth tracked the flight of tracer rounds coming from below the attacker's cockpit as they lit up the night sky for brief, violent moments.

The DC-3 shuddered as it absorbed rounds from the fighter. The staccato sound of bullets as they ripped apart the DC-3 were deafening. Flying bits of metal zipped and popped in the cabin, sending tufts of seat cushions and bits of baggage through the air. The airliner began an aggressive descent, sending personal belongings streaming down the main aisle and under the seats, to the front of the cabin. A chorus of screams erupted from the passengers each time the airliner made a sudden move.

Once more, the attacker made an approach on the same side as before but from a higher altitude, the roar of its engines growing louder with each passing second. Longworth saw the plane's nose guns light up again, its rounds directed at the fuselage of the slow-moving DC-3.

Several more rounds pierced the DC-3's outer skin, filling the cabin with the smell of cordite, which acted like head-clearing smelling salts. The singular, distinct realization that he was seconds away from death shattered all his worry about not completing his mission. A trickle of warm liquid ran down behind his ear, and he reached up and dragged his fingertips through a patch of sticky blood. He could tell that the wound was not deep, but the attack was not over.

The airliner went into another steep dive. The screams of passengers and the piercing pitch of the radial engines as they descended were deafening.

Longworth looked at the inside of the cabin above and around his seat and could see where the rounds had pierced the fuselage. The Royal Navy officer who sat beside him clutched his left bicep, blood seeping through his fingers. A stewardess with a small first-aid kit rushed to attend the officer, stumbling over the dislodged personal belongings that covered the DC-3's floor and struggling against the aircraft's steep descent.

The roar of the attacker's engine grew again, trailed by the sound of its guns. Longworth shut his eyes tight, held his breath, and readied himself for what could be his last moments. The sound smothered the screams of the passengers. A round blasted through the fuselage, followed instantly by the roar of the attacking plane as it passed overhead. The shrieks and screams from the passengers crested.

Longworth opened his eyes and quickly surveyed his body for other wounds. Nothing. The stewardess was collapsed against the bulkhead, her uniform blotted with her rapidly escaping blood. She looked pleadingly at Longworth, her arm extended, and mouthed something to him in a language he didn't understand. He closed his eyes for several moments and opened them again. The stewardess lay motionless, her white blouse now a crimson red.

Longworth looked down to see a stream of blood running below him to the front of the aircraft. The sound of air entering the cabin through the holes made it difficult to hear anything except for the DC-3's own engines as they continued to carry the plane to a lower altitude.

The aircraft leveled off, and there was no sign of the attacker. The cabin quieted except for the whimpering of the passengers and a man praying loudly in Spanish. The pilot came on the intercom, breathing heavily. Longworth could hear the panicked voice of the copilot in the background. The copilot didn't stop yelling until the pilot, still on the intercom, shouted at him to shut up. The praying man in the cabin ceased his appeals.

The pilot spoke for less than ten seconds, his words clipped and harried. He reported that the single German fighter had broken off its attack, which had caused damage to the radio and the starboard engine, but he expected a safe landing in Lisbon. He asked all to remain calm. But few in the cabin listened to his request, as the praying man resumed his conversation with God and many others shouted questions, not waiting for answers.

Longworth was in shock and not well. His head throbbed, and his surroundings swirled about him. But he was alive. He was convinced God played a hand in that because the communists were the enemy of His church, and he was an enemy of the communists—an extremely powerful enemy.

He held a handkerchief to his wound, sat back, and closed his eyes in an effort to tame his vertigo.

CHAPTER FORTY-TWO

1900 Hours, Thursday, October 15, 1942
Whitchurch Airport, Whitchurch

The storm that battered the region had passed through, leaving behind clear skies. Thorn maneuvered the spirited Morgan, cheerfully loaned out by Benny, up a circular drive, past a small, practically vacant parking lot, to the front entrance of the terminal building. He remembered little of the terminal and its surroundings from when he'd passed through after his arrival from Lisbon over a week ago. He did recall that his great relief at being on firm ground was quickly overwhelmed by his concerns about his reassignment meeting with Donovan. So he noticed for the first time that the façade of the building was painted a gleaming white that shone brightly despite the setting sun. He detected no interior light coming from the terminal's windows and assumed that blackout curtains were in use.

While nearly shouting at each other in the open-air Morgan, Thorn and Emily discussed Maggie's reluctant agreement to keep the Longworth story under wraps. Emily doubted Maggie's ability to sell the story of an invite from Clementine Churchill to Chartwell to cover her absence, even with Emily's enlisting Clementine's backing of the story. But Thorn laughed off Emily's worries, assuring her that Maggie could sell eyeglasses to a blind man.

He stopped abruptly, and the car's narrow tires protested with a shriek. Emily smoothed the hair she'd fought with for the entire ten-minute drive, and as she collected herself, Thorn jumped from the car and headed into the terminal at a brisk pace.

Inside, several small groups of people were milling about, many of the travelers looking as if they were settling in for the night in the rows of chairs that were scattered around the terminal. He scanned the line of airline counters along the back wall. All the counters were deserted except two: the British Overseas Airways Corporation counter and one with a brightly lit sign for KLM Airways. He headed down the concourse with Emily at his side.

Thorn found the terminal quiet compared to the last airport he'd been in—Lisbon's Portella. In spite of the few flights that Portella offered, it attracted throngs of people that wanted to put Lisbon in their rearview mirror. "Where is everybody? Why aren't there more people here?" Thorn asked.

"Since the war started, the government has restricted access to flights to diplomats, military personnel, VIPs, and anyone else with government approval. That leaves out a lot of people." They arrived at the KLM counter and found it staffed by two women, one in her twenties and one much older, both in faded-blue uniforms.

"Hello, ladies, do you have a minute?" Thorn asked.

The older woman, who had gray hair and seemed to be in charge, balked and looked at her coworker.

Thorn realized that he and Emily didn't look official in their cobbled-together outfits. Thorn resembled a classic English farmhand, with his scratchy-wool shirt and blue gabardine pants. Emily was the spitting image of a scullery maid.

As Gray Hair approached, the younger woman stood behind her, peering over her coworker's shoulder.

"What can we do for you today? I hope it's not a flight you're looking for."

"No. No, it's not," Emily said.

"Because the last flight left here a few hours ago. Civil aircraft can only fly in daylight hours. And there aren't any more flights until tomorrow afternoon."

"Yes, I know. Are you Mrs. Stevenson?"

"That would be me," the gray-haired woman said. "And you are?"

"I spoke to you earlier. I'm—"

"Ahh, yes, that crazy lady from the government. Oh my, but aren't you the pretty one?" Stevenson said, giving Thorn a sly wink.

Emily smiled and lowered her head.

"I suppose you're here about flight 777. We've quite a mess on our hands, I fear."

"What type of mess?" Thorn asked.

"We've been trying to reach the pilot to recall the flight ever since we got a call from some bigwig in London. But we still can't make contact, I'm sorry to say. We're all quite worried."

Thorn's lips pressed tight as he leaned against the counter on his hands, both arms extended. His shoulder protested.

"So the storm is still an issue?" Emily asked.

"Honestly, we don't know. The last time we tried, instead of static that came and went, we received nothing."

Damn it. It's not just the storm working against us. Thorn pushed away from the counter.

"I'm sorry. You said 'nothing'? I'm not sure I understand," Emily said.

"They've lost their high-frequency radio, Emily," Thorn explained. "Lightning strike, electrical fire, equipment failure—who knows?" he said. He turned to Stevenson. "One more question: How long is the flight?"

Stevenson turned to look at the wall clock, but the younger woman stepped forward. "Usually around four and a half hours. But bad weather would have some effect on that."

"Yes, Felicity is correct," Stevenson said.

Thorn nodded. "Hmm . . . when exactly did the flight leave?"

"Three forty-five," Felicity said.

"Thank you, both. You have been very helpful," Emily said as Thorn stepped away from the counter, but then he stepped back.

"I have a favor to ask. May we use your phone? It won't take long."

"If you're looking to get a connection back to London, it may take some time. Patience is the key." Stevenson moved a handset from below the counter and placed it in front of Thorn and then left them, with Felicity in tow.

"So the flight left early, 1545 hours, and let's say that it takes about five hours with the bad weather. That has it landing—"

"At 2045 hours, an hour and thirty minutes from now," Emily said.

"Right," Thorn said, pushing the handset toward Emily. "You need to update Section Five with the estimated arrival time. They have plenty of time to get into position."

Emily picked up the handset and dialed. In a minute, she'd related the new flight information and answered some questions about her location and the time of their arrival back in London. Thorn heard her say goodbye to Philby. She slapped the handset back into its cradle with a bang and turned to Thorn. "Conor, what if he gets through somehow? What if he does head to Rome? We can operate in a neutral country like Portugal, but operating in an occupied city like Rome is just not possible. We need a backup plan, one that works this time. There's too much at stake."

"You're right—we need to think about the worst-case scenario." Thorn leaned over the counter; its thick, lacquered finish gleamed. "I need some air and a moment to think."

Thorn walked toward the terminal's exit, lightly massaging his wounded shoulder as he went. Outside, he took a seat on the Morgan's front fender; heat from the engine seeped from under the hood. He watched a flight on the last stage of its approach and craned to make out the paint scheme on its fuselage. It was a British Overseas airliner. When it disappeared behind the terminal building, Thorn began pacing.

If Longworth somehow made it past MI6 in Lisbon and headed to Rome, into the safe hands of the Abwehr, it would be an intelligence bonanza for the Nazis. If it became necessary, could Longworth be stopped on the ground in Rome before he could do any more damage? The logistics of getting into Rome undetected confounded him. Thinking about how to get back out if they made it in practically short-circuited his brain.

Several minutes later, a handful of people, chiefly military types, exited the terminal. Most waited for transportation, including a priest, his white collar visible in the setting sun. Thorn stared at the priest for a good thirty seconds. "Father Sean Sullivan . . . *and* his associates. Yeah, that could work," he muttered. He headed back into the terminal and found Emily, still standing at the KLM counter, engaged in a conversation with Stevenson.

"Any luck?" she asked.

"Think so. I have a backup plan. Or at least a half-baked one, if it comes to that."

"I'm listening."

"Not now. It's still . . ."

"Baking?"

"Yeah, baking, that's it," Thorn said. "I need to get through to Bruce and report in. Wait in the car. I won't be long."

#

Emily sat in the Morgan, pulling her hair back and holding it there when Thorn emerged from the terminal. "Did you get through?" she asked as he settled into the cramped confines of the vehicle.

"I did. Bruce said Colonel Donovan is back from Casablanca. Donovan and Bruce want to see us right away."

"Us?"

"Your boss will be there too. Something's up. Bruce sounded rattled. He almost couldn't get a full sentence out."

CHAPTER FORTY-THREE

1930 Hours, Thursday, October 15, 1942
German Embassy, Rome

When Bishop Heinz looked at Hitler, the führer's eyes returned his gaze with overpowering intensity—the intensity expected from the leader of National Socialism. The portrait of Hitler was more or less as large as the fireplace it adorned and depicted an imperious Hitler from the waist up, his left hand resting on his hip while his right hand gripped the back of a chair. A red armband emblazoned with a black swastika was wrapped around his upper left arm. His face showed an unhealthy, pale pallor, which placed it in stark contrast to the dark, brooding skies that were featured behind it.

"You are late, Bishop. I expected you over five minutes ago. You think it wise to keep me waiting? Would you keep the führer waiting?" Major Kappler asked, motioning to the portrait of Hitler.

"Certainly not, Major. Please accept my apologies." Heinz watched as Kappler paced in front of his massive desk, which was completely bare except for two phones and a lone dossier that sat open.

"Sit down." The uniformed Kappler maneuvered around the desk, its bleached wood complemented by ornately styled gold trim, then stopped. He stood stiffly beside an enormous desk chair. Everything in the office sparkled, including Kappler's knee-high black boots—their spit-shine reflected the room's main lighting, which flooded from an enormous crystal chandelier hanging from the vaulted ceiling. "Have you received word from Longworth?"

Heinz, wearing a black cape with an intensely red lining, removed his wire-rimmed spectacles and cleaned them with a cloth that he'd pulled from inside his sleeve. His trepidation over delivering a mixture of welcome and unwelcome news produced a queasiness in the pit of his stomach.

"Well, answer me. Have you heard from Longworth? Admiral Canaris is growing impatient. As am I."

Heinz placed his glasses on his nose and wrapped the wire temples around each ear. "I have, indeed, heard from him. In fact, I have received two letters, one yesterday afternoon and yet another late this afternoon. Which is highly . . . irregular."

"Go on."

"In the letter I received yesterday, he includes nonspecific information regarding the second front," Heinz reported with a dismissive wave of his hand.

"Meaning?"

Heinz withdrew a letter from a pocket inside his cassock and cleared his throat. "The information in his letter that I just received took me three hours to decipher, as it was much longer than most of his previous letters. It was the reason I was somewhat late."

"Yes, yes, stop wasting time. Get on with it."

Heinz cleared his throat, not once, but twice.

Kappler tilted his head back and shook it.

"Bishop!"

"I am pleased to report that Longworth is, as we speak, on his way to Lisbon. He reports that he has high-level Allied in-telligence that will greatly satisfy the admiral and you, Major." Kappler's look of surprise and satisfaction pleased Heinz. Heinz cleared his throat again. "But it seems that risks taken to obtain the intelligence, which he does not share in this letter, have led to him being exposed as an agent of the Abwehr. That's the reason he gives for asking that the Abwehr make arrangements for his safe travel to Vatican City, for his safety and so that he can hand off the intelligence personally, ensuring, he states, that it be taken seriously." Heinz held up the letter as if it were an encyclical from Pope Pius XII.

Kappler's satisfied demeanor vanished. "Let me see that."

Heinz rose and slid the letter across the desk. Kappler studied the decrypt, his lips moving as he read. Finished, he sat back in his chair, still tightly grasping it. "He's on the run," Kappler said as he looked up at the brooding Hitler. "But what happened in the span of two days to explain this second letter?"

"Might Churchill have finally taken the cabinet into his confidence?"

"Yes, that is possible." Kappler sat silently thinking. He began to wave the decrypt slowly back and forth. "Don't misunderstand me, Bishop. I am gratified at the mention of new intelligence, but news of the loss of an asset so deep in the Churchill government is news that will not please Admiral Canaris."

Heinz deliberately repositioned his glasses on his nose. "I am sure, Major, there is much to be gained by welcoming Longworth to Rome. He must know a great deal that he has not . . . shared. Wouldn't you agree?"

"Possibly . . . possibly," Kappler said, sitting back in his chair. "When is he expected to arrive?"

"I believe he should be arriving in Lisbon in an hour's time. I am sure with the assistance of the Abwehr, Longworth will have no difficulties making his way safely to us."

"That does not worry me."

"Major, I must point out one word that he used to describe the intelligence that did strike me."

"What is that?"

"*Authenticated.*"

"Yes, I saw that—*authenticated*," Kappler said, drawing out the word. A moment later, he reached for his phone and barked into the handset. "First, connect me with the Abwehr station in Lisbon. I must talk to Muller. Then, connect me to Admiral Canaris. Ring me back as soon as Muller is on the line." Kappler hung up the phone. "You know the man personally. Do you trust him?"

Heinz rose from his chair and pulled his cape tightly around his torso. "Major, I place my trust only in God."

CHAPTER FORTY-FOUR

2045 Hours, Thursday, October 15, 1942
Portella Airport, Lisbon

"What the hell is going on?" asked James Burton, the MI6 Section Five agent in charge of the detail to identify and bring in Henry Longworth. Emergency vehicles, all with their lights flashing and most with their sirens blaring, had been speeding toward the main runway ever since the KLM airliner first started circling the skies around Portella Airport with a steady stream of black smoke trailing from its starboard engine. Ground and maintenance crews darted frantically across the tarmac in front of the main terminal. What started out as a quick identify-and-snatch operation was now a completely fouled-up mess. "Jones, what is going on here?" Burton asked again of one of the two other men in his detail. All three had donned KLM ground-staff overalls to pull off their infiltration of the airline's service personnel.

"I just heard one of the baggage guys say that the tower can't establish radio contact. But it does look like they're in some sort of trouble."

"How did this get so cocked up? There are too many people running around out here. It's mass confusion. And I don't have enough men," Burton hissed under his breath. He looked around and could see at least twenty men in various emergency garb, along with a number of fire department vehicles, two ambulances, and airport security, in addition to KLM staff. If he could wrangle the KLM overalls, so could German agents.

"Jones, we need to be prepared in case there are any injured passengers. Slip one of these medical staff workers fifty escudos for a white medic's jacket and blend in with the medical teams. Remember, if you get close to Longworth, make sure you search him. I don't care what anybody tells you. You hear me?" Burton asked.

Jones nodded. "Loud and clear. But…ah, who's going to search his luggage?"

"No worries there. KLM told Broadway he didn't have any luggage. But they didn't mention anything about a briefcase, so I'll check for that," Burton said.

He leaned against his sedan and watched the landing lights of the DC-3 grow larger and brighter as it slowly approached the terminal, emergency vehicles trailing closely behind. The starboard engine, still smoking badly, had been cut. He noticed a Mercedes sedan following the DC-3 in from the runway; it slowed to a stop on the far side of the airliner, which gradually came to a full stop in front of the terminal. The damage to the plane's portside fuselage was now clearly visible.

The moment the pilot cut the DC-3's portside engine, the sirens ceased and the ground crew sprang into action, placing chocks around the plane's wheels while another crew doused the starboard engine. Three additional ground crew rushed to open the rear door of the plane and drop the stairs into place. Two men in dark suits carrying black bags were the first to enter the aircraft, followed by a medical attendant.

As they went to attend to the passengers inside, other white-jacketed members of the medical team, including Burton's man Jones, moved their stretchers onto the tarmac, close to the plane's stairway, ready to receive the wounded. Burton held a photograph of Longworth, ready to survey the passengers as they disembarked.

The first to emerge was the Royal Navy commodore, who was able to walk down the stairs with minimal assistance from a medical attendant. Next was a stretcher that carried a body draped with a white sheet that was quickly absorbing blood from the victim. Burton caught Jones's eye and nodded to the stretcher. Jones scurried over to the stretcher, which now lay toward the aircraft's tail section. While the stretcher-bearers ran back to the plane's stairs, Jones bent over and lifted the sheet. He rose and made his way back to the stairs, shaking his head.

Another medical attendant emerged with a man who had his right arm draped over the attendant's shoulder and his left hand holding a handkerchief to a wound near his ear. The injured man was guided down the stairway and loaded onto a stretcher.

Burton looked at the photo, then at the tall, gray-haired man lying on the stretcher. "That's the bloke," Burton mumbled. He gave Jones a sharp nod.

Jones moved alongside quickly, and as the medical attendant that brought Longworth out of the plane returned to retrieve more wounded, Jones searched a swooning Longworth.

Burton moved closer to Jones, who looked up at him and signaled with a shrug that there was no document on Longworth. Two other medical attendants came over to Longworth and began to move him into the back of one of the ambulances. Burton motioned Jones to go with him.

The ground crew, yelling at one another in Portuguese, climbed over the left wing of the aircraft, inspecting the damage caused by the attack. Two additional wounded passengers were escorted from the airliner and placed on stretchers. The rest of the passengers disembarked. Most hadn't reclaimed their natural color.

When it became clear that there weren't any more passengers to disembark, Burton took two steps at a time up the stairway. As he entered the cabin, he looked back out one of the windows and saw that Longworth's ambulance was pulling away, siren blaring and emergency lights flashing. Burton was told to assume that a top-secret document wouldn't leave his side. He needed to quickly determine if Longworth had a briefcase with him, then head off to the hospital before any Abwehr agents showed up. He raced up the aisle, checking for any valises that were left behind, deducing that one of them must have been Longworth's.

He located a tan leather bag adorned with the initials *H. L.* He opened the case and sifted through its few contents. In a side pocket, Burton found a small flask inscribed with the same initials. He shook the flask to be certain it contained only liquid. Lying at the bottom of the valise was an unsealed envelope emblazoned with the Royal Coat of Arms of the United Kingdom along with the name of Henry Longworth, written in a calligraphic style. Burton pulled out a single sheet of heavy bond paper. It was a letter permitting air and train transit "for the Minister of Public Works, Henry Longworth, for the purposes of conducting business for His Majesty King George VI." Not seeing any other document, he took a penknife from his pocket and slit the inside lining. When his efforts proved unproductive, he headed back down the aisle. But before he reached the open cabin door, he heard two gunshots in the distance. He rushed outside.

When he jumped off the stairway, he saw that the ambulance carrying Longworth had been stopped at the gates by the sedan he'd spotted trailing the DC-3 earlier. For a moment, Burton froze. Things were happening too fast. His plans were blowing up in his face.

Burton ran to his sedan to give chase, looking over the tarmac for his other agent and swearing when he didn't see him. He had no time to look further. When he got to his sedan, he stopped dead in his tracks—all his tires had been slashed. "What is fucking going on here?" he shouted.

Burton saw an ancient airport tug used to tow planes sitting nearby. He jumped in and started it up, discovering it had only one low gear. He floored the accelerator, and the engine whine filled the air.

As he closed the distance, he saw two men transfer Longworth from the ambulance into their sedan and then jump into the vehicle. Fifty meters from the ambulance, Burton pulled his pistol from his pocket and fired four times at the swiftly retreating sedan.

When he arrived at the ambulance, he found that the driver and two medical attendants had been shot. Jones was lying facedown on the stretcher. Burton could see the exit wound in the back of his agent's head. The round, fired at close range, had taken half his skull with it as it exited.

"Good God!" Burton moaned as he watched the sedan vanish in the distance.

CHAPTER FORTY-FIVE

2130 Hours, Thursday, October 15, 1942
Claridge's Hotel, Brook Street, London

When David Bruce answered Thorn's knock, he did a poor job of hiding the look of utter astonishment at seeing Thorn and Emily standing there in their best English countryside attire. "Come in."

Donovan was seated on his couch, an open file in his hand. When Thorn and Emily walked into the suite, Donovan, who appeared to give them a pass on their wardrobe, rose and gave Emily a hug, which caught Thorn and Emily off-guard.

"Emily, so glad to see you again. It's been quite a while." Donovan extended his hand to Thorn. Thorn shook it, but not without betraying a wince of pain. "What's wrong, Conor?"

Be careful. You don't need to give Donovan any reason to pull you off the mission and put Emily in the hands of some dope.

"Colonel, we got roughed up a bit dealing with Longworth." Thorn saw that Emily did her best to avoid giving away her surprise at the understatement. "But I'm fine. Getting better every hour." *I'm not lying. I almost can't feel the pain anymore. Almost.*

Donovan studied Thorn for several moments before he nodded. The french doors to a bedroom were open, and Thorn heard the raspy voice of an Englishman handling the short side of a conversation with someone. "Yes, sirs" and "I understands" could be heard every few seconds. The discussion ended with the sound of a handset dropping into its cradle. As they settled into club chairs that surrounded a glass-and-brass coffee table, a natty-looking man in a blue pinstripe, double-breasted suit emerged from the bedroom. He was in his fifties, and a large forehead signaled a retreating hairline. His sparse moustache was graying.

The blue-suited man took a seat. Introductions were not forthcoming, but as the man sat, Thorn shot a hasty quizzical look at Emily and mouthed *C?*

Emily responded with a bob of her head.

"Anything to share?" Donovan asked, looking at C.

C turned to Donovan. "That was the PM. I have my instructions."

Donovan nodded slowly. "I understand."

"Conor, you're up," Donovan said.

Thorn rushed through his report, starting with the foul-up with their backup team. He addressed questions from both Donovan and C regarding the involvement of Toulouse. He ended by placing great hope on MI6's efforts to intercept Longworth.

"If he gets through, he isn't planning on coming back ... is he?" C asked.

Thorn smiled. "No, sir. He can't. To follow up on that, he's not safe in Lisbon. But in Rome, with his friends at the Vatican and inside the Abwehr, he thinks we can't touch him."

After a moment of silence, Donovan turned to C. "A cabinet member working hand-in-hand with the Abwehr. Whatever he hasn't told the Abwehr, the Gestapo will sure get it out of him. That can't happen." The phone in the bedroom rang—a shrill double ring, pause, another shrill ring. It startled everyone except C, who slowly rose and strolled toward it.

"Hold on a minute," said Bruce. "How the hell did he get his hands on the diary page when we couldn't find it?"

Thorn looked down at the floor and shook his head. The sound of C raking someone over the coals forced Thorn to raise his own voice. "I don't have the complete answer. But I have to believe that his nephew somehow got his hands on it. But what's most important is that we know who has it now—Longworth." The whack of the handset slamming into its cradle accentuated the mention of Longworth's name.

The silence that followed was quickly pierced by the sound of C dialing the phone.

Donovan held up both hands to slow Thorn. "I don't understand why he's put himself in so much danger. Why not just communicate the directives to Heinz through the diplomatic pouch?"

Thorn appreciated that he and Donovan were on the same track. "That's been driving me crazy. He wants Operation Torch scuttled. The only thing I can think of is that he needs to somehow prove the accuracy, the validity of the intelligence. That diary page looks authentic because it *is* authentic. If he can pull it off, the Nazis will move divisions and squadrons to North Africa pretty damn quick. He certainly knows that the Nazis must be skeptical, since we've been disseminating all sorts of phony intel on the location of the second front. But frankly, I think there's more to why he's delivering the intel himself. I haven't put a finger on it . . . yet."

"Colonel, there's another reason. A simpler one," Emily said. "We know and he knows that he's betrayed his country. He needs a safe haven. The Abwehr, Bishop Heinz, and the Vatican's neutrality could be his salvation."

C entered the room with his hands buried in his suit coat pockets and took his seat. "The report from the team on the ground in Lisbon is not good," C said, looking at no one in particular. "Longworth was picked up by the Abwehr. It seems the flight had been attacked by the Luftwaffe, and in the commotion on the tarmac caused by the emergency and interference by what appears to be Abwehr agents, Longworth slipped through."

Thorn lowered his head, his chin resting on his chest. *God damn it! The son of a bitch made it.*

"Is the prime minister aware of this development?" Donovan asked.

"He is all too aware, I'm afraid," C said. "This morning it was my task to inform the prime minister that I received a report that directly implicates Longworth in a long-term conspiracy with the Abwehr, indicating he had been passing along logistical information regarding northbound convoys. Apparently, the information was passed along to Longworth by his nephew."

Emily's faced knotted in confusion. "Sir, who reported this to you?" she asked.

"Philby. Section Five. Why?"

Emily lips parted. "Philby? Why would the report come from

the head of counterintelligence in the Iberian Peninsula? What or who was his source?"

"Frankly, Bright, it's none of your concern," C said, then turned to Donovan, a clear signal that he was done discussing it.

"So, do we all agree that he's on his way to Rome?" Donovan asked.

Thorn looked at the four people before him and waited. Again, no one spoke up.

Donovan finally dove back in. "All right then. How would he get there?"

"My bet is he'll use his contact at the Vatican, Heinz, to make arrangements with the Abwehr. But, if I may, sir—what's our next move?" Thorn asked.

Donovan folded his arms and looked at C.

"News of Longworth's defection would be a disaster for the government," C said. "That is the PM's belief and one I share. With the news of our failure in Lisbon, there is no question that Longworth must be eliminated at all costs."

Thorn suppressed a smirk. *Eliminated. Gotta love the English.* He looked around the room. "And how—"

"Bright and you—with Colonel Donovan's permission, of course—will catch a flight to Lisbon immediately. The PM has made his personal plane available to you. It will leave from Tempsford. As far as travel to Rome is concerned—"

"We'll handle that and your cover story," Donovan said, looking at Bruce.

C nodded.

"Colonel, if we're headed to Rome, I have a suggestion," Thorn said.

"I'm listening."

"Rome, and the Vatican, for that matter, could just as well be on another planet. Once we get there, we'll need someone to be our guide. Someone who knows his way around the place and could provide us some . . . cover," Thorn said.

Emily's face lit up with understanding. "Sean Sullivan. Father Sean Sullivan," she said.

"That's right." Thorn nodded. "He's an old family friend assigned to Westminster Cathedral, working for Cardinal Massy.

He spent time at the Vatican working for Cardinal Massy as well. His own cover could be as a courier of the diplomatic pouch. I'm sure we could pull a few strings and get Sean assigned to fill in. We only need to figure out the transportation."

Donovan ran his hands through his thinning, gray hair before speaking. "Hmm, I could see that would be helpful. I'll reach out to Cardinal Massey, Catholic to Catholic, and do a little arm-twisting. I'm sure he'll give me an earful about the Vatican's neutrality. If he does, I'll have to bring up the fact that Longworth was using the diplomatic pouch." Donovan turned to C. "If I could drop the name of the prime minister, that would be helpful."

C gave a quick nod, which Donovan returned.

"And as far as how we get around in Rome or the Vatican, I've been chewing on an idea," Thorn said.

"Go ahead, Conor. You're on a roll," Donovan said.

"I'm a long-suffering Catholic. I set the record for serving Masses and funerals at Saint Catherine's. My mother had a dream that one of her boys would become a priest. Maybe now's the time—with a little help from Sean."

Donovan snorted, and Bruce exhaled deeply, while C actually smiled.

It seems the audience is pleased.

"And Emily? Let me guess. Your companion is Sister Emily Bright?" Donovan asked.

"Colonel, great men think alike."

Donovan rolled his eyes and turned again to C.

"Bright, are you up to it?" C asked. "If not, just say—"

Emily nearly jumped from her chair. "Sir, I am not without my own experience with the good sisters. I'm sure I can pull it off."

C, his lips pursed and back straight, nodded sharply at Donovan. A mere ten seconds later, C was closing the door to the suite behind him.

Donovan rose and moved toward his desk. "When you get to Lisbon, Conor, ask for your old friend Heugle. He'll tell you how you're getting to Rome, and he'll fill out the rest of your cover story."

Donovan opened the bottom drawer and pulled out a pistol that sat snuggly in a tan leather holster. "Are you armed?

"I am, but I could use some magazines," Thorn said.

Donovan reached into the drawer again. "Here're five extra magazines. Emily?"

"Colonel, I could use a PPK and some ammunition."

"OK. I'll get it to you before you leave the hotel. Go downstairs and talk to the hotel manager, Albert Gilles. Tell him you need food and some clothes right away." Donovan looked at Bruce. "David, let's go make some calls. You place a call to the State Department. I'll tackle Cardinal Massy. Let's see if we can sneak these two into Rome."

CHAPTER FORTY-SIX

0130 Hours, Friday, October 16, 1942
On Board B-24 Liberator MkII to Lisbon

As soon as the wheels of Churchill's Commando lifted off the runway, the lights outlining the runway below them were doused. As the B-24 Liberator, which was painted black to hide it from Nazi fighters during its night flights, swiftly gained altitude, Thorn craned to see out a small portside Plexiglas window and noticed that the area around Tempsford appeared to have been swallowed up by blackness. In the plane, the bomb racks had been removed, allowing for modified accommodations that provided some degree of comfort for fifteen passengers. Insulation had been added to mitigate the airframe-shaking roar of the four powerful Pratt & Whitney engines, but not enough had been done to effectively mask the smell of aviation fuel and hydraulic fluids.

Thorn sat back in his seat and closed his eyes. He focused on short, shallow breaths to help tame his mounting anxiety. *Easy, Conor. You'll be in Lisbon soon, and a fear of flying will be the least of your troubles.*

Sean Sullivan sat across the aisle from Emily, his large frame filling every inch of the seat, smoking what must have been his fifth cigarette since they'd boarded. The Vatican diplomatic pouch was shackled to his left wrist and tucked tightly between the seat's armrest and his left thigh. Sean snuffed out the cigarette stub in the tiny ashtray embedded in the tip of the armrest. He immediately pulled another cigarette from the pack and lit up. "Conor, why were they painting over the British insignias on the sides of the plane?" Sean asked.

Thorn leaned forward to look past Emily, who was seated next to him. "That struck me as odd too. The pilot told me that a military aircraft can't land in a neutral country. It's against international law. He thinks that painting over the insignias will buy us a little time on the ground in Lisbon before the Portuguese get curious."

"I see." Sean put out the cigarette and stroked his lips a few times.

"Father, are you feeling well? You look a little under the weather," Emily said.

Sean tugged at his collar with his index finger. "I'm not surprised. Flying and I are not the best of friends."

"Ahh, I understand," Emily said. She began digging into a canvas musette bag, plucked out a vial of pills, and handed it to Sean.

"What's this?" he asked.

"They're capsules filled with ginger. They're supposed to help manage airsickness."

"You are prepared, I'll say that," Thorn said.

Emily huffed and shook her head. "I must admit that I harbor self-serving motives."

"How's that?"

"I simply want to endure this flight without having to witness anyone soiling their shoes and possibly some other priestly garments."

Sean popped two capsules into his mouth and grabbed one of the thermoses that had been brought aboard. "So," he said after he swallowed, "tell me just what the hell am I doing here." He made the sign of the cross as he waited for Thorn to reply. "Cardinal Massy received a call from someone, and here I am, on my way back to Rome with an old family friend who has only told me that he and his associate work for the American and British governments."

Thorn looked at Emily, but before he could answer, the pilot, Captain William Vanderkloot, entered the cabin. He was a tall man and was forced to move about the aircraft in a stoop. "Everything shipshape back here?" he asked.

"Captain, so far so good. But can I ask if there is any way to pick up some speed?" Thorn asked.

"Only if you want to freeze your toes off. We can move up to thirty-two thousand feet and pick up some knots, but it will get damned cold in here."

"How much quicker would we get to Lisbon?"

Vanderkloot stared into the back of the cabin and chewed on the inside of his cheek. "Oh, about fifty minutes or so."

"That would help, Captain. We'll deal with the cold," Thorn said, nodding at Emily and Sean.

"OK, it's your toes." Vanderkloot headed to the rear of the cabin and returned moments later with three blankets. "The prime minister is fond of these." He returned to the cockpit, and moments later, the Liberator nosed up to gain altitude.

Thorn proceeded to explain all that had happened with Longworth, including their need to sneak into the Vatican.

Sean shot a look at Thorn and Emily. "Your guide? That sounds a bit—"

"Crazy?" Emily said.

"I was going to say farfetched. Have you considered how I am to explain you two to the Swiss Guards?" the good father asked.

"At this point, we're merely two members of the clergy headed to the Vatican to conduct business for our dioceses."

"Clergy? Members of the clergy? You must be pulling my leg," Sean said.

"Hey, I was an altar boy for quite some time, Sean."

"Well, I could take that as an insult, but I won't. There *is* a bit more to it than that. But, of course, you know that."

"Certainly. Our cover story will be fleshed out a bit once we get to Lisbon."

Sean shook his head. "What do the two of you know about the Vatican—its ins and outs, its protocols?"

Thorn looked at Emily and shrugged.

"Honestly, we know little. The only comfort I have as far as Rome goes is having a conversant ability in Italian," Emily offered.

Thorn raised his eyebrows at that. *Well, that could be helpful.*

Sean looked peaked. He started to take big gulps of air. "Emily, another capsule, if you please."

"Certainly," Emily said, reaching into her bag.

"Tell me, how are we getting to Rome?" Sean asked before he dry swallowed the capsule. "Commercial flights don't leave on the hour. But I'm sure you know that, correct?"

"We do. We'll learn how we'll get to Rome when we get to Lisbon. I hope."

Sullivan's brow furrowed, and he began rubbing his chin. "Hmmm . . . something . . . something slipped my mind, Conor. Just two days ago, Longworth stopped by the clergy house. It was around nine o'clock in the morning. I remember I was surprised to see him because he wasn't at seven o'clock Mass that day."

"What was he doing there?" Thorn asked.

"Edith said that all he wanted was to drop two letters into the pouch. He did that and quickly left."

"Do you know who the letters were for?" Emily asked.

"No. Given our last conversation about Longworth, I was going to look in the bag, but the pouch had left with the courier moments before."

Thorn paused. *What was Longworth doing? Letting Heinz know of his final plans? He needs two letters to do that?* "When do you think that pouch arrived at the Vatican?"

"Sometime late afternoon yesterday, I would think. Well, thank you for taking me into your confidence. I believe I should pen some notes to help prepare you to some degree for your . . . foray into the Vatican. That along with a few prayers." Sean got up, grabbed a blanket, and moved to the seat nearest the cockpit.

Emily looked at Thorn and began to speak, but Thorn stopped her. "I know, I know," he said. "The chances we get out of this aren't good, prayers or no prayers."

"Longworth has given us no other choice. And, strangely, I take some comfort in that."

"That's not so strange. Me, on the other hand, I feel as if I'm getting closer to repaying a debt to—" He stopped himself. He didn't want to lose his focus by dredging up the past.

"To whom?" Emily asked.

He turned to look out the window and was met with a star-filled sky. *She needs to know this about me. She needs to know what she's getting into.* He turned back to Emily, whose head was tilted to one side.

"Do you remember, about a week ago, when I said that maybe the death of my wife and son may have saved my life?"

"Yes."

"Well, the complete story is that I was called away from my ship, the *Reuben James*, when Grace went into premature labor. I was at her bedside when the ship . . . my ship was torpedoed by a U-boat off Iceland while on convoy duty." Thorn turned away from Emily. "More than one hundred US Navy sailors went down with her," he said, his voice thick with emotion. He cleared his throat, and Emily reached for his hand. He started to pull away, but Emily held tight.

"I am so sorry," she said.

Thorn saw that she was tearing up. "Me too. Given the short notice, they sailed without an executive officer—me. I should have been there. I could have saved some lives."

"You were where you were supposed to be. With your wife."

"Maybe." Thorn held his gaze on Emily. "So if you're right, tell me—why me? Why was I saved? And you know it's not the first time. So why me? Tell me that, Emily." He realized that this was the first time he had given voice to his nagging doubts and guilt.

Emily squeezed his hand. "I can't answer that. But maybe Colonel Donovan has picked the right person for this mission. You had the courage to stick to your convictions, dragging me all the way, I must say."

"Well, I hope you're right. Hell, I hope I'm right. But one thing I know—we'll get this bastard," Thorn said, releasing her hand and slumping down into his seat.

Emily twisted to face Thorn, staring at his hand. "Conor, you took your . . . wedding ring off."

Thorn looked at his left hand. The skin that his wedding ring had once covered was a milky white. It had taken him several tries to remove it. *It was time. Time to move on. But to what?* "I don't know. With everything that's been going on . . ."

She waited for him to elaborate and finally asked, "Such as?"

"It's tough to explain, so I won't even try. At least, not now. I'm still trying to figure it all out," Thorn said, his voice a whisper.

Emily nodded. "Well, promise me this—you will tell me when you have it sorted out?"

"Deal," Thorn said, relieved she didn't push him harder.

#

Two hours later, the B-24 Liberator landed with successive heavy bounces and began to taxi. Captain Vanderkloot came back into the cabin and sat down across the aisle from Thorn. His brown leather flight jacket was open, but its wool-lined collar was pulled snuggly up to his ears. "I don't know why you're all here. It seems pretty strange to me that we're tasked, with no clear explanation, to fly a priest with a diplomatic pouch into a neutral country. But we're here," Vanderkloot said while taking off his flight jacket. "So here's the plan: Once you disembark, we'll close the hatch and play dead for no more than five minutes. We told the Portuguese that we were experiencing some engine problems, but that excuse won't work for long. I'll give you no more than that to figure out if your mission is still on the rails or if you're all coming back to England with us. Once you figure that out, tap out a dot-dash yes or no on the hatch. You do know Morse code, Mr. Thorn?"

"Yes, sir. Former navy."

"Good. But move fast. Airport security can get surly and block our path to the runway pretty damn quick. Remember, I said five minutes. I kid you not, that's all I'll give you. Am I clear?"

"Very. But, Captain, we're not going back. At least not now," Thorn said.

"A lot could have happened while we were in the air. I'm giving you a last chance." Vanderkloot nodded once and made for the rear of the B-24.

Thorn and Emily collected their belongings and met Sean at the rear hatch door, where Vanderkloot was ready to lower the stairs once the plane came to a stop. It took the three passengers moments to disembark from the plane, and the hatch slammed shut behind them. Thorn looked at his watch.

The tarmac was lifeless, yet the airport was ablaze with lights. Terminal, tower, and runway lights shone brightly—a clear contrast to the airfields in Britain. Thorn and Emily stood shoulder to shoulder. Sean stood behind them. A dark-colored sedan approached, the driver flashing the headlights as he got close. Before the sedan stopped, the lone passenger had the door open and one foot on the ground.

"Bright?"

"Yes, here. And you're Burton?" asked Emily.

"Yes. James Burton." The driver shut the engine down but left the headlights on, and then took up a post twenty feet behind the vehicle. Burton, his eyelids heavy and his face drawn, leaned on the sedan's fender and nervously scanned the perimeter. His suit coat was severely rumpled, his tie loosened. He smoked the last of a cigarette.

"It was the Abwehr, right? They took Longworth?" Emily asked.

Burton hung his head and rubbed his eyes with the heel of his hands. "It's been a long night, Bright."

"I don't care how long a night it's been. Where did they take Longworth?" she asked, surprising Thorn with her peeved tone.

Burton stood taller, clearly taken aback by getting a rebuke from a woman. "He was snatched. I . . . I lost a man last night."

Thorn and Emily exchanged looks. "Details," Emily prodded.

Burton rubbed the back of his neck. Up to the point where he said Longworth was taken across the field in the direction of the Lufthansa hanger, Thorn and Bright glumly listened. But at the mention of the Soviets, Thorn stopped him.

"What the hell did you say?" Thorn said.

"I said someone slashed the tires on our sedan after we got on the scene. That's why we couldn't give chase right away. I have no idea who. The Abwehr, most likely. Hell, it could have been the bloody Soviets. Those bastards can't be trusted. They're always fucking with us."

"Soviet agents? Shit." Thorn took a deep, slow breath as a panel truck approached the sedan. It was towing an oversized fire extinguisher, the type seen all over major airports. Thorn made out two men in the cab of the truck. He watched the truck pull up and stop fifty feet from their position. The two men remained in the cab.

Thorn turned on his heels and rushed toward the Liberator.

Another vehicle with emergency lights flashing approached from the same direction as the panel truck. Thorn took his Colt and, with the butt of the pistol, rapped out *no* in Morse code. He looked over his shoulder at the two vehicles.

Something's not right here. He turned back to the B-24 and repeated the message, then spun away from the bomber.

"Where's his bag? I want to see it," Emily said.

"It's on the backseat."

Emily pulled out the valise and began rooting through it.

"Did he say anything?" Thorn asked, looking at the gathered vehicles.

"He was too disoriented."

"Don't look now," Thorn yelled and pointed to the two vehicles. "But we've got company."

A second later, the Liberator's engines fired up. The emergency vehicle pulled to a stop. His Colt still in his hand, Thorn watched the two men in the panel truck emerge, both with a gun. He turned toward the other vehicle, whose driver and passenger did the same thing. The passenger held what looked like an automatic with an oversized magazine.

"Get down!" Thorn screamed as he took cover behind the sedan's front fender. Burton took up a position to Thorn's left. Sean dove headfirst into the front seat of the sedan, and Emily knelt behind the sedan's rear fender, gripped her PPK semiautomatic with both hands, and began firing.

Thorn aimed at the driver of the panel truck, who was now crouched behind the truck's fender, and squeezed off three shots. The driver collapsed to the tarmac. *Who the fuck are these assholes?* Thorn could barely hear the shots over the engine blast from the B-24 as it taxied to the end of the runway.

Burton's driver, out in the open, fell as a shot smacked into his chest, landing him on his back. Burton, his arms extended on the hood of the sedan, fired off two shots but missed the passenger of the panel truck, who was shifting to the rear of the truck. Thorn took aim. Before the passenger could get there, Thorn dropped him with one shot.

Two down.

The driver of the emergency vehicle fired off four shots, all hitting the side of the sedan. Thorn trained his Colt on the driver, but at just that moment, the driver took a shot in the chest from Emily's PPK.

Just don't move from behind that fender, Emily.

The passenger of the emergency vehicle was the lone attacker left. He slipped back into the vehicle and put it in reverse, both front doors still wide-open. Smoke billowed up from the rear tires, and within seconds, the vehicle was out of range. Thorn stood, his Colt lowered. Burton didn't move as he watched the escaping vehicle speed off into the distance. Thorn didn't see Emily move and started to panic. "Emily, Emily . . . you OK?" he screamed.

Emily slowly stood and walked toward him.

He exhaled and hung his head in relief.

"Yes, I'm fine. I was just loading another magazine."

"Everyone else OK?" Thorn asked.

"I'm OK, but it looks like I lost another man," Burton said, reloading his weapon.

Sean, his face as white as a sheet, sat up in the front passenger seat still clutching the diplomatic pouch under his left arm, a small pistol in his right hand.

Thorn shot a look of surprise at Emily, who smiled.

"Sean, what the hell are you doing?" Thorn asked.

Sean raised the pistol to near eye level and stared at it. His hand was trembling, his face pallid. "Yes. This is out of the ordinary, I admit, but with all the intrigue that you've uncovered, I thought it wise to . . . take precautions." He tucked the pistol underneath his cassock.

"Were you going to use it?"

"I . . . just don't know. To protect the Vatican's diplomatic pouch? Quite possibly. To wound but not kill, of course."

"Yeah, of course. Just go for the legs," Thorn said as he slipped his Colt into his waistband. He gaped at Burton. "Who were these people? And here's another good question: How did they know we were going to be here?"

"I bloody well don't know the answer to either question." It was devastating enough to have blown the capture of Longworth, but it demoralized him to think that maybe they were putting their trust in the wrong people.

Burton ran over to the panel truck and turned over the three bodies. Thorn trotted over to Burton's driver and saw the blood-soaked shirt, a small hole just above his heart. Blood had spread beneath his body, and his clothes had begun to soak it up.

"Let's get out of here, Burton," Thorn yelled.

Burton sprinted back to his driver's body. Thorn helped him drag it to the sedan. Emily opened the trunk, and Thorn and Burton loaded the young agent in. The three agents silently stood looking at the driver. Burton shook his head. The blood-soaked clothing gave off a strong metallic smell. Sean pushed between Burton and Emily and placed a stole with embroidered crosses around his neck. He laid his right hand on the driver's forehead and began praying over the body.

Burton put his hand on Sean's shoulder. "Father, he's not Catholic. He's—"

"A child of God, son. Now let me finish, because I'm sure we do not have the luxury of time."

Atta boy, Sean. But damn if you're right about not having the time. Sean finished up, praying so quickly Thorn didn't pick up one word.

Thorn slipped into the backseat with Emily. Burton got behind the wheel, and as he put the sedan in gear, he turned to Thorn. "Russians. Bloody Russians. You can't trust those sods."

Thorn glared at Emily. "I think you—*we* have a problem somewhere in MI6. And it almost got us killed," he said.

CHAPTER FORTY-SEVEN

0430 Hours, Friday, October 16, 1942
Lisbon

Thorn's sour disposition worsened as he mulled over their setbacks on the drive through the deserted Lisbon streets to the OSS office. Three Soviet agents were lying on the tarmac, and one MI6 agent was in the trunk, gunned down by people who were supposed to be their Allies. Thorn now believed that their worst-case scenario was, in fact, much worse than first believed.

He turned to Emily, who appeared lost in her own thoughts. She had rolled down the rear window, and the chilly, early-morning air rushed through her hair and forced her to nearly close her eyes.

"Emily," Thorn said to rouse her.

She faced Thorn and stared at him blankly. "Conor . . . I don't know what to think or to say." She turned back to the window and watched the lights of the city pass by. The next several minutes, silence filled the car until Thorn leaned forward in his seat and spoke.

"How can you be so sure they were Russians?"

Burton's bloodshot eyes met Thorn's in his rearview mirror. "Look at it this way, Thorn. It's a game. It's like a football league, except this is a league of spies. We're paid to know their players, and they're paid to know ours." Burton's hands tightened on the steering wheel as he spoke. His eyes darted from the road in front to the rearview mirror. "Sometimes a new player enters the game, but we eventually get to know him." Burton's emotionless demeanor shook Thorn. "I'll guarantee you they knew the name of my agent they killed. He was a damn good man . . ." His hushed voice trailed off.

"You OK, Burton?" Thorn asked.

Burton looked in the rearview again and nodded as he pulled to a stop in front of a building on Avenida 24 de Julho. Emily and Sean proceeded to get out, but Thorn sat for a brief moment. "You sure?" he asked Burton.

"Yeah, I'm sure. Just a game."

Thorn slid across the seat, stepped out, and was about to close the door when Burton held up his right hand to stop him. "Wait. What did you mean when you said there was a problem somewhere in MI6?"

Careful, Conor. You don't want to throw too much mud at your friends in MI6. "Just that someone is not making our jobs any easier."

Burton flinched. "Who's the someone?"

"Not quite sure." He cocked his head at Burton briefly. "Ah, I'm probably way off base on this. Thanks for the ride. Oh, wait a minute. Is that mess back there going to get tied to us?"

Burton turned around and slouched in his seat. "No. They'll collect their own assets, as we would. That and a modest amount of money from both sides in the right hands should do it. That's how the game is played in Lisbon."

Thorn nodded and shut the door, thinking that Burton needed to be pulled from the game.

"Oh, by the way," Burton said through the open window, "your old friend Heugle is expecting you. Third floor."

"Thanks."

Burton jammed the sedan's gearshift forward, the transmission loudly protesting its displeasure as he drove off.

Thorn caught up to Emily and Sean, and they marched up to the front entrance of the building, which overlooked the Tagus River. The early-morning river traffic was sparse, and the surface of the water was the color of dark coffee and smooth like glass.

Inside the entrance, an elevator was nowhere in sight, so they took the stairs. As they neared the third-floor landing, Thorn spotted Bobby Heugle.

"Robert L. Heugle, you are a sight."

Heugle smiled broadly and leaned on a brass railing, looking down at his guests. His dark hair looked glossy in the light, and there was a glimmer in his eyes that betrayed his spirited personality.

"Mr. Thorn, the Tangier Terror." Heugle spread his arms wide as they joined him. "Welcome to Lisbon, also known as the White City, but better known these days as the Spy City. Hello, Miss Bright. And this must be Father Sullivan," Heugle said, approaching them and shaking each of their hands with an exaggerated pump of his arm. "Welcome, all. Let's head down to the office, so we can talk some spy stuff."

On the way down the long, dimly lit hallway, Heugle was talking up Sean in his usual animated style. "So what do you have in that there bag, Father? Wouldn't be anything important, would it?"

"Actually, Mr. Heugle, I don't know exactly what's in the pouch. They never tell the courier."

"Well, let's hope it's not my eighth-grade report card from Saint Philomena's. Trust me, the pope would not be happy." Heugle led them through a door to a suite of three offices connected by a spacious waiting area that accommodated two long, leather couches and a desk that looked as if it had been kicking around since the days of the Moors. Thorn and Emily took opposite couches, and Sean collapsed onto the far end of the one Emily sat on.

"Bobby, we need to get to Rome. Fast. Has Wild Bill been in touch?"

Heugle sat on the corner of the desk. "Damn sure has. And he's pulled a doozy out of his hat this time."

"What do you mean?" Thorn asked.

"The colonel's made arrangements for all of you to fly to Rome with Myron Taylor." Heugle turned his right hand over and looked at his watch. "In about an hour from now."

"Who's Myron Taylor?"

"He's FDR's new representative to the pope. He flew in from the States last night. And here's where it gets crazy." Heugle paused long enough to arch an eyebrow and produce a shit-eating grin. "You and Emily get to dress up as a . . . priest and a nun. Do you believe that?"

"Bobby, we know. It was my idea. But what about our cover story?" Thorn asked, taking some of the wind out of Heugle's sails that his announcement wasn't as dramatic as he'd hoped it would be.

"Oh, OK. Well, your cover is that you're meeting with Vatican higher-ups about servicing the religious needs of German and Italian prisoners in the UK, Canada, and the States," Heugle looked wide-eyed at Thorn and Emily. "Pretty good, huh?"

Thorn, Emily, and Sean all exchanged glances, but Sean was the only one who laughed.

"Does Taylor know the real story?" Thorn asked.

"No. No way. The colonel had to go through Archbishop Spellman in New York, a friend of his. Spellman reached out to the State Department. A lot of string-pulling." Heugle slid off the desk, pulled out a sheaf of papers from a drawer, and passed two letter-sized folios stamped with the papal insignia to Thorn and Emily. "Of course, your papers are all in order, thanks to some quick work by some local friends of ours. Forging documents is a growth industry in the Spy City, if you didn't know."

Thorn looked over the papers, which featured a headshot of Thorn in a priest's collar. He looked up and saw Emily showing her identity papers to Sean, who looked impressed.

Heugle then ducked into a side office and came out with the garb of a nun and a priest displayed on hangers. "Here are your getups."

Sean's look changed to one of amusement. "Wouldn't your mom be proud, Conor?" he said.

"You better jump into these. I have to get you back to Portella. Oh, shit—sorry, Father."

Sean shrugged. "I've heard worse, Mr. Heugle."

"Emily, I forgot to tell you that someone from MI6 dropped this off for you last night." Heugle pulled an envelope from his breast pocket and handed it to her. Emily slid her index finger under the flap and opened the note. The color drained from her face. She looked at Thorn and then reread the note, this time taking longer. Thorn expected her to report on the note's contents, but nothing was forthcoming. She looked lost in her thoughts.

"Mr. Heugle, is there a lavatory I could use?" Sean asked.

"Sure there is, Father. Follow me. Are you going to be able to . . . handle things with that baggage chained to your wrist?"

"You'd be surprised, Mr. Heugle." Sean and Heugle disappeared back into the hallway.

Emily rose from the couch and went to the desk, where she found a box of matches in an ashtray. She lit a corner of the note and let the flame dance upward for a moment. Black smoke drifted up to the ceiling, and then she dropped the paper in a wastebasket.

"Anything I should know?" Thorn asked.

"I have orders from C," Emily said.

"What does he want you to do?"

"Eliminate Heinz."

"Hmmm. No big deal. I was going to do that anyway, priest or no priest."

"Right . . . right, no big deal, as you say," Emily said. Thorn heard a proud *stiff upper lip* tone in her voice, like she wasn't going to tell him that she was in deep pain.

CHAPTER FORTY-EIGHT

0730 Hours, Friday, October 16, 1942
German Embassy, Rome

Wilhelm Canaris slumped in a chair in front of Kappler's desk. He held yet another message from Himmler excoriating him for his and the Abwehr's blundering and ineffectiveness. But this time, Himmler went the added distance to accuse him of abandoning his duties, given his excessive travel. Canaris snorted at the accusation. But Himmler was right; Canaris did travel. It allowed him to avoid seeing exactly what Hitler and men like Himmler had done to his country—a country that Canaris was struggling to save.

The knock on the massive office door startled Canaris as it echoed off the marble floor of the office. He folded the message from Himmler and placed it in his breast pocket.

"Come in, Bishop Heinz. And please have a seat." Canaris did not get up, nor did he turn to greet Heinz. He'd never liked the Austrian cleric. It wasn't only his pinched face and shifty demeanor, but also Heinz's perpetual sickness that he detested. Particularly, he found Heinz's germ-spreading propensity for sneezing disgusting.

Canaris remained seated and continued to gaze out the massive office window behind his desk. The sky was becoming brighter. The sycamore trees outside the window hosted a noisy flock of jackdaws. It appeared to Canaris that the flock of cackling blackbirds were looking directly at him.

Heinz angled the chair to face Canaris, sat, and promptly

sneezed. Canaris leaned away from the bishop and muttered under his breath. He got up and dropped into his chair behind the desk, glad to put distance between him and the germ farm of a priest. Canaris was also pleased to put his back to the mocking jackdaws. The bishop finished wiping his nose and tucked a lace cloth up the left sleeve of the dark-purple cape he wore.

"Admiral Canaris, it is a great and unexpected honor to see you again."

Canaris smiled weakly, showing no joy. "Is it, Bishop? Some days, given the tasks that are asked of me, I am not so sure that I would want to meet someone like me."

"Admiral, if you do not mind me saying, that is an odd thing to say about yourself, an Iron Cross recipient no less, who has served his country well for so many years."

"My country? There are days when I don't recognize my country."

"Ah, a beleaguered country must do what it has to do to survive. Don't you agree?"

"A view I share, but a view that extends to individuals. Its citizens must also do what is necessary and expedient for the country's survival."

"Yes, Admiral. No disagreement there," Heinz said, his elbows resting on the armrests and his hands joined together as if in prayer.

"So, I am told that Major Kappler is meeting Henry Longworth. Is that accurate?" Canaris asked.

Heinz pulled a lace handkerchief from his sleeve. "That is correct. He should be arriving at the embassy soon. I pray that the intelligence he carries with him is as valuable as he says it is." He forcefully blew his nose, the *toot* echoing as loudly as his earlier knock.

Canaris pushed his chair away from the desk, stood, and walked to the window, his hands folded behind his back. He realized that if the intelligence wasn't top grade, it would become enormously difficult to fend off the attacks from Himmler.

"Yes, Bishop. You continue to pray. While Longworth's escape from England and his desire to live out his life in the Vatican certainly places a high value on the intelligence he brings, I, on the other hand, will continue to be highly doubtful, which leads me to the concerns I wish to discuss."

"Concerns? Such as?" Heinz asked, dropping his hands into his lap.

"I have received a report that Soviet NKVD agents interfered with British agents that were at Lisbon's airport to apprehend Longworth." Canaris turned to Heinz. "Why would that be, Bishop?"

Heinz didn't hold Canaris's gaze and instead dropped his head. "That is puzzling, Admiral. I have no explanation."

Canaris continued to stare at Heinz. "I do not put it past the British to orchestrate an elaborate show to convince us that Longworth, indeed, possesses valuable intelligence, only to have that intelligence lead us into wrongly deploying the Wehrmacht and Luftwaffe. But the involvement of the NKVD confuses me greatly."

Canaris's voice trailed off as he lowered his eyes to the floor. For several moments, he studied the veins in the marble under his black cap-toe shoes; the path they traveled appeared to lead directly to his feet. "I can't help but feel that trusting Longworth would be a mistake," he said. He fixed his eyes back on Heinz and took two steps to the desk, closing the distance between him and the apprehensive bishop. "This may not end well for him," Canaris said, tapping the desktop with his finger on each word.

Heinz's eyes dropped to the tapping finger and then back to Canaris's face. "He does risk much. I find it challenging to fully understand the motives of risk-takers."

"Well, Bishop, I do have a more thorough understanding of his motives. And they are not—how shall I say?—pure. He's a desperate man, and desperate men are dangerous men."

"I see," Heinz said, nodding.

Canaris pondered if Longworth ever got around to confessing to Heinz any of his carnal sins. "One other matter. My agents in Lisbon have informed me that MI6 and the American OSS are following Longworth's trail. While this too could be part of their ruse, my question is, how will they get into the Vatican—or Rome, for that matter—undetected?"

Heinz's eyes widened. "Well, under normal wartime circumstances, the same way that Jewish refugees and British and American airmen make it out of Rome and back to England."

"And that is by what means?"

"They seek out the assistance of the British ambassador to the Holy See, D'Arcy Osborne."

"Are these normal circumstances?"

Heinz reached for his handkerchief that sat in his lap. "No, Admiral. Mr. Osborne has been in England for several weeks. Absent his help, it escapes me how they could manage travel into and out of the Vatican."

Canaris nodded thoughtfully, and Heinz sneezed, overwhelming his small handkerchief and shooting spittle across to the seat vacated earlier by Canaris. The sight made Canaris shudder.

CHAPTER FORTY-NINE

0745 Hours, Friday, October 16, 1942
On Board Lockheed Model 10 to Rome

Thorn and Emily sat in the last row of the ten-seat Lockheed Model 10 Electra as they sought to put as much distance as possible between them and Myron Taylor, who was seated in the first row of the aircraft. The least amount of interaction was called for until they were more comfortable in their roles as priest and nun. Sean walked down the middle aisle, his large frame hunched over, and took the seat in front of Emily.

"So, Sean, how did we do? Convincing enough?" Thorn asked.

Sean twisted in his seat and looked over his shoulder. "It appears so. But he's not too happy. My impression is that Mr. Taylor is a man who doesn't appreciate last-minute changes."

"Hmph, he wouldn't make it in this business."

"Well, I am sure I wouldn't make it either," Sean said as he reached into his black suit coat and pulled an envelope from his breast pocket. "But, to increase the chances that you make it in my business, I want you both to read and memorize this." From the envelope, Sean pulled two note cards covered with a compact scrawl on both sides and handed them to Thorn and Emily.

"What's this?" Emily asked, giving hers a cursory glance.

"In case we get separated inside the Vatican, you must at least know how to tell a bishop from a cardinal, from a priest, as well as how to address them. So while we were at your friend Heugle's office, I finished my notes regarding descriptions of their attire and how to refer to them."

Thorn looked over the note card. At the top of the list was a vivid description of the pope's day-to-day attire. "There's a chance we could run into the pope? Really?"

"No. But thoroughness is a virtue."

"Sean, this is very helpful, thank you," Emily said.

"You're welcome. But, Emily, I suggest that you don't make eye contact. You are a quiet, shy sister doing God's work. You don't want to spook a cardinal with those big, blue eyes."

"Good thinking," Thorn said.

Emily blushed and shook her head, followed by a slight smile. Thorn returned it.

Sean nodded slowly. "And one more thing—there's not enough time to familiarize you with the layout of Vatican City or even Saint Peter's, so if someone stops you, just tell them you have just arrived from overseas, and you are too overwhelmed to remember anything about where to go and how to get there."

"So, play the dumb-tourist card," Thorn said.

"Yes, that should work," Sean said as he turned in his seat to face forward and tilted his head back, the diplomatic pouch wedged tightly between his thigh and the armrest. The chain that secured the pouch to Sean's wrist was as thick and, like the lock that secured the pouch's front flap, the metal cuffs that were attached to the pouch and Sean's wrist were robust. Whatever was inside was secure. *Safe and secure. Very secure.*

Thorn leaned across the narrow aisle and grabbed the armrest of Emily's seat. The habit she wore hid her auburn hair, which would force an onlooker to focus on her striking facial features— he had to admit that his attraction to her was knocked off balance; visions of every Dominican nun he ever tormented in grade school flooded his mind.

"I think I've figured out some of what Longworth's up to," he said in a somewhat normal volume, banking on the plane's twin engines to drown him out for someone sitting several rows away as Taylor was. "Not all of it, but some."

"Wouldn't be the whereabouts of the document, would it?" Emily asked, an anxious look on her face.

"Yeah, that part," he answered. He leaned into the aisle and looked up toward the front of the cabin. He saw the back of Taylor's head; his graying hair was thinning, and a cloud of smoke haloed it. "So the search of him and his luggage produces nothing, no diary page. Yet he's on his way to Rome anyway. Why go to Rome and meet with his buddy Heinz without it? The Abwehr wouldn't let him rest comfortably in the Vatican without getting something in return, right?"

"Right. But even without the diary page, he has much to offer, being a cabinet member," Emily said.

"Yeah, but for Longworth, it's all about stopping Torch. And the diary page with Torch directives in the hands of the Abwehr accomplishes that. So I'm back to where the document is. That's what I couldn't figure out, but the answer was right in front of me."

"What do you mean?"

He pointed to the diplomatic pouch chained to Sean's wrist.

"The diplomatic pouch?" Emily asked.

Thorn nodded. "Longworth didn't want to risk being searched for the document. It was too dangerous. So rather than be caught with it, he sent it to the Vatican in their own diplomatic pouch, the same way he has been communicating with Heinz."

"He sent it to Heinz?" Emily asked.

"I don't think so. No, I'm sure he wants to hand it off personally. He sent it to someone else. Someone he trusted to hold it for him. Maybe they don't even know what they're holding for him."

"He knows a lot of people inside the Vatican, including the pope," Sean said, leaning into the aisle.

"Well, I think we can rule out the pope," Thorn said. "Longworth's—" he stopped. He heard the portside engine of the Electra misfire for several seconds. He stretched to look out the window; he needed to see that the engine was not on fire or leaking oil or aviation fuel. When the firing of the engine returned to normal, Thorn leaned back into his seat, staring straight ahead. He began nervously opening and closing the metal lid to the ashtray embedded in the armrest.

Sean looked at Emily and cocked his head, his eyebrows knitted tightly.

"Conor!" Emily snapped. "You were saying?"

Thorn stopped fiddling with the ashtray and looked at Emily. He took a deep breath. "Yeah. Uh . . . so I was saying that Longworth's number-one goal is to make sure the document gets in the right hands and that he has an opportunity to personally sell the fact that it's genuine. So it would have to be someone he trusts completely."

"Hmmm. Did he have any love interests?" Emily asked.

Thorn gave her a hard look. *Good question. Leave it to the woman on the team to go in that direction.*

Sean reflected for a moment. "No. At least none that I am aware of. There were rumors, of course. It is, after all, the Vatican."

"Rumors about what?" Emily asked.

"He was seen at a few social functions with the wife of one of the Vatican's lawyers. It got some tongues wagging. I didn't pay attention. But it couldn't be her."

"Why not?" Thorn asked.

"She passed away. Back in early 1939. About a month before Longworth was called back to England."

"Hmmm . . . interesting timing," Thorn said, rubbing his chin. "So who else might be on the list? What about the British ambassador Osborne? They worked together, right?"

"Closely, for a few years," Sean said.

"But that wouldn't work," Emily said. "D'Arcy Osborne is back in London and has been for the past few weeks or so. He's not due to return to Rome until after the king knights him. Longworth wouldn't send the document to him if he's not there to receive it."

Thorn nodded, feeling as if Sister Mary Catherine, his fifth-grade teacher at Saint Catherine's, had just told him that his solution to a math problem made no sense.

A quiet descended on the three travelers, and Sean moved into the aisle. "I think I'll go up to chat with Mr. Taylor. He said he wanted to get some inside information about the inner workings of the Vatican." He scrambled up the aisle, bouncing from one side to the other.

Thorn sat back, discreetly pulled out his Colt, and began wiping it down with his handkerchief—a nervous habit that he felt safe to indulge given that Sean was bending Taylor's ear. "I know one thing—that diary page is sitting somewhere in the Vatican waiting for Longworth to pick it up."

CHAPTER FIFTY

0800 Hours, Friday, October 16, 1942
Littorio Airport, Rome

For the entire flight to Rome, Longworth sat facing a middle-aged Abwehr agent who reeked of garlic and wine. The agent slept the entire flight, snoring incessantly while the handcuffed Longworth sat staring out the plane's window, doubts as to the success of his plan taking root.

Shortly after the three-engine German Junkers transport touched down at Rome's Littorio Airport, Longworth was passed off by his inebriated companion into the hands of two mute Abwehr agents. They marched him off the tarmac, which was rapidly becoming sunbaked, toward a waiting Mercedes that sat inside the gate. Its engine was running, producing exhaust that appeared to cling to the asphalt due to the stillness of the air. One of the agents opened the rear door and then retreated to another sedan parked behind the Mercedes. Longworth stood there as a waft of cigarette smoke escaped the interior of the car and mingled with the Mercedes's exhaust fumes.

Someone barked at the guard from the rear of the sedan to remove Longworth's handcuffs. Longworth recognized the voice; it made him stiffen and clench his teeth. The agent uncuffed Longworth, who massaged his reddened, raw wrists. Longworth hadn't seen Kappler since the major first approached him a week after Maria had died in his bed. That night, in an empty café near the Vatican, was the first time he had seen the photos. Kappler had started with pictures of him and Maria enjoying some wine, followed with photos of gentle foreplay. Things that night, as on most nights, had progressed swiftly—Longworth taking control, Maria fighting back, then submitting, then resuming her fight, ending with both achieving a release that drained their bodies. The photos caught it all. The last one was of Longworth as he stood over Maria's lifeless body. But some things had changed since he and Kappler had first met—now, Kappler had no power over him.

"Come in, Longworth. Please join me." Kappler's thick accent clanged in Longworth's ear.

While he expected to see Kappler at some point, Longworth groaned. Seeing him served to further weaken his resolve. He'd botched killing Bright, was nearly killed in an aerial attack, and had suffered ill treatment at the hands of the Abwehr, and now he had to deal with Kappler. His only source of comfort was that he had killed the impudent Thorn.

Longworth bent down to get into the Mercedes, which produced a throbbing pain above his left ear. He sat opposite Kappler, with his back to the driver. "Major Kappler, I would like to say it's a pleasure to see you again. But it's not."

Kappler greeted Longworth with an icy stare, then gave the order to drive to the German embassy. Kappler, his civilian attire topped by a black hat pushed rakishly to one side, its front brim angled downward, had been reviewing a file when Longworth entered the smoky sedan. Kappler closed the file, placed it under his arm, and pressed it tightly against his rib cage. "Lisbon is such an exciting city, is it not? Full of intrigue and subterfuge. And from my sources, it appears that you have experienced quite an adventure," Kappler said, his face the picture of smugness.

"I was only there long enough to see the Abwehr's subterfuge."

"And yet, here you are. All in one piece. I trust that your wound has been cared for appropriately."

"I believe so. It's no longer bleeding, so that's an improvement."

"Excellent. Excellent," Kappler said, his voice dripping in faux concern. Several moments passed. A sly smile appeared on his face. "You surprise me, Longworth. You took great risks to come through that city—risks to your life and, more notably, at least to the Abwehr, risks to the intelligence that you brought with you."

"The risks to myself were necessary and calculated. I counted on the Abwehr to see to my safety. I did not calculate that we would be attacked by your Luftwaffe."

"Ahh, yes. A clear example of the vagaries of war. It is best if one is prepared to die any day. I do sincerely hope that the intelligence you promised to Bishop Heinz is more ... valuable and impactful than the worthless trash you have been feeding the Abwehr up to now," Kappler said, his tone stripped of its condescension. Longworth now heard anger.

"It is, Major."

Kappler tilted his head back and eyed Longworth through narrowed eyes. "Very well then. I am sure you understand that I would prefer to judge for myself. Let me see it."

Longworth had rehearsed this conversation several times on the flight from Lisbon. "Major, I have taken proper precautions. I do not have it with me."

Kappler lowered his head, his face knotted in confusion.

"But, I assure you, it is in a safe place."

Kappler took off his hat, tossed it on the seat, and placed the file on his lap. His hair was combed straight back and held in place by a generous portion of hair oil. "I do not take you for a stupid man, but you are playing an enormously dangerous game. A game whose outcome is not in your control."

Longworth sighed; he was tiring of dealing with this idiot. "I took possession of a particularly valuable piece of intelligence concerning the Allied plans for a second front. To have that intelligence on my person as I traveled through the English countryside and Lisbon would have been insane. As I said, if you were listening, it is in a safe place."

"Oh, I was listening, Longworth." Kappler leaned forward. Longworth could smell the strong scent of the hair oil. "Must I remind you that we hold all the cards in this game?" The major opened the file and extracted a black-and-white, glossy photograph and handed it to Longworth. It was only the second time he had seen any of the photos of the last night he'd spent with his mistress. Kappler handed over three more, each more graphic than the previous. The images were as jarring and regretful as they had been upon his first viewing. "The stakes are high. The *London Daily Mail* will have no trouble identifying you in these pictures. And if you have any ideas about ever returning to England, you must not fail to deliver this intelligence."

Longworth looked up at Kappler and smiled. He was quite satisfied with Kappler's look of astonishment.

"What are you smiling about?" the man insisted.

"These photos—they no longer have any hold over me." He threw the photos into Kappler's lap. "You, Major, have no hold over me."

Kappler's face reddened, and Longworth noted that his chest was heaving. "Oh, is that so. You—"

"My life in England is over. Hopefully, with the help of friends in the Vatican, a life in Vatican City awaits me. You see, what it has all now come down to is this—killing communists. That is what I want. That is what the church wants. That is what Hitler wants. Without a second front to concern you, how many communists can your German armies kill?"

Kappler stiffened and sat taller in his seat. "Where is the document?"

"I sent it to the Vatican."

Kappler's jaw dropped open, and his eyes widened. "The Vatican is a neutral state. We do not have access."

Longworth ignored Kappler and stared out the window. "Where are you taking me?"

"To the German embassy, of course."

"No," Longworth snapped. "We must get to the Vatican and Sir D'Arcy Osborne's office."

"Why is he involved?"

Longworth looked at Kappler. If he could have killed him now, he would have done so gladly. "I sent the document to myself, in care of his office—my old office. It should have arrived yesterday. The office staff knows that I am no longer assigned to the ambassador's office, so I must retrieve it quickly, before they send it back to England."

Kappler slumped in his seat. He took a moment before replying, "How quickly?"

Longworth looked out the rear window of the Mercedes,

calculating the number of days that had passed. "A return pouch will be leaving tomorrow for Westminster Cathedral. We shouldn't waste any time."

Kappler looked at his watch. "Then we must get Heinz. He will have to arrange for access to the Vatican, so as not to arouse suspicions." He leaned forward and looked around Longworth. "Driver, take me to Santa Maria dell'Anima, the Piazza Navona. Quickly." He sat back.

The depleted Longworth sat with his eyes closed. "Where are the Allies going to establish a second front?"

Longworth didn't respond.

"Longworth!"

"French North Africa." Longworth did not open his eyes.

"Ah, a rumor we have heard all too often. And Norway. And Dakar."

"Wait until you see what I have before you rush to judgment."

CHAPTER FIFTY-ONE

0845 Hours, Friday, October 16, 1942
Church of Santa Maria dell'Anima, Rome

Longworth's eyes were shut tight for the entire trip; he was hoping to squeeze the pounding in his head into submission. Vibrations moved up his spine as the Mercedes traveled over the tightly knit cobblestones of the narrow streets that surrounded the Piazza Navona. Kappler's driver pulled the Mercedes onto Vicolo della Pace, the street—which resembled an alley—that flanked the imposing church where Heinz had an office.

When the sedan stopped, Longworth opened his eyes. It took a moment for his eyes to adjust to the bright morning sun. He recognized the sand-colored façade, which was made up of under-sized bricks, and the stained-glass windows that lined one side of the sixteenth-century church. The windows of the national church of German expatriates were protected by a chain-link barrier that had been built to protect the glass artwork from the stones thrown by angry Romans.

Kappler and Longworth moved down the narrow alley, its cobblestoned surface wet from rain. After entering the rear of the church, they ascended a marble staircase; decade upon decade of foot traffic had worn the surface of the hard stone steps, leaving them indented. At the top of the stairs, a long hallway traveled the full length of the rear wall of the church. Midway down the hallway, Kappler and Longworth entered an office and startled a nun in a black habit crowned with a white headdress. The old woman was bent over her desk, peering into an ancient typewriter and losing a battle with a typewriter's ribbon spools, her fingers stained black.

"*Cosa loro vorrebbero?*" asked the nun, sitting back in her chair as she wiped her hands on her habit.

Longworth conversed with the nun for several moments, then turned to Kappler. "She says that Heinz was called to the German embassy this morning. She doesn't know by whom, since Heinz took the call himself."

"The embassy?" Kappler said, his face taking on an imperious look. "Impossible. Ask if there is a phone we can use."

A short question and answer later, Longworth pointed to a phone on a desk in the corner.

Kappler rushed over, picked up the handset, and dialed. After a long pause, he spoke loudly into the handset. "This is Major Kappler. I am looking for Bishop Heinz, and I have been told that he was called to the embassy." He looked over his shoulder at the nun, who had gone back to fighting the ribbon spool. "Called by whom?" Kappler asked, clearly irritated.

Longworth took a seat near the nun's desk and dropped his face into his cupped hands.

"Admiral Canaris!" Kappler shouted.

Longworth snapped his head up at the mention of the Abwehr chief's name.

Kappler turned his back on Longworth and the nun. "You must tell them, at once, that they must meet me and Henry Longworth at Heinz's office. We must travel to the Vatican immediately . . . No, no, there is no time. We are closer to the Vatican than the embassy is. Tell them." Kappler hung up the phone and stood over Longworth. "We shall wait for the bishop . . . and Admiral Canaris. You can tell your story to the admiral. I am sure that he will not be amused."

#

Thirty minutes passed before Heinz and Canaris arrived. When Canaris entered the office, Longworth rose from his chair.

"Bishop, we require some privacy," Canaris said, scowling at Longworth.

"In here, Admiral." Heinz led the group through a door, steps away from the nun's desk. They entered a cramped office space that featured one large window, the exterior of which was soot stained and keeping the morning sunlight at bay. Behind the desk were two flag stands—one sporting the flag of the Vatican, the other the flag of Nazi Germany, the black swastika centered on a field of blood red. Canaris looked at the flag and winced. No one made a move to sit.

"Admiral, you honor us with your presence. May I welcome you to Rome?" Kappler said, his words dripping with deference. Canaris was surprised to see Kappler out of uniform but pleased that he didn't have to see the lanky major strut about with his ribbons.

"Just tell me what the situation is," Canaris ordered.

Kappler's look changed immediately from cordial to official.

Longworth explained why it was too risky to carry the document with him and that it had been mailed in the Vatican's diplomatic pouch to the office of D'Arcy Osborne. "We need to retrieve it right away, before it is sent back to England," Longworth added.

"Why would it be sent back?" Canaris asked.

"Because they know that I have been appointed to a new post there. They will think it was sent by mistake by someone who is unaware of the . . . reassignment."

"Will they not be . . . surprised when you show up to claim it?"

"I'm sure at first, but I can talk my way through that. I counted on Osborne's absence from the office to help me with that."

"Admiral," Kappler said, puffing out his chest, "I believed it wise to have Bishop Heinz lead us, his guests, into the Vatican and to Osborne's office."

Canaris looked at Heinz and realized that, coming as far as he had, he might as well see this drama through to the end. "Will there be any problems, Bishop?" Canaris asked.

"I do not anticipate any," Heinz replied. "If anyone inquires, I will say that I am escorting some German nationals to the German College to see relatives who are studying there."

"I see." Canaris looked at his watch. "Then let's proceed to the Vatican," he said as he made to exit the office.

"Admiral, there's one more thing you should know," Longworth said.

Canaris stopped and turned back to him, annoyed at another possible twist to the drama that was unfolding. "You're wise to be forthcoming, but I hope it is not bad news."

"There were two agents on my trail. One OSS agent and one MI6 agent. While dealing with them, in a moment of . . . of rage, I revealed much of my plan."

"Good God, man, why would you do that?" Canaris blurted.

"I was about to eliminate them. They would have posed no threat. But things did not go as planned. I killed one, an OSS agent named Thorn."

"And you believe that MI6 is still in pursuit of you?"

"I do."

Canaris looked down at the floor, pondering the possibility of interference from MI6.

"He would be awfully foolish to enter Rome. It is a German-held fortress," Kappler said.

"She. And she is exceedingly persistent, Admiral," Longworth said.

The Abwehr chief ambled over to face Longworth. He sensed that Longworth was holding his breath. "It should be your hope that her persistence has its limits—as does my patience."

CHAPTER FIFTY-TWO

1000 Hours, Friday, October 16, 1942
Inside the Papal Limousine, Rome

When Thorn observed the four officers from a security detail mounted on motorcycles that were to escort their limousine into Rome, he realized that, for the first time since the start of the war, he was in enemy territory and in plain sight. *If I can pull this off, I want an Academy Award.* The flags of Pope Pius XII on each of the sleek front fenders snapped in the wind as the limousine, a black 1940 Cadillac with curtained privacy windows, hastily made its way to the residences of Santa Marta, located inside Vatican City.

Both Thorn and Emily fiddled with their disguises; Thorn tugged at the stiff, white collar that was too tight, and Emily was constantly adjusting her habit. Thorn worried that they would not be able to limit his and Emily's interactions with Vatican officials. A nosy official anxious to preserve the Vatican's neutrality would not hesitate to expose them as interlopers.

Thorn and Emily sat in the middle seat, facing Sean and Taylor, who sat in the back. Only four feet separated the seats, making private conversation impossible. Thorn detected the smell of incense, and it brought to mind the queasiness he had always experienced when he served as an altar boy during funeral masses. Sean answered questions from the weary-looking Taylor, who expressed some nervousness over meeting the pope later that day. Thorn and Emily talked in low tones about their contrived mission regarding prisoners of war.

Thirty minutes into the trip, Thorn pulled back the curtain on his right and could see that they had pulled into a large square, where the limousine parted a sea of pigeons as it sped forward.

"Father, where are we?" Thorn asked.

Sean pulled back the curtain. "Ahh, here we are. Saint Peter's Square. We'll be at Santa Marta in a matter of minutes."

"Well then, this might be the appropriate time to wish you, Father Thorn and Sister Bright, much luck with your assignment." Myron Taylor slid forward in his seat and reached out for a handshake. "Be sure to give my best to Archbishop Spellman when you report back to him."

"We will, Mr. Taylor. And good luck to you with your discussions with the Holy Father. May they be fruitful," Thorn said, hoping that his forced sincerity wasn't too over the top.

"I am sure they will."

Their Italian police escort had disengaged as the limousine entered Saint Peter's Square and approached the Petriano entrance gate. The driver pulled up to the gatehouse and produced a pass, after which the guard entered the information into a logbook and let the car pass. The limousine drove past the German College and a moment later pulled up to the entrance of a six-story building, its exterior a warm, light-yellow stucco. The driver was the first to exit the Cadillac, and he promptly opened the passenger door closest to the entrance. Another attendant came from inside the building and opened the trunk to retrieve Taylor's bags. They stood outside the entrance in a cool, late-morning breeze that played havoc with Emily's habit. An anxious-looking Taylor stood close by, hat in hand.

"Well, good-bye to you, Father Sullivan. Thank you for regaling me with tales of life in the Vatican. They were very enlightening as well as entertaining."

"My pleasure, Mr. Taylor." A moment later, Thorn, Emily, and Sean were left standing in front of the entrance to Santa Marta with no one else in view.

"Get back in. We've got to get to Heinz's office," Thorn said as he opened the driver's door and slipped behind the wheel. Emily climbed into the backseat.

"But, Conor, I have to get the pouch to the secretary of state's office now. It can't wait," Sean pleaded.

"It has to. We don't have the time. Now get in, Sean."

"Bloody hell, Conor." Sean ducked through the open back door and slammed it shut as Thorn put the limousine in gear and executed a hasty U-turn that flung Emily into Sean's lap, knocking her habit's veil off. As they pulled away, Thorn noticed the limousine driver exit the building and begin to give chase, his fist extended high into the air in protest.

#

Thorn parked the Cadillac in front of the Church of Santa Maria dell'Anima; its width virtually blocked the narrow street that ran past the building. Sean led Thorn and Emily into the church and down the center aisle, to a door to the right of the altar that ran to a back staircase. The three sets of feet clambering up the stairwell produced a ruckus that drew the attention of a nun who stood outside a door in the hallway. As Thorn neared her, he noticed a black smudge on the nun's left cheek. Sean introduced himself in Italian and began to converse with the suspicious nun, who didn't take her eyes off Emily and her slightly askew habit. When they finished, the nun opened the door and entered an office, but not without shooting a disapproving glance at Emily.

"It seems that Bishop Heinz is not here. And he is not alone," Sean reported.

"Who is with him?" Thorn asked.

"A Major Kappler and two other men that Heinz's assistant did not know."

"Did she describe them?" asked Emily.

"No. Let me press her for that." Sean entered the office. Thorn looked at his watch and began pacing. Emily leaned against the wall and fumbled with her headpiece, stuffing strands of hair back underneath. Sean exited the office and shut the door behind him.

"Well, one description fits Longworth. The other she described as a short man, gray-white hair, bushy eyebrows, and frail looking." Thorn looked at Emily.

"Bloody hell," Emily said.

"What?"

"Canaris . . . Wilhelm Canaris."

"Holy shit," Thorn whispered. "That's great—a chance to bag Longworth, Heinz, and Canaris."

Emily's creased brow and pursed lips showed that she didn't share Thorn's glee.

Come on, Emily. Talk about contributing to the war effort. "Where were they headed, Sean?"

"She had no idea."

Thorn grabbed Sean's upper arm and pulled him toward himself. "What's your best guess? Where would he go?" Thorn pressed.

"Well . . . first guess—the German College. He's in charge of the place. That's where I would bring a couple of Germans."

Emily was quiet. The creases in her forehead deepened.

"All right, that's the next stop." They all turned around and went straight back to the street and their limousine. As they were about to exit the church, Thorn saw three security guards walking around the limousine. One peered into the windshield; another pointed to the fender flags and let loose with a rapid stream of words.

"Don't say anything. I'll handle this," Sean said. Thorn and Emily followed him into the street. Thorn gave the guards a timid bow of the head and slipped in behind the wheel. Emily got in beside him, her headdress hitting the top of the doorframe. Sean engaged the older, more senior guard in a spirited conversation, while the other two continued to examine the Cadillac closely, chatting excitedly between themselves. Thorn saw the senior guard nod, throw his hands skyward, and shrug. Sean shook the guard's hand and rushed to join Thorn and Emily.

"Let's go. Before their curiosity gets the best of them," Sean said, slamming the back door.

Thorn fired up the sixteen-cylinder engine and engaged the transmission. "What did you tell them, Sean?"

"That we were sent to pick up Bishop Heinz for a meeting with the Holy Father, but the bishop was not feeling himself today."

Thorn squinted into the rearview mirror. "How quickly lies come to the lips of an Irishman."

"If that is your way of thanking me, you're welcome."

CHAPTER FIFTY-THREE

1030 Hours, Friday, October 16, 1942
Office of D'Arcy Osborne, The Vatican, Rome

Excited at the notion of getting his hands on the directives for Operation Torch again, Longworth took the steps two at a time as he led Canaris, Kappler, and Heinz up the staircase to the fifth floor. All the rooms on the top floor of the Santa Marta annex featured fifteen-foot ceilings. The ceiling height coupled with the stone floors made sounds carry.

Kappler ordered him to stop at each landing, to allow Canaris and Heinz to catch their breath. Once on the fifth floor, Longworth traveled down the hallway at a brisk pace to D'Arcy Osborne's office. He did not wait for Canaris or Heinz to catch up but instead entered the spacious office and left the door open. When Longworth entered, with Kappler behind him, he noticed one of Osborne's assistants seated on a plain couch with another woman, a tray with a pot of coffee on the low table in front of them.

"Sophia, good morning to you," Longworth said.

The assistant, given the absence of her superior, seemed startled to see anyone, much less Longworth. She jumped from the couch with a start and spilled some coffee on the oriental rug that covered the marble floor.

"Mr. Longworth, I . . . I am surprised to see you," the assistant said as she folded her hands and brought them to her chest. Her English, with not a trace of an Italian accent, was better than

Longworth remembered it. "I'm so sorry to say that Mr. Osborne is not here. He is—"

"I know, Sophia. He is in London, being knighted by the king."

Sophia placed her cup on the tray and spoke quickly in Italian to her friend, who then cleared away the tray and disappeared into an adjacent room. Sophia, in a light-blue dress that stretched down to the top of her ankles, strode toward Longworth, now wringing her hands as Canaris and Bishop Heinz walked through the door.

"Yes, isn't that marvelous? So deserving, don't you think? Oh, Bishop Heinz, we have not seen you in some time. I hope you are well?"

"I am, my dear. Thank you," Heinz said, forcing out the words between short breaths. Canaris strode toward the windows, separating himself from Longworth and the others by several feet, and turned back toward the group as if he were an audience member watching a passion play.

"Sophia, I come on official business, a part of which requires me to claim a letter that has been sent to me in care of Mr. Osborne's office. It should have arrived within the last two days. Have you seen it?" Longworth asked. Despite the heat-starved room, Longworth could feel perspiration run down his sideburns.

Sophia's face broke out in a warm smile, and the tension in her shoulders disappeared as if the Holy Ghost had touched her with a bolt of enlightenment. "Oh, yes. I was so surprised to have received it. I was going to have it sent back to Westminster Cathedral in the next diplomatic pouch. Give me a moment."

Sophia turned and went behind a small desk in the corner of the room and entered a closet through a door that was cut into the wall paneling. She reappeared with a letter in her hand. She handed it to Longworth, who took it and saw that he had done nothing to disguise his handwriting on the front of the envelope. Sophia gave no indication that she realized the envelope was addressed to Longworth in his own hand, but he glanced at an apprehensive-looking Canaris, who carefully signaled Longworth with his hand to get on with it.

"Given that Mr. Osborne is in London, may I use his office to review the letter's contents?"

"Of course, Mr. Longworth. May I get you and your guests some coffee?"

"No, that won't be necessary. We won't be long."

\#

Longworth, with Kappler, Canaris, and Heinz in tow, entered Osborne's office. The room was also spacious with a simple desk, two armchairs, and two couches. Portraits of Pope Pius XII and King George VI hung side by side behind the desk. Like the outer office, the room was cold, per the wishes of the pope, who had banned any heating of Vatican City buildings during the war.

Longworth stood beside the desk and opened the envelope; Kappler stood behind him, looking over his shoulder. Canaris took a seat in one of the armchairs, as did Heinz. Longworth pulled a thin paper from the envelope, looked it over briefly, nodded, and then walked it over to Canaris. He stood, looming over the admiral, waving the paper in his right hand.

"This is the communication between the Combined Chiefs and General Eisenhower, signed by Chief of Staff of the US Army General George Marshall. It clearly lays out the directives of the Allies' next operation—Operation Torch, the invasion of French North Africa." Longworth handed the page to Canaris.

Canaris held out his hand. "Operation Torch . . . how clever. And how did you come into possession of this . . . communication?"

"It is a story too long to tell. Suffice it to say that it turned up missing during the microfilming process and made its way to me through people who do not want to see this operation take place."

Kappler moved closer to Longworth and Canaris, his hands buried deep into the pockets of his leather long coat. "What people?" he asked.

"People with ties to the Soviet Union."

Kappler's mouth dropped open. He looked at Canaris, whose expression did not change, then back to Longworth. "Absolutely ridiculous. That makes no sense. None whatsoever. You expect—"

"Major!" Canaris snapped as he held up his hand to silence Kappler. Canaris began to read the document. He held the paper close to the tip of his nose and moved his head back and forth as he reviewed the document. When he was done, he lowered the paper and leaned forward in the chair, as if to stand, but instead remained perched on the edge of the seat. "It seems authentic. But now you tell me that the Russians were involved in . . . stealing this intelligence. That explains why they intruded in Lisbon. But there's the issue of trust. I do not know how wise it would be to trust you and your fellow Englishmen, not to mention the Russians, whom we do not trust at all." Canaris folded the paper, which crinkled like cellophane. "I have no choice but to doubt the veracity of this document. It is the safest conclusion to come to."

Longworth's face flushed, and his breathing quickened. "You incompetent fool . . . such a disappointment."

Kappler pulled his gun from his pocket and slammed the butt against the back of Longworth's head, which sent him plummeting to the floor. Canaris stood and looked down at Longworth, who struggled to get back up. "Listen to me," Longworth croaked. "You must get this document into the hands of someone who fully understands military matters. Get it to Keitel. Let him and Hitler decide."

Canaris smiled. "Mr. Longworth, it's a shame. You have come a long way only to find out that you, and we, are being played as fools by the Russians," Canaris said calmly.

"No. You are wrong," Longworth protested as he raised himself off the floor. "I too am distrustful of the communists. But even they realize that this operation will do little to draw enough divisions and squadrons from the Eastern Front to make any difference in their fight against Germany. Don't you see? They want the Americans and British to invade France. If this operation is betrayed to the Germans, the Allies will be forced to cancel it. And that will give Hitler more time to focus on destroying Stalin without worrying about a second front to his rear."

Longworth was lightheaded from the blow to his head and grabbed the edge of the desk for support. "They know I have the document. They know, by now, that I am in Rome. But you must finish what I have started. You must get this directive into Keitel's hands."

Canaris stared at Longworth, whose contempt for Canaris rose up like acidic bile from deep in his stomach. The thought that all he had to do was get the document into a high-ranking Nazi official's hands had rattled around his head ever since it had fallen into his lap. He realized now that would not be enough.

Canaris handed the page to Kappler. He motioned to Kappler that it was time to leave as he put on his hat.

"Where are you taking me?" Longworth asked.

Canaris took his time securing his hat. "To the German Embassy, to have a deeper conversation—one without hysterics, hopefully." Canaris turned toward the office door.

"I'm not leaving the Vatican. That was what I asked for—safety in exchange for this intelligence."

Canaris waited several beats. "Safety in wartime is a very valuable commodity. Its supply is finite. Your . . . intelligence . . . does not come close to matching the value of the safety that you request." He turned and left the office.

Longworth looked at Heinz, who tightened his cape and bolted from the office. "Heinz! You scum!" Longworth shouted.

"Don't worry, Longworth," Kappler said as he poked the nose of his pistol into Longworth's back. "I am sure the Abwehr can keep you safe from your countrymen—your betrayed countrymen."

He had done all he could, and there was nowhere else to turn. Long ago, his life had taken a turn for the worse inside the Vatican, and it seemed it had again.

They walked out of Osborne's office, and Longworth, walking unsteadily, saw Sophia study him as he clutched the back of his head, blood clearly visible seeping through his fingers.

"Mr. Longworth, are you injured?"

Longworth turned as he approached the hallway door and looked back at Sophia. Her image moved in and out of focus. He left without uttering a word.

CHAPTER FIFTY-FOUR

1130 Hours, Friday, October 16, 1942
Inside the Papal Limousine, Rome

For Thorn, every sound and vibration was amplified as if he were back on the flight from Tangier to Lisbon, except now he was in control. Sort of. He eased up on the accelerator as they approached the Petriano entrance gate.

"Shit, are you ready for this, Sean?" Thorn pounded the steering wheel. "Damn it, we should have discussed how we were going to talk our way back into Vatican City with the pope's car."

"I think I can handle this," Sean said, peering out the windshield. "I know this guard. He's a sergeant. Pull up to the gate slowly."

As Thorn pulled up, Sean rolled down the rear left window and attracted the guard's attention before the man could engage Thorn. "Sergeant Graf. A pleasure to see you again."

The guard recognized Sean and smiled all too briefly. "Father Sullivan. You have returned."

Thorn was taken aback by the guard's accent. He'd expected an Italian accent but heard something different. *Of course, Swiss guards.*

"Yes. Yes. We are—"

"Father, what are you doing with the Holy Father's car? The driver reported that someone drove away with it earlier."

"Ah, yes. A miscommunication, I'm afraid. My Italian is a bit rusty. You see, the Holy Father was kind enough to send his car to pick us and the American representative Myron Taylor up from the airport."

"Yes, I am aware. You were checked in a while ago."

"Well, Mr. Taylor asked that we retrieve Bishop Heinz from Santa Maria dell'Anima for a meeting with Mr. Taylor, before he meets with the Holy Father. But it seems—"

"Bishop Heinz and guests checked in at this gate about thirty minutes ago."

"Ah, yes. So we were told. A wasted trip it was, I'm afraid."

Emily cleared her throat, getting Thorn's attention. She pointed to her watch and raised her eyebrows. Thorn responded with a timid shrug.

Graf bent over and peered into the rear of the limousine. "Father, shouldn't that diplomatic pouch be dropped off at the secretary of state's office?"

"Yes. That is the next stop."

Graff gave a halfhearted nod. "And who are these people?"

"That would be Father Thorn and Sister Bright. Is it all right to pass through, Sergeant Major?"

Graff gave his jaw a firm rub. "This all seems rather unusual, Father, but go ahead."

"Thank you for understanding."

Thorn rolled slowly though the gate, gravel crunching underneath the Cadillac's tires. On the other side, he took a slight turn to the left and headed through the Piazza del Santo Uffizio, toward the German College. As Thorn brought the Cadillac to a stop in front of the German College, he noticed Longworth, his tall frame putting him a head above two other men and a third who pulled up the rear of the group, as he was getting into a long, black Mercedes.

Mark this day, you bastard. It's your last.

"Well, look at that, would you?" Thorn said, motioning with his head. "Over there—it's our man Longworth. And take a look at who's behind him."

"It's Canaris," said Emily, her voice tinged with wonder and dread.

"And the short man in the frock and cape—that's Heinz," said Sean.

Heinz stood on the periphery of the group, uninvolved in the conversation but looking intently at the Cadillac.

He looks plenty alive to me. Someone should tell MI6, Thorn thought, fighting the urge to drop the car into first gear and bury its hood in the side of the Mercedes and be done with it.

"I think they spotted us," Emily said.

With the Cadillac's engine still running, Thorn grabbed the gearshift and pulled it toward him, then down. A dull clunk, and the car was in first gear. *Don't be stupid. The Swiss Guards will be on you in seconds, and you won't get the diary page. You need to jump them on the streets of Rome. Not here.*

"No. They can't see inside the car from that distance. They most likely recognize the car. The fender flags are kind of a giveaway," Thorn said, putting the Cadillac back in neutral.

Longworth was the first to get into the back of the Mercedes. The other three men stood outside the car for a moment and conversed among themselves before they joined Longworth and drove off, headed in the direction of the Petriano gate, passing the papal limousine.

Thorn's mind raced. The sight of a Churchill war cabinet member with the head of the Abwehr was chilling.

"Conor, that's where D'Arcy Osborne's office is—on the top floor," Sean said.

Thorn turned around to look at Sean. "Of course it is," he said, the pitch in his voice rising. "Longworth knew that Osborne was in London."

"Of course he did—the cabinet held a lunch for him in his honor," Emily added.

"And he knew that Osborne wouldn't be here to raise questions about a letter or about Longworth's appearance in Rome. The timing of Osborne's trip to London fit into his plan perfectly."

Thorn got out of the limousine and yanked the flags of the Holy See from the fenders, jumped back behind the wheel, shoved the gearshift into first, and sped forward. He took an abrupt right turn in front of the Sacristy of Saint Peter's and another sharp right after passing the German College, then headed straight through the Petriano gate, drawing a stern look from the sergeant. Thorn could see the Mercedes up ahead, a flock of pigeons scattering into the air before resettling on the cobblestones as the vehicle raced along.

Longworth's been a few steps ahead of us for too long. I think it's time to catch up.

#

Longworth regained his composure as the Mercedes turned off Via Paolo VI onto Borgo Santo Spirito and picked up speed on the wide boulevard. Canaris and Kappler peered over their shoulders.

"What's happening?" asked Longworth.

"It appears that we are being followed—closely," Kappler said.

"That's the Holy Father's limousine," Heinz said. "It was parked across the street from us moments ago. But he couldn't—"

"I don't care whose car it is. They're following us," Kappler shouted.

Longworth considered what would happen at the embassy. Canaris's reaction to the document was deflating. Would they interrogate him? Would they torture him to collect other classified information? He had lost control of his plan. He was falling into an abyss.

"Longworth, could this be the persistent agent that has been after you?" Canaris asked.

"I have no way of knowing, but it's your problem now."

"Perhaps it is the NKVD coming to your rescue?" Canaris offered.

Longworth gave him no reaction except for an unrelenting stare.

"Admiral, should I try to take out one of their tires?" Kappler asked.

"No, let's try to lose them in some traffic."

"Driver. The black limousine behind us—pick up speed and lose them." Kappler, seated opposite Longworth, took out his gun and placed it in his lap.

Longworth stared at it as Kappler turned to look out the rear window.

#

"Where are they headed, Sean?" Thorn asked as he guided the speeding Cadillac down the Borgo Santo Spirito.

"I don't know. They aren't headed back to Heinz's office. But they could be headed to the airport or the German Embassy."

"Well, they're not going to get to either place. Hold on," Thorn shouted. He took a right off of the Via Paolo VI onto Borgo Santo Spirito and saw that the Mercedes had picked up speed. He buried the gas pedal, and the Cadillac's sixteen cylinders effortlessly closed the distance.

"What's up ahead?" Thorn asked.

"If they stay on this street, it runs into the Piazza Pia. If they take a right as it gets close to the Tiber, they'll go across the Vittorio Emanuel Bridge."

"What's the plan?" Emily asked as she pulled her headdress off and took out her PPK .

"The diary page has to be in that car. All we have to do now is stop them."

The Mercedes slowed as it approached the intersection of Piazza Pia and then took a right onto the Vittorio Emanuel Bridge. Thorn did not slow when he made the same turn, forcing Emily to slide across the seat toward him. Sean held on to a strap above the door.

The Cadillac, its tires squealing, was now less than fifty feet behind the Mercedes. The two-way traffic was flanked on each side by wide sidewalks, and a white, decorative marble railing three feet high ran down the length of the bridge on each side. The traffic on the bridge was sparse—a bus, a delivery truck, and a sedan in the oncoming lane. A two-wheeled cart pulled by a donkey was thirty yards ahead of the speeding cars.

Thorn swerved into the middle lane and pushed the Cadillac's V-16 engine, pulling alongside the Mercedes.

#

Inside the Mercedes, Longworth saw that Kappler, Canaris, and Heinz were all riveted as the Cadillac pulled up. Mere moments ago, he believed that he might bargain his way into the safety of Vatican City. But that hope, as feeble as it was, was smashed by the relentlessness of their faceless pursuers...yet maybe all was not lost.

Kappler, his gun in hand, screamed at the driver to pull ahead. Longworth lunged at Kappler, trying to wrestle the gun away from him.

"Get off me, you fool." Kappler pushed his foot into Longworth's chest, propelling him back into his seat. As Longworth's hand was wrenched away, a shot thundered inside the cabin, Longworth's ears ringing as it smashed through the glass partition and hit the driver in the shoulder.

\#

"What was that?" Thorn shouted.

"Not sure. I think the driver's been shot—he's slumped over the wheel," Emily yelled over the revving V-16.

On the right sidewalk, a woman held a baby, its carriage nearby as she stood at the bridge's railing, looking out over the Tiber River. Thorn gasped as he realized the Mercedes was careening directly toward her and her baby.

The woman turned toward the sound of the approaching vehicles, and Thorn saw her face twist in terror as the Mercedes bore down on them. Her expression triggered an image of Grace as she held their son while he took his last breath, Thorn by their side, powerless to help in any way.

No. Not this time.

There was a loud bang as the Mercedes's right front tire slammed into the curb, popping it. The delivery truck, bus, and sedan in the lane of oncoming traffic screeched to a halt. If Thorn mistimed what came next, he would launch the Cadillac over the railing and into the Tiber.

He reached out and grabbed Emily's arm, yanking her away from the passenger door. Clenching his jaw, he spun the wheel of the Cadillac sharply to the right. The car collided with the Mercedes with a deafening crunch, launching it up onto the sidewalk, hurling Emily to the roof and then back down into her seat. The scraping sounds of metal on metal filled the air.

The Mercedes's front end smashed into the marble railing. Parts of its grill and headlights showered the sidewalk and its chrome bumper slid across the sidewalk and crushed the baby carriage, coming to rest inches from the woman. The Cadillac jolted to a stop.

The woman screamed, sprinting down the sidewalk away from the crash, clutching her baby just as the Mercedes's radiator ruptured and released a hissing cloud of steam. Thorn pulled ahead and up onto the sidewalk in front of the Mercedes. He glanced over at Emily and saw she had her PPK trained on the car.

The driver began to stir and moved as if reaching for a sidearm. Thorn grabbed his Colt. From the driver's seat, he leaned toward Emily and, with his Colt inches from her left shoulder, fired a round, piercing the windshield of the Mercedes and killing the driver.

Thorn and Emily leaped from the Cadillac, guns aimed at the Mercedes's back left door. Longworth was the first to stumble out of the car, followed by a man in a long, black leather coat with a gun pointed at Longworth's back. Longworth looked as if he'd laid eyes on Satan when he saw Thorn.

Thorn smiled. *You fucking bastard. You tried to kill me. Now it's my turn.*

"Thorn. Another bloody mistake surfaces," Longworth said, shaking his head. "You have no idea what you've done."

Emily took several paces toward the bridge railing to separate from Thorn, getting a better angle on the man holding Longworth hostage. Thorn saw her stoop and peer into the Mercedes, where Canaris and Heinz remained, which prompted Thorn to momentarily think of Sean. *Stay put, buddy. I may need you.* Leather Coat took two steps backward toward the Mercedes, his gaze jumping between Thorn and Emily.

"And what is that, Longworth?"

"You've only made it possible for Stalin to overrun the Germans in the east and take over most of Eastern Europe."

"A fascinating statement. The way I see it, I've kept a top-secret document from reaching Berlin while capturing a traitor to his country along with the head of the Abwehr."

"Conor, we don't have much time. We're too exposed here," Emily said, holding her PPK with both hands.

Thorn barely made out the sound of a siren above the hissing of the Mercedes's radiator.

"You're both bloody idiots. I am the true patriot here. I am the one that clearly sees who the true enemy is. Do you think I'm the only one working against the inept government of that Stalin-appeaser Churchill? I am not. Do you hear me? I am not alone."

"God, that's enough. Which one of you has the document?" Thorn asked.

"That would be me, Mr. Thorn—Major Kappler of the Abwehr." He said it with the Germanic tone of arrogance that Thorn loathed so much, and as he did so, Kappler circled Longworth, putting the man between Emily and himself.

"Bucking for a promotion, are we, Major?" Thorn asked.

"Your humor betrays your fear," Kappler said, a smile emerging. "I must say, if you are so anxious to reclaim the document, traveling so deep into our territory, it must be authentic. The admiral had his doubts. I'll just hold on to it for the time being, because in a matter of minutes, this street will be swarming with German and Italian security."

Canaris emerged from the backseat and stood near Kappler, whose attention bounced between Thorn and Emily. "Give it to them," Canaris said. "It is nothing but another English ploy—worthless intelligence that will not be believed by the führer."

Kappler's focus on Thorn and Emily shattered, his gun shaking as he stole looks at Canaris. Thorn spied Longworth inching toward the railing.

"What are you saying? Have you lost your mind? How can it be worthless if they risked so much to retrieve it?" Kappler said, his face turning red. Spittle built at the corners of his mouth as Longworth moved closer to the railing.

"Longworth, sit tight. You're not going to swim for it. And enough of this. Drop the fucking gun, Kappler, or I'll put a round in your boss's chest," Thorn said.

Canaris put his right hand on Kappler's forearm. "Do as he says, Major."

"Admiral—" Kappler pleaded.

"Just do it."

Kappler lowered his gun and placed it on the roof of the Mercedes.

"Emily, search Kappler," Thorn said.

As she moved toward the major, Thorn glanced over his shoulder and could see that some of the bus passengers had gotten off and were gathered on the opposite sidewalk, taking in the show.

"Conor!" Sean yelled from the backseat of the limousine.

Thorn spun back around as Kappler made a move for the pistol. Thorn squeezed off two rounds—both landed in the man's chest and he crumpled to the ground, blood gushing from each wound.

Kappler's pistol hit the ground and skidded toward Longworth. Canaris dropped to the ground and Emily crouched for cover. As Longworth bent to pick up the gun, Thorn noticed movement in the back of the Mercedes. *I shouldn't have let it go this far. I should have come out blasting everyone in sight. Another mistake.*

Heinz crept from the backseat holding a small-caliber revolver. As Thorn opened his mouth to warn her, Emily jumped up, drew a bead on Heinz, and fired off two rounds. His body fell atop the bridge's railing before sliding into the Tiber River. As the sound of Heinz's body hitting the fast-moving water echoed off the bottom of the bridge, Longworth raised his pistol at Thorn—but Thorn already had his gun trained on Longworth's head.

"You—"

Thorn fired. He was done talking—he was done with Longworth.

Longworth fell to the pavement, then onto his side. His eyes fluttered, his face tightening in pain. Thorn fired once more, the bullet driving into Longworth's skull. *That's for Churchill.*

Canaris struggled to his feet as Emily combed through Kappler's tunic and pulled out an envelope. She held up a thin piece of paper and looked it over. "This is it!" she shouted, smiling and wide-eyed as she slipped the envelope under her habit.

The tension in Thorn's shoulders released. He saw faces—the crewmates from the *Reuben James*, Grace, his mother. He had been spared for a purpose—one that was becoming clearer to him. Save and protect. He took a deep breath.

"Grab any identification from Longworth's body—wallet, rings, anything," Thorn said.

Emily rifled through Longworth's pockets.

"Check around his neck," Sean said, leaning out of the door of the Cadillac. "There should be a Saint Christopher's medal inscribed from Cardinal Massy."

Emily quickly loosened Longworth's collar, reached inside his shirt, then yanked a chain from around his neck.

Thorn slipped his Colt into his waistband in the back, bent down, and grabbed Longworth's body under the arms. Longworth's head bobbed as Thorn dragged his body to the railing. He gripped Longworth's feet as he tipped the body into the murky, swift-moving waters of the Tiber.

He turned to Emily. "Now grab Canaris and put him in the back of the car with Sean. We have to get out of here."

Emily began to back away from Canaris, her PPK in her hand. "Conor, I…I can't do that," she said.

Thorn's jaw dropped. He wasn't sure he had heard her right.

Canaris smirked.

"What? What the hell are you saying? Grabbing him would be a windfall for the Allies. We're not leaving him here."

"I have orders that he is to be left behind—and left alive."

"From whom?"

Emily looked at Canaris, who looked back at her, patiently waiting for her answer. "From C."

Canaris stared at Emily and nodded as if he had seen the script beforehand.

EPILOGUE

When Thorn and Emily entered the foyer of 70 Grosvenor Street, Thorn saw the two ever-present armed guards flanking the elevator. Between them stood Lieutenant Colonel Duncan Lee. His wire-rimmed glasses were slightly bent out of their normal shape, sitting lopsided on the bridge of his nose. He looked agitated. As Thorn and Emily approached, he tapped his watch.

"Colonel Donovan and guest are waiting."

"Well then, let's get going," Thorn said with just the right amount of pseudo-excitement to annoy Lee.

Emily tapped Thorn on his arm to bring him into line.

The elevator ride to the third floor was spent in silence until Lee cleared his throat. "The colonel wants to see you tomorrow morning, Mr. Thorn. Alone. At eight o'clock," he said without breaking his gaze on the elevator panel.

Thorn stood behind Lee and noticed that the man's ears protruded to the point where they looked as if they were trying to fly off the sides of his head. "And that would be about?"

"To put you back to work, I imagine."

"Ahh. No rest for the—"

"Wicked," Emily said, a glint in her eyes.

"I was going to say *weary*. But wicked works," Thorn said as the elevator doors parted.

Entering Bill Donovan's office, Thorn saw that neither of the two men present was speaking. Donovan sat behind his desk holding a saucer and sipping from a steaming cup. Another man, dressed in a blue pinstripe suit, had his back to the group, looking out the window behind Donovan's desk.

"Emily, Conor. Good to have you back," Donovan said as he rose and came around his desk to shake hands. "Please sit. Can we get you anything?"

"No, sir," Thorn said as he reached into his pocket and pulled out a roll of film and passed it to Donovan. "Colonel, we took some shots of us burning the diary page. Just thought someone would want proof that it was destroyed."

"That wasn't necessary, but thanks," Donovan said.

Pinstripe turned around and moved toward Donovan's desk. It was C. His face was less ashen than when Thorn had first met him.

"Conor, you remember Stewart Menzies, head of MI6," Donovan said.

"Yes, sir. I do," Thorn said. "Hello, sir."

Menzies wordlessly recognized Thorn with a nod and a soft grunt as he placed his cup and saucer on Donovan's desk. He approached Emily and shook hands, lingering and sharing a warm smile. "Emily, you have my undying gratitude."

Menzies was dressed as if he were going to a coronation. Thorn watched him stroke his impeccably trimmed mustache as he returned to his position beside the desk.

"Would you prefer to sit, Stewart?"

"No, Bill, I will stand, if you don't mind. Too much time behind my own desk. My legs are rather creaky today."

"Fine. I echo Stewart's appreciation for your efforts. As does General Eisenhower."

"And the prime minister," Menzies said, with a couple of sharp nods for emphasis.

"Your success fills many key people associated with Operation Torch with the confidence they need to strike a decisive blow against the Germans and the Vichy French," Donovan said.

"Thank you, both. But can I bring up something that has been bothering me? Emily begged me not to, but I have to," Thorn said.

Emily glared at him.

"What about?" Menzies asked.

"Why we left the head of the Abwehr on that bridge when we could have either taken him with us or put a bullet in him, like we did to his friends."

Menzies, his mouth pinched, folded his arms across his chest. "It makes no sense to me."

"It doesn't have to, Mr. Thorn. It only has to make sense to me, who gave the order. And . . . it does."

"So, let me get this straight—he's either the most incompetent head of an intelligence service, or he is an asset that—"

"I refuse to discuss this matter any further, Colonel," shouted a red-faced Menzies.

Emily took a deep breath as she gripped the armrest of her chair, her knuckles turning white.

"Very well, Stewart," Donovan said.

That's it? No more discussion? Just because this guy throws a tantrum, we can't discuss why we left the head of the Abwehr alive?

"But," Donovan continued seemingly unfazed by Menzies's childlike stubbornness, "I do want to discuss something in your report, Conor—the statement from Longworth about not being the only one working against the Churchill government? Did he say anything that is not in your report?"

"No, sir. I didn't let him," Thorn said. "Things needed to move along, given where we were."

"I understand," Donovan said.

"But I *have* been thinking about what Longworth said, and I have some . . . concerns," Thorn said. *I don't work for C, so I don't have anything to lose.*

"As in?"

"Lisbon was a mess when we got there, and we almost didn't make it out. Why the hell Soviet agents were there to stop us and how they knew about us being there is something I can't figure out. We weren't only dealing with Longworth. Something, *someone*, else was trying to trip us up."

"Just what are you inferring, Thorn?" Menzies asked.

Emily held up a hand. "Conor, not now."

"No, Emily, I think now is a good time," Menzies said as he clasped his hands behind his back and rocked back and forth on his heels.

Thorn leaned forward. *Here goes.* "I'll just say it. I think someone inside MI6 was working against us. I think someone from Section Five—Philby's section."

"Wait a damn minute here." Menzies sprang forward and stopped at the edge of the desk. "With all due respect to Colonel Donovan and his organization, you, sir, an agent for all of six months in an organization less than a year old, have no right, no right at all, to accuse one of my top operatives of working against the Allies. Have you considered the possibility that someone inside the OSS might be to blame? Have you considered that?"

"Stewart, Thorn was there. He was on the ground," Donovan protested.

"I don't care. Emily, do you share in this . . . mad theory?"

"I . . . I can't help but think that something, some information, made it into the wrong hands. Those Soviet agents in Lisbon could be working both sides. We've all seen that happen. I just know that it's…unsettling."

"Emily, you disappoint me. You are both far off base. And, Thorn, you should be . . . cautious before you make outlandish claims against MI6."

"So are we done here?" Donovan asked as he rose from his desk chair, seemingly anxious to short-circuit the tension.

"There is one more item, Colonel, if I may?" Menzies said.

"Certainly, Stewart."

"In order to quell any probing from Fleet Street newspapers that might sow uncertainties about the Churchill government and to explain Longworth's absence, there will be a funeral service in two days for Longworth, who, it will soon become known, suffered a devastating heart attack on a trip up north. It will be held at Westminster Cathedral and presided over by Cardinal Massy and Father Sullivan. Colonel, your presence is requested. But I do not think it wise for either of you to be there," he said, looking at Thorn and Emily.

"You're kidding. You have no body," Thorn said as he looked at Donovan and Menzies.

"First, Mr. Thorn, MI6 does not kid. Second, do not concern yourself. We have already found a body."

#

Outside Donovan's office, Thorn and Emily put on their coats and stood silently looking at each other. Thorn shoved his hands into his pockets and shrugged.

"That was the strangest meeting I've ever been in. What about you?" he asked.

"If I said that I'd been in stranger, you wouldn't believe me. If I said I didn't see it as strange, you wouldn't believe that either," Emily said as she took his arm.

"Ever the diplomat," Thorn replied as he looked intently at a broadly smiling Emily. "You know, the fate of Canaris aside, we did a pretty good thing in Rome."

Emily smiled and squeezed his arm tightly.

He spied a calendar on the wall behind Lee's empty desk. "In four days, task forces set sail."

"And, it's my hope, in as much secrecy as they'll need to be successful."

"Well, that sounds like something to raise a glass to," Thorn said.

Emily suddenly grabbed his arm with both hands. "There is one matter that I haven't brought up about our time on the bridge."

"What's that?" Thorn asked. He felt the warmth of her hands through his shirt.

"Your quick actions saved the life of that mother and baby. She and her child are alive because of you. You realize that, don't you?" Emily asked.

"Yeah, I've been thinking about that. A lot." He drifted for a moment in his own thoughts, an image of Grace appearing, this time as his beaming, pregnant wife—the happiest she had ever been. It was her happiness that stoked the fires of his own happiness, but those fires had long since been doused by loss. Would that be the last time he would allow himself to be happy? Maybe he needed to lay the groundwork for it to happen again.

Maybe it was time to let her go.

"Let's head over to the Savoy," he said. "Maggie and Dad are waiting for us. A 'welcome-home bash' I believe Maggie called it."

"A wonderful idea. We'll toast to a young Italian mother and her baby, alive and well."

"Yes. A wonderful idea."

AUTHOR'S NOTE

Being a work of fiction, much was imagined in *The Torch Betrayal*, but much in the way of real people, events, and locations were incorporated into the story as well. What follows details some of the more significant factual elements.

The inspiration for *The Torch Betrayal* was found in the book *My Three Years with Eisenhower: The Personal Diary of Captain Harry C. Butcher, USNR*, published in 1946. The entry for Monday, September 7, 1942, cited that, during the microfilming process of documents that were to become General Eisenhower's personal war diary, one document was lost. It was "the page of the first TORCH directives to Ike to clean up the North African coast." After exhaustive searches, the missing page was never found. This piece of unsettled history sent my mind racing, which led to *The Torch Betrayal*—my story about what happened to that missing top-secret document. For purposes of elevating the dramatic tension, I took liberty with the discovery date of the missing document, placing it closer to the dates that were set for the embarkation of the Eastern Task Force on October 22 and the Western Task Force on October 23.

For the setting of Tangier and the activities of agents in chapter 2, I relied on the enthralling work by Hal Vaughn titled *FDR's 12 Apostles: The Spies Who Paved the Way for the Invasion of North Africa* (2006). Over a year before Pearl Harbor was attacked, FDR sent twelve vice consuls to North Africa, specifically, to Algeria, Morocco and Tunisia. One of these vice consuls was a World War I veteran named Colonel William A. Eddy. Their official task was, with the Vichy government's permission, to supervise the delivery of US goods at ports in North Africa, which gave them the needed freedom to monitor shipping, the French order of battle, and enemy agent activities. The group reported to Robert D. Murphy, who worked closely with "Wild Bill" Donovan. The informant Tassels was a real-life character who was a Moroccan leader that provided valuable information regarding French military activities.

Dean's Bar, the setting for chapter 3, was a celebrated nonconformist watering hole opened in 1937 by Joseph Dean, who was compared to Rick, the Humphrey Bogart character in the classic film *Casablanca*. It was frequented by the likes of Ian Fleming, Errol Flynn, Ava Gardner, Barbara Hutton, Samuel Beckett, and many other notable characters.

The Bureau Central de Renseignements et d'Action (BCRA) was an intelligence organization created by the Free French government-in-exile and was headed by Major Andre Dewavrin. In 1942, the level of distrust of the Free French, particularly Charles de Gaulle, held by the Americans and the British was extremely high. Great efforts were made on the part of the British and the US to keep any information from the Free French, as they believed that it would make its way back to Vichy France and then into the hands of the German Abwehr. In Anthony Cave Brown's biography of Bill Donovan, *The Last Hero: Wild Bill Donovan*, he cites an investigation by Donovan in the summer of 1942 that discovered the BCRA had established an "inquisitorial chamber" at their No. 10 Duke Street headquarters in Mayfair, London. In chapter 17, Bright mentions rumors that circulated through the intelligence services in London about torture and even the murder of suspected traitors carried out at No. 10 Duke Street. This information was gleaned from Douglas Porch's *The French Secret Services: A History of French Intelligence from the Dreyfus Affair to the Gulf War*. Toward the end of chapter 5 in the *Torch Betrayal*, Toulouse mentions the British attack on the French fleet at Mers-el-Kebir, French Algeria, which took place on July 3, 1940. The British launched an air and sea attack to keep the fleet from falling into the hands of the Nazis after the French signed an armistice with the Germans following the defeat of the Allies in the battle for France.

Flight 777 from Lisbon to England's Whitchurch Airport

was a regularly scheduled British Overseas Airline route, staffed by crews from Dutch airline KLM. At the time of the German invasion of the Netherlands in May 1940, there were several KLM airliners that were en route to various destinations. Some of these crews escaped to Britain. Respecting the neutrality of Portugal, during the early stages of the conflict, both Germany and Great Britain left each country's civilian aircraft unmolested. As the war progressed, Germany changed their policy. When Flight 777 left Portella Airport on its way to Whitchurch it was shot down by eight German Junkers JU-88s on June 1, 1943. British actor Leslie Howard was among the passengers on that flight.

Hedy Lamarr, the Austrian born actress whose Hollywood career spanned the late 1930s to the 1950s, was proclaimed by the MGM Studio to be the "world's most beautiful woman." Lesser known is the fact that she, along with her friend George Antheil, invented a frequency-hopping system that, when employed, would make the jamming of radio-controlled torpedoes impossible. However, the US Navy did not adopt the technology during World War II.

The air crash that Conor Thorn recounts to Lamarr happened on September 22, 1922. Air shows were a popular form of entertainment in the 1920s and 1930s. This particular air show attracted a crowd of approximately 25,000.

In chapter 7, Bill Donovan speaks of Conor Thorn's service aboard the *Reuben James*. The destroyer *USS Reuben James (DD 245)* was a four stack, Clemson class ship that was torpedoed and sunk by U-552, commanded by Erich Topp, on October 31, 1941, while on convoy duty in the North Atlantic. Casualties numbered 115, including the ship's full officer complement.

In this same chapter, Churchill first mentions the name of Emily Bright. The character of Emily Bright in *The Torch Betrayal* is inspired by a woman named Joan Bright, who, according to William Stevenson's book *A Man Called Intrepid: The Incredible WWII Narrative of the Hero Whose Spy Network and Secret Diplomacy Changed the Course of History*, "typified the adventurous, emotionally stable, selfless youngsters attracted to dangerous work without the reward or encouragement of public acclaim." Joan Bright, with a high security clearance, toiled deep below Whitehall in "the hole in the ground" where Churchill conducted the day-to-day planning for the fight against the Axis. (A tour of the Churchill War Rooms is a must for any student of World War II.) She worked with the Joint Planning Staff and the Joint Intelligence Committee. In the 1930s, Joan Bright was offered a job teaching English to the family of Rudolf Hess, which she turned down. She also dated Ian Fleming, who, according to her obituary in the *Independent* (January 28, 2009), she found to be "awfully attractive and fun, but elusive."

Also in chapter 7, during the October 4 dinner scene between Eisenhower and Churchill, reference is made by Churchill to a letter sent by Joseph Stalin to AP correspondent Henry Cassidy on October 3. The quote is taken from the letter verbatim.

We first meet Kim Philby in chapter 8. Philby, NKVD code name "Sonny" (later changed to "Stanley" in 1944), headed MI6's Section V with the responsibility of counterintelligence on the Iberian Peninsula. The wily Philby managed to navigate the labyrinth of British intelligence as a Soviet spy undetected from the late 1930s to 1963, when he boarded the Soviet freighter *Dolmatova* in Beirut bound for Odessa, but not before admitting that he was a member of the spy ring known as the Cambridge Five. It's a bit of an understatement to say that much has been written about the enigmatic Kim Philby and the organization he betrayed—MI6—and the organizations he loyally toiled on behalf of for nearly three decades—NKVD and the KGB. I referred often to Ben Macintyre's *A Spy Among Friends: Kim Philby and the Great Betrayal* and strongly recommend this well-researched book to anyone with a thirst for understanding the double agent Kim Philby.

Conor Thorn and Bobby Heugle head to MI6 headquarters to meet Emily Bright in the bar deep in the bowels of MI6 headquarters located at 54 Broadway (chapter 11). The revelation of the existence of a bar in the headquarters of a major power's spy agency was, at first, too difficult to be believed, until I learned, from Macintyre, that the "most secret drinking hole in the world" regularly entertained the spies of MI6. According to Macintyre, "the spies were spectacular boozers. Alcohol helped blunt the stress of clandestine war, serving as both a lubricant and a bond."

Admiral Wilhelm Canaris, head of the German intelligence, fought a valiant battle to save Germany from total destruction at the hands of the Allies. He recognized early that Hitler was leading his countrymen down a deep, dark path of annihilation unless Canaris and other similarly committed Germans could find a way to convince the Allies that it was possible to depose Hitler and take steps to sue for peace. Richard Bassett's *Hitler's Spy Chief: The Wilhelm Canaris Betrayal: The Intelligence Campaign Against Adolf Hitler* was an invaluable resource regarding the role that Canaris played as the clock on the Third Reich ticked away. Staying in place at the top of the Abwehr was crucial to allow Canaris more time to pull together the necessary support for an attempt to depose Hitler.

In chapter 18, we learn of Otto's demise. Otto, code name for the Soviet's chief recruiter in Great Britain, was Philby's first handler. His real name was Arnold Deutsch and his fate is shrouded in mystery. Stalin's paranoia-driven purges were notorious for the rounding up of anyone with foreign ties who was serving the Soviet cause. According to Ben Macintyre's *A Spy Among Friends*, while some Soviet agents defected, many willingly complied with Stalin's orders to return to Moscow to their bleak fates.

The composition of Churchill's war cabinet fluctuated during the war. In Churchill's *The Second World War, Volume IV: The Hinge of Fate*, Churchill wrote, "I have solved the problem of representation of the Upper House in the War Cabinet by the device, already introduced, of having several ministers who, though not formally members, were actually in practice 'Constant Attenders.'" Feeling strongly that I couldn't make an actual cabinet member a spy or traitor, I created Henry Longworth, a fictional character, but one that represented an actual ministry—the Ministry of Works and Planning (later changed in 1943 to Ministry of Works).

In chapter 23, Father Sean Sullivan mentions Longworth's letter writing, most notably to Bishop Augustus Heinz, the "Brown Bishop." This character is based on Bishop Alois Hudal, also referred to as the "Brown Bishop." The Austrian Hudal was strongly anticommunist, as was the Catholic Church. He was named rector in 1923 of the Collegio Teutonico di Santa Maria dell'Anima, a theological seminary for German and Austrian priests. In 1937, he wrote *The Foundations of National Socialism*, praising the policies of Adolf Hitler while taking aim at some Vatican policies. After the war, Hudal assisted former Nazis in their efforts to relocate to other countries. While the real Brown Bishop lived until 1963, I took the greatest creative liberty in seeing that the character based on his persona did not survive the scene on the bridge over the River Tiber.

Saint Ermin's Hotel, the setting for chapter 27, was indeed the home to the Special Operative Executive for a spell during the war. The SOE occupied an entire floor of this beautiful hotel. The Caxton Bar was frequented often by agents from MI6, MI5, and Naval Intelligence. One of the Cambridge Five, Guy Burgess, used the bar to hand over top-secret files to his Soviet handlers.

Eleanor Roosevelt arrived in England on a goodwill trip on October 23, 1942. She toured factories, hospitals, and camps, where she met with American servicemen. For purposes of suiting my timeline, I moved up the date of her arrival.

In chapter 32, Churchill tells Thorn and Bright that D'Arcy Osborne, Envoy Extraordinary and Minister Plenipotentiary to the Holy See from 1936 to 1947, was in London to be knighted by King George VI. Osborne was actually conferred the KCMG (Knights Commander of the Order of Saint Michael and Saint George) by King George VI sometime between April 6 and June 18, 1943. The plotline for this story required Osborne to be away from his office for an extended time. The awarding of his knighthood fit that need, but I again had to adjust the timing of this event to suit the story.

Conor Thorn, Emily Bright, and Sean Sullivan hitched a ride to Rome with Myron Taylor in chapter 49. FDR appointed Taylor, a Protestant and former chief executive officer of US Steel, his representative to the Holy See. Taylor was to act as the channel of communication between FDR and Pope Pius XII. Taylor made several trips to the Vatican. One such trip had Taylor leaving New York for Lisbon on September 2, 1942, arriving in Rome several days later, on September 17. He was met at Littorio Airport by the papal limousine and was driven to Vatican City with, to Taylor's great surprise given that he did not have formal diplomatic status, cars belonging to the Italian security police leading and trailing the limousine. I used this scenario to get Thorn, Bright, and Sullivan into Rome but, again, altered the date to suit the timeline of the story. My research for this particular aspect of the story took me to the fascinating eyewitness account of Harold H. Tittmann, Jr., *Inside the Vatican of Pius XII: The Memoir of an American Diplomat During World War II*. This book chronicled Tittmann's service as an assistant to Taylor and his family's life in Rome during the conflict.

Menzies, in the epilogue, stonewalls Thorn when he presses him on why they left Abwehr chief Wilhelm Canaris on the bridge in Rome. A supporter of Hitler until 1937, it is well known that Canaris became quite disillusioned with Hitler and his policies. What is less well known is Canaris's attempts to reach out to the Allies, more specifically to Sir Stewart Menzies, head of Britain's Secret Intelligence Service, also known as MI6. In Heinz Höhne's tome *Canaris: Hitler's Master Spy*, Höhne gives details of a meeting in the summer of 1943 in Santander, Spain, between Menzies, Donovan, and Canaris. (There was a mention in Richard Bassett's *Hitler's Spy Chief: The Wilhelm Canaris Betrayal* that a meeting between Menzies and Canaris took place in December 1942.) Canaris presented his peace plan, which involved a ceasefire in the West, a deposed Hitler to be eliminated or handed over, and a continuation of the conflict in the East. But FDR swiftly squashed any chance that the plan would move forward, urging Donovan to stand down.

Menzies downplayed his meeting with Canaris. It is not clear if the short-circuiting of these efforts was due to Churchill and Roosevelt's agreement reached at the Casablanca Conference in January 1943, which laid out the necessity for Germany, Japan, and Italy to accept an "unconditional surrender" or if it was due to the fear that news of the liaison reaching the ears of the Soviets would upend the already-shaky cohesion of the three Allies. To be clear, the Soviets' greatest fear was that the US and Britain would sue for peace and then turn their forces on Stalin's armies. The opposite fear was embraced by FDR and Churchill.

Lastly, it was noted in Bassett's *Hitler's Spy Chief* that, while the Abwehr did take blame for not uncovering Allied plans for Operation Torch, some sources implied that Canaris had in his possession but did not pass along knowledge of the operation to the German High Command. It would follow, after hearing Canaris's peace plan in Santander that Menzies, as well as Donovan, would want to leave Canaris, an avowed Hitler opponent, in place, fearing that he would have been replaced by someone like Heinrich Himmler, head of the SS.

ACKNOWLEDGMENTS

I am indebted to quite a few people who provided much needed guidance, inspiration, and just plain help in completing *The Torch Betrayal*.

Firstly, Jennifer Blanchard, author, writing coach, speaker, book marketing expert—just what can't she do? Jennifer provided extremely valuable assistance in fleshing out the first draft. It was a messy process that produced note upon note from numerous phone calls and email exchanges.

Susanne Lakin and John Paine provided excellent editing advice for drafts two through six. They gently pushed me to dive deeper into characters and to devise more imaginative plot twists and turns. I hope I delivered, if only somewhat.

And a great deal of thanks goes to Gretchen Stelter, for her finishing touches to the final draft. She has a sharp eye and ear that proved to be invaluable.

Early comments from J. R. Olsen, a novelist himself and a former officer in naval intelligence, were quite enlightening and helped smooth out some rough passages.

For someone who knows little about guns, the firearms expertise of Chris Grall from Tactiquil was indispensable. The action sequences in this novel are sharper for his input.

Then there's the talented Jane Dixon-Smith, who designed the interior and the cover art for the book. It was quite a thrill to open the email attachment to see the first mock-ups of the cover, and the process from there was an absolute pleasure.

Lastly, to my loving and supportive wife, Christine, and my three wonderful kids, Thomas, Michael, and Riley, all of whom have been nothing but supportive and encouraging of a dream that was long in development.

CPSIA information can be obtained
at www.ICGtesting.com
Printed in the USA
LVHW03s1127260918
591411LV00002B/72/P